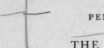

PE

THE

Elizabeth Jane Howard was born in March 1923. After training at the London Mask Theatre School she played with a repertory theatre in Devon and at Stratford-on-Avon. During this period she also modelled and worked for the BBC. In 1947 she left the theatre to become a secretary. Subsequently she started to review and edit books and to write her own novels. In 1960 she was awarded the John Llewelyn Rhys Memorial Prize for her first book *The Beautiful Visit*. Her other books include *The Long View*, which was a Book Society choice, *After Julius*, *Something in Disguise*, *Odd Girl Out*, and *Mr Wrong*, a collection of short stories, all of which have been published in Penguins. She has also edited *The Lovers' Companion: The Pleasures, Joys and Anguish of Loving*. Her latest book, *Getting It Right*, was the *Yorkshire Post* Novel of the Year in 1982.

THE SEA CHANGE

*

Elizabeth Jane Howard

PENGUIN BOOKS
in association with Jonathan Cape

Penguin Books Ltd, Harmondsworth, Middlesex, England
Penguin Books, 40 West 23rd Street, New York, New York 10010, U.S.A.
Penguin Books Australia Ltd, Ringwood, Victoria, Australia
Penguin Books Canada Ltd, 2801 John Street, Markham, Ontario, Canada L3R 1B4
Penguin Books (N.Z.) Ltd, 182–190 Wairau Road, Auckland 10, New Zealand

—

First published by Jonathan Cape 1959
Published in Penguin Books 1962
Reprinted 1975, 1976, 1977, 1979, 1980, 1982, 1984

—

Copyright © Elizabeth Jane Howard, 1959
All rights reserved

—

Made and printed in Great Britain by
Hazell Watson & Viney Limited,
Member of the BPCC Group,
Aylesbury, Bucks
Set in Linotype Georgian

Except in the United States of America,
this book is sold subject to the condition
that it shall not, by way of trade or otherwise,
be lent, re-sold, hired out, or otherwise circulated
without the publisher's prior consent in any form of
binding or cover other than that in which it is
published and without a similar condition
including this condition being imposed
on the subsequent purchaser

THIS BOOK IS
IN GOOD MEMORY OF
DAVID LIDDON HOWARD
my father

CONTENTS

CONTENTS

CHAPTER SIX · HYDRA

CHAPTER SEVEN · HYDRA

CHAPTER EIGHT · ATHENS

CHAPTER ONE

*

1. JIMMY

IT might have happened anywhere, at any time, and it could certainly have been a good deal worse. Paris, for instance, or even New York, before an opening; with Lillian's heart giving us all a bad time, Emmanuel on his first-night strike, and I bouncing from one emotional situation to another, picking up the pieces and giving them back to the wrong people. In fact, it happened in London, two weeks after the play opened, at approximately twenty past twelve last night in the bathroom of the furnished house in Bedford Gardens. It might have been a hotel – it might have been a block of flats – in fact it might have been far worse. Far worse: she might actually have been dead. Sticking to facts, however, Emmanuel had put off sacking her for days: I think he'd even let her think she was coming to New York with us. We always do travel with a secretary, so it would have been quite reasonable if she'd thought that. Yesterday morning, when I tackled him about her, he tried to get me to do it – he even produced the gag about his being paid to be responsible for other people's emotional problems, so why should he face his own? But I knew then that he would do it. She cried a lot; poor Gloria, she's given to tears. He was very gentle to her all day; Lillian was persuaded to keep out of her way, which was the kindest thing *she* could do, and I did my best. She brought Emmanuel his letters just before we went to drink with Cromer before going to see a girl in a play whom Emmanuel thought he wanted for the New York production. Emmanuel offered her a glass of sherry, and we all had a sticky drink together: she seemed all right then – a bit quiet, and puffy round the eyes, poor thing – but on the whole I thought she was being very controlled. In the taxi Emmanuel suddenly said: 'What a pity that girls don't look beautiful, like country, after rain!', so I knew he was feeling bad about her. Then Lillian said: 'I look marvellous after I've been crying – easily my best', which was clever of her, because she made him laugh and it's true.

The girl in the play looked right, but she wasn't – Emmanuel said her voice depressed him, and of course Lillian thought she'd be perfect, so what with the argument and dinner we weren't back until after twelve. We had a drink and Lillian started again about the girl: it's funny how people who love arguing are nearly always bad at it. To change the subject Emmanuel wondered why all the lights were on. They were: in the sitting-room when we got back, and all the way up the stairs. Most people can get depressed or agitated out of their observation, but Emmanuel doesn't: he never stops noticing things, but he only mentions them when he's bored. Lillian said 'How extraordinary!' and dashed upstairs saying something about burglars. We sat on the arms of the armchairs, and Emmanuel looked at me over his lime juice, raised his eyebrows, dropped them with a twitch and said: 'Jimmy. Here we sit on other people's chairs, drinking out of their glasses. I'd like to be at least one of the three bears: I prefer a hotel to borrowing everything.'

'In three weeks you'll be snug at the New Weston,' I said.

He raised his glass. 'I can hardly wait.'

He'd gone blue under the eyes; whenever I most want to comfort him I seem to underline his despair – well, perhaps it isn't despair, but it is so quiet and continuous and often makes him look so sad that I can't think of another word for it. And then, whenever I feel like that about him he always makes me laugh. Now, his eyes snapping with the kind of amusement that people who don't know him think is malicious, he said: 'If we *have* burglars, Lillian is getting on with them rather too . . .'

And then from upstairs she screamed – if you can call it that – the most dreadful sound: I can't describe it – a scream, a howl, a wail of terror with a train of shock in its wake – a thud, and silence. Emmanuel's face had closed on

the instant to such a breathless frozen acceptance of disaster
that I thought he wouldn't be able to move, but he was ahead
of me up the stairs.

Lillian was out on the bathroom floor : the door was open,
the lights were on, and we could see her as we rushed up the
stairs. Emmanuel was on his knees by her: 'She's fainted:
look in the bath.' But he didn't need to tell me. In the bath
was Gloria Williams. Her shoes were arranged neatly beside
it as though she'd gone to bed, but she was still wearing her
horrible mauve jersey and her tight black skirt, and she
looked exactly like the jacket of a crime story. For a moment
I thought she was dead.

'She's not dead, is she,' said Emmanuel. He was hardly
asking and he didn't look up. Then I realized that the heavy,
groaning breaths were not Lillian's but Gloria's. 'No.'

I felt for her heart in an amateurish sort of way: there was
a reluctant, irregular bumping. There was no water in the
bath.

'Help me to get Lillian on to her bed, and call a doctor.'

We did that. Emmanuel put a handkerchief soaked with
something out of a bottle from the dressing-table on to
Lillian's forehead while I was talking to the doctor's wife. By
the time I'd finished the air reeked of eau de Cologne, and
Emmanuel had gone.

In the bathroom he was kneeling by the bath, slopping
cold water on Gloria's face and slapping her hands and he
didn't seem to be doing much good.

'Phenobarbitone,' he said; 'and God knows how much
sherry. *Sherry!*' he repeated with a kind of wondering disgust. 'Doctor coming?'

'About five minutes. I told his wife about the breathing
while he was dressing. Lucky we know a good doctor.'

'We *always* know a good doctor,' he said.

'How much stuff has she had?'

'The bottle's empty, but I don't know how much was left
in it. Let's get her on to the dressing-room bed.' She was
much smaller than Lillian, but unexpectedly heavy, and her
breathing was beginning to frighten me.

'I'm sure we ought to prop her up.' We did this: her head rolled to one side and I heard a little click in her neck.

'Black coffee?' I said tentatively. 'I mean – isn't the thing to wake her up?'

'The thing is to get the dope out of her, and I defy you to do that. How *do* you make somebody sick if they're unconscious?'

'She's not absolutely unconscious – look.'

Gloria had half-opened her eyes, but only the whites showed which made her look worse. They flickered heavily and shut. Emmanuel said: 'Lillian!' as though even the idea of her was his fault, and vanished.

I tried to prop Gloria's head up more steadily, but it resolutely drooped: ashamed and inefficient, I pushed her dry wispy hair off her forehead, and wondered why the hell she'd had to go to these lengths. Love for Emmanuel? Despair? Spite? Sheer bloody-mindedness? Or six vital months spent with one of our leading dramatists? I was just thinking how awful it was that I couldn't feel sorrier for her when the bell rang, and I heard Emmanuel go down. The doctor was coming – and immediately I started to feel sorry for her. Poor Gloria; she was an awful colour: her face looked as though it had been made up over nothing . . .

The doctor looked tired and reliable; Emmanuel followed him into the room and then said: 'Keep an eye on Lillian for me, would you, Jimmy? She's rather confused.'

Lillian was lying on the bed with her eyes closed. She had then, and always has what would once have been described as 'a striking pallor'. Emmanuel had put her mink over her which somehow made her look even more weighted down and fragile – because although she is tall, she is extremely thin. She has ash-blonde hair like short silk, and is not at all like poor Gloria. Asleep, she looked gentle and delicate: she wasn't asleep; her eyes opened smoothly like a piece of exquisite machinery and she nearly smiled at me.

'Shock,' she said. 'Light me one of my cigarettes, Jimmy, like a lamb.'

Her bag was on the stool in front of her dressing-table, and in the triple glass I could see her watching me. She has one of those faces that are all eyes and mouth and white complexion – very attractive at a distance.

'The doctor's here,' I said. I gave her a cigarette and struck a match. The huge black pupils of her eyes contracted from the flame: eau de Cologne and the herbal cigarette were horrible together. Her face clouded.

'Why hasn't he come in then?'

'He's seeing to Gloria. She's not very well,' I added carefully.

Her long thin fingers clutched my sleeve, and painfully, a bit of my arm. 'Gloria! Oh! Is she –? Has she –? Oh, what on earth has Em done now?'

'He's helping the doctor, I think.' I was determined not to understand her, and she knew it, because she wouldn't let go of my sleeve. 'If you're all right, I think I'd better go and see if I can do anything.'

'Jimmy – I got such a dreadful shock – I can hardly remember a *thing*. You know my heart stuff in the bathroom? If you're going to leave me, I think you'd better get it. Don't worry anybody – just fetch the stuff.'

I got it. In the bathroom I saw the decanter with 'Sherry' on a silver vine leaf slung round its neck. It was almost empty. Somewhere in the house a clock struck one. I met Emmanuel on the stairs looking brisk and very sick.

'He's telephoned for an ambulance. How's Lillian?'

Then he saw the bottle in my hand, and the much-worn mechanism of concern marked his face.

'She's O.K. She's smoking. Is Gloria going to hospital?'

He nodded. 'But the doctor says she's all right. She'll live to regret it.'

'Is he going with her?'

'He wants to talk to us first.' He looked suddenly bitter, and good tempered. 'You'll have to do the talking, Jimmy.'

I gave Lillian her stuff, and she said that if someone brought her some brandy, she thought that she could get up.

'You're much better off in bed,' I said truthfully. 'And you'd better lay off the brandy until the doctor's seen you.' I escaped downstairs on that. At that moment, the last thing I could bear was Lillian: the same old Lillian, only this time it would probably be worse, because although several of Emmanuel's secretaries have fallen in love with him, none of them has ever done anything like this. 'I happen to love my husband so much,' it began, 'that I would do *anything* for him. Naturally he needs outside interests, and who am I, constantly ill (etc., etc.), to stand in his way? I know they are not *serious*: his only serious interest now is writing plays – but all artists need a sense of freedom and every kind of opportunity . . .' and so on: whitewashing anything is a messy business. 'He knows if ever there is any trouble, I am always there . . .' was the end of it. He did, indeed. Hell, even if I did think she was a bitch, I was being worse about her than that. She's had her share of disaster – the trouble was that none of us ever forgot it – and her active ambivalence about Emmanuel's work nearly drove him crazy at times. . . .

The doors of the ambulance slammed outside, and I opened up to the men before they managed to ring the bell. They tramped carefully up the stairs with a stretcher, and carefully down again with Gloria, extraordinarily diminished, upon it. Emmanuel and the doctor followed. The doctor went out with the stretcher, and Emmanuel, looking guilty, said where was the brandy, Lillian had got to have some before she would face the doctor. I poured out a small glass, and to my dismay, he drank it – as quick as a flash – and held out the glass again.

'Lillian, this time,' I said. I couldn't bear his mournful brown eyes asking for trouble.

'Lillian this time.' He took the glass and went.

The doctor shut the front door, pulled the curtain across it and walked towards me (the door opens straight into the sitting-room which has always seemed to me to be carrying the English system of draughts about as far as it can go).

'Would you like a drink?' I was nervous: I knew he was going to ask questions, and I felt that some of them might be rather awkward to answer. He said he'd like a small whisky, and I set about it. I was just about to ask him if Gloria was all right, or something silly like that, when he said: 'You are another secretary of Mr Joyce's?'

'Well, in a way. I manage things for him: business, and travelling, and if he directs his plays I act as a kind of assistant.'

'Miss Williams is his secretary?'

'She was.' I handed him his drink, and he nodded sharply at me.

'What do you mean, "was"?'

'She has been for the last six months. We're leaving for New York in a week or two, and he wasn't taking her there.' I felt a kind of nervous patience in my voice; this was like the police, and, if I wasn't very careful, the newspapers. Before he could say it, I said: 'Look – I fully realize that this is a serious matter – we're all most upset by it. Apart from anything else, it was a frightful shock. I'm afraid I don't know what happens about these things, but if you'll tell me how I can help – anything you want to know –' I heard myself make an unconvincing noise – 'naturally I'll do my best.'

He sat turning his glass round and round in his hands, looking at me tiredly and not saying anything. I ploughed on. 'Mr Joyce told her this morning that she couldn't come to New York. She was terribly disappointed and so on. I suppose that is why she took the phenobarbitone.'

'How do you know that she took it?'

I think that gave me the worst shock of the evening. 'She *must* have! She was all alone . . .' The icy trickle reached the middle of my spine – 'I *don't*, I suppose.'

He smiled then, in a finished sort of way which made him look incongruously pathetic. 'Oh, I think she did take it. I wondered why you thought so.'

'She *is* going to be all right, isn't she?'

'She should be all right. They'll be pumping it all out of her by now, and then I shall go and have another look at her. The point is, Mr . . .'

'Sullivan.'

'Sullivan, that people don't do that sort of thing without what seems to them, at least, good reason. And, as you know, whatever the reason, it is an offence to do that sort of thing. Is there any chance that she can have taken it by mistake?'

'I don't know. She *could* have, I suppose . . .' I left that straw in the air where it belonged.

'Was she attached to Mr Joyce?'

'Well – I think she admired him. You know, he always seems a glamorous employer – the theatre, and so on, and all the publicity . . .' I took the plunge – 'and while we're on that subject, it may seem callous to you, but it's part of my job to stop anything like this getting a press. Not that anything like this has ever happened before, of course.'

'Of course,' he agreed. He almost seemed faintly, not unkindly, amused. 'Who found her, and when?'

'Mrs Joyce. It must have been about five minutes before we called you.'

'About twenty past twelve. Where did Mrs Joyce find her?'

'Upstairs. She went up to her bedroom because the lights were on, and that's when she found her.'

'On the bed?'

For some idiotic reason, I just nodded.

'What about her relatives? Have you got their names and addresses? The hospital will want them, tonight, if possible.'

'She lives with a sister. I can find the address.'

I had just done this, when Emmanuel came into the room. He walked straight over to the drinks table, poured and drank another brandy. Then he turned and faced us: his eyes were bright, and he looked unnaturally fresh.

'Give Dr Gordon another drink, Jimmy.' He looked amiably at us, but there was a kind of defiance about him which I knew and distrusted. 'Well, now, where have we got to? Have you got Gloria out of the bath yet?'

He noted the doctor and me – he positively revelled in our reactions before, in an intentionally flat voice, he said: 'I'm sure that Jimmy hasn't made the situation clear to you, doctor. He is under the impression that he has to protect me – annihilate at least one dimension of mine. We found this young woman in the bath having taken all the available sherry and phenobarbitone, because she fancied herself – and very possibly she was – madly in love with me, and having had an affair with her as short as it was unsatisfactory, I was abandoning her. I was not, you see, at any time in love with her. These discrepancies occur – particularly if one is irresponsible and unscrupulous; they are probably inevitable, but one doesn't anticipate them. If anticipation is the thief of experience, every now and then one needs an experience – even if one is just ticking over because of the repetition.'

I knew it all. The way that he could be explicit and pompous, give anybody the other side of the picture with such a devastating honesty that it was the only side they would see. They would end up hating him with all the good reasons for doing so that he had handed them on a plate. He was making for the drink again.

'Emmanuel: you're drunk now, and you'll be hell if you drink any more. We're not amused: have some nice lime juice and lay off talking for a while.'

He stood where I had stopped him, clapping his hands gently together: the doctor, who at least had a kind of hardy convention which was soothing, made a dry noise in his throat and suggested visiting Mrs Joyce upstairs.

'I am sure she would be enchanted to see you,' said Emmanuel graciously.

I started up with the doctor (I was fairly certain that even if it occurred to him, Emmanuel would not make it), and by the time I got down again, he had pinched another drink.

'I was wondering where your courage' – his voice rose – 'your fidelity ... Jimmy, why don't you find me sooner and tell me to stop whatever it is. . . .'

'Drinking?'

He made a shambling, helpless gesture with his hand. 'Further back.'

'I wasn't born far enough back.'

'My fault again.' He leaned forward. 'Jimmy – don't you ever want a life of your own?'

'No,' I said. 'I've thought about it, and I don't.'

There was an unpeaceful silence edged by the rise and fall of Lillian's voice upstairs.

'Do you know how old I am?'

'Yes,' I said; 'you're sixty-one.'

'Sixty-two, sixty-two,' he reiterated more easily.

'According to the files, you won't be sixty-two until the nineteenth of September.'

He glared at me. 'I'm like a century. I like to think ahead.'

The doctor came down, said Mrs Joyce was all right: he'd given her a sedative and she was going to sleep. He'd ring up in the morning and he'd be getting along now.

When he'd gone, Emmanuel looked up hopefully and said: 'Jimmy. Let's go *out* to drink. Let's find a nice bar where our feet don't touch the ground from the start, and everybody but us is drunk.'

'You can't,' I said; 'wrong country; you can't drink all night here. Let's get some sleep.'

He took no notice of this. 'Why *don't* you want a life of your own? A private life? You're young enough.'

'I have yours,' I said gently: he was beginning to look as though he was made of glass, or paper.

'She was so beautiful. She wore a blue cotton dress: it was old, and it had faded on the tops of her shoulders in the sun. Her hair was a real brown, and her skin smelled of fruit and the tops of her arms were round. We lay in a chalk hollow on the downs by the sea, and the air was streaming with poppies over our heads, and the blue air was brittle with larks. I asked her questions and she answered – she never told me anything more than I asked. She filled me to the brim and never slopped anything over. She had the most complete smile I've ever seen in my life. That was one fine day.'

He took his head out of his hands and said: 'Jimmy: now I must have one more drink.'

'We'll have one each.' I got up to get them and he said: 'I've told you all that before, haven't I? It is one of the things I tell you, isn't it?'

'Yes; you've told me before.' The odd thing was that in one sense he'd never told me. The feeling was the same; but the settings, and even, perhaps, the girl, would be different each time. I'd heard about it in a pub – all plush and frosted glass, and they were sharing a bag of hot potato chips with a fog outside; another was on top of an open tram with a tearing sky above them; she was wearing his raincoat and the wind made her hair come down. No – the girl wasn't different, I suppose: he'd simply pick out different aspects of her – her fingers eating the chips – her eyes looking up at the sky – her neck before her hair came down over it. Once it had been a snowy morning at the Zoo, and once a lake and a rowing-boat on a September afternoon, with leaves dropping silently on to the water round them burying her reflection. I knew it was the same time in his life: and the more times that he told me, the more sure I was that there had only been one time. There was a kind of pure joy about the way he remembered her, and a kind of pure grief at the end of his memory. If I'd asked her name, he would have given her a dozen names, but it was the same girl, and each time he told me he added another occasion to that one time. He only told me when he was drunk, anyway, and I don't think he told anyone else.

On the stairs he stumbled, and clutched my arm to steady himself. He stood for a moment clutching me, and then said – much too loudly:

> 'There once was a bastard called Joyce
> Whose shoes on the stairs made a noyce . . .'

He'd gone a bit green by then.

'We mustn't wake Lillian,' I said hopelessly, and he earnestly agreed.

At the bathroom he looked at me as though I hardly knew him and said: 'Jimmy, if you want the bathroom, use it now, because I shall have to be sick.' He gave me the harassed embarrassed smile he usually reserves for actresses he can't remember, and added: 'My heart always goes to my stomach.'

Later, after I had made sure that he finally got to bed, I fell on to my own, but I couldn't relax. The others could sleep one way or another; it was I who was left twisting and turning over the practical problems – soothing myself with the might have been much worse formula. But if I thought much about that, it stopped me cold. Supposing she *had* been given the phenobarbitone by somebody? Not by Emmanuel; he might hit anyone if he got angry fast enough, but he'd never poison them. Not by me – I was all for a quiet life. That left Lillian. She was mad about drugs; she'd probably think that phenobarbitone was a nice quiet death for Gloria. Of course, she *hadn't* had anything to do with it, but I was tired enough, and resentful enough and sorry for myself – all the usual reactionary crap – to consider the responsibility with brutal calmness. It was I, after all, who would have to pack up this particular set of Emmanuel's troubles – all he had to do was to smile; and Lillian could lie on her back racked with nostalgia and the mitral valve in her heart....

2. LILLIAN

I HAVE woken up in so many bedrooms that now I concentrate upon the shape of my body before the shape of the room. There are three kinds of waking for me. One is like being cast from some smooth deep water on to a rocky shore; I am aground and wake with the same shock – the day is hard and slippery under my eyelids and my bones ache from years of wrecking. There is a kind when I move like a ship mooring so unobtrusively to the day that memory of my last dream is not crushed; I come so meekly alongside reality that I can scarcely believe that I have arrived. And there is a third kind – when I seem slowly, imperceptibly to discover myself lying in warm sand, and the water is creeping down my body, leaving it bleached in a delicious lassitude. This last kind is the best, but I only have it now after sleeping-pills, and they won't always let me have them. This is the time when I am devoted to myself; before I have made any false move of the day: when I can imagine actually wanting to eat breakfast; and then dressing – putting on for the first time a pair of simple, but exquisitely made shoes, and a scarf of some ravishing colour that I've never worn: spending the morning with somebody younger, not very happy, who really needs me to be gay and gentle with them; having an exciting lunch with somebody I have never met before; in the afternoon buying wonderful shirts for Em, and some windcheater or windjammer or whatever they're called, for Jimmy (he adores tough sporting clothes although he'd never see the daylight if he could help it); racing back to give everything to them while we have heavenly English tea; Em asking me about some character in his play – the one he hasn't even started writing yet – but he and Jimmy look so kind and secretive that I know that something lovely is going to happen to me, and when they can't bear it any longer they – no Jimmy – goes and gets it, and gives it to Em to give to me. ... a wicker basket and inside it is a golden labrador puppy that I have wanted more than anything else and that Em has never let me have because of the quarantine and he gets asthma with dogs – but he's changed about it entirely, and he chose this puppy especially for me. ...

I am back where I seemed to have begun; the last time that I had a puppy – on my fourteenth birthday, at Wilde, in 1925. That was my last real bedroom and I can remember it best with my eyes shut. I can remember all of that day with its currents of pleasure, its peaks of excitement: I think that it is the only day that I remember which has nothing in it that I want to forget or have forgotten. It was the first time that I had ever had an animal entirely of my own; it was the last birthday before I was ill; it was the first time that I stayed up to dinner (bronze silk stockings and my christening-present jewellery – changed like the grown-ups); it was the last autumn we spent at Wilde, and the whole day had a most lingering beauty which I didn't know that I noticed at the time, but now I can't say the word autumn without remembering it; it was the first time that I thought about the future – 'for ever and ever' – 'the rest of my life'; it was the last time that I accepted my parents as the puppy accepted me. After that day, everything seemed to swoop and pounce and happen too fast; as though I was running breathlessly behind my life – shrieking with the need to choose – out of earshot – in a frantic slipstream of the events which rocketed on before me; a paper-chase of examination papers I couldn't pass, prescriptions to stop a pain I couldn't describe, the death certificates of my father and mother – in the same boat for the first time in their lives, and drowned, the catalogue of books and furniture, of pictures, of silver and glass and the auction of Wilde; a picture lying on a railway-carriage seat – Em looking intelligent and disastrous and so fascinating that although someone had wrapped a sandwich in the newspaper, I picked it up and remembered how horrible my family had always been about Jews ... Marrying Em – papers, papers, papers. I nearly caught up with the chase then; seemed to reach something, but he only stopped a little while to admire the view of me, and then flew on: my heart was affected – I couldn't keep up – I gasped and pounded and had always the weak angry sensation that he could fly; for him, at least, there was no uneven ground. He streamed away, above and ahead of me, scattering a new trail of paper – of plays, opinions, letters, cuttings, invitations, and tickets, tickets – for theatres, for boats, for trains, and aeroplanes; 'I'll go on ahead by plane; you follow by boat in comfort.' In comfort! I seemed always to be in mid-ocean, in the dark, cut off – from the remains of my family who never approved of my marriage, the combination of somebody who was half-Jewish and wholly an artist exceeding the wildest bounds of their worst imagination (they concentrated as hopelessly on his origins as I on his destinations), cut off from Em to the point where I seemed only to discover him through second-hand sources; through reading his plays – through the people he worked with and swung towards with the sudden irascible illumination of a lighthouse – through the newspapers who fired rumours and accounts of his more violent, scandalous doings which lit up his behaviour to me like starshell. And then, for two years, Sarah – but she dies – in such hideous evil agony that I wanted to kill her. I sat with her for seventeen hours, until her small mechanical shrieks ran out and her head was still: then there were telegrams. Hatred; murder; and a great fear of

God: I wanted the doctor's children to be like Sarah; I wanted everyone I knew to suffer for her – to nail them to her pain which they would not stop: I wanted to brand them with the senseless wicked cruelty which had been done to my little, beautiful, dear Sarah. I had been weeping – imploring them to do something – to stop it, and when they had done nothing and it was stopped, I tried to kill one of the nurses. At least I struck out at her and wanted her to be dead. Then Em took me away for nearly a year. We travelled, but he was with me all the time – with such patience for my bitterness that in the end my heart, which seemed so hard and intolerably heavy, suddenly opened, and a great weight of grief gushed out: the exquisite relief, the weakness; the sinking into a single merciful sorrow – that Sarah was dead – it was almost like bleeding to death. It was then that Em gave me transfusion after transfusion of his love; seemed to pour all his life into me – all his creation into my comfort – gave me every breath of his compassion. At first I couldn't say anything about her; then from the morning when he held my head and for the first time since before she died I could weep and say again and again 'I'm so sorry that Sarah is dead: I'm so sorry that she is dead', I couldn't stop talking about her. Then he mourned with me, and gradually he made of it a natural grief – not monstrous, but life-size – until he had taught me to live with her death. He said that her dying was an innocent business: that there was nobody to hate or to forgive for her death – that it had not the terror and dirt about it which there must always be when people were responsible to one another for such things. . . .

These are the things that seep through my mind on the mornings when I have the third and best kind of waking – all past and done with – but in them I have a memory of life, a distant gratitude for gesture, for that committed animation from which I seemed to have died. Out of Em came Sarah; out of Sarah came Em; but I also had something to do with it, and I want so much to have something to do with somebody.

The daily maid who brought my breakfast said that Mr

Joyce had overslept, that he was finishing his coffee and letters, before he came up. There was only one letter for me, and it is curious that only when I picked it up did I remember the extraordinary shock of seeing that woman in the bath the night before. . . .

Dear Mrs Joyce,

I wonder if you have any idea of the misery you have caused me during the last few weeks? But I imagine that you are so completely wrapped up in yourself that it has hardly occurred to you that I existed (by the time you receive this I shan't exist any more). All this time – the only time in my life that has mattered to me – I have been watching *you* – wondering why he ever married you – whether he ever felt anything but pity for your weakness which you have made so dull and dangerous for him. *You* thought that I was just another secretary – there must have been so many, I can see that now – you never realized I was different because I had a heart. I may not have your background, or your looks, but in the end, you know, that doesn't make any difference to what one feels inside. All I asked was to be with him, I recognize his loyalty to you. He'll never leave you, however much he wants to, but you couldn't even let me have that. You have to hang on to both these men – being as bad a mother as you are a wife because that's all that Jimmy wants from *you*. I could have borne anything if only I could go on being with him, but suddenly, for some mysterious reason, I am not to go to New York. I am to be sacked as though I was anybody. *He* would never have done that by himself – not to me – so that in my sanest moments it is hard for me not to guess who arranged that I should be left. Let me tell you that you will do this sort of thing once too often, and then God help you. He must be on somebody's side though apparently not on mine. It's odd that most people are sorry for you because of your past, and the only shred of pity I can work up for you is about your future. Well – thanks to you, I have none, but at least I had a present, once, which is more than you ever had.

Gloria Williams

There was something about those pages being impeccably typed that made them worse – something striking and venomous and machine-made: only the signature was written – sprawling in green ink, like somebody suddenly revealed in the wrong-coloured underclothes. I was still staring at it when Em came in. He walked straight over to the window and stood with his back to the light, but even then I could see that he looked dreadful, and I felt suddenly angry that he, out of all this, should look ill.

'How are you?'

I didn't reply; just looked at him as though I couldn't understand what he meant by such a question. I was thinking of Gloria's shapeless silken knees tilted in the bath; sick that he had touched her, angry that I had no longer an innocent anger with him – that I knew so much that I couldn't understand.

He was picking a matchbox to pieces – seemingly intent – but I knew he was watching me with the acute delicacy of somebody in a fight waiting for an opening to knock me out with pity – to leave me defenceless and protective towards him.

'How is Miss Williams?'

'Not dead. All right,' he added.

I wanted to smoke; my hands were shaking too: I had no matchbox, and instantly he was lighting my cigarette: he looked pathetic and intent doing it, and my anger rose again.

'As far as I can remember, it is approximately eighteen months since you last achieved anything like this.'

'My dear Lillian – nobody has ever been found in the *bath* before.' But his eyes filled with tears, and he sat down on the bed suddenly.

'Well, if you wanted first-hand evidence of a young woman literally dying of love for you . . .'

'I don't want any of it: no part of any of it.' He reached for one of my cigarettes, put it back, and started fumbling for one of his own.

'She *might* have been dead, and I might have died discovering her. What does that make you? Lucky? Apart from being damned irresponsible, of course. But perhaps you think it's *bad* luck. A clean sweep and you could have started making all the nice familiar mistakes, with nobody to watch you. Except Jimmy, of course – he's a real audience – numb, dumb, and devoted ...' Suddenly I heard this thin and savage voice; I had never heard it before – hearing it twisted everything round so that what I was saying sounded reasonable – a better life for him if I had died and only Jimmy was left to care for him. This was extraordinary: I stopped, and thoughts streamed back in the silence. 'I can't admire you.'

'No,' he said at last. 'I don't see how you can.'

'And I don't seem able to help you.'

'Are those the reasons?' He looked sad and inquiring – and intolerably like Sarah, and he was going to twist about like some intellectual fish: I had to make him laugh, or I'd lose him.

'All I ask is that they shouldn't end up in baths. It's so bad for my heart.'

'You can ask more than that.' He spread out his hand, and I pulled the bedclothes round me.

'If I did, you'd say I was blaming you. "Let there be no deserts", you said.'

'Now I say – mind on your own count. Don't fabricate a climate for concern.'

'Do you remember when you said "Let there be no deserts"?'

'Cherry said it in *The Orchid Race*. Just before she goes back on her street.' He sounded preoccupied, which he always does when he's trying to evade me.

'*You* said it after Sarah died. In Florida on the beach in the dark. You simply put it in a play afterwards – like everything else.' The familiar sweet aching was there when I said her name to him. Miss Williams or anybody else couldn't destroy that, and with the life of this feeling I burst into tears. 'You wouldn't have done these things if she hadn't died. If there had been another child! You would have had some difference between real life and what you write – it would not have all been the same. She would have been sixteen – I can't *bear how far* I have to imagine her now. You wouldn't have wanted *her* to have that kind of shock – you'd have conducted your life with more taste – more discrimination – I wish you'd stop worrying about humanity and live more like ... like ...'

'A gentleman? Or other people?' But neither of us even tried to laugh. He picked up the napkin from my breakfast tray.

'Darling, don't distress yourself. Have a quiet morning in bed. Don't race so much.' He was mopping my face, and I didn't mind his touching me now.

'What are *you* going to do?'

'Jimmy has organized the morning to the brim. I've got to lunch with Sol Black, and there's this party at the Fairbrothers', but you can cut that.'

'What are you doing in the afternoon?'

I saw him square himself to be elusive.

'Going to work a little.'

'Here?'

'No – out. Lillian, you know I can't work here.'

'I won't disturb you. I'll take the receiver off. I'll only warn you in time for the party.'

'I've told you a hundred times I cannot work in the house: I must be alone.' He managed to look both angry and patient.

'I'm coming to the Fairbrothers' - I want to.' It would be the only time of the day with him. 'And you needn't think I'm going to lie about in bed all day. I've got a lot to do before we go to America.'

'Rest in the afternoon before the party. How *are* you feeling, really?'

'Perfectly marvellous.'

'Jimmy said don't answer the telephone today – he'll do it.'

'Don't start telling me how wonderful Jimmy is.'

He didn't.

'Perhaps *I'd* better engage the next secretary. At least we might have a lady, while we're at it: they're no more expensive and at least they won't wear such awful stockings.'

'Were Gloria's stockings so awful?'

'All greasy and stretched; panic-stricken stockings.' I felt better that he hadn't noticed. He smiled faintly when I said

27

'panic-stricken'. 'All I ask is that we don't have another neurotic virgin. All their imagination's gone the wrong way.'

He laughed suddenly.

'What?'

'I was thinking how *very* little that had to do with "being a lady".'

'Em; you know perfectly well what I mean.'

'You mean somebody not brought up in a slum as I was.'

'Now you're just being difficult. You're different because you're an artist.'

'That's like the countless dear people who've said to me: "I don't usually like Jews but you're different." '

'There's no point in getting angry with *me*: *I've* never said that.'

He threw the napkin on to the floor. His hands still shook. 'Imagine Lillian – imagine meeting an elephant, and presuming so far. Different from what? From whom? How many elephants have you met? Are you sure that what you met was an elephant? What kind of palsied constricted vulgarity are you employing now? If I am the exception, then I am interested in the rule. You are so much the rule that you can't stand an exception. You're only nourished by being able to take things for granted, and the only things we can take for granted are either not pretty, or totally unreal. Honest intentions, I tell you, are the fertile ground: they edge their way out and make cracks in society. . . .'

Jimmy came in.

'I did knock. Some society in Bradford want to know whether you'll waive the royalty on *Our Little Life*.'

'That awful play. Why do they keep doing it?'

'Seven women, two men, and one set.' There was nothing Jimmy didn't remember about Em's plays. 'They call themselves the Mad Hatters,' he added morosely. He looked ill too.

'What are they doing it for?'

Jimmy picked up my telephone.

'Mr Joyce would like to know why you are putting on the play,' and Em snarled silently at the instrument.

'They say it's to raise money to build a swimming-pool for their Club premises.'

'No. Tell them I haven't got a swimming-pool. Parochial bastards.'

'Mr Joyce is very sorry, but he only waives royalties for international charities.'

When Jimmy had finished, Em said peevishly:

'That play's like a double-bed eiderdown in a cheap hotel. It gets thinner and thinner, but it still slips all over the place. I thought we didn't allow ourselves to be besieged on the telephone anyway.'

'We don't, usually. It's my fault. I just can't help being unnaturally polite this morning. It's my weak character. How are you, Lillian?'

'Displaced. Em's been bullying me about class structure.'

Em got up from my bed. Jimmy said: 'Emmanuel, you'll have to shave before lunch today. Don't you think so, Lillian? He can't go out to lunch like that, he looks like a charcoal biscuit.'

Before I could agree, the telephone rang, and Jimmy was caught between blocks of interminable listening and short bursts of disagreement. Em lit another cigarette and wandered to the window. It was raining: it would probably rain most of the day, with cold, gusty sunshine – like somebody who does not know how to laugh. Suddenly, because I knew then that I could not laugh either, I had a picture of the three of us – back this morning where we started, to our shallow centre made up of ritual allowances for one another, traditional misunderstanding and a kind of idiomatic discomfort. Em turned towards me, and for a moment I wondered whether we were both thinking the same thing, and whether he knew it.

'But those are *twenty-four*-foot flats,' Jimmy was saying: 'you might as well put them in Piccadilly Circus – you *can't*: you'll have to border them till the whole thing looks like the wrong end of a telescope.'

He was tapping his cigarette with his forefinger – not listening to Jimmy – preparing to go. If only Jimmy wasn't on the telephone I might have caught him: we could have talked about telescopes – which *was* the right end, or were they just an instrumental admission of failure, only resorted to when one could not really see anything at all. . . . He left the room and my mind reeled after him: I hadn't even shown him the letter – but weeks later I'd say something about it as though I'd said it by mistake. This kind of restraint would impress him: his face would light on me – already I could feel a warmth like the instant's burning of the piece of paper on which Miss Williams had written her letter. . . .

When Jimmy had finished, I asked him to have lunch with me. He couldn't, he said. He'd got to have a drink with the girl we'd seen last night to tell her that she wasn't right for Clemency in New York. There was a call for understudies at two – he didn't think he'd get lunch at all. He turned all these reasons into excuses with his face. That's when I know about people – with the most bitter, exacting certainty. 'See you at the Fairbrothers'?' he finished hopefully.

'My dear Jimmy, I'm not going to the Fairbrothers' to see *you*.'

'No chance,' he said, and contrived to look defeated. When he had gone, I squeezed the letter into my hand against the sick burning jolt of being humoured. I hate it: I hate that kind of shallow understanding – the allowances made for me and the person who allows himself to make them. I'll make my own allowances for myself: I'd rather he'd taken the trouble to say I was a bitch. But although he thinks in those terms, he'd never call me that. It doesn't go with my liking poetry and Sicilian jewellery and English country life. And after all, I am Em's wife: a kind of holy relic. I looked at the letter, crushed up into exactly what it was worth. Em didn't care about *her*; probably was bored by and disliked her; might even have swung into a violent distaste – so active with him that he would actually have wished her dead. . . . But this suddenly frightened me, fitting too easily into my second picture of Em – not the majestic migratory bird, but the little figure with mournful eyes – on a platform by himself, in the dock; against the party, the crowd, the law, who hate him and do not know why he is here, and he does not hate them but does not know why either. I am the only one who knows, and they cannot hear me, and he won't understand because he is fixed upon the crowd with a kind of reckless grief – indifferent to their judgement. My head has started to ache, and it's raining hard now. The only kind of day that I could have by myself would sound like a schoolgirl's diary. 'In the morning, head ached – am I in love? In the afternoon bought gramophone records.' And then some extraordinary little clutch at a cultivated comparison: Satie with Seurat; Renoir with Roussel – the self-conscious yardstick of appreciation so pathetically employed by the young; such intellectual bathos in the old. I shall stay in bed until I am better, or it is time to go to the party. If I could tell them that simply to know something was only like having keys that will unlock anything but one's private house, they would not write about Satie in their diaries: but Sarah did not even have time to write her name: she just liked colours, and any noise designed to charm her. Remembering her little starting shout of laughter is as sharp as Em's sudden blaze of anger – it seems so extraordinary to be left simply with the anger, and that it should be his. . . .

3 · EMMANUEL

HE left the house with the spurious sensation of freedom that he had come to associate with leaving any place where he had slept. There was no sense of accomplishment – no movement in a better direction; simply an opening, with the streets and the daylight before him. His day had been arranged for him by Jimmy and Lillian – on the usual basis of ought and not. Lunch with Sol Black and another possible Clemency – early, because he had said that he wanted to work all the afternoon. That meant going to the dreary little top-floor room in Shepherd Market that Jimmy had hired for him. He had spent a week actually trying to write in it, but had been defeated by its impersonal cosiness – its almost furtive air of artistic information. With its divan, its cheap bookshelves packed with the *sine qua non* of the last thirty years – its postcard reproductions of Etruscan art and its chipped pottery ash-trays, it had seemed to him the place to be poor and young, silly and serious, and desperately in love. He was sixty-odd; his income bounded precariously ahead of his enormous income-tax; he was no longer silly without an effort, and hardly at all serious, and he had the greatest difficulty in remembering what it was like to be in love. In fact, the room seemed to underline to him everything that he had lost; and so he had used it off and on, but not for writing. Anyway, did he want to write another play? *Poor Man's Friend* looked like running here for a year, at least, and the Broadway production was assured – it only remained to find a girl for Clemency. Somebody of nineteen – like Betty Field; but there wasn't anybody like her. The young actresses today couldn't kick up their heels any more – there were no pretty clowns whom you fell in love with while they were laughing at themselves. Nowadays they were all stern and intelligent about it, and talked about timing – somehow they'd forgotten their bodies: it was like meeting a kitten who turned out to be a ballet dancer. No good talking like that, and worse to think so: nostalgia was a dangerous drug – one developed such toleration to it that even deadly doses failed to stimulate the imagination which ended by living on its own fat with no hunting summer ahead. . . .

He was on a bus – he did not know where he was going – but he bought, as usual, a sixpenny ticket, and allowed himself to be swept, with good-tempered surges and patient moments, down Bayswater Road. It was raining quite hard now, and the park looked its worst. Enormous trees, their new green lumpy and sodden; the grass, soured by soot and frost, had no sense of direction, and all this endured under a sky both dirty and hopeless. There had been some streaks of blue – Lillian's favourite colour – when he had looked out of her window earlier. Poor Lillian. He wished that he either wanted to write another play, or, at least, didn't want *not* to write one. But what on earth was he to do this summer if he didn't write? His inability to think with any hope or confidence so far ahead jolted up more recent events: the last few weeks; last night. Lillian, who might really have had a bad heart attack: Gloria, who might really have killed herself: Jimmy, who might easily have lost his head or washed his hands at the unnecessary shock and squalor of the whole business. . . . But when he came to himself in all this, he was assailed by exactly the pattern of panic that made him have a drink (he'd even got the first drink out of Jimmy by a trick) – such horror of being himself, of consequences spreading like ink on to other people that he had to desert, to abandon himself, to go out of his mind which so disgusted him, and become a man who would naturally do such things. He was feeling sick again – must get off the bus; must stop drinking; must stop seducing secretaries; must stop upsetting Lillian. . . . He got off the bus, took a taxi (he always took them if he knew where he wanted to go), and went to the theatre to find Jimmy. In the taxi he felt such profound, humble gratitude to Jimmy that he wasn't at all sure he could bear to meet him. He had had it before – several times now – and once when Jimmy had actually been there he had said: 'I don't know why you do it. You're worth six of me.' And Jimmy had looked at him – soft and cynical and said: 'Yeah, but there *aren't* six of you, Emmanuel; thank the Lord for that, whichever way you like to look at it.'

He found Jimmy with a photographer arguing about stills. They were both leaning with their heads on a large desk over which the glossy plates were strewn. The photographer was sulking, and Jimmy was discarding plate after plate with a kind of professional petulance. They both looked up when he came in – the photographer assumed good humour and Jimmy winked. 'Don't think that you haven't done a wonderful job, Lionel, in the *main*, it's just that, particularly with Miss Cockeral – I'm looking for a different quality; a kind of . . .' He paused with two fingers held an inch and a half apart; 'you know what I mean?'

The photographer, let loose like a horse in new pastures,

tossed his head, snuffed this meaningless air, and seemed soothed.

'It's elusive, but if anyone can get it, you can.' Jimmy began blocking up the plates. He had metaphorically shut the gate and was talking over it – finishing the job. 'Now look, Lionel. She's filming for the rest of the week as we all know to our cost – she won't be in the mood to cooperate in the way you *need*. I'll talk to her, and fix something for next week, and then I *know* you'll get some wonderful pictures for me. How's that? By the way, have you met Mr Joyce?'

The photographer held out a hand like a fish slice.

'I'll show him the pictures,' said Jimmy, still soothing.

The photographer whinnied, released Emmanuel's hand, and looked reproachfully at the plates.

'He'll understand about them being roughs,' said Jimmy smoothly. 'Be seeing you, Lionel,' he added as an after-thought.

Emmanuel smiled – really with pleasure at being able to see Jimmy so easily: the photographer gave him a yearning, dazzled look, and went.

'He wants to do you, of course.' Jimmy lit a cigarette. 'My God. What's he *done* to Elspeth though. She's a nice, sexy girl, and he's made her look like she's been underground all her life resisting something.' He shoved the plates into a drawer. 'You haven't forgotten your lunch, have you?'

'No.'

'Got the key to your room?'

He began feeling absently in his pockets for the key, but before Jimmy could say 'It's O.K., I've got the duplicate here,' he said: 'I don't know that I want to write another play, Jimmy.'

'Why not?'

' "Why not?" that's not how to do it. I've no statement to make.' He touched the desk – pressed it with his fingers. 'Out of touch: equal proportions of feeling helpless and detached.'

There was a silence during which he knew exactly what Jimmy was not saying. 'Have you got Gloria's home address?'

'She's still in hospital.'

'I want to see her sister.' He waited a moment, and then said: 'I must.'

When Jimmy had given it to him, he said: 'You know anything about this girl Sol's bringing to lunch?'

'Only what Sol said: nothing. She's had no experience to speak of. Of course Sol says she's out of this world.'

'I don't blame her: it's not a very nice world.'

'You come along with me and get fixed up at the chemist's.'

'I'll have to do something, or Sol'll talk me into engaging her blind. Why can't you come?'

'I've got to tell Annie it's no go, and there's a two o'clock call.'

'Annie?'

'You saw her last night. Her voice depressed you.'

'Yes, it did. Didn't it you?'

Jimmy looked embarrassed. 'She's depressed me in other ways.' Then he said almost angrily: 'Pay no regard. I shan't lose any more sleep over *her*. She wouldn't be right for Clemency – I always told her that, but she wanted me to get you to see her.'

'Well, I may have to get you to see Sol's girl. I don't suppose she'll be right, either.'

'If we ever find anyone who is, I'll fall for her. I *love* Clemency. Come on; drug store?'

'Chemist,' said Emmanuel gently. At that moment he loved Jimmy.

Sol Black, who had chosen the restaurant, met him in the padded draught which was its entrance. After they had stood there for a few minutes exchanging greetings and being hit and trampled on by waiters and other clients (they were neither of them large men), Sol indicated a very small, low table jammed in a corner near the bar between two groups of drinkers. Their chairs, higher than the table, were wedged behind it, but with some skill Sol levered them into position and they sat – the table rocking, and Emmanuel brushing potato crisps off his knees. It was almost dark, but otherwise the general impression was red: the air impregnated with scent, French dressing, and damp suits (it still rained). Sol talked, but it was difficult to hear what he said: ice shakers (or bracelets?), women laughing who had no business to do so in public, and the heavy murmur – like distant surf – of men boasting about money, made anything but an exchange of platitudes almost impossible. The air-conditioning operated just above Emmanuel's right ear and he tried to shift himself a fraction towards Sol's white shining face.

'Of course! You want a drink,' Sol said instantly: he had a capacity for looking tragic over imaginary shortcomings. 'Hey! We'll get one ready for Martha, too.'

Emmanuel said he didn't drink at lunch-time.

'You don't say! God! How I admire you people. Sure you won't break the rule – just this once?'

'Tomato juice.' His voice sounded useless – it sank into the padded walls anonymously – without a murmur.

Sol ordered two Bloody Marys and a tomato juice for Mr Joyce, and the waiter moved off like a knight on a chessboard with the order.

'. . . As I was saying . . . about this girl – Martha – she's not the usual run – you must believe me. She looks good, of course, not conventional, mind you, but is that girl intelligent! She's read everything! And she really understands your work: she's said things about it which really made me sit up. Little things, mind you. And you know all those Russians? Well, she's read *them*! Not just the dialogue – the whole works . . .' his face glistened, his voice broke: 'and music,' he said hoarsely, 'boy! has she come out the other side of that!' Their drinks arrived and he waved the bill away.

'Has she done any acting, Sol?' Emmanuel asked gently.

'Well now you're asking. Cheers! Yeah, she's been in Rep: wanted to do it the hard way – she's *cultivated* . . .' he took a deep drink. 'She's twenty, you know – just a kid really – she couldn't have done much of anything. I want to bring her in on the top, because I *know* she's got what it takes – I'm a *hard* man,' he added appealingly: 'Look at me!' he gazed at Emmanuel with liquid eyes; 'Broadway, London, Hollywood, I've been everywhere – they're all the same to me. You can't tell me any more about human nature, and if I tell you this girl's got what the public wants and a great future ahead of her – she's *got* a great future, period.'

'Have you seen the play, Sol?'

'Took Martha last night. It's great: she's wild about it – just crazy about that girl Vlem – Clem . . .'

'All right, stop selling her, Sol. I'd like to see her.'

'Well now: here she comes!'

He tried to get up, and Emmanuel clutched the table. A tall girl in a dark blue suit was weaving her way over to them. The skirt was tight, the jacket was loose on her shoulders; her dark brown hair was neatly scraped back from her face, which was big and well-proportioned. Sol introduced her; everybody smiled, and she sat down on a third chair which seemed to grow up out of the floor. She was wearing a white shirt, very open at the neck, and as she sat down Emmanuel realized that she had the most beautiful breasts that he'd ever seen in his life. This made him laugh aloud which he seldom did: the others looked at him inquiringly, but at that moment, the head waiter, a man with a diabolic expression and shoulders like a grand piano, loomed over them and laid a menu about twice the size of the small table upon it. They protected their drinks like guilty secrets between knees numb with cramp and screwed their eyes in the appropriate directions. The menu was in mauve handwriting hectographed on to rough grey paper; it was written in food French, and Emmanuel couldn't be bothered with it. He watched the others: Sol expansive, generous – struggling with greed and his waistline; the girl – Martha Curling she was called – trying to choose what was expected of her; the head waiter whose features had settled to an untrustworthy cooperation – and then back to Miss Curling's breasts. He had never seen anything like them – he wanted to congratulate her, to laugh again – to celebrate such a delightful phenomenon. He ordered oysters in their honour, and tried to take a more general interest in the proceedings.

'. . . you dig your knife in and all the butter runs out,' Sol was saying.

The girl was fingering one of the buttons that were not done up on her shirt: she had large irresponsible hands, and Emmanuel wished she'd take them away; 'but then I suppose she has to eat with them,' he thought.

'Is it a Russian dish?' she was asking him: 'I mean, Kiev?' she added intelligently. Emmanuel smiled charmingly at her and didn't reply: he never answered a question that bored him. She decided to leave the button alone, and have steak. The waiter went, and Emmanuel realized that unpleasant though he was, he nevertheless created an area of calm.

Eventually they were herded to a table which was not un-like a roundabout on the Great West Road, only smaller, and unless they actually sat on the table, much less safe. It was a good table anyway, said Sol, with satisfaction. He loved people, but they made him sweat – and already he had exerted himself until he looked like a melting candle. They all had lunch: but the girl had a kind of inert self-con-fidence that Emmanuel found dispiriting. She tried to fix him with her large pale blue eyes, which seemed somehow to reflect great wastes of her character: she worked her way perseveringly through his career – comparing his plays with one another – broadcasting her innocuous opinions like weed killer on a well-kept lawn, with Sol behind her rolling the mixture in. Emmanuel ate his oysters and tried not to feel predatory or exasperated. The other two drank a wine foisted on them with expert contempt by the wine waiter: the girl unfortunately added bravado to her repertoire and Sol gleamed phosphorescently in the gloom. She was practically asking for the job now, and Sol was heading her off – he had finesse if you looked at things large enough – by asking about Lillian and Jimmy.

'Your children?' She was deflected: her face composed to that indulgent lack of curiosity which by now he related to that question.

'My wife and Jimmy Sullivan: he directs for me – manages everything.'

'Do you mean to say you haven't *got* any children?'

'We had one: she died of meningitis. My wife is not allowed to have another; she has kidney trouble and something wrong with her heart – it was very dangerous for her to have a child at all – so no – I haven't.' He said this quite mercilessly – to the girl and to himself – so that the girl would never again ask anybody those questions, and so that it sounded to him as though he was talking about somebody else.

The girl looked stunned: then Sol leant forward and said: 'Will you tell Lillian I saw her at the opening Tuesday looking so beautiful I meant to send her flowers for it? *Honest!*' His eyes were like deep velvet; his great soft heart, like a cushion, plumped up to receive them.

They were drinking bitter, boiled coffee. Emmanuel said: 'I'll tell her, Sol, but she won't believe *me*.'

'Then I'll *send* the flowers!' His smile was like an advertising sign. 'What does she like?' He started unpacking his breast pocket – a flurry of leather wallets and books and cases fell out.

'Something blue that smells.'

'Blue that smells,' he wrote laboriously in a tiny book. 'Say, what would that be? Heelio ... Higher –'

'Hyacinths,' said Martha. 'It's not too late for them, is it?'

'Not too late,' said Emmanuel, and smiled at her. He had noticed with his sharpest detachment that he had only upset her about herself and not in the least about him.

He escaped in the end – recapturing his coat for a small consideration, and set off for Finchley Road where Gloria and her sister lived and ran a small typing bureau. His progress was erratic: as usual, he started by taking a bus whose intentions he did not discover, but he did not notice this for about half an hour because, in order not to consider immediate events, he was engrossed with the past, trying to unwrap the layers of choice and responsibility and get to his intentions. ...

Once, at their beginning, they had hardly seemed wrapped at all: the tissue of poverty, gigantic hunger, and being always cold or sweating from enclosure had covered his life, he had shivered and panted his way through it – his private self fortified by the permanent self-appointed post of Prime Minister which he enriched by incidents like the King sending for him: 'Never, in all my career as King, have I known a Prime Minister of nine. There are no lengths to which you won't go, my boy, if you keep this up.' He kept it up and there seemed no need for ambition in terms of life at 492 Napoleon Road. He could even watch the spectacle of his parents tearing each other to pieces with a kind of unquestioning detachment. His father, a small man, strong as a cat; his eyes blazing with abstract convictions: a disposition both fiery and shiftless – mostly out of work, and often mysteriously drunk even then: his mother, soft, and pale and dark, with her lacerating silences – her grief-stricken sense of commitment: she had defied her orthodox family in marrying an Irish Roman Catholic, and so burned her courage down that her spirit guttered like a candle for the rest of her life. He could not remember ever thinking of them as anything but not the same – different – elementally irreconcilable like fire and water. But the night his intentions were born was a memory distinct as the smell of frying sprats which accompanied it, and the heat of his mother's face charged with waiting. She was wearing an overall patterned with flowers too large for her, and her shoes, which she only wore out of doors or on fine occasions. That evening was one of them; the anniversary of his parents' wedding, and, as usual, they were waiting for his father – had been waiting with the sprats unfried, for nearly four hours. His mother had once wept in that time, as her fragile idea of pleasure broke to despair – and he, what he had gone through about those sprats! When the waters of his mouth had given out, he had magnified them, had made each one the size of a whale, big enough to carry him on their backs, big enough to swallow whole somebody he disliked. He had become a sprat himself for a while, surrounded by gleaming friends with fat economical bodies – then he got desperate and tried to count them, to work out what would be his share. ... Meanwhile the air trawled from the hot dirty street, and netted in their small room by the lace curtains, seemed to get heavier – to press upon them like a weight of clouded water – as hopes silted up from expecting something good to waiting for something bad. After his mother had wept, which she did with lamentable discretion – one little cry of sound and a few cold tears – he knew that the evening was spoiled, that the sprats meant nothing to her, and that if he was not careful they would be forgotten. He became inspired – adding up suddenly that his mother responded only to two things, sickness or bullying. Sickness was out of the question if a single sprat was to pass his lips: he got the whip hand of the situation and bullied her. Shaking her head, faintly blushing, smiling at he knew not what family resemblance, she fried the whole lot. He watched the silver fishes swoon in the clear fat (she used a special kind), jig a little as they stiffened, lost their beauty and became crumby and confiding. She had just put a plate with seven fishes on it – five large, two small – in front of him when his father arrived.

Emmanuel, years later, was to divide second-rate actors into those who could make exits and those who could make entrances. His father was essentially a man who made entrances. He had flung open the door so that it hung gaping on its hinges, and now he leaned diagonal and dramatic in its narrow opening: breathing heavily and with a piece of blood by his left eye. Below this eye, and the other one which shone with a purer rage, he was smiling. He paused long enough for this awful incongruity to sink in but not long enough for them to get used to it before he began: 'I've been out after me sense of proportion: I have to remove myself from life to get anything out of it – if I stayed here I'd be the size of a fly on a dusty lump of sugar – that's you my *darling* – sweet and dusty – giving me such a thirst for distance that I can glory in a street corner – anything outside this rotten little hole – have you thought that if we were all dead we'd take up much the same room lying down? Isn't that a damned thought? But as you lay down when you married me and never got up perhaps it's another of the billion trillion things you don't notice ...' And on and on He could not remember all of it. His mother was crying, and as his father lurched past him to her he suddenly thought of his one visit to a circus – the best day in his life – because his father smelt of lions, a hot, tawny, meaty, sawdust smell. 'If you were as far away as the stars I might miss you – but not much, because you wouldn't gleam – you wouldn't twinkle a mile away. You're the kind of woman one bumps up against in a foggy life and spends the rest of it apologizing. I came back from me great thoughts of the utter ruin of this country to the smell of fish, and you snivelling – what's that but a stinking little beano? If you're a poor man your possessions cost money – for me that's you and that little toad – I could keep myself one way or the other when I was knee-high to him. You may be all I have in the world but *by God*, I could do without you! I was worn out with family life before I'd taken a girl round the corner. And what 'ave I got? That mooney young savage – that chewed and spewed out little piece of rope heading for damnation as sure as an egg comes out of a hen – a little knocked-up piece of work without blood or brains; with a future the length of his own nose, and eyes like some lady's dog ...'

Emmanuel had never felt so important. He tried to see the end of his own nose – a squint at the future – but he was already so drunk with language that it made him dizzy. His mother had subsided on to the only chair with arms to it: his father swaying perilously over her – pieces of his overcrowded mind breaking up like a wreck, as below him she shuddered like the sea.

'... I'm like a man with a great weight on his back – but it's no river I'm crossing – no holy child to bless *me*, and no bank in sight: I might be carrying the river itself, you're so like a weight of water, Leah. I could be in America by now, giving meself a fine time of it, but ever since you married me the corners of me life have turned down – there's no smile in it – you're so set on concocting a tragedy out of a chance.

I can walk the streets with me head in the air at the stars –
all over the sky all over the world – that's a spectacle with
some size to it, but I come back here to you jammed in this
little trap of a room, chock-a-block with a thimbleful of
grief – making the worst of me all the time I'm away. One
day the balloon will go up and by God I'll be in it. Is it my
fault your family are like stones to you? Is it my dreadful
sin I'm not a Jew? Have you thought of my poor mother
negotiating the saints about this little heathen?'

His mother uttered one loud wailing cry at this, threw her
apron over her head, and there was a savage silence. He
could not remember how the scene between them ended:
they went into the other room where they slept, and he was
left alone. Words, words, words: he did not consider their
meaning – his heart was so packed with their power. There
was a kind of force about them that stretched his little, open
mind (for the first time he thought of its size, and knew that
it was small because he felt it growing with an irregular
surging excitement). It hurt him, and he did not know why;
he remembered looking at his arms and legs for some mark,
while pieces of his father's language rocketed in his head
with explosions of colour and sound. He seemed to be as big
as the room now – if he moved his hand the walls would fall
down: his eyes were already outside them, and some other
part of him was further than that – higher and farther than
his eyes. He tried to catch this piece by pinning it down.
America? The stars? Negotiating the saints with his unknown grandmother? But this piece was gigantically obliging – if he said America, it was there, and rushed to supply
him with detailed evidence: cowboys eating golden ice-
cream galloped over him; rivers spiked with Indian canoes
poured towards him; mountains, cactus, animals, seeded
like magic. The stars were not made of gold: they were
silver – crisp and pointed, so that if you pulled them together
with your finger, they fitted in one piece of patched and
dazzling beauty, and the dark air round them was warm,
like feathers to his skin. His grandmother – wearing a white
dress because she was dead – carrying an umbrella like a

dame in the pantomime he had seen at Drury Lane, was jabbing it at a circle of saints – all men, with golden beards, bare feet, and heavy holy eyelids, and he laughed because she could not break the circle with her umbrella. ... This piece of him could go anywhere; indeed, he could not stop it – it was like a marvellous machine to him. Did his father, using all those angry, travelling words also have such a machine? He decided not: his father was too angry and despairing: but perhaps his machine had broken down, or perhaps he made it run the wrong way. This was an easy, but frightening thought: if the machine was so very obliging and one went the wrong way with it, anything could happen. ... Oily black underground rivers crept up with a horrible silent speed, so that his feet hugged the legs of the chair: the sun was an enormous red angry stare, and he could hear the blood behind his ears like thunder – he was the size of a drop or a grain – drowning, scorched ... he threw all his remaining weight against the machine – it gave a convulsive shudder and was stopped, and the words lay scattered about like broken pieces of it. They had to be used right: had to be put together, and then they could reach, could cover, anything. He looked down at his hands lying each side of the plate of fish, and saw them, and saw the difference in his sight. His hands were soft, grey, boneless, small, calm, and rather dirty; but they were simply waiting to do what he wanted; he could move a finger, turn a wrist, have any power with them – they were another kind of this astonishing machinery. He felt so wonderfully made that he was easily contained in the small greasy room; he felt now that he was a right and powerful size in it. He looked at his hands again and thought: 'I shall write the words. I'll use them like that,' and a burning shot up in his heart until he felt his eyes alight with it. He went to the small stove on which his mother had cooked the sprats, and opened the fire box. It was nearly out – one layer of red, and below it a powdery bed of grey. The pan of sprats lay on the top; he touched one and it was almost cold. He lifted the pan carefully and tipped the fish on to the fire; it gave a creak of amazement, and rustled to

life. New clear flames with unexpected streaks of an unearthly blue slipped up and down over the fish. The blaze
suited him, and when it began to die down, he fetched his
own plate and fed the fishes one by one to the fire. He waited
until the very end: then pulled out the bottom drawer of
the dresser, which was his bed, turned out the gas, and
plunged into sleep.

Here, he was woken up: the bus had reached its terminus,
and, as the conductor pointed out, he was not now much
nearer Finchley Road than he had been when he boarded
the bus. He became quite passionate about Emmanuel's poor
sense of direction: reproached him bitterly for not stating
his destination; explained to him three or four ways by
which he could have reached Finchley Road by public transport; and made it very clear to Emmanuel that his concern
was the more justified as the situation meant nothing personally to *him*.

Emmanuel apologized, which had a calming effect, and
the conductor asked whether he was a foreigner. He could
not really say that he was. That was funny, because the conductor felt that he'd seen his face somewhere.

'I do go abroad a great deal.'

'Oh well, that must be it, then. You'll have to take a taxi,'
he added pityingly.

They lurched down the stairs together, and the conductor,
with an obvious effort of generosity, remarked: 'Mind you,
I can see the funny side of it.'

Gloria and her sister lived in part of a neo-Tudor gem set
well back from the Finchley Road. He had never been there
before, and he had never seen Gloria's sister, who was older
than Gloria and called Beryl. He waited for her in a small
bleak room which had been furnished for the purpose:
instinct, which had driven him here, seemed to have abandoned him, and he was now trapped with a blank and nervous mind.

She came in dressed as a professional woman of twenty
years ago: the classical navy-blue coat and skirt which were

supposed never to date and did, as indubitably as people's faces. The white shirt with a bow at the neck – stud pearl ear-rings, as far removed from their function as tinned fruit, hair contorted with the same rigid gaiety as a municipal garden, and a face whose energy had all been put into withstanding the unexpected. Her expression now, covering what seemed to be curiosity and resentment, was one of breezy caution.

'It's Mr Joyce, isn't it? I had no idea you were coming.'

'I came to ask you whether you had seen your sister?'

'She was sleeping this morning – so I'm going this evening after work. She's quite comfortable, they say.'

There was a short silence and then she said: 'It was a terrible shock, of course.' She said it not looking at him and as though there was no other kind.

'I wonder whether you could spare me a few minutes to talk about Gloria?'

Her expression deepened. 'Of course. Won't you sit down? I'll just tell my girl to take the telephone.'

As she went out he realized that she was really wearing the same clothes as the girl with whom he had lunched – with a difference which somehow touched him. He sat on one of the uncomfortable chairs and stared at a water colour of some angry-looking jonquils in a gilt basket until she came back. She sat in the other chair and they looked at each other.

'I wanted to tell you,' he began carefully, 'that I had absolutely no idea that Gloria would even attempt to kill herself. I am going to New York in a week or two, and yesterday I had to tell her that I could not take her with me – with us. I hadn't even realized that she had thought she was going until my manager – Mr Sullivan – told me he thought so. I had absolutely no idea that my telling her would have this effect.'

She said nothing, so he asked: 'Did *you* know that she was expecting to go to New York?'

'I knew she wanted to go, naturally.' There was a pause, and she added suddenly: 'You must have had *some* idea of it. You must have known she thought she was in love with you.'

Taken off his guard, he said: 'Thought?'

'People can think about love the same as they think about anything else, can't they? And if you think all the time about that sort of thing you get narrow-minded. Gloria's romantic, of course.' She said this last with a mixture of pride and resentment. 'Mind you,' she added, 'I don't think you've helped much.'

'I think I've done very badly indeed.'

She did not confirm or deny this, but he felt her open a little to the confession. She was thinking. Then she said: 'I suppose you'd give her a good reference?'

'Yes – of course. She's a very good secretary.'

'I usually send her out for the interesting temporary jobs, but there doesn't happen to be one just now. She gets fed up sitting here all day typing manuscripts. If *you* gave her a very good reference, I might be able to find her something to take her mind off everything.'

'Oughtn't she to have a holiday first?'

A complex of emotions came and went on her face: she gave an unnecessary cough and said: 'I don't think that could be managed at present. We're a very small business, you know – just us and a girl, and she's only training. As soon as they're any good, they go, because I can't afford to pay them enough. Gloria does get a holiday,' she added hastily; 'it's just that it has to be fitted in when we're slack.'

'Do you have one?'

'I usually take a week at Christmas. We go down to my brother at Eastbourne: he's married, and I always say Christmas isn't Christmas without children. But Gloria goes in the summer as well.'

'I was wondering,' he said, not looking at her, 'whether you'd let me arrange a holiday for both of you now – any kind of holiday . . .' he searched for what they might like; 'a cruise, or something like that. To Madeira or Greece – or anywhere you like.'

He heard her give a little gasp; saw her hands clench together in her lap; her neck, her face painfully coloured a dark pink, and her eyes filled with tears. She was withstanding nothing at all, and plainly exposed she lifted the whole situation from the cheap embarrassment he had felt in offering to pay for his behaviour, to a most gentle pleasure at being able to afford her delight. He went on explaining that he would help for somebody to run her bureau while she was away, and ended by saying that nothing could happen to it in six weeks or so.

'Six weeks!' She searched for and discovered an inadequate handkerchief. He gave her his; she took it without noticing – crying and trying to explain to him. She'd always wanted to go abroad, but Mother had only died last year, and had been too poorly for thirteen years before that; Mother simply couldn't bear to go away, even for the week at Christmas. She'd started the typing bureau because she'd had to work at home. She'd been engaged for nearly four years but he wouldn't have Mother to live with them, and you couldn't blame him – Mother didn't like him, and Gloria – she was only seventeen at the time – said she'd die if she was left alone with Mother. You couldn't blame Gloria – she and Mother had never really got on. In the end he'd got fed up and gone off, and you couldn't blame him really. She was forty now – no chicken, ten years older than Gloria – so she felt responsible for her in a way, and she'd been trying to save a bit for a rainy day – her heart wasn't what it was – and she hadn't felt justified in taking a holiday – let alone going abroad ... 'Abroad!' she repeated, cramming his handkerchief from one hand to the other with shiny, nervous fingers.

He said he would have some itineraries of cruises sent to her to choose from, and that apart from making her choice, she was not to worry about any of the arrangements. He must go: he got to his feet – she sprang to hers like a clumsy young girl, and his handkerchief fell to the ground.

'Oh!' It was the first time that she was aware of it.

As he returned it to her, she said: 'It's *ever* so good of you to do this – and to think of me. I hadn't thought – I think I'd better talk to Gloria first: she might prefer to go alone. She might feel that you were *her* friend, and that I had no business taking so much from you. Besides, she might feel she'd have more fun on her own.'

'She has to be looked after,' he said firmly; 'she's been ill. Either you go with her, or she doesn't go.'

Her face lightened and she followed him meekly to the door.

'And if I were you,' he ended, 'I should not tell Gloria that I had anything to do with this trip. I would much prefer that you didn't, and I think it will be more of a success if there is an element of mystery about it. Didn't you say she was romantic?' He was smiling at her now, and afterwards – for the rest of her life – this precise and delicate goodness was her secret blessing.

In the taxi he lay back; his body relaxed, and his mind drifting towards the moments that he recognized but could never invite. He felt calm and alert, and he knew he was waiting for something. Somewhere, at an extremity, he was touching it: as though he was adrift in an ocean with his fingers on a raft: the swell was moving him and the raft in its different way, and the difference was at the end of his fingers. . . . Her neck and her face suffusing that painful pink; her clumsy movement to her feet; her acceptance of his handkerchief . . . the machinery of money – use it, abuse it, it was still the same stuff – people only generalized about anything out of a personal lack of grip. . . . 'Her heart was not what it was.' He wondered if she had ever known what it had been. He started to imagine her heart: raw – touched by the man she didn't marry – grabbed by Gloria – squeezed to its death by her mother; the substitutions encouraged, bolstered by provocative whining: 'Beryl's the one with a head on her shoulders: Beryl's strong – she's a good worker': and beneath that we've all got bodies that must be warm and clothed and fed: the rainy days are always with us: where would we be without Beryl – without her heart she won't be able to consider where she might be without us ... and Beryl 'settling down' to earning her bread and spreading it on both sides for Mother and Gloria – always goaded into her place by the unwinking certainty that she was a substitute – doing for them the least that a man might have done on top of the housekeeping-nursing which was her mother's idea of companionship : pinched by circumstances which she had not made but was constantly expected to improve – expected also to be in four places at once, and to 'lose herself' in the process. The outlets: the week at Eastbourne in December; an unmarried sister-in-law exhausted with the maintenance of chronic illness and romanticism, picking gratefully at the crumbs of goodwill that her brother and his wife had to spare. 'It was only for a *week*; it was *Christmas*, after all.' During that week, the continual nag of Mother hating her to be away; of her and Gloria not getting on; of the knowledge that even in a week they could accumulate a bulk of resentment and self-pity that it would take her fifty-one weeks to redeem. The mother had died : Gloria, if the slightest chance offered, would abandon her, and she would be left to her own resources, having served their purposes, and never her own. The spark he had touched in her – its endurance, its dignity in surviving at all – blazed now in retrospect, and illuminated elements with no limit – no horizon but a deeper blue – a rounding off of such distance that the eye could not carry it.

At this moment, like the faint movement of air before a warm wind, the shut red knowledge of sun through the eyelids, like the sudden stroking of a shadow, this kaleidoscopic collection of fact, invention, instinct, and heart, shivered, shook itself, and fell into a beautiful pattern which filled and spread to the edges of his mind. Not to touch or test it – not to move any of his formidable machinery near it – but simply to let it lie there printing itself was like the motionless effort of a time-exposure, and at the end of it he was matchwood and water. He got out of the taxi shaking, and so cold that it took him minutes to find the change.

Even if they rented houses, he thought, they never managed to live in them. The sitting-room had the watchful, un-inhabited air that made him feel rootless and apologetic about it. Upstairs, he heard the petulant sound of drawers being opened and closed – felt steam creep out of the bath-room as he passed its open door – smelled face-powder and scent on the wing. Lillian would have dressed for the party, and was probably late.

She had been to the hairdresser: her head was shining – stern and casual – an expensive business. She was wearing a dress which in a dishonest and conciliating moment he had once said that he liked. It was a floral silk – predominantly blue – with a skirt tightly swathed over her hips, and a low square neck that showed all her delicately prominent bones. It emphasized all her angles without giving an impression of her shape as a whole, and he did not like it. She was adding a pair of diamond clips, diamond and pearl ear-rings, and a pearl collar with a diamond clasp. He was late and she did not like it; she was dressed and he did not like it: she would want to know exactly how he had spent the day and he did not want to tell her; she would want to tell him exactly how she had spent hers, and he did not want to know. 'This is where we start from,' he thought; 'do I want to make any-thing of it?' He said: 'Sol Black said how beautiful you looked on Tuesday and sent his love. He was really struck: I think you'll get flowers.'

Her face assumed the expression of indulgent scorn that a compliment she wanted from a man she despised always en-gendered. 'He's so effulgent!' She sighed, and started to fill her Fabergé box with herbal cigarettes.

'Did you rest?'

She shook her head. 'I don't like being alone here now. Did you work?'

'A bit.' The pattern shimmered in his mind like a heat haze; resolutely he kept it out of focus.

'Em – you're developing a nervous tic. You keep screwing up your eyes. Don't you think you ought to see an oculist? Although I can't see why *writing* should strain your eyes.'

'Nor can I.'

'It worries me,' she said, and looked up at him for approbation.

'Don't worry. You'll upset your head, and it looks very pretty. I've only got to change my shirt: won't be a minute.'

But she followed him into the dressing-room where first Gloria and then he had lain on the bed.

'Where have you got to?'

'Got to?'

'In your new play. How far have you got?'

'Not very far . . .' His temper loomed and changed into an ugly shape before he could stop it.

'Darling, it's not an unreasonable question. People keep asking me, and I feel such a fool not knowing the first thing about it.'

'Well, you can tell them not very far.' He ripped out his cuff-links savagely, and started hunting for a clean shirt.

She said something – he knew what the sense of it would be and didn't listen to the words – by now he had split into three worthless pieces: with an appearance of anger, he was dressing; with an appearance of patience, he was flowing into her gaps of silence; with (was it an appearance of?) despair, he was running over his pattern of deceit with her; his barren periods – of months – when he pretended that he was working; his moments of being part of some truth which he kept inviolate from her; his weeks of writing – hanging on by the skin of his skill to the memory of those moments – endured privately without her knowledge or consent; and the payment for all this. When the work was whole and out of him, he let her read it before anyone else – let her pat and prick it and mark it with L: let her argue and discuss and find the faults which she felt were her contribution – thereby losing to her all the fine flush of a piece of work finished. Because of her, play after play slipped from the heart where it had been building and was cast upon his waters of Lethe – all over, bar the cheering, and there wasn't any of that. . . .

She was almost in tears – he must have lost his temper. He started to lie to her and she looked relieved. As they left the house, she left her centre long enough to say: 'Poor Em. You should have told me you had to re-write the whole act: it must have been awful for you.'

In the taxi she said: 'Well, the least I can do is to find you a new secretary.' And he took her blue-gloved hand feeling deeply ashamed at the appearance of nobility – brittle and blistering on her face.

The day had worn itself into something of a calm – the sky skim milk, the river watered half-ripe wheat; the plane trees along the Embankment whose new leaves had been washed and tossed all the day were fresh and still and golden green – and the starlings like clouds of black ash – fled to their noisy and uncomfortable night in Trafalgar Square. The Fairbrothers gave their party three floors up in a suite looking on to these sights, but the suite was so packed with the blurring agitation of social intercourse that they might not have been there. The party was about show business: almost everyone there had something to do with it, and he thought that this would be apparent to any odd member of an audience. The women were better dressed – on the whole – than the average English party. They had certainly made the most – and in some cases too much – of themselves; their eyes and mouths designed to be seen at a distance, their hair and their hands well groomed, their feet beautifully shod: they wore real scent and a lot of it; artificial jewellery and a lot of that: ingeniously cut brassières or none at all. A few of them had poodles, which, like their handbags, were either very large or very small, and their voices, at whatever volume, were meant to be heard. The men might have been more difficult to place. Sick men, prosperous men, crafty men, nervous men; men who looked as though they ate too much; men who looked as though they never slept; men who kept and understood their bodies like a well-tuned car. Men who hoped they were somebody else; men who wished they were not; men looking for an opportunity; men escaping from responsibility. Men who made things; men who took things; men who broke things. Men who had nothing to gain; and men who had nothing to lose. Their difference from other groups of men was the immediate and thorough knowledge that they had about each other's careers. Sucess or failure could not be concealed from one another, or, indeed, from anybody else: they had almost all had their bad luck, bad taste, or bad judgement confirmed in public: some of them had been on a financial switchback for years; many of them had some startling ability, and there were a few artists.

Lillian was soon swallowed up, and he stood repeatedly refusing a drink and exchanging minima with the immediate throng. The room had a feeling of pressure about it – apart from scents it smelled mysteriously of cold summer food, although he could not see any: there was the usual methylated haze of smoke above the hats and heads, and there was noise spilling, cramming, flooding the room with the windows open like sluices to let some of it out. His hostess had given him some soft drink – the glass was cold and sticky in his hands – she was asking about Lillian, and he looked distractedly round for Lillian to come and give an account of herself. She was talking to a man whose face he knew and a girl whom he didn't. The girl was certainly an odd member of the audience: very young; listening; wearing a cotton dress and a white cardigan and noticeably out of place. Lillian had caught his eye – he indicated her position in the room to Mamie Fairbrother, and they moved towards it. Arriving, he remembered that the man's name was George (George *what?*) and exchanged a cautious greeting with him. Lillian and Mamie were well away, and as he turned from them he caught the girl looking at him with an expression of such solemn, open inquiry that he nearly smiled. Then Lillian said: 'This is Miss Young. She wants to be somebody's secretary, so I've told her to come and see you tomorrow morning.'

4. ALBERTA

TOMORROW morning I am going to be interviewed by Emmanuel Joyce. He is a playwright, and I met his wife at a party last night – on my second day in London. He wants a secretary to go to New York and Mrs Joyce seemed to think I might be suitable. She was awfully nice to me, and I saw him for a moment: I was wondering what on earth I had expected a playwright to look like, and he noticed me and nearly laughed. . . . It would be a wonderful chance – travelling and meeting interesting people, if only Papa won't be nervous about it. He gets nervous at such extraordinary points – he says himself that there's nothing reliable about his fears. But Aunt Topsy'll want me to go (after all it was her idea that I should do a secretarial course) and we shall play at me being Emma, and she being Miss Taylor, and Papa, whether he likes it or not, will be Mr Woodhouse. In the end he'll laugh and agree, and then he won't say anything more – just leave anxious notes in my bedroom: 'Wash grapes before eating them.' 'Do not look at Goya's war drawings alone: they may make you too sad.' That was when darling Uncle Vin took me to Paris. Papa doesn't mind me going about with him in spite of his being an actor (apart from being his brother anyway) because he always plays clergymen (although he sometimes plays wicked men dressed *up* as clergymen in spy films which Papa doesn't see because he hates the cinema and there isn't one nearer than Dorchester) and Papa simply says that clergymen in plays help to make the Church an integral part of people's lives so Uncle Vin is helping quite as much, and more interestingly, than *he* is preaching to about forty people. I can't think what he'll say about New York or Mr and Mrs Joyce. But perhaps when they know that this would be my first job they won't take me. Uncle Vin says there is an awful lot of never-jam-today in the theatre. I must go to sleep. We had the most lovely morning shopping, and I bought all my presents for home. A scarf for Aunt Topsy, and six butterflies from a shop in the Strand for Clem, and a magnifying glass for Humphrey, and a false beard for Serena because she hates being a girl (Uncle Vin was terribly helpful about that), and a diary for Mary because she's got to the copying stage and wants to imitate me, and a marble egg to keep his hands cold for Papa. Then Uncle Vin gave me a marvellous lunch in a restaurant (*hors d'œuvres*, lobster, and Camembert cheese) and let me choose a gramophone record for a late birthday present. I chose Sir Thomas Beecham conducting the fortieth symphony of Mozart – the other side is the Jupiter – and Uncle Vin said jolly good choice. Then he took me out to a huge party at the Savoy Hotel, and that's where I met the Joyces. (The party was simply filled with famous people, but unfortunately I didn't know who most of them were.) Now I must wash my cardigan for tomorrow.

Wednesday. Uncle Vin offered to take me, and I said I didn't want the Joyces to think I was a child, and he drew in his chin and went away without a word. In the end I went to his room. He was in his dressing-gown playing 'If You Were the Only Girl in the World' on the piano with a cigarette drooping out of his mouth. I apologized handsomely (he said that) and we arranged to meet at a place called Notting Hill Gate which he said was near the Joyces' house. Well – then I went. I wore my tidy skirt and the white shirt that Aunt T. made for Mary and didn't fit her. Uncle Vin explained about buses and waved me off with his fingers crossed.

A man opened the door: he seemed surprised to see me, but I told him why I'd come, and then he asked me to wait in the drawing-room (which we walked straight into) and he went upstairs. It was a long narrow room, very smart and full of precious things that matched each other – not at all like home or Uncle Vin's. I got rather nervous, and after a bit Mr Joyce came down. He is a little man, not much taller than me, and he looked tired, I thought, and if he wasn't so famous I would have thought he was embarrassed. I had been sitting down, we both stood, and then we both sat and nobody said anything. Then, instead of asking the questions which I had expected, he said: 'A good secretary has to have a good sense of proportion for somebody else. Have you got one for yourself?' Then he smiled, and said: 'Don't bother to answer; it's my business to decide that about you. Tell me why you want to be a secretary.'

So I told him about Papa, and Clem not getting a scholarship, and Humphrey wanting to go to Oxford and Aunt

Topsy having used her money up on Serena going to Switzerland for her wretched chest, and Mary being what Papa calls an unknown quantity, and Papa not being allowed a chequebook by Aunt Topsy because of inflation which she says he doesn't understand, and Aunt Topsy giving me a course in shorthand and typing. I'd thought then that I'd help Papa, but he'd said that although as a daughter I had become a necessity, that he constantly appreciated, as his secretary, I would be a luxury that he could not afford. So I'd come to London to look for a job. That made it clear that I hadn't had one before.

'You are the eldest?'

I told him my age, and it didn't seem to surprise him which was a comfort. He asked me if I had had anything to do with the theatre, and I told him about Uncle Vin. Then he asked me if I'd been abroad, and I told him about Paris and Uncle Vin again. Then the man who had opened the front door came downstairs, and said that someone called Sol wanted a word with him. He went, telling the man to tell me about the job, and he was rather shy and took a long time telling me, and he was so vague I didn't understand him much. In the middle Mr Joyce came back and listened for a bit, and then interrupted saying that he'd like me to work for him so never mind, Jimmy, tell her later. They both smiled and I did too, because I liked how they were. Then Mr Joyce was staring at me and asked my Christian name. I told him. There was an odd silence as though I'd said something wrong – then he asked me if I had any other names and I told him the other one, and said I absolutely refused to be called it. They both smiled, and Mr Joyce said out of the question, he wouldn't even call a hen that, but would I mind if he thought of a name for me and they all called me by it, but I would have the right to veto. I thanked him and tried to remember exactly what veto meant, but then Mrs Joyce came in and the subject was changed because she hadn't got money to pay for her taxi. The man Jimmy asked for my address and telephone number and I gave him Uncle Vin's and left. Mr Joyce shook hands with me and called me

Miss Young and then Mrs Joyce did the same: she was wearing beautiful gloves but her rings hurt through them.

Dearest Papa,

This is a very important letter so will you and Aunt Topsy both read it and give it your most serious but open-minded consideration?

I have been offered the most wonderful job by some people known to Uncle Vin, as a private secretary. They want me to go to New York with them, but only for about three months, and then I should be back in England. The salary is enormous, for someone of my age, and it works out at more than £500 a year here, but different in New York and even more. Also they pay my expenses of travelling and where I live – probably with them, so you will see that it is a princely sum which would make all the difference to Clem and Humphrey. Also the experience which is of a very good kind would be invaluable to me, and will probably change my whole life. Mr Joyce is a playwright, but a very good one and if you had met him I'm sure you would agree that he is mercifully unlike what you, Papa, might call to mind if you envisaged such a person. Aunt Topsy has probably heard of him as he is quite old and has written so many plays – Emmanuel Joyce is his name, and he has a very nice wife who is rather ill and it was her idea that I should work for them as the other secretary has had to go to hospital. Then there is a nice quiet man called Mr Sullivan who is a manager and who will tell me what to do. He has a kind of American accent, but he is very shy. This letter is becoming ill-expressed, but you can imagine my heartfelt excitement at the prospect very possibly before me if you, dear Papa, will consent to it without too much private anxiety. Uncle Vin says it would be madness to refuse this offer, and although he rolled his eyes, he really meant it. He says that it is time I saw something of the world, and that most people have to pay to do that, and I am so lucky I don't have to pay anything at all. The only thing is that *if* you agree, will you please do so with as little delay as possible? The Joyces go to New York at the end of this month and want to make their arrangements as soon as possible. Of *course* I should come home to say good-bye to you all and pack my clothes, and write to you frequently all the time I am away. Uncle Vin has read this and says that no time must be lost, and did you see him in *Death*

LONDON

Takes a Dance which of course you didn't but he is trying to shame you into more interest in his career. Give my love to Clem and Humphrey and Serena and Mary and Mrs Facks and Napoleon and Ticky – and, of course, Aunt Topsy.

Your loving Sarah

CHAPTER TWO

*

I. LILLIAN

I NEVER feel more alone than on the day that I leave a country. I should like to leave lacerated by my departure from one place, and throbbing with the adventure of discovery or return to another. I should like the last day to be spent with all those people who haven't seen enough of me while I'm here recognizing their regret – ringing up, trying to have lunch with me, and in the end sitting on my bed while I finish packing – filled with affectionate, envious speculation about where I am going. I would like more friends to come down to the airport with us and we would all be very gay with champagne to conceal our feelings: they would wave to me at take-off – people *do* do that for personal reasons with just a bit of waving to the aeroplane thrown in – and I would not simply be part of the aeroplane, but Lillian Joyce waving back to particular people and then settling in my seat, unstrapping my belt and looking forward to my welcome at the other end of the journey. I have been on so many journeys: I must have watched hundreds of greetings that I would have liked: faces like a sunburst; two people literally running into one, the kind where they walk off together asking questions and squeezing arms, stop for a moment, and laugh before they walk on. Em once met me like that – in Geneva: I was over half-way having Sarah, and we were going to see a doctor because my back which ached all the time I was pregnant got so much worse, and he was supposed to be a great authority on kidneys. Em had been on an exhausting journey for the opening of one of his plays in Denmark, and then came straight to Geneva to meet me. Aeroplanes made me feel as though I was having jaundice then, and what with the sickness and my back I got off the plane feeling like a queasy barrel. Somehow, he managed to join me in the Customs. He came straight over and put his arms round me and his hands on the small of my back, and as he touched me the pain melted so suddenly that I thought I was going to float from the ground, and Sarah gave a little leap on the instant: he felt it, and said: 'What a welcome – like meeting Elizabeth.' That was such a meeting that I didn't care when the doctor looked gloomy and said the same things as all the other doctors: that I shouldn't be having a child; that I must expect to feel more and more sick, and my back to feel like breaking in two – a long list of things I mustn't eat and the usual injunctions about leading a very quiet life. He couldn't know that compared to now I'd never led a life at all; that I didn't care what I felt like so long as the machinery of my body was working and Sarah was being made. The thought of her life was such a centre of strength that I never cared – even during the last long weeks – about the continuous sickness and pain and my possible – I told Em afterwards, probable – death. I lived that time: in the beginning as months; then weeks, and in the end I was aware of an hour in my life, but it was all without impatience or fear.

Now, since there is no chance of his meeting me like that, I have insisted on flying with Em and the others going on a separate flight. But that hasn't altered the desolate day of departure: I'm leaving nothing here that matters and there is nothing in New York that I want. The worst of it is that I am taking so little with me – am travelling so light – it is such a spectral business. Everything is done: the packing – the arrangements – the agents have looked over the house; Jimmy's girl has made a scene on the telephone which shocked poor little Miss Young; Em disappeared for nearly the whole of yesterday and nobody knew where he was which always frightens me so much that I'm horrible to him when he comes back, and some people we hardly know have been badgering us to have a drink with them some time before we leave this evening. And that is exactly how it is when we leave anywhere. The only new ingredient is the girl: she's been with us a week now, and they say she does letters well and seems intelligent. I suppose New York will grow her up a bit, but at the moment the poor thing looks like a typical little English frump. Anyway it's better than a plastic blonde, or some ghastly would-be actress trying to get at Em. I gave her an old jersey I hadn't got room for yesterday, and she was really sweet about it – as though I'd given her a marvellous present – I must say she has nice manners.

And now I've got the whole day to fill in, until the car comes for us at six o'clock. Em likes going for walks on these days, and Jimmy – if he hasn't any work to do – goes to films, and I oscillate between fiddling with my appearance and fidgeting round picture galleries, or bookshops to find something to read for the journey. At least I suppose we might all have lunch and spin that out for an hour or two: Miss Young – Alberta is her extraordinary name – has the day off: she really doesn't look as though she's called Alberta, but except for plays people are seldom right for their names ... Anyway we wouldn't have to have her, which is a relief, because she shows signs of being starry-eyed about the journey and that's very difficult to take if one is as bored as I am.

2. JIMMY

'MAKE it fun for her, Jimmy,' he said this morning: 'She's never done it before – make it an occasion.' It was almost as though he wished he was flying with her himself, and, considering his alternative, one can't blame him. Madam's luggage! I've never known a woman with so many impersonal possessions; she even travels with her private picture gallery, which is why we always have to be at airports early – to get through all the Customs forms and excess baggage. I spent the afternoon with her to give Emmanuel a rest because she's always jumpy before a journey. We met at Wilton's for lunch and she was late which was the best way round. She'd got us a table at the back, and I could tell by the way she came in that she wanted to enjoy herself ... a smile of conspiratorial exhaustion, followed by a little sigh of potential gaiety – '*What* a morning!' and left it to my imagination. 'Let's have a *delicious* lunch.' We did: Lillian has always had a fine feeling for food and loves ordering it, so I let her choose for me as well. We talked of this and that, and then she suddenly shot at me: 'Jimmy! what do *you* think of Em's play?'

I knew what she meant, but I said: 'You know, Lillian, I think it's a honey – the only problem is finding a girl who can do that sort of thing.'

'You know I don't mean that one. I mean the new one.'

I didn't say anything – so she repeated: 'The new one. The one he's had to re-write a whole act of.'

'I didn't even know that about it.'

'*Didn't* you?' She sounded incredulous, but a little pleased as well. 'I thought that if things were going badly, you'd be the first person he'd tell.'

'Well, he hasn't. I haven't seen it, he hasn't discussed it, and I don't even know what it's about.' I managed to sound resentful (Lillian is an authority on resentment); it covered my embarrassment about a play which, so far as I knew, he hadn't even begun.

She raised her eyebrows in a commiserating manner and was silent for a minute before saying: 'I wish he *would* talk about it – to one of us – before it's too late.'

The waiter brought our sole, and I didn't reply, ostensibly until he had served the fish, hoping really that I needn't say anything; but she adores intimate criticism – she doesn't see it as destructive gossip – more as a means of measuring her intelligence by the yardstick of her inside information.

'I mean that the whole idea of that play is fantastically difficult for anyone to do – the inversion of a Cinderella with the girl getting plainer and poorer all through the play. No amount of spiritual growth is going to compensate for that with an audience – they can't *see* it, unless you make her some sort of a saint, and he won't do that. I told him all this the first time I read it.'

It's no good: I can't keep out of it. In that much time she'd swept me along her current – past the danger notices – the drum of my own temper roared ahead and I hadn't the strength to get back. I'd had to deal with Emmanuel the night after she'd read the play, and at the memory of him then my detachment snapped.

'In the first place the girl does grow inside – in exact proportion to her external changes. In the second place, I don't know what you mean by some sort of saint, but he's made her a significant force on the credit side, I should have said, if you think of the last act. In the third . . .'

'You *do* know what I mean. People don't laugh at saints; you can't make them ridiculous – the girl's almost a clown.'

'In the third place I don't even agree about her getting plainer or poorer. It simply depends what you mean by those words.'

'I mean what everybody means. I *don't* mean Hollywood stuff – wearing well-cut rags and all that glossy simplicity racket. Really, Em's plays are above that.'

'He doesn't mean that either. He means a different kind of beauty, a different kind of richness' . . . I realized suddenly how loud my voice was by the expression on her face, felt even angrier, and dropped it. 'The right actress can convey these things – it's all written for her.'

'Exactly! The *right* actress, but he hasn't found one. The girl here plays for laughs all the time, and now we're going to New York for endless auditions, and you know as well as I do that there isn't anyone there young enough who can do it : it's crazy!'

We were right on the edge; she was breathless, and her hands were shaking. It was Emmanuel who was flying with her, and I was supposed to be giving her a pleasant run. I started to hand us back along the banks.

'I agree that the girl here isn't right. She's been a great disappointment.'

'But it was obvious from the start that she never would be.'

'Well – we hoped. I know you realized that before we did.' I was sweating now with the effort and shame that I had made it necessary. I tried to smile and leaned towards her.

'Please eat your fish. Emmanuel would be furious if he knew I'd taken you out to lunch and then argued with you so that you couldn't eat it.'

'But we're not arguing,' she said, and slit her fish from the bone. 'You agree with me really.' She looked quite gay again, and poured us both more wine. 'There isn't anybody to play Clemency, and if Em had talked about the play before he wrote it, we might have got him to see that.'

We were going her way somehow or other. I had rejected violence – had dragged us into calm water, and now she tied me up and let us both down quietly until we emerged at the level she had determined. The only way that I could defend Emmanuel was to agree with her. By the time I had agreed with her that one could tell Emmanuel how to write plays if only he would listen to what she said, we had finished our pineapple, and she proposed that we drink some Kirsch by itself. It was too late to go to a picture, and I had a desire to sleep which nearly overwhelmed me, but she looked wonderful. Warmth and enjoyment always brought the faintest, most delicate pink to her cheekbones; her eyes, which were chiefly remarkable for their size, sparkled with an affectionate ease – she liked being with me and visibly it did her good to like anything.

I'd forgotten her question in the sudden memory of the first time I had seen her – been struck by her, you might say – for she was a dramatic and beautiful sight. It was just after I came out of the Army, in America: Emmanuel had offered me my job and asked me to week-end with them in Connecticut – they'd rented a house for the summer. I'd changed and gone down to the sitting-room. It was a hot June night – *Aida* was pouring out of the radiogram, and the windows were open on to the garden, but the room was empty. It was a large, pleasant, quite ordinary room – books, low tables, and well-shaded lamps scattered about, and an enormous fireplace for burning logs; but it was the first private house I had been to since my discharge, and it had a kind of haze of luxury and civilization over its comfort. There was a tray with Bourbon and orange, cherries and ice, etc., to mix an Old Fashioned, and I was just wondering whether I dared to start on one – when something made me turn round to face the window.

She was wearing a long dress of some finely pleated material – a very dark blue – bare on one shoulder and caught on the other by a swag of wonderful pearls. She was facing me; her arms were lifted to draw the curtains behind her, her face and all her skin had the most astonishing radiance, and her hair looked as though there was moonlight on it. She smiled, and said: 'I'm Lillian Joyce', and at that moment something strange happened to me. All through the war, in various godforsaken places, I'd listened to men talking about what they'd left and what they were going back to. Women; their wives, their mothers, their jobs, their homes, or just women – women they'd slept with, women they'd never seen – the usual reminiscence of sentiment, sex, swagger, and plain homesickness; and I'd mostly listened because I'd never had a home or family and (although I never told them) hadn't even had a woman. They called me Orphan Annie – I was Annie for years – and I didn't want to add to that. I'd listened because I always hoped I'd understand why we were fighting the war, but I never did understand for myself – although sometimes I thought I could see why they thought they were. But when I saw Lillian like that and she smiled, I suddenly knew. I wasn't in love with her; I didn't even want her, but I was struck by a kind of adoration. I'd have done anything to keep her as she was then: there was nobody like her, but at the same time she was every woman. I felt that all these years I'd been helping to preserve her, and my whole war seemed natural in that moment.

The waiter was standing over us with the Kirsch, and I asked for coffee.

'What was it, Jimmy?' she was asking.

I wondered whether to tell her.

'You looked so sad and tender. Were you thinking of Annie?'

How the hell did she know about Annie – a secret I had made sure died with Private Sullivan?

'Don't worry about her. She was only making the stock scene; she'll get over it.'

'Oh – that one. I'm not worried about her.'

'Well – what was it?' She was asking in the best kind of way: gentle, and flatteringly curious.

'Do you remember when I met you?'

She shut her eyes and opened them again. 'In America, after the war. Do you know, Jimmy, I don't exactly. In New York, was it?'

'No – in Connecticut: that house you had for the summer – in 1946.'

'I remember. That was the summer they stopped me bathing. My God, there didn't seem to be anything left that they'd let me do.' She lit a cigarette, and then asked: 'Why – do you remember it especially well?'

There was no point in telling her something that happened to me; she would only see it as something much smaller which she had not noticed happening to her. I finished my coffee and smiled: 'How could I forget such an occasion?'

Dimly she seemed to sense a loss – that she had missed – a compliment? An effect that she had made? She asked for more coffee, and while it was being poured into her cup said: 'Well, I'm glad it's not Annie anyway. She simply wanted that part, I'm afraid, Johnny – she's hell-bent on her career.'

'Yeah: I know. After nine years, I should know.'

There was a short silence, and then she asked me whether I thought the flight with Alberta was going to be trying at the same time as I asked her whether she minded leaving England. Then we both smiled and disclaimed any concern on either count. After a moment I repeated that I wasn't going to stay awake all night whatever Alberta might do, but that I didn't think she'd be any trouble and I liked her. 'She's very conscientious – a funny little thing – very English with all that prim enthusiasm.'

'Like me? You once said how English I was.'

'You are – but it's different,' I said lamely. It was difficult to attribute enthusiasm to Lillian, and primness didn't seem to apply either.

We had an argument about paying for lunch which somehow felt so meaningless that I said so.

'Nor do I. It's because we're leaving the country tonight,' she answered. 'I'm only determined to pay because I want you to do something for me, so don't thank me: try to feel a little in my debt.'

Outside, she said that she particularly wanted to go to a certain picture gallery where there was a private collection of French pictures being sold – the owner having died. She knew pictures bored me, but she asked very nicely, and I felt she really wanted to go. We walked there slowly: it was fine for a wonder, sunlight, and in St James's Square the traffic sounded like a dusky murmur of summer. I knew she was thinking of Emmanuel before she said: 'He chooses such funny bits of London to walk in!'

When I took her arm to cross a road she said casually: 'I don't really mind leaving this country in the least because there is nothing in it now that I really care about available for me, and I'm far too feminine to care without that. You know the people who bought Wilde were really building contractors in disguise? Well, they pulled it down for the materials, and so far as what remains of my family are concerned, I might as well be dead.'

I went on holding her arm when we were on the sidewalk, with the pangs of being too hard about her on my conscience. Whenever I spent a few hours alone with her I felt something like this: she was no more entirely composed of affectation than most people; she was simply somehow out of her element, and if one can't throw a fish back into the water one gets a kind of guilty irritation when it doesn't keep still. I made a resolve to try and like her pictures – at least to take an interest in them.

Well – I tried. I told Lillian to go ahead at her own speed, and I would take one or two pictures slowly and see if I could get something out of them. The first was called *Lundi Matin*, and was of two women sorting laundry in a rather foggy-looking room. They wore drab Victorian clothes and had untidy buns and rather blotchy faces. The whole thing had a dusty shut-up appearance: then I discovered that it was done in those dusty chalks that come off on everything, and supposed the poor man couldn't afford paints. The next one was very small and macabre – a row of gentlemen in dress clothes in a theatre box – all laughing. If you got too far away from it, their faces looked like a set of false teeth, but even close to they looked a nasty lot. Then there was an extraordinary picture of what looked like a huge wooden tiger in an overgrown field. Everything was very carefully, and I thought badly, painted in this one, including the tiger who had a kind of glassy squint, but at least the colours were a bit brighter. I'd just reached a huge picture of hardly any pears on a red table with a green background, when Lillian joined me. She looked dreadful – there was no pretence about that: I put my hands under her arms – they slipped trying to grasp her fur – and practically lifted her on to a seat. Her handbag fell off her wrist as she sat down, I seized it and struggled with the clasp. 'Push, Jimmy,' she said. I could only see salts in her bag, unscrewed the stopper and gave them to her while I hunted for a capsule. She made a small choking cough which meant things were better, but meanwhile the gallery owner was standing over us, spinelessly concerned.

'Would you get a cab?'

'Shall I ring for one?'

'Any way you like.'

Some people who had been looking at pictures were turned now with far more interest, to us, except one – a woman – who was quietly engrossed.

'I'm afraid they're engaged.' He shook the telephone and looked hopelessly about him.

Lillian had leaned her head against the wall: she was still a bad colour, and she was trembling, but I think the pain was dying down. I looked hard at the woman's profile and said: 'I wonder whether you'd be so kind as to get hold of a taxi?'

She turned round, saw Lillian, nodded, and went out of the gallery.

'Shall I try to get hold of a doctor for Mrs Joyce?'

This increased the crowd interest; an expression of distaste crossed Lillian's face and she murmured: 'No – home.'

The gallery owner's secretary appeared with a thick white cup of water which I gave to Lillian. She couldn't hold the cup, but she drank some. The woman came back.

'The taxi is outside.' She had a foreign accent.

I looked at Lillian; she smiled faintly and nodded.

The gallery owner hovered: 'Is there anything else I can do?'

I thrust the cup of water into his hands. 'Do you want to walk it?'

She did; but when, with the woman on one side, we got her to her feet, I felt her legs giving way; picked her up and carried her out to the taxi. The woman opened its door. Lillian, with a tremendous effort, said: 'Thank you so much.'

'Where to?'

I gave the Bedford Gardens address, and we were off, but Lillian, looking suddenly very frightened, said: 'I'm perfectly all right; I just want to go home.'

'That's it. We're on our way now.'

We rattled and swayed along in silence until we came out of the maelstrom of Hyde Park Corner, when, as though she'd been considering it all the time, she said: 'Isn't it funny that all I want is to go home, and you understand that, and we haven't really got one?'

I said: 'Yes,' and she went on:

'Poor Jimmy, you've never had one, and mine is demolished; I don't know which is worse. It's a bit underprivileged of us, isn't it?'

'Don't worry about it: collect your strength.'

She gave a little laugh and said: 'It takes some looking for.'

I put my arm round her, and she looked pleased. A little later she said: 'You ought to get married, Jimmy – then you'd have a home – and it's very kind of me to say that, because I'd miss you.'

Because I was loving her courage, I said: 'You *are* kind, Lillian. You're one of the kindest people I know.'

By the time we got back to the house she was O.K. – a bit

blue under the eyes, but relaxed, with that kind of quiet elation she has when she gets through one of these things.

Emmanuel wasn't back, so I put her to bed, and turned on her electric blanket and fire for her. She lay down without a murmur, but I saw her eyeing the open suitcases which were all over the room, and I said: 'Sure you want to go tonight?'

She gleamed at me. 'Why not?'

I bent down and kissed her forehead, and she made a little settling of contentment into her pillow.

'I'm all right, Jimmy, I promise you – there won't be any more troubles. Thank you so much.'

It was what she'd said to the foreign woman, but she was saying it quite differently.

'I'll be downstairs if you want anything. Wake you at 5.30? Yes?'

'Yes please.'

As I went out she called: 'At least we managed to keep off Miss Williams.'

'That was quite something.' I shut her door and went down to wait for Emmanuel, hoping he'd get back before I had to wake her up.

He did – looking so pleased with himself that I wondered where he'd been. I told him quickly about Lillian because I had to, and I was accurate about it because I knew that as usual he would have to make a decision – or try to make one if Lillian would let him. He stood motionless while I told him – Emmanuel's full attention is of a kind that I've never had from anyone else – and when I'd finished, he held out his hand for a cigarette.

'She ought not to go, of course.' He thought for a moment, then added: 'You remember when I stopped her?'

'I do.'

'Do you think I could persuade her to follow us by boat?'

'No – I think she's had that one.'

'Even if we left Alberta to travel with her?'

'She's not a trained nurse; she's just a kid – it's not fair on her.'

71

'Well then, I must do it, and you'll have to start the Clemency hunt.' He saw my face and said: 'Come on, Jimmy: ring up our friend in Cunard, and see what there is – tomorrow if possible. No – I'll do it. Is the telephone switched on downstairs?'

'As far as I know.' Then I felt ashamed, and said: 'I'll get through for you.' He loathed telephones, and he didn't want to travel by boat.

While I was working my way through the switchboard to his secretary to the man, I was feverishly assembling my objections to Emmanuel arriving six days late in New York: at least six days – it might be more. There might not be a sailing, or they'd be booked up – but if there *was* a sailing, I knew he'd get a passage. Emmanuel always got everything he didn't particularly want. It wasn't just the auditions. He had a television appearance on the series of authors introducing their own plays: there were two public dinners being given for him and the people who were giving them, at least, thought they were important, and there was a first night of the big musical of one of his earliest plays – all this within the next week – he *had* to be there . . . I was through; he was at my elbow, and I left him to it. It was a quarter past five, and as I went upstairs it occurred to me that I could wake Lillian early, and get her to insist on flying as arranged – and then what? She might be very ill on the plane – she might even die, and then how would I feel? An interfering lunatic, and not having a life of my own didn't give me the right to interfere with other people's. It wasn't even fair on the air-line: I'd got morose by now about the whole thing. The door bell rang: it was Alberta back – with her luggage. I helped her in with it, and noticed irritably that she was wearing a completely shapeless camel-hair coat, and looked as though she had been crying. I told her briefly what was going on, and she said: 'Would you like me to cancel their aeroplane?'

'It's probably too late, and Mr Joyce is calling someone anyway.'

'Mrs Joyce likes very weak tea. Shall I make her some?'

'Yes, do.' I tried to sound pleasant, but I wasn't. I was mad, because I knew what I had to do, and I did *not* want to do it.

Emmanuel came back. 'All fixed: we're lucky. The *Mary*: sailing the day after tomorrow. They had one spare, and they've had a cancellation of another – double state rooms. I'd better go and tell Lillian. Will you call Claridges – we're supposed to be out of this house this evening?'

'Wait a minute.' I told him he'd got to go that night, and why, and then I said I'd stay and go with Lillian if she really felt she didn't want to fly. He looked impatient – almost angry – when I said that, and interrupted: 'It's not a question of what Lillian feels. It's what has to be done.'

'Well, I'm telling you – I'm prepared to do it!'

He looked at me coldly. 'The way you are at the moment, I wouldn't want to go to Hatch End with you – let alone New York. Nor, I should think, would Lillian.'

His loyalty was engaged, he would be immovable, and it was all my fault.

'I'm sorry. It's just that I don't take kindly to sudden changes. We had a very good lunch together, and I'll make it a good trip if you'll let me. Could I tell her about it?'

He looked sweetly at me then, and I felt good again. Then Alberta came up with the tray.

'You take it, I'll be up in a minute. And don't argue with her.'

I left him giving Alberta instructions about calling Claridges and the airport.

Well – that's how it was in the end. The funny thing was that we *all* drove to the airport: there was an argument about it, and I suppose all you can say is that some natures are more human than others – in this case Lillian's; she flatly refused to be left behind. We drove in a huge Daimler – a ponderous calm journey. Emmanuel reminded Lillian from time to time of other journeys they had taken, and got the minimum response: Alberta sat staring out of the windows at the Minibricks houses and coy flowering trees, but she didn't say anything, and I sat trying to remember what I'd forgotten. I'd given her Emmanuel's engagement book, and told her that she must get him to everything on time. I told her this in front of him; she looked nervous and impressed, and she smiled and said wasn't it extraordinary about time – the only moments when it was important one didn't notice it. We were past the last Tudor pub – the last cheery injunction to eat, smoke, or drink alarmingly cheap, quick, nourishing commodities, and into the tunnel on the airport road. I did remember something, and gave Alberta a ten-dollar bill – she hadn't a dime – and she put it away in her bag saying in a nervous practical voice that she'd remember how much it was. Poor kid; she looked terrified – or maybe just excited – but ever since she'd been told that she was flying with Emmanuel she'd been speechless.

The bonus about London Airport is that they're all as nice to you as people are before you have an operation, and as you aren't going to have one, it makes you feel good. They met us with the information that the tourist seats for Alberta and me had been rebooked. The Press also met us and took some pictures of Emmanuel and Lillian getting out of the car. We weighed in the luggage and the Press took some pictures of Emmanuel and Lillian waiting while it was being weighed in. The tickets were checked and we all went up the escalator, and the Press came too. They wanted farewell pictures, and as we were drinking, a picture of Lillian drinking to Emmanuel. She was the only one who wasn't drinking, but she seized a glass of water and smiled at him with the right kind of gay devotion. They asked who Alberta was, and we looked round for her, but she'd left us and was talking to a man in an overcoat with a mothy fur collar who looked a typical English heavy. Lillian raised her eyebrows, and Emmanuel said: 'Her Uncle Vincent. Let her say goodbye to him in peace,' and then we got rid of everybody and sat down to wait. Lillian was being alternately gay and querulous: Emmanuel was abstracted, and I was just wishing like hell that we were all going. The thought of going back – of Claridge's – of the train to Southampton – the whole measured business filled me with impatience and despair. Years ago, when I began living with them,

Emmanuel had said to me: 'Three is not an easy number for people, so don't try to do anything in that context unless you are able.' I'd said O.K. and put on my most successful expression of obedient comprehension, and now I was just beginning to see what he'd meant.

Lillian was saying: '... really – it's ridiculous. I could perfectly well be flying. I do *wish* that you wouldn't all make plans behind my back – it's much more nerve-racking in the end.'

Emmanuel was stubbing out half-smoked cigarettes and smiling at her, when a boy came up with a Cellophane box of flowers.

'Mrs Joyce?'

She looked at Emmanuel, and opened the box, and I gave the boy a shilling. It was a spray of bright mauve orchids and they came from Sol Black. Lillian looked at them with exaggerated horror.

'My God. They might be all right forty feet up a tree in Brazil, but can you *imagine* pinning them on to your dearest enemy?'

Emmanuel said: 'He just knows you like flowers.' He was beginning to look hurt; as though he'd given them to her.

'But these *aren't* flowers: they're some other diabolical form of life masquerading as flowers to lull everyone's suspicions. I wouldn't be seen dead with them.' She turned to Emmanuel. 'For goodness' sake see to it that I'm *not* seen dead with them.'

He took the box from her without a word, and mercifully at that moment his flight was called. We all got to our feet, and looked round again for Alberta, who advanced from the other end of the hall rather shyly – with Uncle.

I saw the expression on Lillian's face, but Emmanuel must have felt it, as he put the orchids on the table and walked forward to meet them. They talked for a moment or two, and Emmanuel shook hands with the Uncle and then turned back to us: the other passengers were through the door by now. He kissed Lillian with such kindness that there was something compassionate about it; nodded to me, and stood

75

aside for Alberta, who had hugged her Uncle and now said in her rather high clear voice: 'Good-bye, Mrs Joyce. I do hope you have a good voyage.'

Lillian was staring at Emmanuel, but she said: 'Thank you so much.'

Then Alberta said good-bye to me and went through the door, and before Lillian could say anything, Emmanuel had nodded to both of us and followed her.

I took her arm and we walked back past the table with the orchids on it to the escalator, down and out to the car. The driver wrapped a rug round our knees: I told him to pick up the luggage at Bedford Gardens, and we were off. As soon as the car started to move, Lillian broke into a flood of tears. I leaned forward and closed the limousine glass, and, as I did this, I realized that Alberta's Uncle had vanished at the barrier, and we hadn't had to offer him a lift. Lillian had thrown herself rigidly against the seat – she was crying with her hands clenched to her sides. I found a handkerchief and put it on her lap, and waited. Overhead I heard a plane, and wondered whether it was his – it was funny what a curious sense of loss I had when he went somewhere without me.

Lillian was subsiding. I pulled her head against my shoulder and said: 'Poor sweetheart. You have had a day of it. What would you *like* to do now?'

She'd stopped crying – she must have been exhausted, and now as though she was half-asleep, she said: 'I should like to be a round little woman with healthy pink cheeks and no figure, with three children and a husband whom nobody thought was wonderful but me. I'd like to live in one of those little houses and go to the seaside with the family once a year, and have a mongrel dog who was very faithful, and be very good at making cakes and knitting patterns like the magazines say. I should like a cast-iron routine with me being the variant – instead of endless variations with me being the routine.' She stopped a moment and then said: 'Of course I only want that sometimes – or with part of me.'

'You aren't a routine, Lillian: you're full of surprises.'

'Like my behaviour about poor old Sol's orchids. I recog-

nize that: I call it routine. Did you know I hoped Em had
sent them?'

'No.'

'It doesn't excuse me in the least though. I didn't even
think of giving them to Alberta. She might have liked them.'

'Oh come,' I said – groping for a lighter note: 'poor
Alberta; you said you wouldn't even pin them on your
dearest enemy.'

She moved her head so that she could see me: she looked
suddenly worn to her age.

'When I saw her going through that door with Em following her, I did hate her: I'd been dreading that moment, and
I hated her.'

3. EMMANUEL

She chose her sweet off the tray with care, and, on impulse,
he took another of the same kind and gave it to her. She was
still wearing her bulky coat, and her seat belt would hardly
go round her, but the stewardess, with a kind, professional
smile, had seen that it was fastened, and now she would have
to stay hot and uncomfortable until they were up. They had
taxied to the end of the runway, and the engines were being
run up, one by one – he had explained this to her with the
first of them – and now she sat tense and expectant, staring
out of the window at this roaring dusk. After a moment she
unwrapped a sweet and ate it thoughtfully. The engines were
collected together; with a small shudder of release they were
moving into the short race for speed to become airborne.
He felt her attention to the ground; her second's astonishment when she realized that imperceptibly they had left it;
her amazement at the dwindling houses dropped like
pebbles into the bottom of the air. They made a circuit, and
below them were houses no longer, but lights marking the
earth with intricate chains and swags, and an occasional
rolling glint of water like sheet iron. They were climbing –
up into a melting sky cropped with milky hesitant stars, and
the sun gone – leaving a flush upon the air like the scent of

heat. The cloud was as distant as mountains in an allegory: the sensation of speed settled to movement with the lack of comparison: they were in the air, and then, as with the crackle like a mechanical clearing of the throat it announced its course, height, and cruising speed, they were in the aircraft. Belts were unfastened; cigarettes were lit.

'Would you like to take off your coat now?'

She nodded: she was calm again, but her eyes shone and there was something friendly about her excitement. Her coat was taken away, but not before she had extracted a battered book from one of its pockets. She was wearing a white cardigan over a blue and white checked shirt, and her absolutely straight hair was smoothed back from her ears by a black velvet snood. He looked at the book in her lap: it was a Victorian copy of *Middlemarch*.

'Is that a good book?'

And she answered briefly: 'Marvellous!' Then she added: 'but I don't think I can read it now,' and put it into the rack in front of her.

'No – you can't. You'll be very busy for the next hour or two.' Drinks and *hors d'œuvres* were being handed and wheeled about, and now approached them. She said: 'I'm very inexperienced about drink: my opportunity for it has been rather limited.'

So he chose some sherry for her, and had a glass himself. He watched her choosing *hors d'œuvres* until he said gently: 'Of course you can have as much of this as you like, but there is a seven-course dinner coming later.'

Her hand shot back into her lap and she went very pink. 'I didn't know. Goodness! I thought this was dinner. Thank you for telling me.' She took one canape off her plate and handed the rest back to the stewardess. 'I'm so sorry. Is that all right?'

'Does your father disapprove of drink?'

'Oh no. But we don't have it very much at home because he gives it to everybody who comes to the house and it's gone in a trice. My aunt says that he does not discriminate about his generosity. Do you know that all my brothers' clothes have to be locked up to stop him giving them to people? And Papa's clothes are very clearly marked because my aunt says that this discourages people as it is known that he only has two suits left.'

'And what about your aunt's clothes – or yours, or your sisters'?'

'Well, he only asks for them. He never routs about in our rooms. It's only the boys who are in constant danger.'

'What else does he give away?'

'Oh – food, and books and furniture, but he's got down to the big pieces now, so we tend to hear him at it. But once he gave all our winter blankets away in the autumn before we'd started using them. It depends what people ask for. Hardly anybody *asks* for a dining-room table. But fruit and vegetables! We've simply had to give them up.'

'People must impose on him.'

'They do, of course, But he says it is much better to be a fool than to miss somebody who really needs something.'

'There might be something between the two extremes.'

'There is: but my aunt advises us not to argue with him. He gets deeply distressed.' Her face changed at the thought: 'You see, to agree with us about that would mean altering his principles, and he feels that one should determine these as early in life as possible and then act on them. If one kept altering one's principles, one would be acting from expediency or chance, and he says that one is short-sighted and the other of incalculable distance. What do *you* think about that?'

'I think that relatively few people have principles. They can be expensive to maintain, and most people aren't prepared to pay enough for them.'

'Papa says that the great examples help in forming them – and after that he says that appreciation is a very good thing.'

'*Does* he!'

She looked at him and went pink again. 'I'm sorry. It's probably rather dull hearing what somebody else thinks when you haven't even met them.'

'It is not in the least dull. Your father sounds the most

interesting man I haven't met for years. I should like him very much.'

'Oh – everybody *does*; they almost love him – well, a few really do and the rest think so. Even the gypsies round us do. They used to steal the most enormous goose or turkey to give him for Christmas every year. This worried Papa because naturally he accepted it, and he couldn't always find where they stole it from to give it back. He said Caesar seemed to live farther away each year. So in the end he went to see the wife of the head gypsy and told her all about his rheumatism and she said that she would cure it, and he asked her to do it instead of a goose which anybody could give him but nobody could cure his rheumatism. So now he gets a jar of greenish brown paste to rub on or drink with hot water.'

'Does it cure him?'

'Well, it makes him much better; I don't think it actually cures him.' She looked suddenly round her: people were being served with dinner. 'It seems so *odd* to be talking about him here. He says that only the great man or the bore are totally unaffected by their environment . . .'

'It depends which environment: one would not say you had been unaffected by yours.'

She flushed again. 'Wouldn't one?' and he realized that it was with pleasure.

They had dinner, which took a long time, as Alberta was deeply impressed by it and ate everything. During it, she asked him about New York and the work she was to do, and he explained that they were going first to a hotel and afterwards, possibly, to an apartment which friends often lent them; and as soon as they had cast Clemency, to the country somewhere. In New York she would do all his letters, make the appointments, and accompany him to auditions – at least until Jimmy arrived. Then his wife might want various things done for her – shopping commissions, telephoning, and letters. 'But you'll have some time to yourself,' he finished; 'there is a great deal to see there, and the shops are irresistible to women. There are two warnings: you told me that you're inexperienced about drink: a little drink goes a long way in New York until you're used to it. Secondly, a number of people will want to play Clemency and will stop at nothing to get an audition or to see me at the hotel; and still more people will want to know who *is* going to play her, or even looks like doing so. You must never let either of us be bounced by surprise tactics – especially out of working hours, and you must never know anything about what is being decided.'

She listened so solemnly that he said: 'That sounds pompous, but it is not meant to be more than necessary instruction: the American theatre doesn't work quite like ours.'

'I'll do my best. If I get stuck, may I ask you?'

'Me or Jimmy. Don't worry Mrs Joyce with anything unnecessary. We have to look after her: she has a heart trouble.'

She looked at him and her face changed again, as it had for her father. Her face, which was very young but not remarkable, was sometimes unexpectedly beautiful because of the simplicity of expressions upon it. Whatever she was feeling was occasionally to be seen – fresh, and entire – like the difference between looking at clear or muddy water.

Their tables had been removed, and now she was fishing in a battered handbag for a handkerchief, and he noticed punctures on the leather flap where there had been initials.

'We must get you a new bag,' he said gently: he was touched by her thinking of this detail in connexion with changing her name.

She pushed it under her seat again. 'It is worn out really – I've had it since I was fifteen: I would have got a new one anyway.'

Passengers were being offered brandy, etc., and he asked her if she wanted any.

'No thank you. But I enjoyed the wine enormously; more than any I've ever had.'

'Jimmy told you why we wanted to change your name, didn't he?'

'Yes.' She was silent a moment, and then said: 'I suppose that must be one of the hardest things to accept.'

In spite of himself, he said sharply: 'She hasn't accepted it. That's the trouble.' This was the trap of travelling: the surge of illogical, unreasoning intimacy: to spread it, he asked unseriously: 'What would your father say about that, do you think?'

She thought for a time without answering. 'I don't know. He says that experience is like food, and if one's system is working properly it uses some kinds for nourishing and others should just be eliminated. He says that the most unhappy people are the ones who can't get rid of the useless experience.'

He was past the small personal confidence, and interested again.

'Perhaps good experience – like food – can go bad on one.' She laughed and said: 'Yes – one musn't blame the experience too much: it doesn't make itself.' She was silent again; then she said diffidently: 'Do you know what I think?'

He leaned back in his seat thinking: it's infectious – my fault, I asked for it – let's have it. 'No,' he said.

'The whole of life – for people – is like an enormous unfinished carpet with loose ends hanging out, and some people spin a few more inches of a strand, and some weave in one of the existing strands, and very occasionally somebody does both those things: that makes a piece of new pattern in the design which goes on and on. And other people spend their lives trying to see the whole roll of carpet that has been made in order to see what must be done to finish it.'

He was caught by this: laughing at himself for his shady little fears and delighted with her. '*Do* they see it all? Those last people?'

She hesitated: 'I'm not sure. If they do, they can go on to something else: they don't have to be carpet makers any more.'

'You've left out the unpickers. They are often sadly diligent.'

'I have: indeed, they are.'

'Then you could have some who are like moths: they simply eat carpet. It is amazing that any carpet gets made at all.'

'It should be amazing,' she said seriously. He looked at her; recognized the amazement, and there was no more to be said.

Lights were being dimmed in the aeroplane; chairs were being flattened; people were settling for the night, and she went to wash. How she avoided the little mantraps of personal remark and confidence, he thought: she had made the climate for their conversation – he had simply responded, because for once, and unusually, he had felt in good company.

She came back with freshly brushed hair, washed face, and shining eyes. 'Goodness! Isn't it all beautiful – neat luxury – like an egg!'

When she was sitting in it, he said: 'Now: this thing is called a Slumberette; they will bring bits to fit on to it for our feet, and the rest of it subsides under one until one is helplessly comfortable. You press this and lean back.'

She pressed the knob and shot backwards with a startled gasp, but 'they' were instantly on the spot – rescued her, and packed her with blankets into a comfortable mummy.

'Do you want to read for a bit?'

She shook her head, so he turned out her light, and adjusted her air-conditioning so that it did not ruffle her hair.

'If you can't sleep, there is your reading-light.'

'Thank you so much. Are you going to sleep?'

'After a little neat luxury.'

When he returned, she was already asleep, and he felt suddenly alone, and crowded by the thoughts he had by himself. This was the time, he knew, to make the adjustment that this kind of travel hardly allowed: of time, and place, of work, people, incident, and country. The end of a day which one has physically left behind one is a different end. Poor Lillian: she had made the worst of his departure, and she would be suffering for it, and, possibly, making Jimmy suffer with her. The confounding thing about Jimmy was that just when one was getting irritated by his creed of vicarious living, and watching his comfortable selections from one's life with mounting resentment, he engaged himself for one so thoroughly that one was touched all over again. He didn't like boats; he was raging to find a Clemency in New York, he was worrying about the TV performance of *The Molehill*, and he found days and days of Lillian's company difficult. Well – by the time they arrived he might have fixed up the apartment; that would be better for Lillian – for all of them. Alberta was too young in some ways to manage hotel life by herself, and Jimmy always lived with them wherever they went. Then they would find somewhere in the country for a few weeks: not by the sea because it made Lillian miserable not being able to bathe, but in good, deep country – Massachusetts, for instance, would be about right: then he would be able to get down to New York from time to time if necessary. Then, for a few weeks, they would have what the Friedmanns at lunch today had called 'a lovely home'. It gave him pleasure to think about the Friedmanns – partly because they knew so clearly what they wanted – partly because he had been able to give some of it to them. He had enjoyed his lunch today more than usual – although he always found it interesting, but, possibly because he had not on this occasion seen them for nearly a year, the effects of their continuity and change had impressed him more than before. The house was the same: comfortable, beautifully kept, and furnished more heavily than ever with a kind of imaginative vulgarity. Thus, to strike a match you went through some mechanical whimsy; to sit down you removed one of the flouncy dolls who used to sit on beds in the twenties pretending to be Gertie Lawrence at the Chelsea Arts Ball; to turn on a light you approached an Elizabethan manuscript in full sail; the lavatory paper was concealed in a musical box which lashed out Swiss banalities at you; the sitting room had the bursting flaccid appearance of an overripe plum.

Mrs Friedmann had received him: she had put on weight, and was generally glowing with material wealth. She had such a sense of occasion that she invariably dressed for it to be on the safe side. Today she was dressed in lavender marocain, with a good deal of angular expensive modern jewellery at key points like road signs, and shoes whose burning discomfort had only to be glanced at to be believed. She was corseted from just below her neck to just above her knees, which streamlined her imposing bulk, and she was heavily made up with blue eyelashes and a purple mouth, but this did not detract from her habitual expression of active delight.

'Come in, come *in*! When we heard you were to come we were so happy. Hans is getting some wine to be prepared, and the children are not yet from school here. But please, please come in.'

In the sitting-room they both sat down: Mrs Friedmann, however, never wasted preliminaries.

'I have been so anxious for you to see our children – they have so much changed in the last year. But first I must again thank you and assure you that I love them all the time as my own, but sometimes I think *more* than that because I have had time to know what the loss is of no children, and these two are so remarkable that it is my honour to care for them.'

'You've thanked me quite enough before, Mrs Friedmann, and really for very little. It is the children who are lucky . . .'

'Children should be above luck! But I know that I can never repay you, but I am happy to owe you so much.'

Here there were sounds of children in the hall and her husband arrived.

'Mr Joyce, I am delighted to see you here. Berta, you will perhaps now go to the kitchen, my darling angel, and finish that our meal may be soon? I have sent Matthias and Becky to wash their hands again.'

She went at once, and he looked admiringly after her.

'My wife is as good as she is beautiful.' He got some sherry and poured it out. 'Mr Joyce: since I do not wish to mix business with family matters I will try to put the business in a nutshell. As you know, at the time that you so kindly approached us with the children, I had no work, no money – nothing. If Berta had been able to have a child I should have been overjoyed, but I should also have been desperate. It is only because of your great generosity that we were able to take Matthias and Becky and do for them all we could wish. Our happiness is extremely good, and Berta has been a different woman with her life so rightly filled. But now is different: I prosper each year and have now twenty-five men working for me and three delivery vans and all premises convenient. I can now afford to educate the children and buy for them everything that they need.' He raised a hand as Emmanuel was about to speak. 'Only for one thing. Money of yours has been saved now for nearly a year: if more of it might be saved I would buy Matthias a good instrument. I have heard of a Gagliano going very cheap, and it is a very fine instrument. I have a friend who knows of these things, and he has tried it and says that it is worth what they ask. When we have bought it for the boy we do not need any more money. Some money I have already put down for the Gagliano to secure it for him but he does not know. Berta wishes to put ribbon round it and make a surprise.'

Mr Friedmann took nothing for granted. Emmanuel could not remember any conversation they had had which did not, so to speak, start at the beginning: each time his situation after the war and his subsequent gratitude was faithfully and persuasively outlined before he arrived at present affairs. Emmanuel also knew by now that it would not do to agree immediately about the money: that he was meant to consider Friedmann's proposals at least during lunch – if not longer. He therefore replied with weighty caution, and Friedmann was delighted.

'Of course! You must have all the thought you could wish,' he said, his eyes blazing with innocent conspiracy.

Lunch – and the children. The girl had grown since he last saw her and was something of a beauty, with a very white skin and enormous slanting eyes. She gazed at him solemnly throughout the meal, but whenever he looked directly at her, she hung her head, her black hair flopped each side of her face, and she gave him a rich slow smile. The boy – he was older – was awkward and very shy: with his gentle, protuberant eyes, elaborate nostrils, and small delicate mouth, he reminded Emmanuel of a young hare – since he seemed quiveringly poised for some convulsive movement which would defy pursuit. Both children spoke German and English indiscriminately, but a guest was clearly an unusual event, and they did not speak unless they were asked to do so. As soon as they had finished they kissed their parents and left the room. Friedmann told Becky to fetch her drawings and Matthias to tune his violin. Mrs Friedmann served coffee, and Emmanuel congratulated them both on the children. Mrs Friedmann glowed.

'They are different. Just has Matthias grown out of sleeping with the piece of bread in his hand. All these years he has needed it, not to eat, but to know that it was there, but lately he has been collecting pictures of composers and musicians – newspapers, postcards, anything – and sticking them to the wall round his bed, and every night my husband goes to see him and they talk about one of the people in the pictures. My husband knows a very great deal which Matthias wishes to know. They were talking about – Schumann, was it, Hans?'

'Schubert, my darling, Schubert.'

'*Ja, ja.* I know nothing at all! Of course Schubert who was so poor, and after as Hans was to go Matthias held out the bread and said: "I don't need bread at night." And since then no more bread.'

The girl, they said, was an easy child. After all, she had only been a baby when she left the camp – a few months old, with nothing, or very little, to remember.

'But the boy does remember, too much.'

'What does he remember?'

'He will not say. He will never talk about it. I know, only from the questions he asks me now – difficult questions with some knowledge behind them.'

Mrs Friedmann interrupted: 'Yes. And you know we gave

them days of birthday as they had none and we did not know how to find them? Well, last June, when Matthias was to be thirteen, on his day he said: "This is not my birthday: then it was cold".'

'Sometimes I cannot *answer* him, Mr Joyce,' said Friedmann. 'I have no good answer for Buchenwald – perhaps I do not wish to find one. He ask why, why, all the time. Why this for one because he is such and such, and that for another. I say to him: "You are a boy; Becky is a girl: you are not the same. You are a Jew, and your friend" – he has one friend from school – "Martin is a Gentile. You have music, Martin wishes astronomy, Becky likes to draw. You are not born the same, and therefore injustice is nonsense." He is passionately concerned with justice: everybody must have the same, but I think when the mind is very young there is a confusion between having and being. But I think also he will learn because he wishes to know.'

'And Hans will tell him,' Mrs Friedmann looked at her husband with a certainty that went to Emmanuel's heart: 'because he is knowing so much of everything.'

Friedmann smiled at her, but said nothing until she had gone ahead of them to the sitting-room, when he smiled again at Emmanuel and said: 'As you see, Mr Joyce, the philosophical responsibilities of this great household are entirely mine.'

In the sitting-room Matthias stood by the piano with his fiddle, and Becky lay on the floor with a drawing-block. They had hardly sat down before Matthias said 'Bach', and began to play.

It was a long time since he had heard any unaccompanied Bach, and the sound was a royal shock to him; waking suddenly some part of the heart that keeps awe and adoration locked: charging and changing his body with a stream of joy. Then he looked to see it coming from the boy, but the boy had changed too: he was no longer shy or awkward; he had now a kind of gallant stability – he was struggling with music too difficult for him and an indifferent instrument, but his eyes were luminous with intention, his mouth still, his whole face and body serving one purpose. He was too young to conciliate or to compromise with his instrument: he treated it sternly as though it was the best, and made his own whole in spite of it. Afterwards, nobody said anything, until Becky looked up from her drawing, and said: 'Well done, Matthias, you can very nearly play that piece now.'

He had left soon after that, but as he sat now in the air-craft the boy's playing occurred all over again and shed light on his memory either side of it. He had promised the Gagliano, and said that he would write about the rest of the business from New York: but in the taxi he had had other thoughts – of regret, envy, and confusion. These were the children who were connected to his worst mistake with Lillian: so sure had he been that she would want and love them that he had gone far in the arrangements before he told her, and when he did they had both suffered a bad shock – as they fought their way through layers of dishonest objection and justification to the raw bone of his wanting to pay for the war which he had not fought, to her wanting nothing but their child. To wanting Sarah back, in fact, or another Sarah. He looked at the girl sleeping beside him, and for a moment, imagined that she might be his daughter. He would only have had to marry Lillian three years earlier ... But Lillian's daughter had died, and so had the parents of Matthias and the parents of Becky – if this girl had been his daughter she would be dead now – if he had been the father of either Matthias or Becky he would be dead now. These were matters of fact – of accident? Where would little Alberta put that in her carpet? When he had left the Friedmanns he had said to them that he did not think the children could possibly be in better hands, and meant it, and Mrs Friedmann's blue-fringed eyes had filled as she said: 'We *love* them: but Hans will see that it is wisely.' What he had really meant, he discovered, was that he and Lillian would not have done so well even if she had wanted them. 'We're really not fit for it,' he had thought, churning along in his taxi, and then the boy's music had come back – he had accepted his unfitness, and wondered whether when one thanked God for Bach, one did not also thank Bach for God. Compassion for Lillian filled him, because she did not see their unfitness, and he made a promise to look after her well on the journey. And then, accident, which trod softly on anyone's dreams with the confident deliberation of a cat, had prevented Lillian and substituted Alberta, and it was he who had been looked after in the end. Interesting – that the best parts of the day had been the boy and this girl beside him. Two children . . .

He was tired, and empty now of reminiscence – the small domestic lights of his day went singly out, and thoughts recurred in faster and more distant fragments, until – mere pin-points of light – they too were gone, and blankness rolled slowly over his senses like a blind. But when the darkness seemed complete – just above the reach of his daily mind there was a light – more clearly to be seen as it shone alone: he knew he must turn towards it and climb until he touched it in order to work again, and it was then that he began the slow ascent.

4. ALBERTA

New York

DARLING Uncle Vin,

This won't be a long letter, because in spite of there being so much to say, I seem awfully tired, and I haven't even written to Papa yet. There is one trouble. It is about my flying here with Mr Joyce. As you know, this was a last-minute plan because poor Mrs Joyce was ill, and I asked you at the airport not to say anything to Papa about it, as I know it would worry him and I am too far away to put him at his ease about it. I suppose if I wasn't so far away, he wouldn't worry, but I am, and he would, and so I have decided to deceive him. This is wrong, but to tell him now seems wronger. Isn't that odd? I don't think I've ever been in this position before. Please write to me about it and write to me anyway. We had the most enormous and grand dinner on the aeroplane you can imagine: *hors d'œuvres*, cold soup, salmon, chicken, ice-cream, and little chocolate things, cheese fruit, and coffee and a pale yellow wine (not champagne but still delicious) and sherry first, and brandy afterwards but I didn't. Mr Joyce is very interesting to talk to. He listens, for one thing – that was when I told him about Papa – and he sticks to the subject so that one doesn't just stop at the beginning things people usually seem to say. He told me a bit about what it would be like here, but it is too soon to tell you how accurately. But he made it all sound much easier than I had been feeling it would be, and he was charming about Papa, and said he would like him. Quite soon after dinner I went to sleep like a hedgehog I was so full of food. You sit in wonderful chairs that fall over backwards to make you comfortable, but I woke up very early because I was cold and rather stiff, and Mr Joyce got my coat and most kindly wrapped it over my blanket. He looked awfully tired – as though he hadn't slept at all, but he said he had a little. It was light again : the sky is quite different when you are looking out into it and not simply up – you can love it instead of just admiring it. It was misty below, so I couldn't see America even when it was beneath us, but Mr Joyce said we don't come over New York – just a rather dull beach. We had coffee and orange juice – a whole glass-full – and then we started to come down, which hurt my ears in spite of swallowing and blowing my nose. Suddenly through the mist I saw land quite near, and the airport buildings slanting up at us. When we came down the rubber tyres *smoked* as they touched the ground, and in the end there was a kind of ticking noise when we stopped. It was seven in the morning (quite different for you Uncle Vin) and there was a feeling of us all starting a new life. The airport didn't seem very different except for people's voices. Mr Joyce was photographed getting out of the aeroplane, and it took us ages to get through the Customs, but then we had a car to drive us into New York. Enormous advertisements – really as big as houses – and the most beautiful bridges and sometimes the traffic goes at different levels so you can't work out where you are going to be, and the sun had come out so that from a distance New York looked like a bunch of upright needles glinting, and the newborn feeling went on when one looked at them. All the traffic seemed deliberate and silky, but Mr Joyce says it isn't in the city. When we got there it was like being in a ravine sometimes, but with sky at the end as well as above, and that somehow makes one feel more on the surface of the earth and very small. At the hotel the girl in the lift was a terribly pretty black girl, and everybody says 'You're welcome' when you thank them for anything. We are on the sixteenth floor. I have a small room with a bathroom and shower and telephones. I've unpacked and had a bath and some breakfast – America is a land swimming in orange juice – and I have to go to Mr Joyce's room when he telephones me. I'm writing to you because unpacking made me feel too far away from home to write to them just yet. I think aeroplanes are rather breathless. I looked at *Middlemarch* to see if it had stayed the same; Mr Casaubon's begun to be ill and without wanting to I'm sorry for him. Do you think some people are *meant* to be ill? I wasn't thinking of poor Mrs Joyce: she looked dreadfully unhappy at being left behind, but as though she often has bad luck of that kind. Oh what I most wanted to say: it was so sweet and good of you to come all the way to the airport – I was missing you dreadfully in the car on the way there – and it was much better seeing you again without *soaking* your rheumatic joints through your clothes, darling Uncle Vin I must say you do take family relationships with all your heart, and the least Papa can do is to go to *Death for Breakfast* when it comes to Dorchester. I'll write to them tonight – the telephone – I must go.

Your loving Sarah

20 May, New York

I have written to Papa, at last. So much has happened, that it was quite easy – I simply said 'we' all the time, and it is only five days now until the others arrive here. It is curious, though, what an oblique difference deception makes: it made me write all the time about events and not my feeling about them. I tried to describe New York but did not succeed at all well. I think this is partly because apart from being here for the first time, everything that I am doing here is new as well – so I haven't had a chance yet to see more than the obvious differences. I've met so many people in such a short time (counted it up – it's thirty-six hours – far more than one new person an hour) and they are all kinds of people I haven't met before, so that now I've reached a point where I can hardly understand what they say. Our life has been like a very crowded map, and we have had to go to all the places as quickly as possible. I don't know how Mr J. stands it – except that he's not as old as I thought –

he's four years younger than Papa – and I suppose he's used to it, but on the other hand he's had far more to do than I have. So far we've spent two hours on the letters that were waiting here – goodness! the people who write to him! – and three hours on auditions for the girl called Clemency in his play, which I haven't had time to read yet, although now I nearly know one scene by heart, we've watched it so many times. None of the auditions were any good, but it was very interesting to watch. One poor girl was so frightened that she sat looking at her script and not saying anything until she burst into tears, and Mr J. was very nice to her and asked her to come back, although he said afterwards that she was much too tall anyway. He is an extremely kind man. Then we had an extraordinary picnic lunch in an office with two men who had been at the auditions. They just ate yoghourt because they were dieting, but they talked about what they would have liked for lunch all the time we were eating ours, until I must say it got quite difficult and hard-hearted to go on eating it. They asked me if this was my first time in America, but otherwise they talked to Mr J. about the play. Then we went to Rockefeller Center which is just like a whole town going on in one building with lifts – no, *elevators* – being the transport, like trains. Mr J. had to rehearse his introduction to another play of his they are doing on television. That is a whole other life too, and fearfully complicated. Mr J. only had to sit in a chair and talk, but it had to be the right amount of time, and they wouldn't let him read from the piece he'd dictated to me in London. So that took much longer than it was meant to, and we didn't get away until half past six, and he sent me to telephone some people to put off a drinks engagement, and that's when I realized to my horror that he was taking me with him to the public dinner at eight-thirty that evening. It was evening dress, and I haven't got one because the green net that Aunt T. made two years ago was really too childish to bring. I felt so miserable about this, that I didn't dare say anything until we were outside Rockefeller Center, waiting for a cab. I didn't want to go to the dinner in the least and

I was feeling awfully tired, but I knew he didn't want to go either – and not having Mrs Joyce must be making it far worse. The trouble is that none of my clothes seem right somehow. I've got my silk dress here, but honestly it's the kind of dress that secretaries seem to wear after breakfast – it no longer seems to have an element of festivity about it. Well, I told him in the end: I was afraid he'd be angry, but I explained that I would let him down even more if I went in my dress. I always gabble when I'm nervous – and I went on explaining about my dress sense being unformed, and the dress only just not having puff sleeves because Aunt T. finds them easiest to do, and all the time he was looking at me and I had no idea what he was thinking. (Partly I think that's the heavy lids to his eyes.) Then he said: 'Good. You've provided a perfect opportunity for both of us. We'll go and buy you a dress and a bag and things this minute. I refuse to go to the dinner by myself, and secretaries aren't expected to have evening dresses as a rule, so don't blame yourself. Here's a cab, come on, let's enjoy ourselves.' In the cab he asked the driver what big store would be open late, and the cab man said it depended what our requirements were, and when he was told he thought most seriously and then said he recommended Bloomingdales. (He turned out to be a man who thought seriously about everything.) It was open late that night and he could recommend it personally because his daughter bought her best things there and looked like a million dollars. Mr J. said fine, and thanked him. The driver said we were welcome – Lexington and 60th, and we set off. Somehow Mr J. had stopped me wanting to cry, and both of us feeling tired, and now he smiled at me and said he'd always wanted to do this. The driver said he strongly advised me to make a list of what I wanted to save time. Mr J. began to make a list: he put down a dress and a bag and shoes, and then said what about stockings? The cab driver said that was no way to make a list if one was dressing a lady: we should start scientifically from the skin up – if one was organizing a project one must use plain English and that meant girdle, bra, and panties. Mr J. said he was quite right.

The driver said it beat him how some people administered their simple every-day lives. We got wars, and psychiatrists and traffic jams just because none of us stopped to check the efficiency of our motivation – he'd been saying this to people for years now and it was surprising how little difference it made, and did we know why? Mr J. said no, why? Human nature, said the cab driver. He didn't speak for a moment and then he sighed and swerved the taxi away from a woman who was trying to cross the road with a dog. It wasn't that human nature ever changed, he'd concluded, there was just too damn much of it. Take atomic energy. That was quite predictable if one was an educated guy, but you could go through every college in the world and still not get the other side of human nature. This was why he had no regret about not going to college although he'd sent his daughter; not that he guessed it would make much difference. Mr J. said it probably wouldn't. Then he got more cheerful, and said well, how was the list? I said we hadn't been doing it because we were so interested, but that was no good. Did we realize, he said, that Mozart could write down a whole symphony of classical music and play a game of chess simultaneously? So couldn't we even fix a shopping list and *talk*? So far as he could remember, we'd omitted perfume, make-up – there was a new non-greasy clingstick foundation selling in five shades in two sizes – jewellery, Bloomingdales were running a line in charm bracelets just now and his daughter had gotten one with miniature bottles of deadly poisons all round it which seemed to him cute, and by the way, what was my name? They sold handkerchiefs on which they would instantly print your name or nickname, but perhaps the British weren't so hot on nicknames – anyway, here we were. I said my name was Alberta and he said it was a swell name. Then as Mr J. paid him, he said have a good time mister and he sure hoped I'd be a social credit to him. Then he hooted with laughter, and said forget it – just a political sally, and drove off.

We bought a terribly pretty dress. It was a heavy corded cotton, pale mushroom colour with a little apricot velvet on it. It wasn't the kind of dress I'd even imagined, but it was the only one I tried on; we both thought it was the prettiest, and suited me. We bought a stiff petticoat for it covered with roses and very pretty too, and shoes that matched and *four pairs* of stockings (I've never had so many good ones before) and the two bags. A gold one for the dress, and a black one for day with A.Y. on it in gold. Then Mr J. said what about an evening coat – even the cab driver had forgotten that – and we went to the coat department – up again – and he found a peacock blue velvet coat which he said would be good with my dress. Then we went down again and bought gloves for the coat. Then last of all, he bought me a white handkerchief with strawberries (white ones) embroidered all over it and a bottle of scent which he said he liked and I must trust. It was terribly hot in the store and we both had to carry our overcoats. All our parcels were being packed together: he said that he would go and collect them and then he suddenly thrust some money at me and told me to go and buy underclothes while he got the parcels, and meet him at the entrance we had come in by. 'You must have everything new at once for once. Just spend that, and get as much as you can.' It was a fifty-dollar bill. It seemed a lovely meaningless amount – I realized then that dollars weren't being money to me at all, and we'd bought so many things so quickly that the whole expedition seemed a mixture between an adventure and a game. I spent all the money except for a few small coins, and got the most lovely things I've ever seen in my life. It wasn't until we were in a cab, and I saw the great pile of parcels, and remembered Jimmy giving me a ten-dollar bill yesterday in London, and my saying that I'd keep careful account of it that I suddenly realized that all these things must have cost a great deal of money – much more than I was earning, and anyway I'd planned to keep that for Humphrey and Clem. I don't think I've ever felt so suddenly and completely dreadful – so burning, and ashamed, and caught out by myself. I couldn't say anything – and there seemed nothing that I could do – except wear the things, and thank him for taking so much trouble, and pay him back for them by degrees. He was smoking quietly, and then, as though I had been thinking aloud, he leaned towards me and said: 'Don't worry so much. This was my idea, my responsibility, my pleasure. I am not in the habit of doing it, but it was necessary this evening. It has nothing to do either with conventional scruples or your salary, and if I have overdone it, it is a reflection upon my character, and not yours. Will you please remember what you told me about your father giving away clothes to people who needed them?' I said people didn't need evening dresses, and he said I shouldn't be too sure of that. Then he said: 'Because Mrs Joyce isn't here, I am asking you to do far more than either of us expected of you. This' – he indicated the parcels – 'is all part of that. Do you understand now?' I think I do. At least I felt very much better – as suddenly as I had felt worse. At the hotel, he said we had only got three quarters of an hour to change, and would I come to his suite as soon as I was ready, because he was a quick changer? So I put on all the wonderful new clothes, and powder and lipstick and my locket, and brushed my hair a lot, and scratched the soles of my shoes and put the ten-dollar bill in my new golden bag, and some scent behind my ears. Aunt T. says that ladies should only wear a touch of scent, but although it smelled delicious in the bottle, I couldn't smell a touch on me at all – so I put on a whole lot more until I could smell myself quite easily.

He was quite ready and standing by the window. He said: 'Take off your coat: I want to inspect you.' He looked at me with careful kindness – very like Papa. 'Well, I must say, I think we both have excellent taste.' He touched my locket with his finger. 'What is that? Topaz?' I explained that it was my mother's and Papa had given it to me for the journey here, and that there was a beautiful ring as well, but that Papa was keeping that for me until I was married, and he asked immediately: 'Are you going to be married?' I said I didn't know, but that if I didn't, Mary or Serena would, and that there was only one ring. 'You have no plans about it then. It is a distant point.' I said it was out of my sight, and he put on my coat, smiled, and said: 'You like the scent.' I said yes, and explained that I had only Aunt T.'s hearsay to go on about the right amount, and that I hadn't agreed with her. I asked him if he could smell me properly, and he said: 'Distinctly,' so that was all right. When we got to the lift, I thanked him for all the beautiful clothes and everything: he looked very pleased and said that he was enjoying them just as much as I. As we went down in the lift, it felt as though we had been doing that for weeks, and not at all since this morning, and I asked him whether he found the measurement of time more of a convenience than not. He was feeling in his pockets for something, and asked the lift girl (another one, not nearly so pretty, and they are called coloured, not black) to go back as he'd forgotten something. 'Notes,' he said: 'I've got to make a speech.' I keep forgetting that he's the kind of man who has to make speeches and gets photographed. While he was away, the girl asked me if it was my first time over, and I said yes, and she said she hoped I was enjoying it, and I said yes. When he came back he said he found measuring time more *in*convenient than not – that it was a scourge for writing plays, and either dull, or nerve-wracking in the rest of his life. 'Like this evening – you'll see,' he said, and looked somehow bitter, and friendly at the same time.

I did see. I can hardly write about it – it was so terribly dull. Boiling hot – and so much to eat that I couldn't taste anything after a bit, and people who seemed to have known each other for years not at all well. He was very kind, and kept introducing me to people, but they only asked me if I was an actress, and if it was my first time over and whether I was enjoying it. In the end I wished I *was* an actress, just to make a change in the conversation. There were a lot of cinema men and their wives and the whole thing was in aid of something, but I couldn't see how we could be helping anyone by having a huge, dull dinner. I couldn't even sit next to him at dinner, because he was the guest of honour and I was fearfully dull for the men sitting on either side of me. I asked one of them if they had read *Middlemarch*, but he said he hadn't – he hadn't even time to get through *Reader's Digest* so a book would be out of the question. He must be dreadfully busy, because even Mr Asquith, when he was Prime Minister, had time to read at least fifty pages of a new book every day. He asked me what my ambitions were about two courses later, which seemed a funny way to put it, and I said I wanted to be a good woman, and he stared as though I'd said something rude, and then said I sure looked good to him, so I suppose he misunderstood me and thought I meant good in his moral sense and not in the Christian one at all. So then I tried the other man, who looked older, and asked him what interested him most and he said golf, but his heart had packed up and he'd had to fall back on painting. I said what an interesting and lucky way round, and then I realized that I was being narrow-minded about golf: conversation is much more difficult than I thought. I've hardly ever talked to people I haven't known in some sort, excepting Mr J. and of course he is different. He smiled at me twice during dinner, and that was much more like speaking than anything else. After dinner, there were *two* speeches before his, and I felt awfully sleepy, and couldn't understand what they were talking about – they seemed to veer without any warning from vast generalizations to something that happened to them last week, with people fidgeting or laughing so that one couldn't hear. Mr J. was the best: he didn't talk for very long, but he was much easier to understand. Then there was another long time after the speeches, and then I had to queue to collect my coat and had to get change for the ten dollars to give something to the woman, and didn't know what to give her. I gave her a dollar in the end (this was too much) and then we got into a car which was waiting for us and my head ached. Without meaning to, I went to sleep in the car, and Mr J. woke me up when we got back to the hotel. Well – I *have* written about it. But it's clear that there isn't going to be time here to write the kind of diary that Mary and I write at home. I shall have to try and select the salient points – if I understand which they are in time. Mary will be disappointed, because she will be writing hers (she was terribly pleased with the one I gave her) and we were going to have a tremendous read to each other when I go home. It has taken me all afternoon to write to Papa and write this. One thing is clear. I am very lucky to be working for Mr J. because he is the most considerate and kind man. He has given me the afternoon off to rest before we go to the opening tonight of the musical version of his play called *The Orchid Race*. Extraordinary name – what can it be about? I have never been to a first night in my life – and to go in these rarefied circumstances will certainly rank high in my experience of the world. But then, my dear Sarah, your experience is laughably little. I feel like Celia: can it be possible on such a sudden, I can fall into so great an experience? My goodness, I couldn't have managed without my lovely new dress. I've just thought: accounts of places are not very interesting, unless one has some idea of the writer's feeling about them – or their feelings generally. There seem to be two kinds of life going on, then, and when very little seems to be happening is when one has a busier life inside. So much seems to happen here to everybody, that I wonder how they manage the inside part. It seems to have got the wrong way round somehow – it is the skyscrapers who seem so calm and immovable and they are filled with scurrying people, instead of the people being calm and scurrying inside. Scurrying is the wrong word: I must say I'm glad I'm not a writer. What am I? Somebody on a brink, I should say – like thousands of people – so is the brink private, or universal? I think the *idea* of a brink is universal, and the actual brink is always a private one. Clem would say this is half-baked philosophy – but I don't think I can manage yet with ready cooked.

CHAPTER THREE

*

1. EMMANUEL

ON the morning of the day that Lillian and Jimmy were to
arrive he went for a walk. He went early – because he was
sleeping badly: the ship was due to dock at half past ten,
and he needed refreshment for the day. He started uptown,
along Madison Avenue, with no particular sense of direction; but the faint, elusive liberty which always stirred
when he left a night, stretched now in the early air and encouraged him simply to go on. He had left a message for
Alberta that he would breakfast with her at 9.30 before they
went to meet the travellers. In a sense, he was meeting them
now : apportioning appropriate pieces of himself to the cut-
up artificial day which lay ahead. Their arrival, which ought
to be a beginning, was seeming, somehow, an end. Had he
enjoyed Alberta's company so much? It was hard to say. He
had liked the alternating solitude and company of somebody undemanding, eager, and new to the offerings of his
daily life. He had enjoyed being kind because his kindness
had been so simply enjoyed. I am not so kind as she thinks
me, he thought – yes, to her I am that: and she is one of the
very few people who accept what I am to her uncharged by
what I am to anything else. She had made an ordinary, tiring
week interesting and worth the candle at both ends. Or
perhaps he simply enjoyed the freedom from intimate
routine difficulties. No Clemency: Lillian loathing hotels
except when they were on holiday – the hunted expense of
privacy ... Supposing one bought one's oxygen for the day
every day – that would be a nice direct way of paying for
existence, instead of having it clothed in State taxes, with
privacy like mink; a luxury to be flaunted by people who
didn't know what to do with it. But perhaps there were
animals – like the mink – who could wear privacy for free.
The trouble was not so much that one was trying to avoid

paying for things, it was trying to find out how to pay. When you buy something – on the whole you choose neither the price nor the currency. Some people seemed to spend their whole lives trying to pay for one thing without knowing how to do it – and probably I am one of them. If they know, of course, there is an element of dedication – there is more height and light about it – a little dignity and the possibility of something more than mere behaviour. The passionate interest now commonly displayed in the subconscious was probably due to the fact that hardly anybody's behaviour rose above that point. It was therefore natural that they should pay large sums to see anybody who had achieved even partial control of their bodies – let alone anything else. Am I, in any sense, a dedicated man, he wondered? Jimmy would say that I was dedicated to the theatre – to writing plays. Lillian would say that I ought to be dedicated to making a life with her. I don't think either of them would stop to consider these purposes: why should they – they are supposed to be my purposes, and I haven't stopped to think about them much. He stopped now in the street to consider them, but arresting his body, he lost his mind: it noted that he was on the corner of East 57th – it reminded him that this was Lillian's favourite street because of the picture galleries, and then it asked him why he had stopped at all. At that he went on; observing the morning and the scene set in it – the sky a startling blue – air like soda – the light freshly minted by sun – the streets clean and almost empty – too early yet even for people walking their dogs – the scene not yet swelling with its crowds: an empty city has an innocence which country, inhabited on a much larger scale, has not, he thought. He was back to how they were to inhabit this city that day – the four of them. After Lillian and Jimmy had arrived they would go straight to the apartment on Park Avenue. Lillian would start to unpack – would say she couldn't possibly face it, and that she wanted her favourite morning drink of champagne and orange juice – and then they would all sit in the sitting-room exchanging little canapes of news until it was time to decide where they should lunch, which meal would compromise between a festivity for Lillian and a business-like snack for Jimmy. Then he and Jimmy would go off on the audition racket, and Alberta would help Lillian unpack and hang her pictures. Once he and Jimmy were in a cab and on their way to the west side, Jimmy would relax and ask him all about the week. He'd ask about *The Molehill* and what cuts they'd made; he'd ask about *The Orchid Race* (it looked like a smash hit and he'd enjoyed it in a detached sort of way); and of course he'd ask what the Clemencys had been like. Then he might ask if the new play was shaping, and he would answer no, it wasn't. Finally he'd ask how Alberta had made out. And he would tell Jimmy that she had done very well considering that she hadn't known her way around at all: that she was conscientious and enduring and good company. Then he'd tell Jimmy about the expressions on the faces of Messrs Rheinberger and Schwartz sitting each side of her at the dinner, and leave it at that. They'd go back about six and he'd see Lillian who would have been resting and she'd have an 'at last' expression and ask him all about the week. He'd tell her who had called them up, and what places they'd been offered in Connecticut and Massachusetts, and explain about not going south because they had to be near New York until they'd achieved Clemency. And then she would want to know how Alberta was getting on, and he would tell her that she was very clever to have found Alberta, who was quiet and nice and had very good manners. Then she'd ask if he was getting on with the new play and he'd say yes, he was; that was why he wanted to move out of New York as soon as possible. Here, he broke down: he was cutting a poor pair of figures out of this – the only difference between him and a chameleon was that the creature had real reasons for its behaviour, and he hadn't. He could not say that this flickering dishonesty and failing in either saved his life or earned him his bread – so why do it? Because, of course, they were not the only reasons for doing anything. Right: if he was not, as a medical friend of Lillian's had once said, an integrated personality, he could at least indulge in a really personal argument – Joyce *v.* Joyce – or perhaps it was Emmanuel *v.* Joyce. Very soon after his first success he had discovered that women who were certain of seducing him nearly always said how marvellous it must be to be Irish and Jewish if you were a playwright, and the ones who wanted to seduce him but lacked self-confidence always asked him if it wasn't very difficult for a playwright having so many points of view – sympathy, in fact, was a more tentative approach. This was more than thirty years ago – in England, when class consciousness was more or less confined to the upper and upper middle classes, and had not spread democratically to all 'income groups'. (How the Indians would howl with laughter at this childish equation of money with caste.) The point had been that, with success, he had met a lot of people who didn't want to sound rude or patronizing about his background, were incapable of being anything else, and therefore picked on his mongrel blood as a safer alternative. He hadn't minded; he hadn't wanted to talk about his background either – he had discovered at one attempt a number of shocking platitudes. If your parents had been well off, or even comfortable, it was quite in order to hate them; but if they had been damned poor, and you'd been brought up in what they called a 'distressed area' – the thought of their two rooms and 'area' still made him smile – any breath of criticism was disloyalty and being stuck-up: your parents became characters and you were expected to have a character attitude towards them. So he had never told anybody but one how much he had hated his father in the end ... by the time he had outgrown the dresser drawer and had to sleep always on his back in it – in winter with his knees drawn high up – in summer with his legs lolling over the end so that the wood bit into the soft place under his knees – he used to lie there and imagine his father dead: in winter of pneumonia – in summer of prickly heat which he had read about and sounded awful enough to kill anyone. But his father lurched and jabbered on; charged with disastrous vitality – bored by everything but his own imagination of himself and haunted by all the chances he might have had. By the time he was eleven, he had been earning more regularly, at least, than his father: by the time he was twelve he had caught his father pinching these wages out of his mother's pocket and had knocked him against a gas bracket which had knocked him out. This random shot – which had astonished Emmanuel – had terrified his mother and produced a kind of angry respect in his father for a day or two, but when this was succeeded by a menacing swagger, he felt it was time to leave. . . . That was one morning he would never forget – November; raw and foggy; six o'clock, the time when every other morning for months he had lit a candle, wriggled out of his drawer, pulled on a jersey over his shirt (he slept in all his clothes but his jersey in winter), eaten the piece of bread and dripping left out for him over-night, and trudged off to the stables where he worked. Fifteen milk ponies: they all got a small feed before being harnessed for their rounds, and he used to pinch a pocketful of oats to eat while he fed them. The stables were dark but comforting after home; he liked the warm smell of manure and the ancient smells of dirty harness and dried sweat, and the animals welcomed him with confidential nickers as they stood in their line in patient cynical attitudes waiting the day's work. Daisy, Bluebell, Captain, Lilly, Brownie, and Rose, Twinkle, Major, Melba, and Blackie – good lord, he couldn't remember all of them now – he would feed them – mostly bran and chaff and a few precious oats, and then start lifting their heavy collars down from the pegs on the white-washed wall, and hoisting them on to their shoulders. He was tortured by chilblains in those days; the icy slush of the walk cooled his feet, but his hands were chapped and swollen so that he could hardly grasp the collars, and the men arrived long before he was through. But the morning that he left home he woke even earlier than six, and lay in the dark collecting his final impression of it. Except for the cheap clock with its weary hysterical tick there was silence – dark-ness, and smells: of distant cabbage; of partially washed clothes – his mother took in washing then, and there was a tub in the corner with garments soaking that these mornings

was covered with thin grey ice – the curiously angry smell of
mice, like sweated cheese; the little peevish draughts of leak-
ing gas; his father's clay pipe – a blackened greasy odour
that was in the imagination until one touched it; the rotting
plaster of the walls like damp, sleepy pears; a sour damp-rot
smell from the floor; the purple church smell of the book his
mother had won at school as a prize; the tea leaves which she
kept for the small mat in her bedroom; the faint wafts of
urine from the yard . . . he collected it all, and the wanting
to pack himself with bread and dripping till the yawning
grave inside him was filled. If he had the luck to be ship-
wrecked on an island in the Pacific, like those holy little
nippers he'd read about – if he ever had the chance to go on a
crusade, or the King wanted anywhere discovered for England, by God he'd remember this – because whatever his
luck or chance, he was making a change for himself. First he
was going to earn a lot of money and then he was going to
build a huge house and put his mother in it. She was going
to have a fur coat – several of them – and nothing to do ever,
and the house would be boiling hot and full of Jews because
she liked them best. He'd come for her one day in a
carriage and four horses and silk handkerchiefs for her
tears, and just take her and her book and leave the rotten
rest. . . .

Some of this blind vehemence overran him even after fifty
years, and he bumped heavily into a stranger: they recoiled
with dazed aggression and apology, and he was back in New
York, shivering from the jolt and needing coffee. He looked
round him, having no idea how far he had walked, and made
for the nearest drug store across the street. It was while he
was waiting for the coffee to cool that he saw a headline in
the paper lying on the counter: ATLANTIC STORM: TANKER
COLLISION OFF CAPE COD. 'QUEEN MARY' DELAYED.

The whole day changed: he had been certain of it and
shivering in the heartless spring air of the street – the sunlight cold and dazzling–the angles of the shadows sharp and
deep and crazy and turned at their centre to cavernous
draughts: he had felt heavy and cold and old; hemmed in

by foregone conclusions, imprisoned by mechanical experience, actually 'doing time' with this day: but now, sitting up by the soda fountain with bars of dusty sunlight round him, his hands warm round the coffee cup and the newspaper spread like a proclamation of chance before him, these little currents of warmth and light and uncertainty brought him to life; the atoms of dust were distinct in the sun – each particle seeming to have a gentle mysterious purpose – so that it was like looking at a magnified bloodstream. I am sitting on this stool, a small and ageing man, and at this moment anonymous to everybody but myself – there's balance for you – that's the right way round for once. I have a power, a little beyond me, to design a certain kind of communication for people who have not got this power. I can show them a certain sense of proportion – give them some balance – which is all that design is for – to put something in its right place in relation to whatever lies on either side of it. Proportion is always beautiful: beauty is always significant; therefore design is always necessary, and I am one of the thousands of designers. He felt an impersonal joy about all this, and looked again at the slow unearthly movement of the dust in the bar of sunlight. He was warm and smiling from the centre of his heart and he kept his head very still until the glow had spread to it, as he had learned long ago not to fly to a piece of paper with the first little vestige of an idea, which merely blunts the memory and renders it indiscriminate. He remembered an argument with Jimmy about this, because not immediately recording them meant that one forgot some of the ideas, and Jimmy had thought this lazy and wasteful. He couldn't make Jimmy understand that it wasn't: that it was wasteful and lazy not to make one's memory work for one; it had to select what was worth remembering and then wait for it – instead of premature explosions on paper – like a bird breaking open an egg she has just laid.

He saw the boy who had served his coffee eyeing him with a kind of apathetic curiosity: nothing would surprise *him*, unfortunately. He asked for his check, what the time was, and what street he was on, and the boy provided this dull information as though his customer was drunk.

As he walked back to his hotel he reflected that usually at this point of his walks – on his return – he was consciously bracing himself, storing up his private life to last for the day when he did not expect to have any, and focusing his patience and attention: but that now patience did not seem to be called for, and his attention was not straining after any particular direction but at ease, and therefore ready.

'. . . and so', he finished, 'I thought that as I had nothing worse to do, you and I would spend the day.'

She sneezed and continued to look at him expectantly.

'Until the boat arrives at six o'clock. Or do you want a day off to yourself?'

She shook her head. They were breakfasting in his sitting-room: she was eating waffles with maple syrup, and he was drinking coffee.

'What would you like to do, Alberta?'

'Tell me what there is.'

He told her all the things he could think of – the sight-seeing – going to the top of the Empire State Building, or Radio City – the Frick Collection, the Bronx Zoo, Greenwich Village, shopping – having a Chinese lunch, etc., etc. – and she listened with the impassive but acute attention of a child. When he had run out of what he could immediately think of – and it was surprisingly little – she sneezed again, and he said severely: 'But if you're getting a cold we shan't do any of it.'

'I'm not, I'm not.'

'Well, hay fever. You're probably allergic to maple syrup.'

'I'm not allergic to *anything*!' she said and scraped her plate defiantly, but she had gone pink, and presently she added: 'I'm sorry, but excitement makes me sneeze. I've been sneezing since we got here, but naturally I have tried to be unobtrusive about it.'

'You've succeeded,' he said solemnly.

'I expect to outgrow it, of course.'

'Excitement, or sneezing?'

'Sneezing first.'

'Do you mean that you *want* to outgrow excitement?'

'I – no, I don't mean that. I mean that I'd like to be much *more* excited about fewer things. Perhaps even one thing in the end. May I say what I think about the day now? I wish to change the subject.'

'Do.'

'I think we should do what we have to do first, and then see what happens.'

'Move the luggage to the apartment?'

'Yes, and see if the woman did come and clean it, and everything is ready for Mrs Joyce. Perhaps she has had a horrid time in the ship if there was a storm.'

'You are quite right. Let's go.'

'I'd better see if the letters have come.' She went to the telephone, and looked at him questioningly. He nodded. She was wearing a sweater which he recognized as Lillian's – a very pale fawn which she had said didn't suit her skin in winter. With it she wore a dark grey flannel skirt, very old, but well-polished English brogues and the stockings he had given her. He longed suddenly to take her out and buy her everything she could possibly want – then he remembered Lillian's remark about Gloria Williams's stockings – and a whole set of extremes reared protectively in his mind, hedging any past from this present – forcing all comparisons to such a background that they were barely distinguishable.

She was asking for the bill to be sent up with the letters. Her high, clear little voice had a command about it which was, or seemed to be, unconscious, and therefore agreeable. She projects herself, he thought, thinking of the exhausting hours he and Jimmy had spent trying to get various people to do this in a theatre. The letters arrived, and there were two from England for her. She asked if she might open them, and watching her pleasure in the contents of the first one, he realized that he couldn't remember when he had last had a letter which he was eager to open.

'Are your family well?' he asked when she had finished reading.

She nodded: she seemed so full of their news that he said: 'I like hearing about your family – do tell me.'

'Serena and Mary both have colds which they say they caught by accident, but Aunt Topsy doesn't believe that illness is accidental, so they are in bad odour. Napoleon has had five more children, but we were expecting her to: she is a cat; she was called Napoleon before we realized who she was. Mrs Facks says the world is coming to an end on November 11th and Papa does not agree with her, but he says that the employment of reason would be cruel as she has so little security. Mrs Facks works for us – off and on – because she has so many children. They live on chips and tomatoes, and Aunt Topsy says she keeps them under a paving-stone – they are a very queer colour for people – but they are awfully strong really, because they're always having mumps and things and it doesn't seem to impair their strength. Serena has decided to be a doctor for her career, which is much more suitable than her previous choice.'

'What was that?'

'An Admiral,' she replied briefly, and folded the letter.

'What about your brothers?'

'Humphrey is at school, and Clem is still down from Oxford, but staying with an extremely rich friend in Yorkshire which worries Papa, as he says it is healthy to have ideas above your station, but useless to get ideas which aren't your station at all, and he's afraid Clem may with his friend.'

'And how is your papa?'

'Well. This is my aunt's letter, he has simply put a postscript saying mind the traffic being different in America and his blessing. The other one is from my uncle, and I'm going to save it up for a bit.'

'Well, I – we – are going to save all mine,' he said, and stuffed them into his pocket.

Outside, there was far more wind than there had been on his early walk: the sky was hurried by clouds – the streets glittered – and there had been a shower. When they had visited the apartment earlier in the week they had discovered it all shrouded in darkness by curtains and blinds. It had been hot, as the heating was full on; it smelled of stale cigarettes, and when they had turned on some of the lights they were presented with luxury smitten by contemporary squalor. Full ash-trays, innumerable dirty glasses of every description, coffee cups, a great bowl of dead dogwood, nuts all over the floor: in the bedrooms, unmade beds, tissue paper, crumpled Kleenex and dirty cotton wool: the bathrooms were full of used bathtowels and razor blades, the tiles smeared with toothpaste, and in one a stack of newspapers had been put in the bath on to which the shower – which could not be thoroughly turned off – had dripped. The kitchen was spattered with dirty crockery, cartons of half-eaten food, and open tins whose oil or syrup seemed to have reached every available surface. Over everything there was dust, and above the dust a layer of irresponsibility which was somehow disgusting. 'Really, it's as though they were rich monkeys,' Alberta had said when they had surveyed it. 'I mean not quite sure what anything is for,' she had added. They had seen the porter, who assured them that a woman came every day to clean up, and that all would certainly be well by the time they wanted the apartment. Alberta was quite right: they ought to make sure of everything – see that the right beds were made up, and get coffee and flowers and things like that. . . .

The porter was a different one: he produced a key, put them into the lift with their luggage, and vanished. Alberta opened the door: it was dark; it was hot; it smelled the same. In silence, they switched on the lights: the dogwood was a little deader, and the odour of its decay was the only addition to a scene otherwise unchanged. He felt suddenly, furiously angry. But for the merest chance, he might have brought Lillian back – to this. He walked to the main window in the living-room – he was so angry that his feet hurt on the ground – jerked up the blind, and wrenched open a window. That was not enough: he seized the dogwood and flung it out of the window, and turned round for the bowl which had contained it, but it had fallen to the ground and a sticky green stream oozed from it. That was the last straw. He picked up the bowl, and hurled it into the fireplace where it broke with a cheap dry crash. Alberta said: 'I know exactly how you feel, but this is all my fault, so please don't break any more.'

'That bloody woman – that damn porter – what do you mean, *your* fault?'

'I should have seen whether she came before today. It may not be the woman's fault: she may be ill, and the porter has changed. Anyway, I'm your secretary, it's my responsibility and I'm very sorry. Now we'd better clear it up.'

'I won't have you clearing up this disgusting shambles. I'll call the porter. He can damn well get someone to do it.'

'All right.'

'Well – what are you doing then?' He stared at her aggressively, while he jogged the telephone.

'Opening a few windows: I don't know how else to stop central heating.'

There was no reply from the porter and he went down in search of him. The situation was not Alberta's fault: it was he who had been so confident and airy about the arrangements. His temper cooled in the lift, and by the time he had found the porter, and had a long and dispiriting talk with him, it had frozen to despair. The porter was new – the other man had gone sick – nothing was known of the daily woman, not even her address: in the two days that he'd been on the job five tenants had asked the porter if he knew of a daily woman; he hadn't known one and he didn't know one now. It was not his responsibility to see to the inside of apartments – he had enough to do as it was. Someone had just thrown a bunch of dead flowers out of a window – they had fallen on to a very, very sensitive dog who had bitten a truck driver who had been delivering a monkey at the service door. He was sore because he'd been bitten on the sidewalk and his union only insured him in the truck, and the owner of the dog said it was in the middle of analysis and being provoked to aggression just when it was beginning to understand its social responsibilities was very, very bad for it, as if *he* – the porter – was supposed to be responsible for anything tenants threw out of windows: the last block he'd worked in the windows didn't open and things were more civilized. For all he cared the tenants could throw themselves out – then at least the cops could take care of them and he wouldn't have to sort things out. Meanwhile here was the monkey in a basket cage marked: 'I eat four bananas a day please do not give me more out of mistaken kindness' and no address. Had he, by any chance, ordered a monkey? Well, that left him with a cool seventy-four apartments to call up. Emmanuel looked at the monkey, who, grasping the bars of its cage with tiny grape-coloured hands and glaring hungrily at them, was clearly longing for some mistaken kindness. It did not seem as though anyone was going to help anybody. He gave the porter a cigarette, and the porter said he guessed they both better sort out their own problems.

He decided to organize a laundry and a cleaner and book a hotel for a couple of nights until everything was sorted out, but he had reckoned without Alberta. He found her methodically at work. The ash-trays, glasses, and cups had disappeared from the living-room. The flat was light, imbued with fresh air, and she was on the floor sorting and folding dirty linen and making a list of it.

'There's an electric carpet sweeper and quite a lot of soap powder,' she said cheerfully; 'so if we could find a laundry to take this, everything will be all right.'

'I was thinking of booking a hotel until this was cleared up.'

'I really think that would be the most unwarrantable extravagance.'

'Do you?' She looked so earnest about it that he began to feel light-hearted.

'Yes I do. I mean it really *is* my fault that everything is in a mess, and the least I can do is to clear it up. I do know about cleaning houses,' she added anxiously, 'and feel confident of my success.'

'Do you?' He was smiling at her: he found her language sustaining.

'If you'll trust me: it's the least I can do.'

'I must say I've never seen anybody either confident or cheerful about the least they could do before. I trust you implicitly, but you'll have to tell me what to do.' He suddenly found himself viewing the prospect with enthusiasm: the experience was a new one, and she seemed perfectly suited to directing it.

'Find a laundry, wash up, and make a shopping list are the first things.'

'What about lunch? What about our Chinese restaurant?'

But she said that there wouldn't be time, and perhaps they could have sandwiches. So that, in the end, was how they spent the day, and having decided upon it – or consented to it – everything went easily for them. Years of money, travelling, and Lillian's ill-health had left him ignorant of housekeeping, and he recognized that he was probably unduly impressed by Alberta's practical intelligence over it, but he was none the less delighted with the pleasant results she made before his eyes. They made a shopping list and he went shopping obediently to buy a great many things that had not occurred to him since he was young and poor. Then, having done all she expected, he bought wine, fruit juices, and whiskey for Jimmy: flowers – tulips, lilac, narcissi, and freesias – for Lillian: then he wanted to find something for her – couldn't think of anything that he was sure she would like him to give her – got desperate, and bought a box of *marrons glacés*.

The porter, whom he had not seen on his way out, met him at the door of the taxi with suspicious alacrity, and said he'd sure bought a few items for the home. Emmanuel unwisely asked after the monkey; the porter's face took on an expression of hunted sentiment, and said that he'd called all the apartments, and of those that replied, nobody had ordered a monkey. He carted Emmanuel's load to the elevator and then stood in its door looking uncomfortable. Finally he asked if Emmanuel had by any chance a banana handy. No. It was the monkey's eyes that were getting him down. After all, the notice simply said that the monkey ate four bananas a day: it didn't say that it had already eaten them; there was no chart or anything where you could strike off the bananas as the monkey ate them – and meanwhile it sat in that goddam cage looking mournful and blaming him and he wasn't at all sure how much more he could take. Emmanuel pushed him gently out of the way, and advised him to get bananas.

Alberta seemed to have done so much that he was almost shocked. The living-room was clean and orderly: it was now the charming room he remembered. Two bedrooms were done and their adjoining bathroom; she was just starting on the other two and she'd made up all the beds. She had a large transparent smudge on her forehead, and her hair was tied back from her head in a tail. He said that they must stop to have lunch, and she said that she wanted to finish all the rooms first excepting the kitchen: he felt it would be dangerous to stop her. So he went and sat in the living-room, and wondered vaguely what it would be like to live some-where – to have some roots that he had never had since he had left home that November morning. The digs, the theatres, the top back rooms, the faded shady little boarding-houses, the arty pinched guest-houses kept by war widows who had frozen and starved and ground out of him the pittance for their roofs which was their only hope – the miserable appearances which he had contributed towards keeping up – and the rooms themselves, multiplying now out of his memory into myriad icy draughts from sash windows; wardrobe doors that flew open to flush forth sour sweat and moth-balls; the spilled powder and hairpins in the top drawers of dressing-tables; the threadbare carpets held to-gether by aged dirt and grease; the creaking skeleton beds with fibrous rigid blankets; the chamber pots and sooty lace curtains; the daguerreotypes of Disraeli and Henry Irving and *First Love*; the spotted mirrors and explosive cane chairs; the papers of anonymous flora that roved and climbed, wriggled and wilted over countless walls; the empty grates with paper fans; the cold, the wet feet, the loneliness. ... What had sustained him then? It was easy to remember. The theatres, of course, a new one each week, but above all, the plays; in most of them strong sentimental or melodramatic meat – there was not their equivalent entertainment today even in the cinema – the plots were rich, like dark plum cake, the ideas behind them simple. Right prevailed and there was no doubt about what was right; Love won through; dramatic justice was done to characters who attempted to thwart courage or chastity; motives were declaimed from the start, and the language (except for minor character parts) made no attempt at contemporary idiom. But when he was in his early teens and working with a touring company, these plays and the people in them, this language, these principles, were life – all and more than he had ever asked of it, and for years he lived with this inversion of reality; from the moment each time that the company took possession of an empty dim theatre, and he was on the stage with its menacing odour of size – its dim whiffs of gas – its chalky sweetmeat draughts, he felt, helping to fly backcloths and brace flats, that he was preparing the scene for life. He did not expect to take any part in it: he had been engaged as a general dogsbody – he shifted scenery, did the calling, fetched drinks for the cast, cleaned out dressing-rooms, distributed handbills, packed and unpacked clothes and prop baskets, patched flats, made noises off with tea trays, coconut shells, air pistols, and his own voice, and went on the book for rehearsals. Once, they tried him with a one-line part in a historical drama. He was to come on at the end of the second act and announce the sudden death of a main character to the assembled company. He had no rehearsal for this, as he knew the play by heart and was a last-minute substitution – they simply gave him the clothes and told him to make himself up. This had taken a long and exciting time, and the result had been that at the last possible moment he had shot on to the stage, chalk white, with a spectacular and improbably black moustache, creaking boots, and a cloak several sizes too large for him. He stood for a moment, intoxicated by the dazzling, powdery light, delivered the line, and then, feeling that this was not enough for the occasion, he made a speech – his thin arms whirring inside the cloak like a windmill, his voice, which was breaking, cracked and squeaky with excitement, as he recounted in gory and horrible detail the manner of the character's death. After seconds of paralysis – the hero – a man of considerable, if repetitious, experience, had picked him up and carried him, a small struggling bat, to the wings where he was flung at and fielded by a distraught stage-hand. This was his one and only appearance on any stage, and it was good old Elsie who had saved him from getting the sack. Dear Elsie – she was a good woman, and she'd been his first friend. It was she who tried to explain what came over him to the boss, while he stood speechless and trembling – it was she who gathered him to her exuberant bosom and breathed comfort and stout and Devon violets over him while he cried in an agony of fear and contrition – who made him look at his white and black streaky face in the glass until he gave a watery laugh at the sight – it was she, who, standing like a rock beside him in her corsets, turned the whole thing into a joke with the company. . . .

Alberta stood in the open door saying: 'I've had to stop: I'm too hungry.'

She looked like a cross little girl, and then he saw that it was simply another smudge on her face.

'We'll eat immediately.'

He had brought what seemed to him a simple sensible meal; she made a prim admiring remark about it, and ate for some minutes in an awed silence. Then, just as he was wondering why he was wondering what to talk about, she said : 'May I ask you something?'

'Well?'

'Do the people who have auditions for Clemency read the rest of the play?'

He started to say 'of course they do', and then realized

that in many cases he didn't know. 'Some of them get the whole script certainly. Whether they read it or not is another matter.'

'But all the ones who are just given that scene we had hectographed. *They* don't?'

'No. But they are mostly the shots in the dark: they are expected to go wide of the mark. Why?'

'Because I don't see how they can be any good in that scene unless they know what it is for. Of course I don't know anything about acting. But I didn't understand the scene in spite of watching so many people read it, until I'd read the whole play. Is it different for actresses?'

'Some people would claim that it was. You see, at the moment, we're not looking for somebody who gives the perfect performance of Clemency, we're looking for a certain quality without which she wouldn't ever be Clemency.'

'I should have thought that that quality would make whoever it was insist on reading the whole play before an audition.'

'Supposing you're right about that. Then what would happen?'

She said simply: 'Then they'd know whether they could be her or not. No, thank you, if I drink any more I'll go to sleep.'

'It isn't quite as simple as that. Do you want to know why?' She nodded. 'A good actress can't always be playing inside her emotional experience. But she must play inside her imagination, which is based on her emotional experience. There is always a margin, you see, beyond actual experience, where the imagination can be pure – untainted by the players' false ideas of themselves. It's their business to keep that margin pure – alive – to enlarge it if possible; it's my business to gauge what it is. I'm talking about good actresses now – artists if you like – not just anybody who happens to act. One doesn't write parts like Clemency for them. Of course, I may be wrong about the play. If I am, then however I cast it, it won't come off. It didn't in London.'

'I thought it was a great success?'

'It's running. I mean it hasn't turned out at all as I meant it to.'

'Does that happen often?'

He smiled: she had an unconscious capacity for his sense of proportion which made him laugh at himself and like her. 'No – it does *not*, and I always talk as though it does, or should. Have some grapes now, and tell me what you thought of the play.'

She put a finger gently on the smoky skin and rubbed it clear. 'Isn't that extraordinary? Imagine collecting bloom; it's something you can't *have* – you can only see it sometimes.'

He looked absently at the grape: he wanted suddenly to hear what she thought about Clemency, and he felt that she mightn't tell him. 'You weren't cloaking your opinions in some sort of whimsical symbolism, were you?'

She looked so startled that he nearly laughed. 'Give me your valuable opinion, Miss Young.'

'I liked it. I like the whole idea: it starts and finishes and seems complete in itself, and there is still something on either side of it.' She was getting pink again, round the smudges. 'My experience of play reading is extremely limited, so I don't think I understood all of it, and therefore my opinion must be of little significance.'

'Do you feel that if your experience of play reading increased the significance of your opinion would go up?'

'It would depend ...' she began – saw his face and stopped: 'The trouble is that I think I take almost everything seriously, which really only means taking *me* seriously about them. I'm so sorry: it is such a dreary bad habit – Papa says it is the broad highway to being a bore.'

'It's a crowded highway,' he said, as a feeling of affection shifted in his heart, and he wondered what to do with it. 'Is there any more of your insignificant opinion?'

She looked up from the grapes with eyes that were nervous with honesty. 'A bit more. Why do you want me to tell you?'

'I might find something out.'

'About your play.' She did not put that as a question, so he did not deny it. She thought for a moment, and then said: 'About the beginning. You mean her – Clemency – to be beautiful, rich, surrounded by admirers, friends, and achievements, don't you?'

'Yes.'

'And in some ways she is happy like that?'

'Externally.'

'This is the beginning of what I don't understand. After that extraordinary evening she spends meeting the anonymous man outside the theatre, she wants something quite different?'

'Yes. But she can't have it with her existing life, she understands that.'

'*Yes.* To get what she wants she has to give up the success and admiration – all that. But, as she doesn't seem to value them much in the first place, they aren't much to give up, are they? I mean they might be impossibly hard for some people, but they are so shadowy to her that they hardly count. I don't know what you mean by external happiness, but surely you can't cheat by paying for something you want very badly with twopence – it isn't expensive enough – and if she felt she was really rich in the beginning, she'd have something to pay with.'

There was a complete silence: he was looking at her, and he saw her so clearly that in her was his own reflection: he saw so much of himself that there were no words in his mind for it – the few seconds were filled so that they were round and unrecognizable drops of time. She knew something – or understood that there was something for him to know, because she did not break this moment; having furnished him, she was still, and when it was over she waited for him to resume, or assume what he would. It was much as though she had unerringly laid a finger on something that he found it very difficult to find, and left him to count the beats.

When he stirred, she got to her feet, and took their tray into the kitchen, but the sensation of warmth and lightness remained with him. He joined her; she was rubbing her face furiously with a wet handkerchief.

'Aunt Topsy says that to make really light pastry, you should never let the flour get beyond your knucklebones. I don't know how far dirt should go in good housework, but I'm sure it shouldn't get to one's forehead.'

'Are you tired? You've done a great deal of housework.'

'I'm not, thank you. Fortunately I have a magnificent constitution. That was the most delicious lunch; now I'm going to clean up the kitchen.'

'I'd like to help. Shall I dry things?'

'Thank you. There are some rather queer towels, with verses – what Papa calls pupperel on them. Do you think people really *read* their tea towels in America?'

'I expect the poor bored housewife gets something out of them.'

'I know. Everything about food and kitchens is made so dull, they do need something. It's terribly difficult to feel skilful and indispensable with gadgets and pre-stressed food. It's all boiled down to the least you can do, which is so disheartening.'

They washed up: there was a kind of affectionate ease with her that he had only felt before with anybody after making love. She asked him how he had come to write his first play and what it had been about, and these questions which he had so often been asked and answered with a kind of dishonest brevity, got their full reply. He told her about running away – getting frightful toothache the first day; about Elsie finding him sitting in the road outside a pub holding his head and crying; how she took him to her dressing-room and got the stage carpenter to pull his tooth out with a pair of pliers, made him rinse his mouth out with eau de cologne, and then got him a job with the company. He told her about his disastrous appearance on the stage and how good Elsie had been then – how afterwards she had said 'Write it all down ducks – get it out of your system – it will only make trouble for you if you don't and it won't do anybody any good inside. If you can think of all that you said on the spur of the moment, you might write a famous play – with a deevy little part in it for me.' And when he had asked her what deevy meant, she said it was slang, but very refined.

'Tell me about her – what did she look like?'

'There aren't many people like her now – although then she was quite an ordinary type. She had been a blonde, and she'd played *ingénues* for years until she got too heavy for them. She dyed her hair when it began to fade; she still had a pretty complexion and blue eyes, but I think they'd faded like her hair. She had a fine pair of arms and shoulders – they were much more a point of admiration in those days: women dressed to display them – and for the rest, she enjoyed her food and her stout too much to keep her figure. But besides her ready heart and her practical kindness she combined a sense of adventure with a general cosiness in perfect proportions – at least for a boy of fourteen. She said she was thirty-five, but she must have been well over forty: she only mothered me when I really needed it: the rest of the time she never forgot that she was a woman, and that I would one day be a man. She had a passion for gentility and refinement, but for her they went with high life and romance – she believed in them – she didn't care a damn what the neighbours thought. She'd once had supper with a marquis and it was one of her favourite stories against herself. "Imagine *me*, dear," she used to say, "fancying myself a marchioness because a nice young man liked me figure – the *ideas* we get about ourselves." She thought England was the best country in the world – she loved the theatre, and she was passionately in love with the manager of our company, who treated her pretty badly most of the time, and was frequently unfaithful to her with the string of young women engaged to play the parts she had once had.'

'Did she know about it?'

'She knew. She knew all about him, and it didn't make any difference. You see, she knew a good deal about herself. I only once saw her really down with it, when I burst into her dressing-room one evening and found her hunched under her dressing-gown struggling into her corsets with tears streaming down her face. "He's off with that Violet Everard now. Each time he says it's never going to happen again; I know it is, but I enjoy him thinking it won't." And when I tried to comfort her, she dropped the dressing-gown and said: "Of course he's fond of me, but you help me into these and you'll see what a silly old woman I am to go chasing after what I'm not meant for any more. I've only got to get myself into these to have a good laugh at myself – carrying on like a girl of sixteen inside all this. If I can't learn to be my age, why should I expect him to?" And then she really did laugh at herself, and cleaned up her face and gave her performance – as Violet's mother in the play. It was the only time I ever saw her cry.'

He had forgotten about drying glasses – he was sitting on the table – years away. She took the cloth from him and said gently: 'What about your play?'

He laughed as though he had caught it from Elsie. 'My play. I wrote it: every single character had a title, and most of them were wicked, except for the part I wrote for Elsie, into which I poured all my ideals of womanhood and goodness, and so the most frightful things happened to her without the slightest effect – she might have been a block of stone, she was so passive, so indestructible and dull. It took place in an earl's castle: opened with a shrimp tea in the library, and it was called *Evil Does Not Pay*. One of the characters left the stage on a line which ran: "I must leave your blasted presence: you sully the air so that I cannot breathe it," and the hero poisoned a lot of characters in the last act by putting bad oysters in their champagne. They didn't drink anything else, you see, so that was bound to do for them.'

'What happened to it?'

'That was the terrible thing. They did it – as a farce – instead of a pantomime, at Christmas. They let Elsie play the part I'd written for her; they paid me twenty pounds and I was so excited I didn't realize what was going on. I went out and bought a string of pink pearls for Elsie – she loved pink – they were in a box lined with pink velvet, and I planned to give them to her with a card on the first night. It was she who had given me her bottle of green ink she had hardly ever used for writing letters, and her box of notepaper to write the play. They were shifty about letting me see rehearsals, but they were all laughing and saying how good it was – except Elsie, who just kept saying get on with starting another play, and just before they went up on the first night she called me and said she was very proud of me, and if the play didn't go as I expected I must not fret but see it was all for the best and everybody had to get started somehow.'

He stopped, and said: 'I haven't thought about all this for years, and this is the third time today that I've remembered about it.'

'Go on: what happened?'

'They put me in front, in a box all by myself, and for about ten minutes, until the house lights went, I felt no end of a nob. I saw myself wearing a top-hat and owning theatres, with Julia Neilson, Lewis Waller, Playfair, Dion Boucicault, and others all on their knees to me imploring me for plays. I don't suppose those names mean anything to you, but they meant a lot then – they were the epitome of heroic glamour – thousands of people adored them and collected postcards of them in their famous parts just as avidly as they collect pin-ups today. I'd just got as far as postcards of me, when the house-lights went. From the moment the curtain went up, I knew something was wrong; and when I saw the pink flannel shrimps, the size of bananas, and the house laughed at them, my heart dropped like a small burning coal into my boots, where it remained for the whole performance, while I struggled with my feelings. My feelings!' he laughed: 'you've no idea what they were like – resentment, shame, rage, self-pity, sheer, obstinate refusal to accept the situation – shame and rage again. They went round and round, accompanied by a full house in holiday mood, roaring with laughter at what I considered to be my most heartrending speeches, agonizing situations, and beautiful moments. When Elsie came on in a white nightgown several sizes too large for *her*, and a long wig of golden hair streaming down her back, I nearly burst. The conflict was so awful, you see: a bit of me thought she looked wonderful; and a bit wanted to laugh, because she was somehow a caricature of herself, and there was everybody shouting with mirth, and her entrance was one of my beautiful moments – well, I sat there seething until – I don't remember what made me – but I laughed – by mistake, of course: it made me furious; I was crying as well, without any noise – with tears on my scalding face like spit on an iron. And I thought if they could see me now – the author – looking like this, they'd laugh more than ever: they were the world, you see, and it would be my fault if I gave them another chance to laugh at me. So I watched the rest of the play with a kind of glassy calm – if I was a failure I was going to be dignified about it. And so I bolstered myself until my nose cleared, and I imagined myself facing the company afterwards, with worldly indifference. I hadn't bargained for the end, at all, when they clapped and the cast started to cry for author; Edward Burton – he was the actor manager – sent for me and they hauled me on to the stage and I found myself standing between him and Elsie, unable to look at either of them, as the bitterness of my failure rolled over me all over again. I had set out to do one thing, and the fact that it had turned out to be something quite different, escaped me. I could only see what I'd failed to do.'

He became aware, as he stopped again, of how much he had been talking; he had talked and talked, and she had finished the kitchen. He made a small conclusive gesture with his hands. 'Well: that was that. But it was the classic example of things not turning out as I had meant them to.' He looked round for a cigarette, and she pushed the packet across the table to him.

'You were fourteen when all this happened?'

'Don't you feel I ever could have been?'

'It just seems so young to write a play and have all that happen, and very hard to bear at fourteen. What did Elsie say to you?'

'Oh, she saved my bacon – or sense of proportion – as usual. She talked to me nearly all night till she was dropping, bless her. Had I realized that lots of people wrote plays who never had them performed at all? Of course I hadn't. Did I realize how much easier it would now be to get another play put on? Of course I didn't. I explained that I wanted to write about life, and she said there was nothing to stop me but I'd have to learn something about it. The best thing she said was that one wasn't *born* knowing things, but one had a chance to find out what one wanted to know. She – do you *want* to hear all about this?'

'Yes, I do.'

'She said that as I wasn't living in castles with a whole lot of earls, it would be difficult to write a serious play about them and that I'd written a play out of other plays, and not out of what I saw or knew. Then she said: look at her: could I imagine her behaving like Lady Geraldine FitzAbbot? Not her – she wouldn't be so silly: she wasn't pure and high born – she was fat and rather common; she liked her stout and a good laugh and she dyed her hair and she loved Teddy Burton and there was nothing pure or noble about her – but at least I *knew* her. Then I began to see what she meant, and felt so much better that although it was three in the morning, I gave her the pink pearls and asked her to marry me, and she was sweet about it all – the pearls and the proposal.'

'Did you really want to marry her?'

'It may seem absurd to you, but yes – I did, then. She seemed to me so *good* – such a good, kind creature, and I found that such an attractive quality – I wanted to stay with it. I still feel like that, sometimes.'

'You mean, you still sometimes wish you had married her?'

'Yes – no, that's not what I meant.'

There was a silence, and then she coloured, and said: 'I'm so sorry. Of course that's not what you meant.' She was thinking of Lillian, and her possible implication of disloyalty.

He put his hand on her shoulder – let it rest – and took it

away. 'I know it's not what you meant, either.' He understood her – that she didn't know he had not been thinking
of Lillian.

In the taxi, driving across town to the piers to meet Lillian,
he thought of Alberta arranging flowers and unpacking in
the apartment she had so neatly made habitable, and Lillian
in the boat locking and unlocking pieces of hand luggage,
and worrying about whether he had remembered to meet
her. Out of her country family life, Alberta – in the middle
of New York – could do what was required of her: she could
adapt what she had been bred and brought up to be, because
something else in her was steady – was not rocked by outward changes. But if Lillian made physical gestures her
body broke down, and he did not think that she recognized
any other kind now: her courage was therefore constantly
misspent, and sinking into the parched field of her activities.
She was as pinned by this fixed image of herself and her
desperate efforts to serve it, as Alberta was free to be served
by her own imagination. That, he supposed, was the difference – and he hovered above it, uncertain where he should
stand. . . .

2. LILLIAN

THE restlessness started the night before we were supposed
to dock. Up until then, it hadn't entered my head – I don't
know why not. Jimmy had been his sweetest – really I'd
enjoyed the trip – even when he got seasick, which he always
does, poor thing, he was so pathetic and good-tempered
about it, and so grateful for being looked after that somehow even his being prostrate for two days hadn't spoiled
the journey. I read to him – he still likes C. S. Forester and
almost any poetry I choose best, and we had delicious little
picnic meals in his cabin although the poor creature couldn't
eat much. But he adored being looked after – I think that's
never having had parents or a proper home – and it was
heavenly to be the nurse for a change. He said I was good at

it, and he meant that, which was so warming. He told me about his life in orphans' homes which he's never talked about before, and it sounded awful – much worse than he realized. The sense of being a collection – of everything being based on justice rather than feeling; everybody dressed the same, having the same, acting the same, and knowing everything about each other. He told me that he was sent a tin motor-car anonymously for Christmas, and he kept it buried in the garden so that the others couldn't share it and told everybody it was lost and dug it up to touch and look at it by himself. Of course it got all rusted and fell to bits, but he said it was worth it to have a secret. It was the only secret he managed to have, he said, the others all got found out in spite of telling lies. He said that even at the time he felt disconnected from his life – as though he was watching somebody else go through the motions of it. I understand that: that's why he is so useful to Em and adores him so, and I really must *not* be jealous of that. But the night before we were supposed to dock there was fog and we reduced speed and everybody was talking at dinner about how late the fog might make us. It was then: it came over me just like the beginning of a disease or fever that perhaps in a week Em had become attracted to her and seduced her because that would be the easiest thing in the world to do. And immediately I thought what nonsense – think of her – she's just a dull little schoolgirl, and if he wants to seduce somebody, he can do better than that. Then I thought of that horrible Gloria Williams – mincing lethargic creature with those hideous legs – a genteel martyr if ever there was one – if he could get off with *her* he might do anything. The vulgarity of my thoughts about him sometimes appals me, *and* the language in which they are couched, which, of course, is in keeping. After all, *I* picked her, and God knows I have learned to consider this squalid little possibility. After dinner, I asked Jimmy to walk on the boat deck with me, and while he was getting our coats I resisted the urge to confide in him – to share this apprehension: I don't want Jimmy to discover that Em talks to him more than he talks to me, and so I have always pretended to Jimmy that I know everything, and understand, or don't care. But while we were pacing up and down in that curiously heavy, billowing air, I asked him what Em had had to do all the week in New York, and when he told me, I felt much better, because really there would hardly be time to start a new affair as well. Only I do hope we don't get delayed too much by this weather, and nobody will say anything definite about that. After a bit, Jimmy said would I like to go to the movies – they were showing *The African Queen*, which we'd both seen, but it is Jimmy's beloved Forester, and I adore Katharine Hepburn, so we went. Afterwards, Jimmy had a drink and we talked a bit about where we would be in the summer, and I said I wanted to go to Greece, which shook him, but it's quite true – I do, and Em has promised me for years. Jimmy looked miserable, and said he loathed sight-seeing, and wouldn't it be too hot, and I explained about my idea of living on an island, and having a really simple life. I also told him that I thought that an island would be a good place for Em to write and be away from the theatre or contacts with it. I begged him not to put Em off, and he looked shocked, and said of course he wouldn't dream of it. Then, suddenly, we had nothing more to say and he suggested going to bed. I couldn't sleep. I read and read: in the end I took a pill, and it was like falling slowly into a heavy warm sea – silent and colourless; dark and empty and immeasurable. At the very beginning of my waking, I dreamed of meeting Em. I could float, which made my movements most gentle, and he was standing on a very small island, with one tree beside him. I felt my hair shining, my skin moist as I rose out of the water and turned to him, nearer and nearer, until our eyes were almost fused in our meeting. Then I saw that his island was floating also – away from me – and that I was not to reach it – that I had come up out of the sea on to my separate island, but with no tree, and I sank on to the pale sand which darkened as the sun went slowly in and I woke. It was late – if there had not been fog we should have docked by now. I rang Jimmy, and he'd had breakfast and knew that we should dock at six. At least we knew. In eight hours I should see him – *if* he was there to meet me – *if* the fog did not get worse – *if* he had news of the time we were to dock. Jimmy came and talked while I had breakfast and was very calm and stern, and said I was working myself up, and he'd call Em's hotel and make sure that he knew we were due at six. He tried to make the call while I thought how funny it was that I couldn't even *enjoy* being excited any more. The call was no good: everybody was making them, and by the time we were through the delay, Em had checked out – which at least means the apartment is on. I wondered what on earth he and the girl were doing, and started to feel bad about her again. Perhaps I get excited by the wrong things – or perhaps excitement is no good anyway. Really I would like to meet him much more like the first half of my dream – with a kind of beautiful, calm confidence – and very quietly. As it is, I can't keep still: can't eat lunch; get more and more breathless, and a pain inside ticks over like an engine ready to start; the palms of my hands sweat, and I keep thinking that I've forgotten to pack something. And yet, whenever I feel like this – right up to whatever is going happen – the event seems, as it were, to start without me: I am not in it – all my imagination of it is dislocated and there seems nothing to take its place. Once, I remember him meeting me (also in New York), and within a few minutes, we were having an argument about some dreary people we hardly knew, and I told him how excited I'd been about meeting him, and he said: 'In order to talk about the Smithsons?' And then I remembered thinking that excitement was useless. That's the trouble with me: I hardly have any real feelings – just awful substitutes – intellectual imaginings, and physical anti-climaxes. Yes, but how does one *have* real feelings, and how can I have them about Em if he doesn't have them too? I *did* have them about Sarah. Oh! Sometimes I wish she had lived a little longer so that I would have more of her to remember now; her two years seem so short that I've nearly lost the taste of them: all my memories are coloured with the pain of losing her. Surely that was real – that wrenching, aching loss? Afterwards Em once said to me: 'Only joy is unmistakable: remember your joy in her.' He said it in the kind of way that made me feel it was true, but I couldn't understand him; I didn't accept what he said, because not having been allowed to suffer instead of Sarah, I refused not to suffer as well as she. It's very odd: I think so much about these things – but I hardly ever think about them in this way: it is something to do with the ship being late, and these eight hours being slipped into my life – not how I expected or meant. I understand what people mean when they say: 'I would die for her'; in certain circumstances, not being able to becomes a kind of outrage. There is something weak and dangerous about making a person the centre of your life: people are damaged and die too easily – but *where* is anything indestructible? My chief feeling about Em is fear that I may lose him, and as I've never really had him, this is absurd. It is funny, the way I'm always trying to give things I haven't got, and am terrified of losing something I've never had, but I don't seem to laugh at it enough to do any good. I think it was sometime after lunch, when Jimmy had gone off to tip our stewards and people, that I made a solemn promise to myself that I would honestly try to be kind and generous to Alberta – try to understand and make the best of her; and having made this promise, something of the calm – the dream-like calm was there, and it didn't even seem difficult to do. When Jimmy came back, he went on treating me as though I was terribly strung up – he didn't see any difference: it made me angry that he couldn't see – and that's how I lost my short-lived calm. We had already made the arrangements – I was to go straight off the ship with my dressing-case and meet Em, and Jimmy was to wait behind, see all our luggage through the Customs, and follow us – but we made them again. Jimmy said why didn't I have a rest, but I couldn't. In the end, I decided to change; I had a new suit of very pale blue silky tweed which I'd never worn, and a dark blue silk jersey, and some shoes which were very plain, but exactly the same colour. I sent Jimmy away, and he said he was going up to look down on the sea, and he'd meet me at five.

I spun it all out as long as possible: had a bath, painted my nails, massaged my hair – but even so, I wondered how countless women manage to keep quantities of men waiting while they bath and change. Perhaps their minds aren't on it like mine seems to be: as some women are about houses, so am I about my body. It is my house, and I enjoy cleaning and grooming and decorating it; and to do it in an orderly, thorough – almost detached – manner, is pleasant exercise. . . .

Time: it fidgeted and jerked; it clung drowning to the last straw of each second; it hung, breathlessly, over my smallest movement. I thought of railway-station clocks that move every minute with a comforting convulsion – of slow-motion films, of speedometers, of sand running through an hour glass, of my hair growing, of the sundial at Wilde whose shadow never seemed to move when I watched it, of the only time I saw the Derby, of my forty-five years (I am more than forty-five!), of the way Em can give the illusion of a whole afternoon and evening in a forty-minute act, of the seventeen hours with Sarah ... the whole business seemed inexorably elastic.

I tried to read. I thought of all the people in the ship who had expected to arrive this morning – the atmosphere of impatience and frustration had been noticeable at lunch – I thought of the extra drinks that were being consumed to fill in time, of the patient crew answering the same questions for hours, of the New York skyline, the Statue of Liberty, and the number of people who had never seen it before. . . . From my porthole, I could see that there was much more wind – the fog had almost cleared, but I would need a scarf for my hair – a white one, if I could find it. . . .

The time had its life – somehow – it seemed to me always to have been dead, but in the end, it had to make way for more of itself that had been waiting and that I had waited for. There is the curious sensation in a large ship: when she is moving, her engines, however discreet, pulse like the circulation of blood in a body, and all the people in her seem to move over her with the scurrying, soundless activity of ants – they seem nothing to her mainstream of life and movement: but when she is stopped, these activities break into sounds, she becomes simply a hive for people and their noises; cabin doors, luggage shifted, voices, breaking glass and changing money, greetings and farewells, footsteps going down to collect trunks, and up to the seagulls. She is no longer moving the moving water; it heaves and slaps against her with time to repeat itself; the air moves round her with a kind of intricate liberty which was not apparent during her journey.

As I was walking off the boat – leaving the concentrated turmoil of crowded passages and doorways for the spread-out confusion below on the quay, I suddenly saw myself, as though it was the beginning of a film. A tall well-dressed woman picking her way down the gangplank – what is going to happen to her? Is she going to meet somebody, and who will they be? She looks apprehensive, and either she is rich, or it is a very bad film, because she has a mink coat slung over her arm. The camera looks for a moment with her eyes at the scene before her – a casual sweep, and then more searchingly. As it is a film, she is looking for a man: and she is either desperately afraid of him, or desperately in love. There he is – the picture hovers at its distance, and then approaches him; he was in the background, and he does not know we have seen him. He is standing with his weight on one leg, staring at the ship. He is a small man; hatless, wearing a blue muffler, and the breeze is raking up his thick, dark hair. His eyes, screwed up a little against the cold air, are not characteristic like that: they should be still, and very bright, but he does not know he has been seen. The woman – we go back to her – has smiled, and perhaps it is a better film than we thought, because it is not possible to tell from her smile whether she is afraid or in love. Supposing, at this point, as much were to happen to me as must happen to the woman at the beginning of a film; some great change, some violent alteration which illuminates the purpose of

itself, so that at the end of it I can see where I am placed. . . .
While I was waiting for the Customs to clear me, and Em
was out of sight, I wondered what change there could be. In
a film the change could only fall into one of two categories:
the external, and some engagement of the heart or body. I
didn't want my externals changed, I suddenly realized, excepting my wretched health – and that would not be merely
a change – it would be miraculous. With the help of that
miracle, I might even have another child. And yet what
were miracles? They seemed generally to be events which
the people who benefited from them totally failed to understand. If my health were now suddenly to improve, I should
not understand why; I should only know just enough about
it not to be able to attribute it to some new drug, because
I know that there are no new drugs for me. It was then that
I discovered that I had lived all my life on the supposition,
the hope, that things would be different; that I lived inside
as though I was the person meant for these changes, and
was waiting to live in them – in fact, as though I was someone else.

'Have you anything to declare?'

I felt my suspicion reflected in his eyes. He held out his
hand for my passport, and I resisted the melodramatic impulse to say: 'I have these papers, but I do not know who I
am, except that I am not what I seem: isn't that a declara-
tion?' But he pushed them back into my hand and said:
'You've come to the wrong place, lady. This is for American
citizens.'

Still wondering who I was, I asked him where I should go.

'You're an *alien*,' he said, as though that answered everything.

So it was a long time before they let me through to find Em
with a taxi, and by the time I did find him, his familiarity
was so welcome that I actually ran to him.

'There, darling,' he said, 'there,' and I clung to him knowing all the clothes he was wearing and the smell of his skin,
and wanting that moment to tell him everything that I had
been feeling and had discovered.

'I wish we ran into each other like two drops of water.'

'Then you wouldn't be able to tell me anything: I'd know it already – you wouldn't like that.'

'Perhaps you do know.'

He signed my face with his finger: he was smiling faintly. 'Is Jimmy going to bring the rest of the luggage on?'

'Yes.' We moved towards the taxi – he was holding my shoulders, and I said: 'Admire my suit.'

'It's charming – I have been.' I looked down myself with him to my shoes. 'They are pretty, too. And you've washed your hair, and look at your hands. You take so much trouble, my darling, do you know why?'

I wanted to tell him, but I couldn't, because I also wanted to surprise him with my answer. Instead, when we were in the taxi, I said: 'Jimmy was terribly sick – for two days.'

He laughed; 'You sound so proud of it. Of course, *you* weren't.'

'Of course not. I looked after him, extremely well. We both enjoyed it.'

He looked pleased. 'I hope he's recovered: he's going to have to go to work here.'

'Have you found anyone for your play?'

'No one. The only possible is tied up with a film contract – she can't leave for long enough.'

'How is Miss Young?'

'I left her covered with dirt. The poor girl has had to clear up the apartment. They'd lent it to some people for a party, and it was a shambles. It's a good thing you didn't come at ten – she's been at it all day.'

'What have you been doing?'

'Oh – buying flowers and things – and walking about.'

'And thinking?'

He looked suddenly guarded, and I added: 'Not about my arrival – I didn't mean that.'

He said: 'I never know what quality one has to reach in one's thoughts to constitute thinking. I have been remembering – do you count that?'

'I do it all the time.' I felt a fleeting contradiction in him, although he had not moved: then he took my hand gently, and said: 'Perhaps "remembering" is the wrong word. I don't mean that I have been recalling exactly what happened: I mean that I have been reminiscing with a selection of events and my impressions of them.'

'Why?'

'I've been trying to find something. The curious thing is that one doesn't just start with revolt – one has a clear, innocent reason for it. At the beginning, something seems valuable: one desires it; it seems necessary and possible and worth fighting for. Then the whole plot of this thickens, and by then one has the experience of activity and struggle and one forgets what the whole thing was for.' He was silent.

'Have you forgotten?'

'Very nearly all the time, but I remembered a little this morning.'

We were both very quiet: then, it costing me, I said: 'Em, I'm not sure that I ever knew.'

He turned to me as though I had said something marvellous, kissed me – and at that moment I could remember his earliest attention and care – 'Yes, you did once; everybody does a little, but they don't make it last, and I don't think I've helped you.'

'It wasn't *you*.'

'It was nobody else,' he said sharply, and Sarah flared up and began to die painfully, as he dismissed her. He took my hand again, and my fingers felt stiff against his. 'Lillian: don't cast yourself on that reef any more. Remember you are here, with me, and that there is more to come. Move in your time: feel what it is – now. You will be so unbearably alone if you live in that other time.'

'I *won't* forget! I don't want to.'

'I'm not asking you to forget anything – only to remember more.'

'Tell me something to remember, then.'

He thought for a moment, put one of his large handkerchiefs into my hands, and said: 'I will tell you. When you were a child – I think you were about ten – you had your tonsils out. Afterwards, your parents sent you away with your nurse for a holiday, and as your nurse came from one of the Scilly Islands, that is where you went. The first evening that you arrived, you were put straight to bed. You were very tired from the longest journey you had ever done – a train from your home to London; from London to Cornwall; a boat to the main island, and finally, a little boat run by your nurse's uncle to the small island which was her home. You didn't notice anything that night: but next morning you woke very early with the sun filling the small whitewashed bedroom. You found yourself in a feather bed, which had a kind of bulky, silky softness, and that was as strange as it was charming. You put on your clothes, lifted the squeaking latch as quietly as you could, and went out, because you couldn't wait to start being on the island. Your house was on high ground, and you could see everything. It was rocky, with green turf – like bice, you said, in your paintbox – and gorse, and slender strips of land brilliant with flowers: you had never seen whole fields of flowers growing in your life. The sky was blue, and the sea streamed and creamed round the edges of the island which had rocks and little shell-shaped bays of shining sand. There were no roads, and this made you feel wonderfully free, but not lonely, because there were a few other clusters of cottages and the air above them had delicate veins of chimney smoke. You walked where you liked, up the hill until you came to a smooth grey rock shouldering out of the ground. And there you found a little hollowed place in it, filled with slate-coloured water. You sat down on your heels beside it ...' He stopped. 'Wait a minute – yes, and put your hands face downwards on the rock. You'd never left England before, and you thought of this island having been here all the time of your life – which seemed a very long time – rooted in the sea, rising up to the sun, complete, and the perfect size for an island, and you had never known about it until now. The air smelled of salt and honey: the little basin of water shivered from invisible winds, and you were singing inside as though you had several voices. You looked into the little basin – it was glittering –

just containing your face, and you felt so new on the island that you decided to christen yourself. You said your name aloud, and marked the water on to your forehead, and it was softer, and colder, than snow. Later in the day, when you were out with your nurse, you came upon another rock, and it also had a little basin, but with hardly any water, and your nurse said that these rocks were the first places on the island to be touched by the sun, and that the bowls had been made a long time ago for sacrifices. You didn't tell her, or anyone else, about your rock, until you told me.' He waited a moment, and then, still in the same, quiet story-telling voice, he said: 'There you are. I remember so well your telling me that, you see, and when you told me I think you meant to share it, but perhaps you gave it to me by mistake.'

'You've kept it very well.' Indeed, he had: that morning which I had not remembered for years was back with me in its true language – fresh and unfaded, as when I had told him first, as when I had felt it. The taxi stopped: he said: 'We have arrived. Have you arrived, darling?' Before I could reply, the porter had opened the taxi door.

'You read that notice on his cage. So I gave him four bananas and what does he do? He *eats* them! He peels them like he's tired and his mind's on something else, but he eats them so quick and hands the skins out to me that in a few minutes it's like there never were any bananas at all, and he's back to his staring at me like I was illiterate. He *dominates* me.'

Em finished paying the taxi and took my arm. The porter followed us to the lift, and asked if I wanted a monkey. Em pinched me and said: 'My wife is allergic to monkeys.'

'I adore them,' I said, 'but they give me a rash. Lobsters and monkeys.'

The porter said forget it – he'd still got twenty-three apartments to call.

In the lift Em said: 'He isn't absolutely crazy. He really got landed with a monkey that doesn't seem to belong to anyone, and, as you see, it's preying on his mind.'

I think I smiled at him, but I was in full possession of the peace he had given me in the taxi, and so warm with it that I would have smiled at anything he said. He was saying something else.

'... worked to get the apartment straight for you – ever since ten this morning. Will you say something nice to her about it?'

I remembered then that in a moment we would not be alone together, and had to use some of my precious warmth to say: 'Of course I will.' But I had the warmth – and at least I could say it.

3. ALBERTA

New York

My dear Uncle Vin,

I am answering your letter at once, because I feel you are worried, and also because I find the nature of your anxiety distressing – this last, I do promise you, not on my account. You have so often said to me that a great deal of gossip goes on in the theatre, and that if people took less notice of it they would be much happier. I have now spent a week here alone with him – Mrs Joyce arrived this evening – and I don't think anyone could have been kinder, more considerate, or more interesting – in fact the things you say sound incredible. Apart from his charming behaviour to me, you seem to have left out the fact that he is married, and from the trouble that he took today it is clear that he is devoted to Mrs Joyce. He spent hours – while I was tidying up this flat in which we are all to stay – buying her favourite flowers, and champagne, and a box of something called *marrons glacés* (chestnuts in sugar) which she fell upon when she arrived, and said were her favourite sweets. He went to meet her himself, and when they came back, they both looked happy and as though they'd achieved something. I would also like to point out to you, Uncle Vin, that he is sixty-one, and could therefore quite easily be my father, and if it wasn't for Papa I wish he was. I hope it is clear that I like and respect him very much, and that is why I hate your believing those horrible idle rumours about him. As for me, you know I have never been in love in my life, and cannot easily imagine what that would be like, but at least I do know that the kind of vulgar intrigue which you imply has nothing to do with love, and cannot start at all unless both people are disposed towards it. When Papa said to me 'It doesn't matter what you do, as long as you are thoroughly aware that you are doing it', I think I understood him. How could I – even supposing it crossed his mind which I am certain it never would – how *could* I encourage him to make poor Mrs Joyce unhappy when she is ill, and has already had so much unhappiness? If I did, it would not be what Papa meant at *all*, and what good could come out of such idiotic irresponsibility? I am sorry to employ this vehemence, but I do feel so angry and sad that people like him should be subjected to such gossip, and although I know that this is nearly always so of remarkable people, the gap between theory and my experience of it is a very large one. So please, Uncle Vin, if you hear anything more of this kind, say that you know better from first-hand evidence.

Now I've read this to see if I've said what I meant, and realize that I haven't once thanked you for worrying about me, which I know you have done with the best reasons. Please don't worry Papa with any of this, though. I'm writing this in bed: the others have gone out to dinner, including Jimmy Sullivan, who had to wait to get all their luggage through the Customs, and didn't arrive here until half past eight. They asked me if I wanted to go with them, and I said no, because I thought Mrs Joyce would like to have dinner alone with him, but then in the end Jimmy went too so it wouldn't have made any difference. This is a beautiful flat and I have a room with so many cupboards that my clothes get lost in them. Mrs Joyce has two *enormous* trunks full of clothes, apart from suitcases. She is very glamorous, in an interesting way – you feel she really *is* – not that she can sometimes manage to be. I am going to help her unpack tomorrow. Finally, to put your mind thoroughly at rest, I may as well tell you that I am not alone in this room, but am sharing it with an unusually gloomy little monkey. He somehow came up in the lift with Jimmy by mistake, and he glares at me all the time in a moping sort of way. I've given him some grapes, and he ate them as though they were wasting his time, and spitting the pips out over his left shoulder, and now he's bored to death and is sitting in a kind of hunched up elegant heap – although Jimmy said all he needed was company, which clearly I'm not managing to be. He shows one quite simply that material comfort is *not enough*, which is interesting, because it's much harder to see about people. Mrs Joyce wanted to let him out, and she did – in the sitting-room. He broke a lamp, upset three vases of flowers, tore some curtains, and made four messes; he did all this frightfully quickly and then ran up the curtains and it took ages to catch him, and even Mrs Joyce said that perhaps he was better off in his cage. It's a pity monkeys can't read, because they look as though they can, much more than a lot of people who actually do. Oh well. Much love, darling Uncle Vin – and please don't worry about me – and I promise I'll tell you if I have any difficulties or get ill or *anything*.

Sarah

4. JIMMY

LOOKING back, at the end of it, on that first week, I realize that we didn't come to what seemed a crazy decision at any one point of it. I say we, because I'm not even sure now who had the idea, I only know that neither of us would have dreamed of it at the beginning of the week. I didn't have a chance to talk to Emmanuel until the morning after we arrived, because the evening was devoted to Lillian, and somehow everything goes wrong if we talk theatre in front of her, and she'd been so excited at meeting Emmanuel that I'd been afraid of her having another attack – I still was – all evening. She was really lit up – not with drink – pure gaiety, and he was responding. He seemed much better than he was in London : less tired and edgy – serene somehow. I guessed he'd been writing, but I didn't ask, and then when she did, he said yes, and I knew he was lying – so it wasn't that. But at least he seemed to be over Gloria, and I'd been afraid we'd have the dregs of her with us for weeks. The new girl – she really *is* the new girl personified – seems to have done her job well. He doesn't seem to have broken any dates, got drunk, or trodden on anybody's toes; he's managed to make the apartment *and* the ship on time, and I haven't seen him so smooth with Lillian for years.

I left them after dinner; they wanted to go home, and I wanted to walk the streets a bit and show myself the town. It was too late to go to a theatre, and I walked around looking for a movie, and wondering why, whenever I come back here, I always feel like this. I mean, I know the feeling so well, you wouldn't think I'd have it any more. It's all right in England: I tell myself I'm travelling – I'm a foreigner, and I don't even have to tell myself that in France: but here, I look forward to coming back, and then have a kind of resentment that it isn't my home: I feel it ought to be – it's just that most of the ingredients are missing. Twice a year they send a letter from the home where I wasn't born: they ask for news I don't want to give, and give a whole lot of news I don't want. I had a drink on the way back to the apartment and tried not to feel resentful about not being able to spend the evening with Emmanuel, which would have made everything O.K. What was it Annie had said in London? The Father Figure, and I was so nuts about him, transferred, I think she said – she was showing off her Freud – that I'd never have a satisfactory affair with a woman. I don't suppose I shall; it seems to me a dreary, interim arrangement. I'd rather lay a woman and never see her again, or be in love with her. I had another Scotch, and started trying to imagine the kind of girl I could be in love with. Slender, but not too tall, with beautiful hair and a low voice – gentle and ready to trust me; someone to whom I could show the world in exchange for her showing me herself. I looked round the bar and imagined myself waiting for her to walk into it: in a sense, I suppose, I *was* waiting for her – and then I thought of the number they'd written into Emmanuel's musical: *Fate Made a Date with You and Me* which they'd scored now to merge into the first act finale number – a waltz: 'The Time and the Place and the Loved One'. Emmanuel had said it was very good and looked like being a hit number. Well, she hadn't turned up, my girl, whoever she was; no sense in looking for her (after all, most of the time I didn't need anyone else in my life), but one thing I knew, and that was she only had to walk into the bar – any bar where I was, and I'd know it was she. It was a little like finding the perfect actress for a part, which perhaps Emmanuel and I would be doing together tomorrow...

The first thing we did when we got shot of the apartment

was to go to the drugstore we always went to when we wanted to think aloud together with no chance of being interrupted. There was nothing unusual about it except that we always went to it. We got coffee and I bought a pack of Luckies, and we sat and looked at each other. Then he said: 'Well, Jimmy, it's just as difficult as we thought. Neither of the ones we wanted is available. There are about six whom various people want to star in something – I've seen four of them and they're no good: two to go. And of course they've put us through a lot of the routine stuff – agents who want to give a girl the impression they're working for her – or want her to have the experience of an audition.'

'Have you tried Alex?'

Emmanuel smiled. 'I didn't have to try. He was round at George's office like a flash with what he described as his greatest discovery in years.'

'Was she?'

'Her appearance was memorable. There turned out to be only two small snags. She hadn't one word of English, and she'd done no acting in any language whatever.'

'She must have been some eyeful.'

Emmanuel said impassively: 'It was extremely difficult to look at her for long.'

'What does Mick say?'

'He's sympathetic, but he feels I can't have written a play with a girl who doesn't exist. He's beginning to take it as a slight on America that I can't pick anyone. He has a new agent on the Coast who he says will turn up something if we give him time. The point is this, Jimmy. I like actresses who know their job. I like them professional, at least, with a pinch of dedication about them. But if we can't find one of them who would be right – and with Luise and Katie out of it, we look like not finding one – then I like the field wider open than these people – Mick and George and so on – are prepared to open it. The bunch of models, call-girls, and bit-part kinds is the wrong kind of wide. I'd rather pick a girl off the street who looked right, and have you teach her to act.'

'Yeah, but we're suppose to open this fall, and I can't teach anyone what they need to know in three months.' I thought a minute, and then added: 'Unless they were exceptional, of course.'

He looked at me, his heavy eyelids belying the amusement in his eyes. 'Well, Jimmy – then they've got to be exceptional.'

I got up to pay our check. I know better than to argue with him then.

That was our first conversation about it.

We spent the rest of the morning seeing George's two girls – the last of the six that he'd got together. We let the first one do the whole scene. She was tall, with what Emmanuel described as a voraciously wistful expression, but she had a good voice with a lot of colour in it. Then when we got to the bit where she goes around taking the pictures off the walls, he said: 'There's a bird that walks like that – a large bird.' So it was for me to get her a nice bucket of clean sand and hold her head in it; she was out, thanking me in anticipation.

Mick was there, and I could feel the whole situation getting on his nerves. Nobody likes to get into real casting trouble, and Mick likes to do everything fast and brilliantly: if personalities advertised, he'd be the done-overnight, solved-while-you-wait problem man. There was a break after the first girl left, because the second girl hadn't shown up. The actor who had been reading for us lit a cigarette, and finally went to sleep on three chairs which he arranged in a row for the purpose. Mick came over to where we were sitting, and did some sales talk on me, and Emmanuel stared at the top of the proscenium arch where a batten wasn't properly masked, and except that he wasn't listening I didn't know what went on in his mind.

Mick's parents had been Polish, and I think he still thought in that language. He had a head like a bullet, a crew-cut, a merry sly smile, and he loved you to agree with him, but it brought on such bouts of gaiety and energetic appreciation that you couldn't stand it for long. If you didn't agree with him, he sulked, and his enterprise in that direction was such that in the end you were responsible for his never having seen Poland which was palpably killing him. But he was a good fixer if he could fix fast, and the set-up that employed him worked on the principle that almost everything could be decided fast if the right man was taking the decisions. Like almost everyone else in the business, Mick resented Emmanuel's control over his plays, and the fact that by sheer weight and merit he could uphold them. Mick knew that experienced and prolific playwrights don't grow on trees, but just now he was kicking up. Emmanuel, having borne with it for some time, stopped looking at the corner of the proscenium arch, and speaking under Mick, but distinctly, said: 'Jimmy, take him away and talk to him, he's beginning to take my mind off something else.'

'Mick?'

'Sure, sure I'll talk to you. Let's go.'

We went to a small room that he used as an office, and he let go. He'd been fifteen years in the business – he'd worked with some difficult people; he named them and there was hardly anyone left when he was through; but he'd never had trouble like this. He'd read the play – it was just great, but what had got into *Mister* Joyce that he couldn't seem to visualize anybody in what was after all a straight lead? What was so out of this world about it that he hadn't already catered for? Sure, he understood about quality – if I liked he would agree that Mister Joyce was a genius – the play was a work of genius – *I* was a genius – so what? Weren't there, wasn't there one single *female* genius who could just play one itsy bitsy part in one goddam play, or must we all kowtow to genius Joyce as though he'd written the Bible and nothing less than Sarah Bernhardt would do? Mister Joyce gave him the feeling that we were all wasting time, and whereas it would make him happy – it would make him *delirious* to go on providing Mister Joyce with an endless succession of beautiful girls to look at day after day if it gave his power complex a kick, there was just one little thing that world genius Joyce was not taking into account, and that was that his, Mick's time *was* money. The stark revelation of this final statement seemed to strike him afresh as he said it, and he had to take in some breath. Then he said there was just one more thing that he wanted to know. Would I just tell him how we had found somebody in London for the part who didn't make Mister Joyce sick in his stomach?

'We didn't,' I said. 'The girl we wanted went sick, and we had to make out with somebody who's upset the whole balance of the play. That's why he's so anxious to have the right girl here. He knows what he wants, and he's quite right.'

'Yeah – with one detail hardly worth mentioning – she just don't happen to *exist*!'

'Snap out of it; you've only been on it a week.'

'A week!' He looked as though he was going to burst. 'He thinks I've been on it just a *week*! I tell you something else. It'll end up by his picking some little girl with no sex appeal, no box office, no record, no nothing. And I'll have to try to sell her to M.C.A. – she's spiritual – Mister Joyce is in love with her – we *all* love her – little Miss Wide Open Spaces 1958 – do you think they'll buy it? I can tell you now what they'll tell me to tell you to tell Mister Joyce to do with her and that won't make a news story, and while he's living happily ever after for five minutes, they'll withdraw and he'll be landed with the play *and* the girl . . .'

'Mick, you're making me tired.' He really was: I could feel the pricking at the back of my neck which is the beginning of getting angry. 'He can always find backing for a new play and you know it. Don't get too big for other people's boots. Be your age and keep your job.'

They called through to say that Miss Harper had arrived. I slapped him as hard as I could on the back and as he fell against the filing cabinet I grinned at him. 'Maybe this is it.'

Of course it wasn't. She was a nice girl, but dumb as they come – she didn't know what she was doing – she just looked good.

We had a weary lunch with Mick and George. It was agreed that everybody perfectly understood everybody else, and was hopping with confidence over everyone else's ability.

George gave Mick the job of lining up a whole lot of screen tests to be run through for us; Mick cheered up quite horribly and started loving us all again, and I watched Emmanuel staring at things and not eating his lunch and going blue under the eyes and I thought goddammit do they *really* think he's in it for his power complex? He was just trying to finish a good job, that's all. When we got to coffee, there was a call through for him: I went to take it, and it was Alberta with a message from Lillian to say that she'd fixed the evening for all of us with the Westinghouses – so would we be back not later than seven? I asked if Lillian was there, but she wasn't – she was out lunching with some Russian princess who knew a lot about herbs – and that meant we'd have to go to the Westinghouses'. Then Alberta said she was sorry if she'd distressed me and rang off. She has a sweet voice, but she says some funny things with it. I told Emmanuel about the Westinghouses and he screwed up his eyes and then said unexpectedly: 'She has a pretty voice – that girl,' and George and Mick became galvanized and said which one, and when he said it was his secretary they lost interest.

After lunch, Emmanuel said: 'I have an overpowering desire to sleep. Where can I go?'

He said it to me and very quietly, so I knew he wanted to get away from George. Then he got up from the table, nodded amiably to Mick and George, and walked out. I didn't take time to care for the check, I got up to follow him: 'He'll jay walk himself into hospital,' I said. Mick smiled slyly; George said: 'Or revwire.' I grabbed our coats and caught up with him a few yards down on the sidewalk. 'Lillian's out.'

He looked at me expressionlessly: 'Let's go home.'

In the cab, he said: 'Do you know that girl found what was wrong with Clemency?'

'What girl?'

'My secretary.' He still looked like nothing.

A bit later he said: 'I've a damn good mind to chuck the whole business.'

'Not put the play on at all?'

147

'Not put any play on.'

'What for?'

He looked at me then, and suddenly smiled. 'That's just it, Jimmy. There has to be a reason one way or another. I haven't found it.' He yawned. 'On with the play.'

I didn't answer. He always started a depression this way: wanting to sleep all the time, and making elliptical damaging little stabs at any project in hand, and if you took him up withdrawing to somewhere you couldn't reach him. But I knew then that something would have to be decided somehow, and thought that I would put a call through to Katie and see if there was no way of hooking her.

When we got to the apartment, he waited while I found a key, and opened the door, and at once Alberta came out of the living-room. Emmanuel walked firmly up to her and took her by the arm. 'I want you to do something for me. Would you take the calls, Jimmy? Now – where can we go?' He pushed her gently into the kitchen, and turned back to me. 'I want to try something. Stop Lillian from stopping me, will you?'

I nodded, and went into the living-room. A minute later, Alberta came in, picked something off a table and went. I shut the door, and put the call through to Katie in California. The time was half past three. While I was waiting for the first call to come through, I made a list of all the others that could be any use, and wondered how that kid had managed to upset him about Clemency. Of course, she wouldn't have meant to – the people who did, moved him not at all. But this kind of thing had happened before: somebody, something, had shifted his view of a completed work, and then there was the devil to pay until he got it back to his satisfaction. Once or twice he hadn't, and they were the worst times of all. That was when I earned my salary: when he lost money, made enemies, and really got down to influencing people. Then it had to be a case of my country right or wrong, and I had the curious sensation of what it cost to believe in anybody. Then I not only had to stand people calling him a fool – a swollen-headed bum perfectionist – a capitalist who didn't care about the security of the workers in the theatre – a sadist who liked to use his power to revenge himself upon some producer or star he'd fallen out with – I had to stand him agreeing with them. 'Why not?' he once said. 'There is no doubt that I have been a fool: that's a useful word; it will cover almost anything. They are quite rightly worrying about the consequences, as I, too late, concern myself with the cause. A fool is somebody who will not keep still, but cannot possibly be responsible for his actions. I am a fool.'

Oh well – it hadn't come to that.

The call to Katie came through at last. At the end of two minutes she had really convinced me that she was tied up, and after that she was free-wheeling on her reasons. Her studio had suspended her a few weeks back: she was scheduled to make two big pictures: she was suing her third husband for failure to pay alimony, and anyway she couldn't leave her hypnotist who was trying to stop her taking sleeping pills. This took another eighteen minutes of her beautiful voice. She couldn't, she said, even work Las Vegas for a week on account of her studio, when God knew she needed the money, and life was twice as expensive as it had been what with lawyers and the hypnotist who hadn't managed to stop her taking sleeping pills yet so any minute she might be suspended again – for good. We exchanged a lot of abstract emotions and hung up. She was an actress, though: she had the lot: and I knew it, even while I caught myself wondering how on earth we ever thought she could play Clemency. I was just starting to call a couple of people I just liked, and thought I'd call, when I heard Lillian, and put the receiver back just as she came into the room. She was not alone.

'Hi, Jimmy. This is Princess Murmansk – you've met, haven't you, Della?'

'Why yes – we certainly have. How are you?'

The Princess – I didn't remember her – had an accent straight from New Orleans where she must have been some landmark – she was well over six feet tall.

'The Princess has been explaining to me how you can do absolutely everything with herbs.'

The Princess smiled, exposing a large quantity of well-kept teeth. Only Cinerama, I thought, would do justice to her. They exchanged herbal cigarettes, and we all sat down.

'You look at a loose end, Jimmy: where's Em?'

'In the kitchen.'

'What on earth is he doing?'

'He's working with Alberta.'

'Why in the kitchen? Why not here?'

'Because he doesn't want to be interrupted.'

'What's he *doing*?'

'Search me. Working.'

Lillian gave an angry little laugh. 'How extraordinary. Well, Della's dying to meet him, and anyway we came back to make some of her marvellous tea.'

'He specially asked me to take all calls and see that he wasn't interrupted,' I said, and noticed that we had both instinctively got to our feet. I tried to smile. 'Don't say I didn't warn you.'

She went. The Princess stretched out a yard or two of leg and said: 'Does it get to be part of your reflexes protecting the great man?'

'It gets to be.'

Lillian came back followed by Emmanuel: I took one look at him and wished I was somewhere else. Lillian said: 'I've got our secretary to boil water and get a tray together, but the actual *skill* will have to be you, Della. My husband – Princess Murmansk.'

'I'm so happy to meet you.' She extended a hand and Emmanuel shook it.

'I do hope I haven't disturbed your inspiration.'

'I have never been fortunate enough to have any. If I had, neither you nor anyone else would be able to disturb it.'

Lillian said: 'Really, Em, that's rude of you.'

'Not rude – just hypothetical.'

I couldn't take it. I went to see how Alberta was making out with the tea. She looked flushed, and when I came in she gave me a quick little smile as though if she didn't smile she'd cry.

'Can I help any?' I said: she was putting cups on a tray.

'I just have to wait until the kettle boils: thank you, Jimmy.'

'I'll stay and watch it with you.' I felt suddenly that she was getting the rough end of something she knew nothing about. She looked at the two chairs where they must have been sitting, and pushed her hair back from her forehead.

'Has he been working you hard?'

She looked bewildered. 'Not working *me*, exactly. He's been making me read to him. He said he wanted to hear something.'

'Yeah – he does that. Has he found it?'

'Some of it, I think – but of course, I haven't asked.' She waited a moment, and then said: 'Mrs Joyce was angry when she came in and then he was very angry.' Her voice was very low. 'I don't understand.'

'He didn't say anything, did he?'

'No – but that made it worse. Jimmy – do you mind me asking you something?'

'Go ahead.'

'Who am I working for?'

'You're working for him, and sometimes that means working for her. Sometimes it doesn't.'

'It isn't that I mind doing *anything*. But if they tell me to do something, and it makes the other angry that I do it . . .'

'Like this?' I indicated the tea-tray, and she nodded.

'Forget it. Listen: they're not beautiful simple people, so they make difficulties from time to time: just don't get involved – it irons out – but whatever they do, you keep it small. O.K.?'

'O.K.,' she said carefully. 'Thank you, Jimmy. I expect it sounds stupid to you, but my experience of married people is unfortunately superficial.'

'What about your parents?'

'My mother died when I was nine. The kettle's boiling. Do we take it in, do you think?'

'I'll find out where her highness wants it.'

I strode into an atmosphere you could cut with a knife and said: 'Alberta wants to know where you want the boiling water?'

'Tell her to bring it in here with the tray.'

Well, we had tea – if you can call the sickly. bitter stuff that woman made tea. Lillian chattered – the princess answered questions about her herbal rest-home; and Emmanuel sat almost silent, and fidgeting, until he suddenly smiled at her with great charm and said he had to go.

'Darling – you can't go out now. The Westinghouses!'

'Tell them I'll be late.' He'd gone.

Lillian looked desperately at me. 'Jimmy – do explain to him, the party's being given for him. He *can't* be late.' As I left the room, I heard her saying: 'He's always like this when he's working on a new play; I do hope you'll forgive him, and understand.'

I caught Emmanuel waiting for the elevator: without looking at me, he said: 'One shouldn't meet that woman indoors: she's too big.'

We both got into the elevator. I said: 'I couldn't have stopped that.'

He gave me a bleak smile. 'I could.' He shrugged. 'Well – it's done now. And the only thing that would put it right again, I can't do.'

I was silent.

'I did it last night. It takes a kind of energy I don't seem to keep for long. Or can't afford. Or won't. I have something else to do.'

Then he said angrily: 'It's like marking *sand*. The tide comes in, and you might never have done it.'

'Are you going to show up at this party?' I asked desperately. I didn't want to ask, but I had to.

'You take her to it. If I'm not coming, I'll call them. I promise.'

I put their number on a piece of paper and put it in his pocket.

'I've lost my temper. It's like getting drunk: you know it's going to poison you, and you don't stop. Freedom! We all talk about it, and don't know the meaning of the word!'

The elevator, which had reached the ground floor some time back, suddenly started up again. He laughed.

'You see, Jimmy? It's just like this. We go up and down, up and down, without the slightest control. Where's the break? What the hell can we *do* about anything at all?'

He spread out his hands – they were shaking – small, nervous, blotched on their backs with large freckles. 'See? I haven't the control of a *cat*!'

'They have a lot,' I said.

The elevator stopped, and a wooden-faced couple got in. Their collective gaze shifted over us and the floor and the walls. They only knew how not to look at each other. I pressed the button for our apartment floor, and said: 'Well, I'll take them both to the party, and hope to see you there. And I'll fix somewhere good to work tomorrow.'

He looked at me, and his look went to my heart. 'Bless you, Jimmy.'

I gave Lillian his message dead pan, and went to my room. Alberta had already gone to hers like a sensible girl. But I knew that Lillian would get rid of her lady friend and come after me. She did.

'What do you mean, Jimmy, he'll call if he's not coming?'

'I don't mean anything at all. It's what he said.' I was lying on my bed with the beginnings of a headache and closed my eyes, but she closed the door and went on: 'Does that mean he *isn't* coming, do you think? Because if so, I must call the Westinghouses . . .'

'He said he'd call: I should leave it to him if I were you.'

'If you were me, of course you wouldn't have interrupted him in the first place when he was "working". And if I were you I wouldn't have interrupted him either.'

'That's true,' I agreed amiably, but that only made her dangerous.

'Doesn't it strike you as odd that I'm the only person who's *capable* of interrupting him?'

'Perhaps you're the only one he cares for.'

She didn't know how to take this. Then she said: 'He wasn't working, anyway. He was just listening to the girl reading.'

She wasn't that stupid – surely? But I looked at her, and saw that the only bit of her that was working at the moment was. I decided to have one real try, and then give up.

'Lillian – honey – you're wrong there. If Emmanuel says he doesn't want to be disturbed that's good enough: we don't decide whether he's working or not – *he* does. It made him mad today because he's got something on his mind, but he'll come back all right if you don't grow the whole thing up meanwhile. Be sweet to him – apologize.'

She looked at me, and I saw she was finding it tough. With an effort, she said: 'I'll think about it.' Then she gave herself a little shake, and said: 'I don't blame you for talking to me as though I was a child: the whole thing has become such a storm in a teacup. I want to leave at seven fifteen.'

'Does Alberta know?'

'She ought to. I told her the arrangements this morning.'

Well – that was not the end of it. I went to tell Alberta: she was sitting on her bed writing in a big book, and she just nodded, and went on writing. I wondered what – and guessed it was a novel. Young girls write novels nowadays like they used to press flowers or make candy. At seven, Emmanuel came back. At eight, we left, in an atmosphere nobody could want to call their own. The party was some blocks down on Park Avenue, and except for Lillian saying how dirty the cab was nobody said anything.

The Westinghouses were a nice couple – around their fifties – with a son in the business and several other grown-up children who usually showed up at parties. He was a good-looking man – always sunburned – with an appearance of nobility that had somehow never got around to attaching itself to anything. The prototype for heroic theory, Emmanuel had once said: but Emmanuel was fond of him – they even went once on a disastrous fishing trip together – Emmanuel was nearly drowned, and the rest of the time so bored that he got drunk and stayed that way for nearly two weeks. Debbie Westinghouse was one of those women you only see here – half doll, half little girl – she'd never had a thought in her head, and that went for the nasty ones too – she was crisp, and silly, and sweet and simple, and so clean you could have eaten off her. She loved her family; the room was littered with snaps of her grandchildren, and she understood that books were for other people. She cried very easily, but not for long, and she told everybody that Emmanuel was a genius with the kind of gasping credulity of a child talking about a magician. Van Westinghouse was always very kind to her, and she certainly made him feel a man.

They had collected about thirty people to meet Emmanuel, and they must have known why they were invited, as nearly all of them turned to look at him when we came in. I knew Van Westinghouse would take care of Lillian – he had a lot of old-world charm for other people's wives – and Emmanuel would be swamped, but the poor kid, Alberta, looked out of it all: she had on a dark blue dress that wasn't right for her or the party, and she looked as though she knew it. There was nothing I could do about it: we were plunged into large-scale and paralysingly efficient introductions. A collection of well-groomed, intelligent, successful people – for some reason they made me think of a whole lot of shiny new automobiles – powerful, well serviced, fitted inside with all kinds of modern gadgets – like insomnia, contraceptives, equality, and fright. Emmanuel once said that no talk was too small for opinions, they were only the suburbia of intercourse, and cocktail parties were their rush hour, and I was in a mood this evening for that kind of remark to stick in my mind. I had two drinks rather fast and listened to three people – Debbie Westinghouse admiring Lillian's dreamy clothes, an intense young woman who'd written a book all about emotional freedom, and an old, rather nice guy who seemed stuck on English furniture. Usually at these parties, I do at least get myself an attractive girl, at least to drink with, but tonight there seemed two good reasons why that would not make a gay evening. One was Alberta, for whom I felt kind of responsible, and the other was Emmanuel. Alberta was answering questions about England, and looking like a schoolgirl up for an examination, and Emmanuel was listening to a journalist who'd just been on a three weeks' trip to India, and who was telling him what an opportunity the British getting out was for the Indian people. What the hell was a party *for*, I wondered. Van Westinghouse was bringing out a cheap edition of Emmanuel's plays – Johnnie, his son, came over to tell me about it: three volumes to start with, with three plays in each: they had galleys, but they were still waiting for a preface and could I turn on some heat to get it? Not tonight, I said. Who was the girl we'd brought – was she an attachment of mine? For some reason this irritated me: I think because I knew Johnnie thought she looked odd, and because I agreed with him. I explained why she was here, and Johnnie said O.K., O.K., he'd only been asking, and got his sister Sally from across the room. She came over, smiling, and looking so good that I felt better just looking. She'd become a model since last time I'd seen her, and she'd changed. I told her she looked wonderful, and she smiled her wide smile and said clothes certainly did something for a girl. Johnnie said: 'Oh, come on, Sal. Tell him you're in love.' 'He's a photographer – I certainly am. He's a genius!' She said it just like her mother. She gave her glass to Johnnie, and smiled again at me and asked me who was the girl I'd brought. Somehow she didn't irritate me asking – so I told her about Alberta and said she was a sweet kid, and was just going to add how young she was, when I remembered that Alberta was at least a year older than Sally. 'She hasn't been around very much – lived in the country,' I said instead – and wondered why everything I said about Alberta seemed wrong or patronizing. That was just when Johnnie knocked against a bottle which fell over Alberta's dress. Sally saw it, and gave a little throaty gasp and went to the rescue. She took Alberta away at once – Johnnie made me an apologetic face – but at the far end of the room, I caught sight of Emmanuel. A good many people had gone, and I could hear that all was not well. He was leaning against the piano, and I didn't like the easy, angry look on his face. I went over '... this *extraordinary* illusion you have that we all know what we are doing?' he finished, and as an after-thought emptied his half-full glass of what looked like Scotch.

The intense dame who'd written the book about emotional freedom gave him a winning, intellectual smile, and said soothingly: 'But surely, Mr Joyce, it is the duty of the more knowledgeable person to inform and guide the common man.'

'If you deal in such an inflated view of humanity, possibly it is. Personally, I have never met anyone in the least know-ledgeable, and I don't think I'd recognize the common man if I stumbled up against him in the street where I believe he lives. I think society is made up of cranks and morons.' He smiled pleasantly round the room, embracing us all, and somehow managed to get Johnnie to fill his glass again without a word. There was an indiscriminate outcry – of people claiming to be common, etc., out of which the man – whom I recognized as the journalist – said: 'You'll be telling me next that you don't believe in progress!'

Emmanuel smiled brightly: 'That's what I'll tell you next. But *you* think information is progress. You think a lot of cranks telling a lot of morons what they ought to think constitutes education. There are a few little worms turning in England, but that is only because they want even their emotional lives for free – they can't even face paying for *that* – they want it on the basis of free milk and public lava-tories, and they simply illustrate the rot of private irre-sponsibility – this is what makes most of us cowards ...'

The journalist was high anyway, and he lost his temper. 'Is this a social message out of one of your plays?'

'I don't write plays with social messages. It is a misuse of the theatre.'

'But surely, Mr Joyce, you consider yourself knowledge-able?' Emmanuel didn't reply, and the journalist said again. 'I repeat – surely you're under the impression that you're knowledgeable?'

Emmanuel said: 'I am attached to the notion that if one is below an impression, it is a false one.'

'You see? You're just evading my point: you damned artists, you think you can run the world. You just think you know everything – for God's sake. Give me the days when the artist was a workman with a job to do and knew his place in society.'

Emmanuel said smoothly: 'I am sure that we all wish that you had lived two hundred years ago,' somebody laughed, and Emmanuel held out his glass to Johnnie.

At this moment – mercifully – Alberta returned to us: Emmanuel saw her first, and although his face did not seem to change, I knew there was a reason for looking, and turned my head. I don't think I'd ever looked at her before – at any rate, now I hardly knew her. She was wearing a black dress with a high Chinese collar, and very short, tight sleeves; her hair was sleeked back – smooth and shining – and her skin made the other women in the room look as though they'd never been in the air on a fine morning. Even Sally, beside her, looked as though she'd lived it up a bit. Emmanuel said: 'Here, at last, is somebody who will answer your question.' He held out his hand with the glass in it, she hesitated, and came over to us.

'Do you consider that I am a wise man?'

She looked at him with unselfconscious steadiness, and said: 'No I do not.' Then she added gently: 'But I think such men are very rare: It has not been my fortune to meet one.'

Emmanuel smiled and inclined his head to her, and there was something like a triumphant recognition about his face and the movement. The sour smell of calamity seemed to have gone: the journalist offered Emmanuel a cigarette, and Johnnie rushed to get Alberta a drink. Sally winked at me and murmured: 'Clothes certainly make a difference to a man about a girl, anyway' – and then I saw Lillian, with an expression on her face like a stubbed-out cigarette. Whatever Lillian may be, she certainly *isn't* supporting cast. Johnnie had given Emmanuel another slug, and he was reciting something to his host and hostess: Debbie was taking it seriously, and Van looked uneasy. I caught Van's eye, and after exactly the right interval, he moved casually over to me.

'I hate to say it, Van, but do you have any further plans for this evening?'

He looked around. 'When the numbers got to around ten, Debbie wanted us to go some place to eat.'

'They're around that now.'

He made a count, during which I noticed that the journalist had got hold of Lillian and was pouring his opinions over her like a bucket of sand on to a chemical fire.

'If you could include Lillian in your care, and your literary pals, perhaps Johnnie could bring the rest of us in due course.'

'Fine.' He went to tell Johnnie: he knew quite a lot about Emmanuel.

Well – the first part of the arrangement worked. Lillian went quietly – she'd decided to behave well about it all, to invest her anger for private distribution I guessed. But when it came to moving Emmanuel everything broke down. When I got back from seeing the others into the elevator, I found him sitting on the floor, making Sally and Alberta compare their childhoods: they became like a couple of kids telling him, and Johnnie was listening and watching Emmanuel's face respectfully – he was a kid with an eye for memories. As soon as there was a chance, I said: 'How about moving?'

Emmanuel said: 'Where?'

'Johnnie's driving us to Patrick's for dinner. We're joining the others there.'

'Well, at least we know where they *are*.' He turned back to Alberta: 'Have you changed your clothes recently?'

'Yes. This dress belongs to Miss Westinghouse. Mine had an accident.'

Emmanuel looked approvingly at Sally and then at Alberta. Johnnie stood around waiting to go, but nobody seemed to take any notice of him, and then Emmanuel started to tell a story about a dress his mother had told him she wanted, and how it had seemed to cost so much money that he imagined it had been made for Queen Alexandra. 'Of course, she never got it,' he finished, and watched pity bloom on the girls' faces like the moon coming out. But Johnnie began feeling the strap of his wrist-watch and looking nervous, so I said again that we should be going.

'Where?'

We went through it all again.

'Call them, and say I'm terribly drunk and it's delaying us. If you point out what an embarrassing evening they would have with me – shouting and spilling my food and breaking things, they might not want us at all.'

When Johnnie and I went to make the call, he said: 'I don't know what Dad will say. He doesn't *seem* drunk, at all.'

'He isn't, but if we join them he'll arrive high without drinking another drop. Put the call through and I'll talk to your father.'

'Gee – if he was really like he said at Patrick's, it sure would be exciting.'

'Just dull,' I said. 'Those evenings are all the same – it's just the audience that changes.'

I told Van Westinghouse that we wouldn't be joining them, and said to tell Lillian I was sorry but things weren't working out that way. Would he look after Lillian, and I'd call him in the morning? He would. He was, as Emmanuel once remarked, in that minority who were at least wiser after other people's events. I turned to Johnnie, who had the look of an expectant schoolboy about to break bounds.

'No more Scotch for anyone – and some small place to eat.'

And that was it. We did go out and eat at Giovanni's, and it was a good evening. All the strain and tensions seemed to have dropped from Emmanuel and he charmed us all – making Sally tell stories and asking Alberta what she thought of them, improvising a preface for Johnnie in the language of a well-known American weekly: 'Slum-born mongrel-playwright Emmanuel Orchid Race Joyce stabs at self-analytical artistic processes as taking people out of themselves and putting them back wrong' etc. But mostly he listened: every now and then he told a story – something very small, but the way he told them they were irressistibly fascinating, and we sat like a bunch of kids, round-eyed, begging for more.

It was not until after the zabaione, when we were all drinking coffee, that Sally began asking about the new play. Emmanuel answered her, and I had the feeling that he was having a final conversation with himself, and also with me, about it. He told her very simply the kind of play that it was; the difficulty about Clemency – what we had done and how we had failed to find her: Johnnie and Alberta were listening too, but the collective attention seemed not to interfere with our privacy. Johnnie, very diffidently, suggested Katie for the part, and I said yes, but she couldn't do it – I'd tried her again that afternoon. Emmanuel was looking at me now, and I knew the feeling – of private summing up, of conclusion – was true. It came into my mind that he was going to scrap the play; that he'd found the reason for doing so which he had said was necessary, and I blotted up this inky fear until I must have changed colour with it. . . .

'. . . and so, I have decided to make an experiment, if the victim is willing,' and both he and I turned instinctively to Alberta, who had been very still, whose eyes, clear and astonished, were the only sign she gave of this news. There was a long, full silence; then she said: 'You know that I know nothing about acting.'

'Jimmy will teach you all you need to know.'

She looked at me: I was seeing her for the second time, and entirely different again.

'I'll teach you,' I said, 'if you're willing to learn. Are you willing?'

She put out her hand, as though she was in a dream, and

must touch somebody, and Emmanuel and I both put our hands on the table.

'I will try to learn,' she said. Emmanuel touched her then, and she smiled.

And that was the end – or the beginning – of that.

CHAPTER FOUR

*

I. ALBERTA

My dearest Aunt Topsy,

This letter is partly for Papa, because it seems that the moment one is in a position interesting enough to warrant writing letters, one has very little time for them. You are the *most* reliable correspondent, and keep me thoroughly in touch, although I'm sorry to hear about Jemima Facks – I must say I should have thought it was extremely difficult to fall down a well *head* first – I mean one would have to be so neat about it : but then I suppose falling runs in the Facks family, and she has had a good deal of experience. Anyway, it's a good thing she had such presence of mind and thick pigtails.

We have just moved into an apartment and I have spent this morning helping Mrs Joyce who has just gone out to luncheon with a Russian princess (not a real one – she's just married a Russian prince). You asked me to describe Mrs J., and I'll try, appearance first, because I've seen more of it. She is very tall and thin and extremely *elegant* – with rather knobbly bones and thin blue veins which show out of the sides of her forehead and on the backs of her hands (like Lady Gorge, only not so useful looking – prettier). She has very fine hair which is a mixture of yellow and white – grey, I suppose, but again, pretty, cut short and waving carelessly about in what turns out to be a very expensive manner, and huge rather pale blue eyes with black pupils. Her skin is very white and looks thinner than most people's – almost papery, and her mouth droops slightly downwards but is a beautiful shape. Her hands and feet are what Clem would call pre-Raphaelite – very long and faint looking, and altogether, if she had long hair one could imagine her in a garden of carnations, or sitting in some banqueting hall; she is very much like a heroine – someone to be rescued or saved. She is extremely delicate, as she has something wrong with her heart, and she had a daughter who died – it is still all very sad. I had to do her unpacking – goodness! – she has two cabin trunks with hangers for dresses down one side and drawers for clothes down the other – apart from countless suitcases. She also travels with her pictures, drawings, and paintings – nearly all portraits, I wondered if any of them were of her daughter, but naturally didn't ask. Most of the morning she was in bed talking to people on the telephone, while I put things away until there wasn't any more room to put them. I suppose they are all the consequence of a glittering life, but it must be rather sad not to have anywhere permanent to keep them. Mrs Joyce said I must buy some clothes here because pretty ones are so cheap. I have got one or two things. ... Then she suddenly *gave* me a summer coat: it is a lemon colour, and a little too long for me, but it is beautifully cut – it is loose and absolutely simple and she said it was a French one but she had cut out the label. This evening we are all going to Mr Joyce's publishers who are giving a party for him. I don't think I could possibly have been more lucky in getting this position. The work is not hard, varied, and nearly always interesting, and the Joyces are so very kind about including me in all the things they do. They seem used to doing things with Jimmy Sullivan, and I just get added on; this is a great help against homesickness, which I'm afraid assails me from time to time. Please tell Mary that I am writing my diary as much as I possibly can, and that I look forward to hers also.

I do not know how long we are to remain in New York – it depends upon the casting of Mr J.'s new play which proves a difficult matter. When that is settled, we are to go somewhere to the country, as Mrs J. wants a holiday and Mr J. has to write – but no certain plans are made. Tell Papa that I quite agree about experiences knowing their place if only one will let them, and that I am trying to remember this. I must add that I find the vast luxury in which I am now living enjoyable; it is rather like *being* a parrot, instead of just looking at one – but perhaps you don't think parrots are luxurious birds? Humphrey says my taste in birds is vulgar – but I suppose one's taste in anything is conditioned in part by one's curiosity about it, and I have never managed to care for little brown birds one can hardly see. I am saving half my salary: this can be certain, the rest is a constant battle between what I need and what I want. You would not like the food here at all. It is either foreign and tastes like it (which I like) or else it looks like ours, only larger, and does not taste at all, so that you have a kind of dream of what you're eating. It is no good my trying to describe New York as I did in my first letter. It would get dull, because I don't know where to begin or what needs describing and what doesn't. I shouldn't worry too much about Serena wanting to be a doctor – it takes such ages she'll probably end up by being a nurse – think of Florence Nightingale – you wouldn't mind that, and you *have* brought us all up awfully well, and, as Papa says, once we're up there isn't much you can do about it. I do hope your hay fever hasn't started: give my love to everybody – including Napoleon and Ticky, but most of all to you and Papa and Mary and Serena and the boys.

Your loving Sarah

This is after tea, and there is such a feeling of tension, that I have escaped to write this in peace. Even the monkey has gone: his owner has turned up at last, and I am quite alone for a bit, which one certainly couldn't be with him. I don't understand people at all well: or just when I think I'm beginning to, they change into someone else. Or do I change? Everybody has turned out unexpectedly today – so perhaps I have too. Take Papa: anybody who really wanted to meet him could do so, and at the worst he's simply shades of himself: one might say: 'He's rather pale today', but he would still be a recognizable colour. I think this is unusual though – there are fewer people like Papa even than I thought. This morning, helping Mrs J., the thread that seemed to run through her morning was her feeling for him. She asked me endless questions about what he had been doing all the week, and whether I had been with him or not, and when I told her about all the shopping he'd done before her arrival she seemed pleased. (I didn't tell her about his buying me clothes – even when she asked me whether I'd got any new ones. This is another piece of deceit, which begins to sit on me rather too often, I think.) But then, when she came into the kitchen, and I was reading to him, she seemed an entirely different person who neither loved nor cared about him – and he was different as well; I didn't know either of them, and had a miserably insular feeling that I wasn't used to people treating each other like that. I was making tea with these bleak thoughts, when Jimmy came in, and *he* was different too: I suddenly felt I could tell him about it, and did, and he made it all the right size with a flick of consideration.

He seems to be both experienced and kind, and I do admire him for that. The pear blossom will be out at home, and the magnolia will be right out. They will be having tea in the dining-room with drops of water on the pound of butter and white crystals on Aunt T.'s blackcurrant jam, and Ticky on the picture-rail shrilling for sugar. But of course, it isn't the same time at home as it is here. That is a curious separation – the hours as well as the miles. This morning Mrs J. asked me whether I'd ever been to Greece in exactly the same voice as she had asked me earlier whether I had been to Saks – a shop on Fifth Avenue – I haven't been to either. Jimmy has just come in to tell me the time of the party tonight. I have never met a publisher. I did ask Mr J. about them, and he said that nearly all publishers hovered uneasily between a business and a profession, that they suffered from the most unpredictable raw material, and that most writers were like a zoo masquerading as a circus with one or two societies for the prevention of cruelty to authors. Then he laughed and said he was a member of the zoo; but none of this – although memorable – is really illuminating. I have no suitable dress for this party, and this makes me wish that I was not going to it. It was so odd, reading the play today, to reach that scene that I have heard so many people read. It made me see how, in a well-made play, everything depends on something else. We got a little way into the third act before we were interrupted – I'd stopped feeling nervous ages before, and when we stopped I realized that my throat was aching, which I hadn't noticed at the time, at all. I have never known *anything like* his attention: it is as though he is listening, seeing, almost breathing in the play – as though the words as I read them were falling into his body, and as though everything outside the play had been turned off and didn't exist. Somehow it is impossible not to be drawn into this attention – not as a person – but as a path between it and him. Sometimes I seemed to be nearer the play, and sometimes nearer his attention to it. He hardly spoke at all: once or twice he repeated a line after me, and I realized that I'd got some of the words wrong – even one word – but he always knew and always repeated them right. Ordinarily, I think I'd have felt confused at being corrected – would have wanted to interrupt with apologies, but as the play grew, these personal feelings diminished, until afterwards I wondered whether all apologies weren't simply to oneself for failing to be the marvellous creature one wanted to appear. It is so much more interesting to be a vehicle – transporting something – because one seems to have a place in relation to so much else, instead of being a tiny over-emphatic full stop. Mary will not understand this, but whom does one write a diary for? I think to save oneself a few conversations with oneself. I do hope he finds the right Clemency. I almost feel that I'd know her now just by looking. I think Jimmy feels this: the best part of Jimmy is his recognition, and that is not a small thing to say of anybody. Must go and put on boring dress for glamorous party.

This is twenty past two – too late for opinions or fears, but they want me to be Clemency for the play. They know that I know nothing. I have undertaken to try and learn.

2. EMMANUEL

HE woke in the night – eyes burning, hands clenched – as though he'd been fighting with himself to stay asleep, and lost. I drank a good deal, he thought, as another part of his mind started to fidget and jeer. 'No sooner said than done!' it began; 'now we'll see the result of all that grandiose simplicity!' His body seemed to be stretched, strained out, weightlessly over the bed. Now, if only he knew exactly what to do, he would leap out of bed and it would be done. It was a quarter to five. 'Just think what you can't do at a quarter to five – or a quarter to anything come to that.' By eight o'clock he would be wrapped in lead, his head throbbing like an electric pump, his eyes little pinpoints of self-pity: but now some feverish energy remained from the evening and the decision he had taken in it; now he could tackle Mick, even Lillian – work through the traffic of their reactions to the business of getting the girl right on a large enough scale. In practice that would be Jimmy's job, although he'd keep an eye on it: he wasn't sure whether Jimmy had seen what he saw in Alberta. We can't stay in New York once the news has been broken to Mick and the boys, he thought – they'll scare the lights out of her: that means finding somewhere quiet for a month or two – where Jimmy can work with her, and I can work, and Lillian can – somewhere that Lillian wants to go. That is all that has to be *done*, he reflected irritably; but he wanted the whole thing settled now, while he lay there – to be handed a little public peace so that he could afford some private excitement. I'm getting old, he thought, to need favourable conditions for everything. It's time we lived somewhere: travel as well, of course, but have some point of departure, some deeper shades to our behaviour – a home for Jimmy, some possible responsibilities for Lillian, and a key to his own cage for himself. This idea – suddenly presenting itself from above and beyond any immediate action – coloured his bleak and crowded mind, softening considerations, lighting necessities, touching up his distant fleeting pleasures; and like magic slides, pictures of Lillian in an element he could provide – hedged in with roses, aired with music, with her own library, with parks and trees and far-off animals – soundlessly, speechlessly – jerked and slipped to his attention and out of it. ... He leapt out of bed.

Her room was grey and cold and smelled faintly of lemons, and he heard her make the small undergrowth movement of someone caught awake in the dark who means to be woken. If she had been very angry, she would have sat up, switched on the light, and stared at him until he was breathless. ... Patiently, he roused her.

'What is it?'

He sat on the bed shivering.

'I have a plan. You must hear it now.'

She switched on the light. One thing that always surprised him was how she looked in the morning – fresh and gentle, and years younger than her age. Now, any resentment for his abandoning her at the Westinghouses' was neutralized by her curiosity – her hair was ruffled like silky waves in a primitive picture, and her eyes, shining, were waiting, poised for him to begin.

'We are to live in a house: I have been thinking what we need, and the first thing is for some external structure which does not change. It would give us better chances, and provide us with the necessary sense of commitment. We are living like twentieth-century savages in hotels and boats and aeroplanes. It is bad for your health, and my work, and does not give us any sense of adventure or freedom any more. You are deprived of many things that you love. You could have a garden, and animals, collect your books and gramophone records. I have been thinking most carefully about all this,' he added, and the second time it really felt as though he had, and as though he had never thought of it before.

She laid her hands one upon the other and leaned a little towards him: 'I could have a walled garden.'

'If you like.'

'And a wilderness, and grapes and nectarines – and a proper herb garden and those charming cows with bruised faces . . .'

'You could have anything you like.'

'I think they are Guernseys: and you could have a beautiful room to work in – Oh! what about Jimmy? He hates fresh air.'

'He loves the sun. He'd come and go.'

'He wouldn't count English sun.'

'Are we to live in England?'

'Where else do you want to live?'

He felt her reach the edge of her pleasure and look down. He said: 'I hadn't really thought about that. But I'd thought we might as well pick a good climate.'

'Where had you thought of?'

He said again: 'I hadn't thought of anywhere really. I mean I hadn't even considered whether it should be here or somewhere in Europe.'

'Only not in England?'

'My experience of English country has been as limited as it has been unfortunate. Skies like saucepans and a smell of gumboots and damp tweed. Don't you remember staying with the Maudes and your hot-water bottle steaming in the sheets?'

'It doesn't have to be like that – truly.'

'And tremendous damp dogs smelling of haddock, and all the food served at blood heat and mice trying to keep up their circulation at night. Don't you remember that frightful mouse that was running to and fro simply to keep warm?'

'Em, that was just Clarissa. She couldn't run a house anywhere.'

'And servants. The only ones we ever saw were at least ninety and raging hypochondriacs. Don't you remember that dreary butler of Clarissa's who changed all our meal times because of his injections? And the housemaid who was on some kind of diet that made her faint all over the place?'

'You're exaggerating now.'

'Only just. It wouldn't surprise me. Accident is so calamitous in the English countryside. Calamitous and dull.'

'It would be just as difficult to get servants here.'

He made an effort not to be irritated by her gravity. 'You really want Wilde back, don't you darling?'

And responding to his affection, she answered quite simply, 'Yes.'

There was a silence – then they both spoke at once; both smiled, and he said: 'What little reflections of our own uncertainties we do provide. Yes, of course I want a house. That's why I broke in on you so early. I asked *you* whether it was what you wanted.'

She looked at her hands upon the sheets in another silence before she said: 'The trouble is that I don't know what I'm *for*. That makes it very difficult to know what I want, because I never want the same thing for long. It is different for you.'

'Is it?'

'Isn't it? You have your plays to write.'

'I agree that that means I can get by a good deal of the time in a smug frenzy of activity.'

After a moment, she said: 'But sometimes you can't?'

He nodded. '*Why* I write them – what I'm for, or even what plays are for: there are layers of those two questions about everything, so that one can't answer one layer in terms of another.'

'Do you remember when you were a child saying that you lived in a house in a street, in London, England, Europe, the World?'

He shook his head. 'Our childhoods were not the same.'

'It always stopped at the world. The world was one's total horizon of one's address. Now, it doesn't seem enough.' She sighed, and then smiled to dismiss it.

'Well?' His head was beginning to drum, and his skin felt like a hot, dry leaf. He did not want his fiery resolutions to drift into a haze of her nostalgia.

She looked up again from her hands.

'Shall we start looking for a house?'

'What? Immediately?'

'Yes. Go back to England, hire a car, and start looking.'

'I thought we were here to cast your play, and couldn't leave until we had.'

'That is something else I have to tell you. We've drawn such a blank that Jimmy and I have decided to try out Alberta for Clemency. So we can go anywhere.'

'*Alberta?* The *secretary*?'

He explained, and she was silent. Then she asked questions, and he explained again. It was a little like the course for the Grand National, he thought – twice round, and every obstacle presenting a different problem. Then she was silent again. At last, she said: 'Well, the whole idea seems preposterous to me: I don't think it is fair on the poor girl, who knows nothing of what she is in for. Jimmy, at least, must think very highly of her even to try and sweat her through it. I suppose he's fallen in love with her.'

'What on earth makes you think that?'

'He's susceptible and he's got strong protective instincts, and she's at an age when she'd fall in love with anyone who suggested it to her.'

'Why do you dislike this poor girl?'

'Why should my thinking she'd fall in love with Jimmy mean that I dislike her?'

'I haven't the faintest idea, but it seems to.'

'I'm not against her,' she said after a pause: 'I simply think that what you propose doing with her is silly.'

'I need coffee,' he observed; 'and a hot bath. Could we leave this arrangement, now? I can't think of anything more to say about it.'

'Well – don't say I didn't warn you.'

'About Alberta being no good? I am taking that possibility into account.'

'About Jimmy falling in love with Alberta – and Alberta with Jimmy.'

'So far as Jimmy is concerned, he's much more interested in my play. And Alberta is *not* a suggestible little school-girl.' He said this with an almost venomous conviction which surprised him.

She was lighting a cigarette: he felt in his dressing-gown pocket – then thought that if he smoked now his head would get worse, and squeezed the packet regretfully.

Suddenly, she said: 'Em! *Don't* seduce her – anything else – but not that. *Please* make sure of that.'

He looked at her: she had spoken as though it was hope-less – as though it was already important and true. He took out a cigarette, tapped it on his finger nail, reached for her lighter, and used it before he had designed an answer.

'Lillian – I know what put that into your head, but I am old enough to be her father, I am married to you, and I don't think she is in search of sensation. She has told me enough about her family for me to feel responsible to them for her. Will that do?'

He felt the climate between them change.

'No, it won't. The first two reasons are laughable, and the last one frightens me. Do you mean you *respect* her?'

'One hardly ever respects people, does one? It's not such a personal business. Sometimes one can respect what they stand for.'

'And you do?'

'I hadn't considered it before, but yes.'

She said coldly: 'I fail to see the difference between Alberta and thousands of other girls.'

'Then you have no reason to respect her.' He got to his feet: his head was pounding, and beyond their familiar air of destruction something unknown was building of which he was afraid.

'Em!'

As he moved back to her, he felt her change her mind, and because of this, he said more gently: 'What is it?'

She said rapidly: 'I do agree about the house – but not now – not this summer . . .' He waited.

'Will you do two things for me?'

'What are they?'

'Will you make us both some coffee and take me to Greece?'

And because this made him smile, he promised.

3. JIMMY

It's no good saying Greece before seven – they won't change their minds, they've decided, or rather *she* has, and I suppose he had to trade Greece for Alberta. Oh well! Join the Joyces and travel, or travel and see the Joyces – it comes to much the same thing. It's stupid to feel sore about it, when it doesn't matter to me where the hell we go. I suppose I can as well train that girl on a Greek island as I can train her any place else. *If* I can train her at all. It began with Lillian. I was taking a shower and she came into my room and called out to me. I wrapped a towel round me and found her, fresh as a daisy, sitting on my bed with a tray of coffee and orange juice beside her.

'I've come to have more coffee with you: I've had some with Em.'

'Is he up?'

She nodded. 'He's having a long, hot bath.'

'What's the time, for heaven's sake?'

'Just after eight. Em couldn't sleep – he had so much to tell me, and we've made a lot of plans.' She gave me my coffee. Somehow I knew that he *had* told her, so I said: 'He's told you about our plan for Clemency?'

'He has. Jimmy, seriously – which one of you had this idea?'

'It wasn't either one of us. We both had it.'

'But one of you must actually have made the suggestion?'

'We just sort of looked at each other and arrived at it. He asked her if she'd do it. Naturally, I leave that kind of thing to him.' I looked at her carefully. If she started upsetting Alberta, I'd never get anywhere with her. 'It's only an experiment, you know. It may work – it may not. But we had to do something.'

'What do you think of her?'

Wondering exactly this, I said: 'I think she looks as though she may be able to learn. Otherwise she has the intelligence, and, I should say, the stamina.'

'Do you think she's attractive?'

'She's got something of what is needed for Clemency – that's the main reason why we are trying her. Lillian – I'm sure you think it's a crazy idea, but you could make a lot of difference to whether it's a success or not.'

'How could I?' She was off her guard – engaged – any appeal would do that to her if there was a shred of truth in it.

'I shall have to work her very hard – voice mostly – to get it to come across and to get it to last for a possible eight performances a week. She'll get tired and depressed and nervous. If you could give her a bit of confidence, be kind to her, help her with her appearance, and so on – it might make all the difference. You know what I mean. Any little thing. Get her hair cut properly – not curled – and tell her what an

improvement it is.' There was a pause, and then I added:
'Then if she's no good, help me to help her out of it. She's
in for a tough time whichever way it goes.'

She smiled then, took my empty cup away from me, and
looked at her watch. 'All right, Jimmy. I'll help, if you'll tell
me what to do. There isn't much time to have her hair cut
because we're going to Greece.'

'*When* are we going to do that?'

'As soon as possible. I want her to arrange the tickets this
morning.'

'Oh Lord!'

'It doesn't matter to you. You can work as well on an
island as anywhere else. You love sun and swimming.'

'It seems crazy to me.'

'It's no more crazy than all of us coming all the way over
here in order to make a decision we could perfectly well have
made in London. Oh Jimmy, please be nice about it. I *do* so
want to go, and Em doesn't mind as long as we find a house
to live in and he doesn't have to work in some hotel bedroom.'

'O.K.'

'It would be silly to go all the way back to England –
think of the *rain*.'

'I see the only solution is Greece,' I said, trying to sound
pleasant about it.

Lillian went and I dressed, wondering why her saying 'It
doesn't matter to *you*' stung me somewhere – why should it?
– I had always prided myself on not caring where we went
as long as we didn't go too far away from theatres for too
long and I could work with Emmanuel.

I found him sitting on a chair outside my room pretending to read a paperback.

'You can't see to read in that light.'

'I can't see to read in any light; Jimmy, for God's sake
before we do anything – take me to a chemist.'

'Drugstore,' I said gently. 'Stay where you are a minute.'

Alberta was cleaning up the kitchen: when she saw me, she
sneezed.

'We're all going for a nice holiday to Greece. That'll mean four plane tickets for Athens as soon as possible. The travel agent's name and number are in the green book. Would you call them? I'll be back in half an hour if you have any trouble.'

She sneezed again, and said: '*Greece*! Goodness! When?'

'As soon as possible. From tonight onwards. Have you got soap powder up your nose?'

'No.'

'Well, I might as well warn you that from now on I shall take a personal and very disapproving interest in any cold you get.'

'I am quite certain that I have not got a cold, but considering the rate at which we are changing climates I may hardly escape.'

'You don't get asthma, do you?' Visions of certain terrible hours with Emmanuel reared up in my mind. She would be no good if . . .

'I don't get anything.' She sneezed again. 'Greece! I simply sneeze sometimes – it is an entirely private and quite insignificant affliction.'

'That's all right,' I said kindly. 'Everybody has to have some private life. Back soon.'

We went out of the apartment, down the elevator, into the street in silence – anxiety and dissatisfaction dividing us: I had begun to feel unduly irritated with Lillian, and I knew that – whatever he was feeling about her – this would annoy him. I sat him down in a corner, got him a draught and coffee for both of us. When he had swallowed the draught, he said: 'How commonplace we are to be sure. Three little mechanisms jostling against one another and ticking away to no purpose. Either we regard the fact of our existence as miracle enough, or we suffer from the delusions of that fool last night. His education and progress don't seem even to improve our mechanism. I could undoubtedly put my foot in my mouth soon after I was born, and I fail to see what I have gained to compensate for the loss of this honest achievement.'

'Perhaps we aren't here for any purpose,' I suggested; 'so it's not surprising that we're commonplace.'

'Do you know, I think that is very unlikely?'

'Why?'

He thought for a moment, and then said slowly: 'Because I detect signs of order wherever anything seems to know its place.' He leaned forward. 'That's the trouble, Jimmy: we don't know our place. We have been told what chaos that used to create in the Servants' Hall. Lillian said this morning that she didn't know what she was for: I have a nasty feeling that this is true of nearly all of us.'

'Well, how do we find out what we are for?'

He looked at me with amusement. 'Jimmy – you're just stringing along: you don't really want to find out because you think you know, don't you?'

'I suppose I do. I know for myself – I wouldn't go any farther than that.'

'But supposing you were wrong. I mean, we take ourselves so fearfully for granted. We allow that certain muscles can be developed, and certain parts of the brain, but all the rest is just dubbed lucky, instinctive, or unlucky: we don't question what else we are besides muscles and brains, and certainly not what we might be. We behave like ready-made products trying to grab at change out of circumstances – as though they were the only variable factors in our lives.'

'Well, they do make a difference. I mean, if I hadn't happened to meet you I would never have been ...'

He looked at me then – curiously intent. 'You didn't "happen to meet me".'

There was a silence into which I tried to follow him. Then he said: 'Do you believe in magic?'

I thought carefully.

'I don't mean white rabbits. I mean something marvellous that you can't understand, that as you are, you couldn't understand and if you even began to have a glimmer of its meaning you would already be different. I mean that kind.'

I thought again: 'No,' I said at last: 'I don't think that kind of magic is for me.'

'Quite right,' he said, 'but *you* might be for that kind of magic, and not know it. That might be what you are for.'

'Are you?'

There was a kind of ache in his face as he said: 'I hope so, Jimmy. I can't tell you how I hope that.'

Getting to his feet a minute later, he said casually: 'So you see Jimmy, it doesn't really matter whether we go to Greece or not. We can make some use of it or not, but it won't make "all the difference" like they say in books.'

It was much later, when thinking over this close talk, I realized that he'd referred to three mechanisms. He'd left the girl out of it.

It was the next morning, in fact, when I thought of his leaving the girl out of it. We were due to fly to Athens that evening – Lillian had taken her shopping and arranged to have her hair cut the day before, and now I had to get her photographed. I still hadn't told Mick and the boys that their worst fears were to be realized, and I wanted to have a picture to warm them up a little. So it had to be a good picture. I had a friend who sometimes took that kind if he liked what he saw: I'd called him and told him what I wanted, and now we were on our way there. I'd done Stanley one or two favours in the past, and he was great on paying up favours or dues – I think he preferred dues – it was how he saw life. Alberta sat beside me in the cab with her hands in her lap and her head a little bent. Lillian had done a very good job on her hair; now that it was cut one could see the shape of her head and the back of her neck. She hadn't said a word since we got into the cab, so I asked: 'Anything on your mind?'

'Not my mind exactly.'

'What is it on?' But she didn't answer.

'If you're nervous or worrying about the part – don't. We'll start on that when we get to Greece. Once we're there, and anything worries you, speak up, and if I can straighten it out for you I will.'

'Thank you, Jimmy.'

'But don't start worrying about it now. Emmanuel said

178

you read the part very well, and understood what it was about: well – that's the main thing.'

'Yes.'

She was so quiet, she made me feel a fool – as though I was the one who was nervous, and perhaps this was true.

'You're not nervous about the picture being taken?'

She shook her head, and said: 'I've never had my photograph taken, excepting for my passport. But there is nothing surprising about that. I hardly do anything nowadays to which I am accustomed.'

'You don't sound happy about it.'

'Oh, I am not *un*happy about it. But it is a little like having meals every day of food you've never seen before in your life. Very interesting,' she added primly, 'but a lot of the time I feel rather full.'

'I must get to know you better, or I'll be a wreck myself. First I think you have asthma, and then I think you're scared, when really all you do is sneeze and have indigestion.' She smiled and did not reply, but just before we arrived at Stanley's studio she said: 'There is one thing that I should very much like to ask you.'

'Go ahead.'

'Is it – would it be possible for me to telephone to my father to explain to him about going to Greece? He is not very young, and I don't want to cause him unnecessary anxiety.'

'Will our going to Greece worry him?'

'Oh no – I don't think so. He may regard it as a bit fidgety – but that's all. But I should like to tell him – if it is possible.'

'We'll put a call in right after your picture has been taken.'

'Thank you, Jimmy.'

Stanley had a curious act, or attitude towards his sitters – I never knew which it was – he never spoke to them – he just didn't say anything at all. All the other times I saw him, he talked all the time: softly, almost inaudibly – but that way he didn't use much breath so he never needed to

stop. The moment he saw you, he fixed you with expression-
less pale blue eyes and started right in telling you what had
happened to him since he woke up that morning. He never
expressed an opinion, or asked you what you thought; he
just quietly, confidently unrolled a record – it was like hearing a newsreel of someone's life – consecutive events with all
the commentator's time-honoured adjectives removed. But
whenever I'd taken people to him for pictures, he hadn't
said a word. He'd greet us with a soft, absent smile and
immediately go to the other end of his studio and fiddle
interminably with equipment whilst I and his sitter carried
on an uneasy conversation until we'd said again everything
that we'd said on the way to him and had subsided into an
edgy silence. Then he would advance upon us with an
ancient lamp and a slightly menacing expression, and the
sitter – agog for some notice to be taken of her – would turn
to him expectantly . . . This was his cue for dragging out a
dirty, hideously uncomfortable chair – half-heartedly up-
holstered in khaki plush: he patted it invitingly, and the
sitter, mesmerized by his indifference, invariably sat upon
it. He took his photographs with an air of reckless gloom –
if he wanted his sitter to move he came and moved her, but
with an expression on his face of it not making much difference. When he had finished, he smiled again and went into
the only other room he had which I knew was a bathroom,
kitchen, and darkroom combined, locked the door very
noisily, and turned on all the taps. And that was that.

As we climbed the stairs of the old brownstone house
where he lived, I nearly told Alberta; then curiosity about
what they would make of each other intervened, and I said
nothing, except that he was the best photographer I knew –
which was true.

Stanley occupied half of the top floor, and his studio (he
called it that) had a kind of anonymously international
eccentricity. It was drab and rather dirty – filled with spiteful
draughts in winter and hot, dead air in summer. It was
packed with incongruous objects nearly all of which were
being used for some makeshift purpose not their own – and

some seemed to have none at all, except the doubtful chance of their owner having at one time thought them decorative. A small gong hung on a nail on the door, and almost as soon as I struck it, there was Stanley ready in his smile with the overpowering smell of carraway seeds behind him. Inside, he left us to the usual problem of where to sit: today it was a couple of shooting sticks stuck into the wide cracks between the floorboards. He had acquired several new things – a large, old-fashioned birdcage which was stuffed with dead lamp bulbs and his bed in the corner was covered with yards of window-dressing grass – but all the old pots made out of twisted gramophone discs were there and the child's playpen with rocks and sand and the old gopher tortoise: the collection of hats on pegs arranged in a serpentine pattern on the wall, and several volumes of the *Encyclopaedia Britannica* spread open on the floor.

Alberta – unlike anyone else I had brought there – did not walk about in search of a mirror and end by furtively jabbing at herself with a powder puff out of her handbag; nor did she run her fingers through her hair and talk to me with one eye on Stanley – she simply sat and looked round the room with a frank accepting interest. So I lit a cigarette and watched them and didn't talk. The silence was preserved while Stanley took three or four pictures: he moved her for each one, but somehow he was doing it differently – he did not manipulate her as though she was material that he knew all about: once he lifted her chin and looked at her with a kind of tentative searching, and after that, he took three more pictures with – it seemed to me – a tender attention in his treatment of her. I knew then that the pictures were going to be good. When he had finished, he did not immediately escape but stood by his camera staring at the floor, and she sat still with her head bent as she had sat in the taxi. Then at the same moment they both looked up at each other and smiled; he moved and we got to our feet: there was a curious feeling in the room – as though they were talking so privately that I could not even hear them.

I had explained when I called him about our going to

Greece, and now I gave him a piece of paper with 'American Express, Athens', written on it. He read it, patted my shoulder, nodded, and stuffed the paper into a pocket of his filthy old leather jacket. Alberta held out her hand and said 'Thank you.'

He bowed over her hand and replied: 'I recognized you: the pictures should be good.'

'Shall I see you again?'

Still holding her hand, he was absolutely still for a moment before answering: 'I'm not sure,' then he let it go, waved his own, and we left.

Outside, I took her arm to guide her across the road, and asked her what she thought of Stanley, and she said: 'I don't think he is an ordinary man.'

'He certainly liked you.' I noticed at the time what a lame reply this was.

I took her to a bar I knew nearby where she could telephone: 'It will be more private for you than the apartment, and we can eat here if we want.'

'Would you mind very much helping me to put through the telephone call? I know it sounds silly when I'm supposed to be a secretary, but I've never made a call like this before.'

'We'll get Frank to put it through for you – all you'll have to do is take it. Write down your father's name and telephone number, and I'll give it to him.'

She wrote down The Reverend William Wyndham Young in full with a place and a number.

I gave the piece of paper to Frank, and sat down opposite her at the small table.

'How long will it be?'

'He's getting through now to find out. What do you want to eat?'

She shook her head.

'You've got to eat. Have some – have some Littlenecks.'

'Some *what*?'

'Clams. Special American food.'

'Oh! Yes please.'

Her immediate enthusiasm made me want to smile. 'Are you very fond of them, then?'

'I've never had them. But I don't suppose they'll have them in Greece, will they? So it would be a waste not to try now.'

We had them, and some beer, and talked. The clams were a success, and while we talked I watched her – trying to feel what she was, what stuff she was made of and how I could use it. She had the most extraordinary dignity: at least I couldn't figure it out alongside her extreme lack of sophistication – her English schoolgirl appearance (except when she had been wearing that black dress, I suddenly remembered) – her funny, prim way of expressing herself, and her admitted inexperience in any field I knew about anyway. It wasn't exactly self-confidence – she was shy except when she was alone with you and even then you had to be careful – it was more as though she was collected – all in one piece – no acts, no exaggerations, no trying to make out she was different: she didn't get in the way of whatever she was talking about. I asked her if she had wanted to be a secretary who travelled – she said she never thought about it – it had just happened. 'If my uncle hadn't taken me to the party where I met Mrs Joyce, I don't suppose I would be a secretary who travelled.'

'And what about becoming an actress?'

'I had not considered that at all. And, after all, you may find that I'm not one. In that case, you need have no consideration for my feelings, because I shall probably know myself.'

'Will you be disappointed?'

She looked at me then. 'I don't think so, because I didn't appoint myself. I haven't any imagination of myself as an actress – either way.' She smiled – with her eyes as well – and for a moment I felt connected with her: there was some warmth, and a warning in it. . . . Then her call came through, and I watched her in the glass booth talking to her father – talking, listening carefully, explaining, listening – her laugh – her moment's tension before she hung up. She came back.

'Everything all right?'

She nodded, and her eyes filled suddenly with tears.

'He wasn't at all surprised to hear me – not *at all*! He sounded exactly the same and clearer than if I was ringing him up from London!'

'What did he say about Greece?'

'A prodigious piece of good fortune.' Her tears ran down with a kind of momentous ease: then she said: 'It's simply that I've known him all my life.' There wasn't anybody I had known like that, and I felt it then.

I said: 'There isn't anyone I've known all my life.'

'Are you an orphan?'

'I don't even know. My mother died when I was born. She wasn't married to my father whoever he was.' I felt my angry smile splitting my face: 'At least I *know* I'm illegitimate.'

'Are you English or American?'

'You may well ask. I'm not anything, really. I've got a British passport, brought up – if you can call it that – in America.' Something in her practical attention eased me, and suddenly I *wanted* to say it all. 'When my mother died, she kind of left me to her sister. The sister married an Irishman who was emigrating to the States. They took me along – the sister died almost as soon as they got there; her husband married again, they didn't want me, and managed to farm me out to an orphanage. That was when I clung to my having been born in England and being different from the rest of the kids. When I was sixteen and I'd been working in a store for some time saving the money for a trip to England, Emmanuel suddenly wrote to me out of the blue and said he'd pay the expenses for the trip. It didn't seem strange at all. I was crazy on the theatre – I'd known about him for years, I'd saved ninety dollars and thirty-five cents for the trip, and I knew I was going in the end, anyway, but it never struck me what an extraordinary piece of luck it was for me that Emmanuel should have picked me out and offered me exactly that. That was in thirty-nine: late summer – the war hadn't started, and Lillian had taken Sarah away for a long seaside holiday – I didn't meet her then. I spent five weeks in a hotel with Emmanuel and he showed me London. They were the best weeks in my life. We went to the theatre every night, and sometimes in the afternoons as well – he gave me wonderful meals with wines which I'd never had before, and in the mornings he showed me London, thoroughly – every single thing I wanted to see, and a great deal that I'd never heard of. And he talked to me! He treated me all the time as though I was human and adult and interesting; he taught me by listening to my resentment, by not arguing with my opinions, by encouraging me to walk down each one of my little dead alleys and waiting for me at the open end. I'd gotten a grudge like a house on my back – I was against pretty well everything you can think of from Mick O'Casey, my aunt's husband, to Dr Heller who ran the Home where my childhood had been spent for me – to the President himself – anything, anyone – but in those five weeks it all peeled off – like having a new skin. He once said to me: "After you've given up something which seemed difficult to give up, you find out it wasn't ever there – you feel much lighter and a little foolish": it was just how I felt about the chip on my shoulder. He showed me the play he was writing, and asked me what I thought of it; he bought me decent clothes; he offered to send me to college or university – it was all set that I could stay in England if I wanted.' I stopped and she said: 'Why have you stopped?'

'I don't know why I started. Oh yes: I was trying to explain why I'm such a mongrel. I don't even have me an accent that either country would call their own. *You'd* think it was American, and most Americans would think it was English.'

'Yes, but what happened next?'

'When?'

'After the five weeks? What happened then?'

'The war. I'd paid no attention to it, you see – I was in such a trance, and it just sneaked up on me. He sent me back to America. I didn't want to go to college, so he sent me to learn my profession with a man he knew in Chicago who owned theatres. He promised me a job after the war, and to keep in touch. He wrote to me and I came straight out of the army to him.'

'He's really become your family, hasn't he?'

'*He* has. I only told you all this so that you wouldn't cry.' This wasn't true: I had wanted to tell her and liked it. I asked Frank for the check, and she said: 'Did you ever know Sarah?'

'She died that fall. Just after I left. I didn't meet Lillian till after the war.'

She said she wanted to pay for her call. 'No – this is part of the expense sheet: honest. We couldn't abduct you to Greece without your father's agreement – you're under the age for that kind of consenting.'

'And I suppose now you're well over the age of resenting?'

'I do hope so.' I was smiling when I said that, and then I remembered Emmanuel's face when he had said the same thing about his magic.

Outside, she said: 'What do you think Greece will be like? Or do you know?'

'I don't *know*, but I suspect that it will be hot and yellow and dusty with everybody arguing about money, and flies on the food. We shall all get dysentery and sunstroke and be eaten by sharks.'

'*Sharks?* Are there really sharks?'

'The sea is studded with them – all half-mad with hunger because there aren't nearly enough fish to go round any-where in the Mediterranean.'

'Sharks,' she repeated dreamily – she sounded pleased. 'What else?'

'Isn't that enough? Well, ruins, of course. The whole country's lousy with ruins, and a lot of rocks so you're worn out climbing. I just can't wait to get back from Greece. I suppose you're looking forward to it.'

She nodded: 'I really am. It may be better than you think.'

I shrugged, but she persisted: 'Or different.'

'I'll tell you if it is either.'

She laughed: 'You won't have to tell me – I'll know.'

4. LILLIAN

CONTRAST – opposites – extremes – how I am fed by them! New York in the early evening of early summer, shrugging with a moonstone mist, chilled, subdued, chalky; filled with a hurrying irresolution – the business day over, the professional night not begun – slung in this hour of waiting for the end of the end. The time for illicit love, for the uncharacteristic event, for killing with a drink or some duty duologue, for playing with the children: to spend, to lose, or to waste – the travelling is over, but nobody has arrived. . . . In the aeroplane we have become a giant: everything below us diminished, cosy, twinkling, melted into the distance of our feet, until, at our giant's level, the sky is our country – pleasing with enormous detail and endless resource. We fly away from the sun which retreats like a beautiful calamity with such majestic movement and tragic colour that I know it is its silence which moves me. When we are above the clouds that reflect this crisis of the sun, they lie in soft apricot waves – the smaller ones sharper hit, red and seedy like split pomegranate, and above us the fine, blue air is already impregnated with stars who are born into the dying blue with little starts of light. Soon the air will have that unbreathing colourless purity that I love and cannot communicate, and I turn to Em sitting beside me because I wonder whether all communication is, after all, only a refuge? This starts some consideration about silence in my mind – the nearest I get to it is with music, when sometimes I am attending to sound outside myself, and if the attention is enough, I am silent inside. I turn to Em again – illogically, even thinking of silence has made me want to talk to him, but at once an avalanche of food and information pours through the aeroplane, quenching all sparks of hunger or need of any kind. Em asks me something but I only hear 'glad' and 'darling': I lean towards him and he repeats: 'Are you glad that we are going to Greece?' and I smile, and start to imagine Athens – but I get caught by the beautiful name and can see nothing. . . .

Athens – stepping out of the plane on to the hot ground into air brilliant, burning at such a pitch of light that my eyes cannot reach it. It is noon; and we walk into the Customs with the heat like an arrow between our shoulder blades, and wait for our luggage amid the usual shuffle of languages and a knot of people becoming resigned to impatience. The stalls sell sham pottery, sham jewellery, and doubtful peasant costumes, real silk and beautiful cigarettes; the airport officials have that Mediterranean inability to look serious in uniform. Alberta is looking at a priest: he wears black boots below his greasy gown, but it is his head that fascinates her. After the wealth of his beard it seems impossible that his long hair can screw into so small a bun – it is no larger than a ping-pong ball skewered below his huge stiff hat. His face is shrewd, savage, and joyous. Then we are in a taxi – a huge old American car which thunders loosely along the coast road into Athens. To our right are mountains bleached and shimmering in the hot distance, and to the left the sea – like a stroke of summer – filling and quenching our eyes. We all look, and say very little – the long flight is beginning to catch up on us: we none of us speak any Greek, and are to depend on my French, but when the cab driver points and says 'Akropolis', and there it is, crowning a hill in actual unwinking splendour, there is a different silence – we smile at one another, and I wonder what the others are thinking until Alberta says: 'My father has a picture of that in his study, but it is rather spotted with damp': and Jimmy says: 'Yes: I've seen pictures of that some place too.'

We are into Athens – the air is white and dusty – every other road seems to be up – buildings are being demolished, being built, and traffic is either charging at full speed or hopelessly jammed. Our driver becomes dramatically concerned with getting us to the hotel – he sweats and sways and groans over his wheel – he hoots and pounces whenever he can take anyone by surprise – he swerves round pot-holes and shoots down side-streets muttering the breathy, liquid language – his face tragic with resolution – I see Em watching it in the driving mirror and take his hand, but it is too hot to touch hands. The hotel is very cool and dark and antiseptic: the man at the desk speaks English, and Jimmy is visibly cheered. In a spurt of excitement at our arrival, we decide to go out to lunch...

Now – in the early evening I lie stupefied in the darkened room. We walk back here from the restaurant after lunch, and suddenly I am so tired that I can hardly bear it – the air feels like a hot curtain falling over my face – I wonder why I wanted to come here and how quickly we can leave this sordid stew of heat and glaring concrete and the ashes of antiquity all casually stirred together and simmering with clouds of dust. The lift does not work and I stumble up three flights of stairs with Em holding my arm – making me wait between each flight – my ankles hurt – I am horribly breathless and I know I am behaving like a weak, angry child. Disappointment! I am encrusted with it like the grit from the streets: I think the pain is starting, and clutch Em's arm, but it is simply that I am aching to cry: I say 'Athens' to myself and remember what I had imagined. 'You are simply exhausted,' Em says and, because I want to scream and hit him for saying it, I know he is right. He puts me to bed – as he shuts the door I start to cry and immediately fall into sleep.

Now – I am slowly waking – remembering our departure from New York, the lovely first minutes in the aeroplane, the long, uneasy night, the early-morning stop at Orly – French breakfast and we bought brandy (it was raining there and we all huddled in our overcoats) and then our dazzling arrival in Athens. The word sounded beautiful again; all the afternoon horror had gone, and from the blissful lassitude in my bones now, I knew how tired I had been.

There is a gentle knock on the door and Alberta stands in its entrance saying 'Mr Joyce told me to wake you at seven. Shall I open your shutters?'

'Please do.'

When we could see each other she came over to my bed: 'Do you feel better now?'

'Much better: marvellous – I must have slept for four hours.'

'We should not have walked back from lunch – it was terribly hot: they say it is unusually hot for June.'

'It's nothing: when I get overtired I just get the horrors, like retired pirates.' I was looking for my bag, and she fetched it saying: '*They* got them from too much rum trying to forget their wicked deeds – not at all the same.'

'Are you fond of Stevenson?'

'Some of him: but I haven't read all. My sister has – she likes him better than anybody – *my* knowledge of him is partly vicarious.'

I lit a cigarette, and she said: 'Would you like me to unpack for you? Just what you need for now, I mean.'

'Tell me what has been happening while I've been asleep.'

'Well – quite a lot, really. Jimmy and I have got tickets for the boat tomorrow morning which goes to the island. We've been to American Express and cashed an enormous sum of money. We've arranged for a taxi to take us to the boat – it's quite a long way. Mr Joyce met somebody he knew in the street who said he knew someone who might lend us a house on the island and they went off to somewhere called Monestarike and then to the Acropolis. Then we met them and I've just been having a shower. I think the others are sleeping, and,' her eyes widened, 'apparently we are all going out to dinner to eat fish with our feet in the sea.'

She seemed so pleased at this that I could not help smiling back: 'You sound as though you have been very busy. Did you get a picture for your father?'

'I have sent him a postcard; it's *wonderful* here – I can't possibly thank you enough for bringing me. Shall I get out your pleated silk dress – the one that screws up like rope? that won't be in the least crushed, and it is still hot.'

'That would be a good idea: thank you.' I lay and watched while she unpacked my smaller case: whenever I was alone with her, I felt utterly disarmed into a liking that was almost protective. She was simply a nice child – she could almost have been my daughter – excepting that she was not physically how I imagined Sarah would have become. Sarah had had Em's heavy-lidded eyes and the same curling mouth, and her hair had been dark, but otherwise she had been too young to tell: she might have become anything. This girl had a restful quality which was graceful beside her extreme youth. She could have been drawn by Holbein, I thought – she has that well-bred homespun appearance which he would have translated into beauty. She was unwinding my sea-green dress – stroking the fine pleats and laying it on Em's bed. She saw me watching her and said: 'It *is* beautiful – like pale green pearls.'

It was. 'I get them in Venice: there is one man who makes them there, although you're supposed to be able to buy them in New York.'

'It is such astonishing silk. It really would go through the eye of a needle, like the princess's shifts.'

'So it would. Is the gold belt there?'

'Yes; and the shoes – everything. Would you like a bath run, or do you want a shower?'

'I'd like a bath. You're spoiling me, Alberta: I'm not an invalid and you are not meant to wait on me.'

'I really like to do what you need. Shall I go now, or wait and talk to you when you've had your bath?'

'Stay and talk to me. I'll be quick – I want a cool one.'

The dress, which was just a pleated tent from neck to hem, drawn in at the waist by a gold belt, was much prettier than I remembered – I'd only worn it once when it was new – and Alberta admired it deeply. She watched me doing my face with such solemn interest that I wanted to laugh, until she said: 'I hope you don't mind: there has been next to no opportunity for me to learn anything like this. Do you think my dress will do for this exotic evening?'

She was wearing a brown check gingham, square necked and sleeveless. She was watching me looking at it and said anxiously: 'I took the sleeves out in New York, because my aunt can only make the wrong kind, but perhaps you can see that there *have* been sleeves?'

'What about the white embroidered cotton we got in New York? Wouldn't you like to wear that?'

'Of course. How extraordinary! I'd forgotten its existence. Events in my life have changed scale so much. I'll go and change.'

'If you come back, I'll show you how to do your eyes.'

'*Will* you? Oh thank you. I have not had the courage to try and do them. I'll be very quick.'

When she came back and I had sat her at the dressing-table, I said: 'Tell me something. What do you mean – events in your life have changed scale?'

'Well at home nothing very much happened – a new dress would be a tremendous event: the whole family would notice it. Now, so much is happening that a new dress seems a very small size of event. You know – it's the difference between leading a Jane Austen life and a Tolstoy one.'

'But some things stay the same size whatever happens, don't they?' I was thinking of Sarah.

'Perhaps they should,' she answered after a moment; 'but I haven't got far enough to make them: I'm too variable for my liking.' She brushed away at her eyelashes in silence and then went on: 'I don't mean what one *thinks*, exactly,' she frowned. 'Not the size or importance one thinks something should have in one's life: I mean what one *feels or knows it is* – all the time – it's difficult to keep that the same.' She put down the mascara brush I had given her. 'Except my father: I was thinking of him. I don't think anything changes how he is to me. I'm not at all good at this: that's one eye – what do you think?'

'That's quite enough – do the other one.'

'I wanted it to show: and it does, doesn't it?'

'Most alluring.' She looked pleased and brushed away at her other eye until I said: 'Was your father always more important to you than your mother?'

'Yes. My mother died, you see, when Serena was born. Of course, it was like having a kind of earthquake in one's life:

afterwards, everything seemed changed – but my father kept some bits of it the same by not changing himself.'

'If he loved your mother very much, that must have been a difficult thing to do.'

'I think it was *very* difficult,' she said with emphasis, and I noticed that her voice was trembling. Because I found myself badly wanting to know, I asked: 'Did you find it helped to pray?' I could not help remembering my bitter failure in this direction. The question did not seem to surprise her and she looked clearly at me in the glass.

'Not much: the trouble is that I can't pray – I don't know how to. I ask and thank for things sometimes, but that isn't the point is it?'

'What does your father say about that?'

'Oh – he says that hardly anybody does know. He says it is a difficult thing to do; one hasn't a hope of beginning until one knows one can't, and most people think of it as a method of getting something; it's nice of them to pray and they ought to get something back – anything from peace of mind to some useful object. They think prayer is *for them*, that's the trouble: that's some of what he says, but of course he says it much better.'

'But what *is* prayer for? Did he tell you that?'

'Of course I asked him: he said: "What is air for?" I said: "To breathe," and he said: "Well, try thinking of prayer as another breath of another life" – that was all he said about it.' She looked up at me again in the glass and was silent for a moment before saying: 'I am so sorry that you lost your daughter.'

She said it so quietly, that my face, which had begun to stiffen with its habit of rejection (nobody could possibly know how much I cared – all casual pity is an insult), became calm and I felt at ease with her speaking of Sarah.

When she smiled at me and said: 'Will I do?' I took a handkerchief and evened up the corners of her eyes and we went down to the bar.

Everything went well that evening. For the first time, we seemed all to have achieved the right degrees of intimacy, but our composition had also a freshness, and the place, so old, so new to us, gave us a kind of dream-like gaiety in its evening presence. Evening in Athens: the air is dry and tender; people loiter steadily – not going anywhere – simply content with existing along a street: the cafés are like hives – their interiors violently lit, with customers bunched at tables on the pavements and waiters like worker bees scurrying darkly in and out. We drive to Phaleron, past dusty squares where people drink orange soda under shrill strings of lights threaded through the tired trees: down one long narrow street which had at its end and above us the Acropolis, radiant in the full dress of floodlighting – out on to a wide highway where one notices chiefly the evening sky with land dark below it pollinated with lights. We turn on to a road which has the harbour on our left – the waters have still a dull sheen on them from the sun – like golden oil. There are a few boats anchored and an air of gentle desertion, but to our right, cafés, booths, restaurants are strung out with irregular bursts of cheap savage light and violent music. As we climb, the curve of Phaleron is below us to our left; pretty, laid out with beady lights like a doll's bay which blots out as we plunge into the quiet town above it. Our taxi takes us down to the waterfront and leaves us and we stand in the road where he has put us, a little dazed, the scene is so full to the brim of the water's edge where everybody is eating under canvas awnings and strings of white lights. The food is rushed to them across the road (full of cars, and spectators) from the cafés, which are almost empty, except for a few old men drinking and thinking alone at large bare tables. The harbour is full of yachts and little boats anchored in rows – some brilliantly lit – others as quiet and dark as a bird on a nest. We smile vaguely at each other – we are not yet in this scene which is so chocked with gaiety and pleasure: Em takes my arm and Jimmy Alberta's, and we walk slowly round the curve to choose where we will eat. It is difficult to choose; the restaurants are not all the same, but we do not understand their differences. Finally we go to one which has a table right on the water – a Greek family are leaving it and we sit round their silted coffee cups to find ourselves staring into the despairing eyes of a very old man in a rowing boat. He wants to take us somewhere, but Em tells him that we don't want to go, and like a disillusioned old dog he understands Em's tone of voice – he waits for us not to change our minds and then rows painfully away. We drink *ouzo*, and poor Alberta doesn't like it, but there are beautiful black olives and long glasses of iced water and slices of bread.

A child has come up to Em – she might be about eight or nine, and she is carrying a huge basket in which there are tiny bunches of white flowers. She stands very close to Em without actually touching him, and thrusts a spindly bunch before us: it is jasmine: she says something in a small, hoarse throaty voice. She is not pretty, but her face has a finesse and pride, so that even her begging – her single gesture and one speech – have a kind of casual distinction. Em buys two bunches from her – she does not smile, but accepts his money impassively and glides away. Each flower of the jasmine has been pulled off and fastened with cotton to a stiff stem: the effect is exotic and enchanting and our table is clouded with their night scent. We eat a great deal – fish and rice, and there is resinated wine which we all, in varying degrees, dislike, and baclava and very good Turkish coffee and the most fiery brandy: the stars come out and a ripe moon. More children come round with baskets and bundles of nuts and sweets and flowers – we cannot buy from all of them, but they all seem to have an ageless detachment from our responses – we buy or we do not buy – either event may occur. At our feet are elegant, desperate cats who eat anything they find with sibilant speed – pieces of bread, the heads and tails of prawns, grains of rice – anything. Our talk has been pleasant, easy, small – the size suited to our remembering all the other aspects of this evening. In the end we manage to pay our bill and find our taxi in the road (he has found where we were eating) and drive back to Athens. We say good night to the others and go to our room and I throw myself on to my bed.

'Are you tired now?' I notice how often he looks anxious: how if I think of an expression of his it would be anxiety.

'No – I am just delighted with my evening. Are *you* glad we came here darling?'

'If *you* are glad, I am.'

'Oh – more than that, surely?'

He sat down and lit a cigarette. 'Yes, I am. It is the people here that I like – they are different, and it is a good difference.'

'Different from whom?'

'I was thinking of other countries that we have visited. We have looked at buildings and pictures and sculpture, and it has been rather like going to see a woman because she comes of a good family and dresses well, and because she is old and poor, she'll see *you* as long as you give dinner and anything else you can spare. You have to care very much about blue blood and good clothes to do it – there is an exchange, but it is a dull one. But these people don't feel to me sold out in that same degree. I don't feel that they are struggling to be comfortable at all costs; to keep up classic or baroque appearances – they have some separate, present pride in themselves, and this makes them less divorced from their heritage.' He was silent for a minute, and then said abruptly: 'I felt this very much at the Acropolis.'

'Tell me about it: what was it like up there?'

He smiled: 'I can't: fortunately there don't seem to be words for its appearance. But I sat on a stone in the sun for a while, and I had suddenly the feeling of life without time: that these temples were buildings always – that their whole was implicit in each part of them, that they were never completed, never begun, and never abandoned. It was something to do with the people I had been seeing all the afternoon. Touch the place in them, and they would come up the hill with stone and rope and chisels, and be building under the sun.' He waited a moment, and then said: 'Always.'

'Like the child with these?' I held up my jasmine.

He nodded. 'Do you want water for them?'

'It would be no good.' I showed him how the bunch was made. 'Em. Tell me about the house on the island.'

'It is a house in a village – not the main harbour, but near it. It has two terraces and its own well. But – we do not know whether it is empty or not. There is somebody called Aristophánes who arranges the letting of it and has the keys. We have to disembark and find him.'

'Supposing it is let?'

Sam says that Aristophánes will find us another house: there are also two hotels. Sam was in the house for a month in May, and said that it was one of the nicest there.'

'*If* we get it.'

'I think we will get it: I might not have run into Sam after all. He's leaving for Paris tomorrow.'

'Is he having a show there?'

'He wouldn't say.'

'How was he?'

'Very gay and shaky: bad.' He got up. 'Darling – you must take off your beautiful dress; we have a very early call tomorrow.'

By the time I had taken off my earrings and my gold sandals and cleaned my face, he was in bed. It was a long while since we had shared a room and the speed with which he put on or took off his clothes struck me again with a kind of affectionate irritation. He looked at me over the sheet, and grinned: 'I've cleaned my teeth as well.'

'Have one more cigarette, because I want to tell you something.'

'Yes!' He switched off the light by his bed and sat up.

'Don't sound so wary: it's nothing awful. I saw Dr MacBride in New York.' I was brushing my hair, and moved the glass so that I could see his face: there was no expression on it. 'About swimming. He said that it would not do any harm, to swim a little – not for too long. He said it was pointless to give up everything I enjoyed simply in order to stay alive. So . . .'

'Those are two quite different things to say – and opposite.'

'No, they're not. What he meant was that it would do me no harm to swim a little – might even do some good – but that if I did overdo it it would be my fault, and that might even be better than giving in about it altogether.'

He looked angry now. 'Lillian, you promised me that you wouldn't go to doctors behind my back. We agreed that I should always go too, and that then we should both be clear about what you might or might not be allowed to do.'

'If I'd asked you to go this time, you would just have said that I was torturing myself, and that there was no point. Anyway, you were busy all the time.'

'What did he say exactly?'

'Exactly what I've told you. Don't you believe me?'

He was silent, and I knew that he did not. The fact that I had had to argue with the doctor came back to me now, so that I said what I had said to him: 'After all, it is *my* life!'

And he answered, just like the doctor: 'It *is* your life; no one can argue that.' He was looking for an ash-tray, and I brought him one. He looked up at me peaceably: 'I'll write to Dr MacBride – or send him a cable. Have you brought your painting things?'

'No. It's no use, Em; I'm not a painter, and I can't bear fiddling about with it. I don't see the fun of "enjoying my-self" with paints: I like it properly done, or not at all. I'm not a Sam, and there's no point in my struggling about in a welter of therapeutic sentiment just because it's a nice quiet pastime.'

'If you were Sam you wouldn't be painting either.'

'Well he *does* paint. I know it's getting more difficult, as the shaking gets worse, but at least he knows he can do it.'

'That must be a great comfort to him, as he finds himself becoming steadily more incapacitated.'

He was angry because I felt I was worrying enough about Sam and whenever he exposed me as being selfish I became violent.

'Well *I* know what that feels like as well. We aren't talking about either Sam's or my main creative faculties: we're talking about my spending a few minutes in a beautiful warm sea – fewer minutes than anybody else, of course, but still something that I can do too, after you've all finished writing and directing and acting your play – otherwise why have we come here at all? Or why be anywhere, if one can never have any life in the place?' I was going to cry, and I went into the bathroom to do it. When I came back, he was standing by the window which he had opened wide. He held out a hand, and I went into his arms on a high tide of apology – able, but unwilling to say: 'I've been whining *again*; it's inexcusable, and worse when I hide it by shouting at other people. I know exactly what makes me do it: I hate it, and I always mean never to do it again. Please, just *please*, forget it, and give me one more chance starting from a better point than my reality.'

All I did say was 'Poor, *poor* Sam.'

And almost at the same time, he said: 'My poor darling. My poor Lillian. I don't remember nearly enough what it is like. You shall bathe; of course I understand about the painting – you're quite right about it. My darling: it is wicked to make you cry when you were so happy: come, you've had a very tiring day ...'

He put me to bed for the second time that day, and I allowed myself to be stroked and tucked up. What did it matter? He had taken us both down a peg with these allowances he made for me. What was the good of wanting something sharper than this easy pity, if I never changed from behaviour which was designed to get only that? I lay in his arms: in a little while he made love to me, and I lost not only all presence of mind but presence of heart. I fly back to the good times – enough memory of them evokes some echo of response in my body ... The first time after the separate tensions of fear and longing that I was aware of all of myself – it was like the sun coming out in me, warming and lighting all the cold and dark places into which I'd been divided, so that I was whole, and ready to be part of him. Em's face, looking down on me then, radiant, gentle, knowing what was possible ... my body was like a field of grass and his hands were the wind – I was bowing ahead of his touch. ...

He is holding my face in his hands, the light is on, and I am aware of his eyes, intent and searching. I know what he is looking for, and I wish that I had it.

The time when we had celebrated our knowledge of Sarah coming; when he had discovered the only courage in me, and I was so steeped in joy at my discovery of this meaning of making love with him that desire seemed to change scale: I felt blessed by him. All the times when I was carrying her, becoming sicker and more unwieldy, and wanting him, and his understanding perfectly how my two loves were growing: he used to put me to bed in the afternoons then, and make very quiet love to me and leave me to sleep. ...

He is kissing me – the taste of fruit and charcoal is over my mouth, and I feel his heart knocking on my breast.

And after Sarah – the great gaiety and affections, and lovely, easy, recognizable times. ...

He says my name – asks me little, tender, questions – using my name again for each one. I have no answers, but I think I am smiling.

And after Sarah again – when she was dead – nothing: angry rejection, frozen despair – the sun gone out: nothing but dumb, dark confusion, until that morning when I woke and could say her name to him again – admit that she was dead and that I had lost her and cry to him about her. Then he made love to me, and once it was memorable – as though he was piloting me home after a storm: I was so tired, and he gave me peace. It was very long afterwards that I understood that he had not come to me as Lillian (how I used to love his saying my name – 'like all the pretty flowers at once', he said) but as though I was simply a part of that humanity he found so agonizing, whose pain he wanted to share, to help, to save: that it was then that I began to be an object equally of his ignorance and his compassion. When I remember that, I have to go back to anonymous sunny hotel bedrooms of years ago. ...

He finishes his love and I kiss him: it feels just like greeting him after a separation. I touch his forehead with my fingers and some sense of reality is back again – the affection is real – I am about to say something, but he shakes his head, puts his hand over my mouth, and turns off my light. He is right, there are no words to be said.

CHAPTER FIVE

*

I. EMMANUEL

ONCE they were on the boat, there was an unobtrusive opportunity of being alone. 'I need it,' he thought; 'I am gasping for silence.' Or peace, perhaps, since his internal life was far from silent. He had found a bit of boat-deck, empty and sunlit, and now he sat down on it, leaning against the davits of one of the ship's life-boats and shut his eyes. . . . 'I am too many small, anxious men' – he could see a procession of them, small, shabby, and identical, each holding a placard which yelped 'Joyce will win through'.

'I am one little man who is afraid he's had the best years of his life when he wasn't looking. I am another who, having taken his little secret spring for granted, is now suddenly afraid that it has run dry. I am also a man who has a wife who needs, but does not want him. I have no land or house which is mine for no good reason. I care less and less what anyone writes or says about writing, including myself. I have no children to care for, unless you count Jimmy, and he certainly wouldn't count me as his father – it would ruin his whole romantic structure. He works for me because he thinks I'm a wonderful playwright.' He thought for a moment without words. 'I have a good deal of money and I've almost entirely overcome asthma. My best days have a kind of winter sun about them – there is light, but no warmth. I know enough people to fill Drury Lane, but apart from Jimmy, none of them are my friends – perhaps the Friedmanns almost are. I don't care enough,' he thought, 'my emotions nowadays seldom reach beyond anxiety, irritation, and sometimes pity.' It hadn't always been like this. He could distinctly remember times when he had loved Lillian – when he wanted to use himself and pay for it, he could remember other times too when he had felt that life was marvellous and astonishing, that the future was exciting and unknown, and that he was moving towards it, instead of its overtaking him – whatever happened, he had a hopeful interest in the outcome. Now he felt as though he knew what would happen, and he didn't care. He used to sink himself in some idea – he could leave and lose external problems and live inside a play he was making – he had always been able to draw on that; it gave him his reputation for patience and detachment, for kindness and bad manners. But everything, presumably, had to be fed by something else – there is no absolute everlasting spring in anyone which has no source but itself. Instead of these plays needing him to write them, he was starting to need the plays – or even a play – one idea that would knit these small anxious men together. Twice the thing had unfolded in his mind for a little while, and died – like those white trumpet flowers (what were they called?) that only lived for an hour or two – and the rest of the time he seemed to be travelling at the beginning of some future desert without water or shade. People still moved him sometimes; Gloria's sister, that boy playing his fiddle, and the girl – Alberta. As he thought of her, a scene the previous evening recurred – bringing the same impression, but more deeply cut. . . .

It was when the child had brought the jasmine up to him in a basket. He had been looking at Alberta: she had been wearing a white cotton dress with a low, rounded neck and no sleeves, and her skin was warm against the paper-white stuff – her arms like natural silk, smooth and womanly, their outline from her shoulders to her wrists running in pretty leisured curves. Lillian and Jimmy were showing her something – she leaned forward and the edge of her breasts moved and rose to the shape of magnolias. At the same moment the scent of the jasmine struck him – it seemed to come from her, and he was seized and filled with desire so violent and immediate that it was as though all the breath was knocked out of his body. The child was speaking to him, holding out a bunch of her flowers, and the others were all looking at her: Alberta – the jasmine – they were separate – he felt air choking his lungs as though it was water and turned heavily to the child, whose eyes, impassive and intent, were fixed upon his face. He had bought two bunches of jasmine, one for each of the women, and for the rest of the evening he flung his attention in every other direction.

Now, sitting alone in the morning sun, trying to collect and to see himself; discussing his absence of heart as though it was simply a piece of history, he was faced with this accident (for the moment he could not think of anything else to call it); but at least he would not delude himself that it had anything to do with his heart. He knew better than that. When one was twenty – even thirty – one was open to this delusion; that an unexpected onslaught of desire constituted love. There were even people of his age who continued to think so – whose deadly security lay in frequent and entire repetition: they used the same words to blame the same situations which the same part of themselves had taken the trouble to attract. 'He is not better, he is much the same.' The point about these little generalizations was that they ceased to be amusing when they applied to oneself. But he was a little better – he wasn't quite the same. While far from sure that he knew what love was, he did feel that he knew what it was not. And this attack he had had was not love . . . He made himself consider carefully what it had been, forced some discovery of what his mind had been doing inside his romantically breathless body. This was very unpleasant: he could easily remember what he had wanted – a part of him jeered with words like lechery and pictures of very old men fumbling with shoulder straps – disgust, ridicule, the poor old creatures – he had not come to that – was nowhere near that age: a part of him justified, denied, made angrily reasonable explanations . . . good God, where was the harm in an experienced man being attracted to a pretty young girl? something wrong with him if he wasn't, surely – no *harm* had been done, he had been simply, acutely, susceptible to her charms . . . but by far the most frightening part of him simply repeated the feelings of the night before again; the desire, the intoxication, the panic, and the humiliated withdrawal into diffusion: this last part did not seem to have any opinions or views on the subject; given half a chance it just went through the same motions again as though to confirm that they had been real. The effect of this, physically, was of a deep, internal blush which he had then to endure for the third time before he started to gather up some rational shreds of dignity. The points were that he had been extremely stupid about his previous secretary; the thing had never for an instant been worth what everybody had paid for it. Alberta was not only his secretary, she was very very young, very innocent, and she had been discovered by Lillian, who had a bad heart, who seemed to have lost the mainspring of her life, who on top of that had already suffered a good deal from his infidelities, and deserved at the least his consideration: if he pretended to love anybody, it ought to be Lillian. If he seduced anyone, it should not be Alberta, for whom he had great liking, almost affection, and the feeling that she should be protected. The whole thing was out of the question on every possible count, and what was the point of being his age if one did not face up to and understand this? He remembered then Lillian sitting up in bed, with her enormous, glistening eyes saying: '*Don't* seduce her – anything else, but not that'; and then, immediately, the picture of Alberta sneezing, saying that excitement made her sneeze – saying, too, that she wanted in the end to give up excitement – no, first, she had said that she wanted to be excited by fewer things – he didn't understand the giving-up part of it, but it struck him now that she was damn well right about being excited over fewer things. He had to write a play because on the whole that seemed to be what he was for, and if he needed to replenish his spring for doing it he must find a way which didn't, so to speak, involve pouring alcohol down his throat. She is on good ground, young Alberta, he thought; she seems to stand in the middle of her territory – she may not have explored it yet, but she's in a better position on it than I am, and he had a sudden picture of himself standing just inside the railings of a municipal park with his back to the well-worn paths holding on to the bars and looking out. I will rest here, help her (meaning

Lillian) with her swimming, get some kind of map of this play in my mind, and keep an eye on Jimmy training her (meaning Alberta) for Clemency. And see to it that he doesn't upset her by making passes at her or any other irresponsible behaviour. I'm old enough to be her father, and I am responsible for her, after all. If I want excitement, I must get it out of the play. He felt his mind shift, strain a little at the familiar traces, and settle to this decision. 'I'm tired,' he thought; 'this holiday will be a good thing if I keep it calm and simple – we all need some fresh air.'

He opened his eyes – the ship was well away from Piraeus; there were new lands ahead and to the right. There was something lighthearted and dashing about their progress – they had seemed to him to leave Piraeus at full speed from a stand-still, and they tore along through the marvellous blue water at the same gay and purposeful pace. The sun was getting steadily hotter, and the air smelled sweet; a warm mountain smell, more feminine than the pure smell of sea. Was there no way of making one aim cover all pursuits? To be left less open to chance and casual requirements? That was what he needed; 'and you won't find it by thinking,' he said sternly to himself. One's thoughts were no better than oneself, and worse, they were no different. He watched the mountainous land – brown and grey rock with deep olive and prussian-blue shadows; smelled what might be thyme and verbena, and saw the colours of the sea invariably changing; heard the ship moving the water with a rich creaming hiss above the reassuring bloodbeat of her engines, and felt the hard dry caulked boarding of the deck with his hand. 'Coming to my senses; if I am any kind of artist, it's time I did that.' The senses can help to make a good climate for the heart. This made him suddenly remember writing with a kind of reckless ease when he had been very hungry, and the clutches of hard-boiled eggs that he had used to keep all over the place ... the sun! He put on his dark glasses and the day changed its mood for him: he was warm and thirsty and nearly asleep. ...

There was Alberta standing hesitantly before him.

'Mrs Joyce wondered whether you would like to come down and have a drink?'

He took off his glasses. 'Perhaps I should: I have been dreaming of hard-boiled eggs which is thirsty work.'

'I don't think they have those. They have things called *tiropetas*: hot cheesy things – thirstier than eggs, I should think. Mrs Joyce has had three, but poor Jimmy can't even watch her eat them – he's lying down. I really came up because Mrs Joyce is worrying about how to get him off the ship.'

'Can't he stand?'

'I don't know, but we don't walk *off* the ship on to the island. We are put into little boats, like a shipwreck, and rowed ashore, and Mrs Joyce is afraid they will throw him at a boat and miss; she does not feel calm about his prospects.'

He got to his feet. 'I'd better infuse some strength into him. When do we arrive?'

'I don't know exactly; poor Jimmy went and lay down first on some boxes stacked along the sides of the boat. They made him feel much worse, and then he found that they were full of chickens who were behaving exactly like his insides felt – lurching and fluttering about and uttering low squawks of misery. It is such a pity for him that he misses all this lovely travelling.'

'Is it lovely travelling? Are you enjoying it?'

'Immensely.' As they went down the ladder, she added: 'I'm so sorry to have woken you up – you looked rather tired.'

He was about to deny this – felt his mouth start to curl like an old sandwich with a wry, dry inner sneer – when he recollected the private collection he had just been making of himself, and ceasing to feel tired he said: 'I was tired: I am restored now.' It was much more comfortable to be in one's place, than to have someone – anyone – put one there.

2. ALBERTA

Hydra, Greece

My darling Papa,

Where shall I begin? Where I am, I think, and work backwards and forwards out of it. I'm sitting on a snow-white terrace with my back to a wall eating figs and every now and then looking round me at a scene of unimaginable beauty (unimagined by me at any rate). We are on the island, and the above address *is* a complete one, although you might not think so. We came in a gleaming white boat that was filled and packed and crammed with people and animals. We charged into the harbour and literally stopped on our haunches – in a way, Papa, that you would hardly approve – much worse than how people drive through our village, but I think Greek captains are better than English drivers. He stopped the boat with an anchor which rattled out like gunfire, and then we were collected in little boats – some with motors, some with oars – which they filled until they were practically swamped with old ladies in black and rather tragic-looking men and boxes and chickens and babies and us, suitcases, furniture, everything. The *moment* the last chicken was over the side the ship roared away at full speed. The harbour is small – and the place mountainous; it looks like one huge mountain with rocks right down to the water, and the houses are built a long way up its slope; they are nearly all dazzling white, and look as though someone had spilled a packet of lump sugar from the top of the mountain and most of it had rolled to the bottom. At first there seem to be no trees, but there are, dark spiky cypresses and dusty-looking olives. The harbour front is beautifully paved – I've found out in *pink* marble that comes from a nearby island – and there are wonderful stalls of figs and tomatoes and grapes and peppers, and wineshops and cafés and other shops with sponges hanging in bunches. There are no cars – only a rubbish cart – on the island because after the harbour it is all built in roughly paved steps, but there are donkeys and mules; they were all standing in a row near where we landed. They wear turquoise blue beads and so do children: this is to guard them from the Evil Eye – I don't know why donkeys and children should be so especially prone, but evidently they are. Perhaps grown-ups can take other precautions. We had to wait for a man called Aristophánes who knows all about houses: so we had drinks and olives and white cheese that takes the skin off your mouth if you let it, and very good bread. Aristophánes was rather disappointing when he came, rather fat and nearly bald, but I do see that it is a difficult name to live up to and he was extremely friendly and spoke a great deal of melodramatic English so at least I could understand what was going on, because we embarked upon hours and hours of talking, and waiting, and having various kinds of refreshment. To begin with Aristophánes said that we should at once have the house which we should discover quite perfect for everything we could wish; then he told us so much about it and everything that was happening on the whole island that after we had all had dozens of olives and pieces of bread and cheese and drink we were longing to go to see the house but then he said we must have lunch, as a key was necessary for the house and the key was uncertain. He kept sending little boys off on mysterious errands in Greek – and they always ran off at top speed and came walking back slowly. After lunch he suddenly started suggesting other houses which now he knew us he felt would more perfectly suit our needs – he went on and on about it until he persuaded Jimmy and Mr Joyce to go and look at a house and Mrs Joyce said what a pity he spoke English at all. We agreed that there was something odd in Aristophánes's change of heart about the house, but Mrs Joyce knows a painter who had just been staying in it, so she knew that it existed and was nice, and she said that if we sat there long enough with our luggage round us something would happen about it. We drank little cups of Turkish coffee and longed to bathe. The others didn't come back for hours : and afterwards they told us that the reason Aristophánes didn't want us to have the house was because he was living in it himself rent free, and he wouldn't take money to go : we had to rent another house for him to move into and then it was all right. In case this sounds shocking to you, Papa, I must explain that Aristophánes is an *Athenian* and doesn't live on this island at all. He broke his arm eighteen months ago, and he gets relief for incapacitation (that's what he said); anyhow Mr Joyce managed to get a house arranged for him and he became overjoyed again and rushed off to take his things out of ours. Then two little donkeys were absolutely *laden* with our luggage and we went, with Mrs Joyce on a third donkey. As soon as we left the port there were a great many narrow lanes built in steps for climbing. The houses are *beautifully* whitewashed; they dazzle in the sun ; they all have shutters which were closed and there were very few people about during our walk which was in the middle of the afternoon and the hottest walk I have ever been. The donkeys had a kind of delicate, leisurely stumble, and it seemed to take ages to get to our house, but it was so lovely when we got there that even Jimmy cheered up (he does not really like walking in the sun which is most unfortunate for him). Our house is adjoining a little church – everything snowy white: it has two terraces facing east and west. The western one looks over a small ravine – I think that is the right word – leading down to the sea. You can see the mainland quite clearly – just undulating masses of mountain softened by blue shadows – very beautiful and mysterious, and a sea planted with one or two islands in perfect positions. The other terrace has a well – it's the one I'm on now, and a much closer view so that you can see the colours of the rock of the opposite hill, and there is a small field, only it's not like our fields, with olive trees and one or two figs. There are cactus and sea plants, but I haven't explored them properly yet. I have a dark cool little room on the ground floor. It is a small house, one room for the Joyces, one for Jimmy, and one for me, and a sitting-room between the two terraces: the kitchen is in a separate place, and the privy which really is one is in another little hut.

Dear Papa, and how are *you*? I do hope Mary is proving some use with the Magazine, and that Lady G. is not upsetting Aunt T. too much over the Flower Show. I will go to a Greek church as soon as possible, and describe it carefully to you. I wish you were here, and the whole family. If only I was rich I would take you for a wonderful holiday – do you remember telling me the story every night after Mamma died about you and me going to India? Every night I could choose something to go into the story, and in the end we had so many elephants that when I chose a tiger, you had to make him tame to ride on an elephant to use one of them up. The extraordinary thing about travelling is that it *is* quite as wonderful as you made it – not the same, of course – but not disappointing.

It's very odd, Papa, but I never realized, until the other evening when I was talking with Mrs Joyce, how very difficult it must have been for you to keep up that story every night for so many weeks at the time that you did it. You were the most reliable man, and that was what was needed. Perhaps it is the first thing to be, and on the way to anything else? Anyhow, wherever I am, I love to think that you are somewhere, at least, and particularly when I am not at home. Please give my love to everybody, and tell Aunt T. that I will write to her soon. I've finished *Middlemarch*. *Villette* next: it's nice to have home books with me, and shall always remember that I read them here.

Your loving daughter, Sarah

I wrote a long letter to Papa in the end – but I couldn't bring myself to tell him about them wanting me to play Clemency – I don't know why – perhaps because it looks as though we shall go straight back to New York, and that may make him sad – that I shall be away so long. But if we *do* go straight back, and I don't go home, won't it be just as sad, or will giving him more time to get used to my being away make it better? This is nonsense: I'm just afraid to tell him because I'm not sure he will approve of my becoming an actress in this manner. But then I may *not* become one at all, in which case it will save a lot of worry not to tell him now. Jimmy says that we are to have two days' holiday before we start work: I asked him whether I should learn my lines, and he said no. How do we work, I wonder? It is rather useless to go on asking questions in a diary, as who is to answer them? Perhaps I shall in the end, if I really want any answers. Jimmy is a much more interesting person than he appeared to be at first. An extraordinary childhood – not belonging to anybody – and then the tremendous luck of Mr Joyce sending for him to England. I must say it must be pleasant to be rich and famous if one can do things like that: it simply transformed Jimmy's life – almost too good to be true. Both of the Joyces are very kind to him and treat him as one of their family, which I expect is what he needs. He is illegitimate and does not know who his father is: I wonder whether he imagines that he was a duke or a magician or something notable like that. Oh dear. Papa once said that diaries were generally filled with idle speculations or idle introspection, and I begin to see why. One is poor company in them because one hardly ever objects to oneself: it is far worse than a doting mother with her children – there does not even seem to be a last straw.

Portrait of Jimmy. Medium height, very soft brown hair, hazel eyes (heavens, I'm not getting anywhere), a very nice, wide, curving mouth, and hair growing to a peak on his forehead. *Very* surprising and beautiful hands – each finger interesting. Can't remember his nose enough to describe it. Has an authoritative air some of the time, which seems to come out of standing a bit away from people as though he's just there to watch them. But in spite of that, and in spite of his appearance of toughness, there is something vulnerable about him : perhaps he is afraid of being caught up with people, and feels it is safer to watch. He moves about most neatly, with no wasted movements – like a cat, and he has a funny laugh – a sort of shout – as though he surprised himself doing it. He has an *extremely* kind heart, so that if he stops simply watching people, he becomes very protective about them. This is especially true of Mr Joyce : his voice becomes quite different when he talks about Mr J. – he tries to sound elaborately casual, but he isn't, at all. He believes in Mr Joyce, and that's that. I do hope Mr J. never does anything that upsets him – he would find it so hard to bear. I like him: he is very good when he is not enjoying himself, which, since we have arrived in this country, has been too much.

Evening. Principal animals on this island : donkeys, mules, goats, cats and dogs, and chickens. I do not think any of them have an enjoyable time by English standards, but perhaps, being Greek, they have a different conception of affection and security. The cats come off best, but that is just because they are superior and independent. Jimmy and I went down to the port to arrange about a jar of wine, and on our way we met a very small donkey tied to the third tree in a row. Nothing for him to eat or drink – nothing to do, and no one to talk to. He stood motionless with a slightly lowered head staring at nothing and looking as though that is what happens to him every night. I haven't met any mules yet. Goats look nice from a distance, but when you come face to face with them, they have an expression both cynical and coarse, as though they have just stopped smiling at something unpleasant. Dogs look miserable here – the people seem afraid of them, and they are often tied up. They lie with their heads on the ground, the children kick them and run away. Cats are mostly extremely thin, with large ears and elegant faces; there are all colours, but a lot of black ones. I can think of nothing either kind or revealing to say about chickens. No sign of a shark, but we have not bathed yet, as we have been too busy settling into the house, and the others all slept in the afternoon while I wrote to Papa. Mr Joyce has just asked me to come out on to the other terrace to watch the sunset.

Darling Uncle Vin,

Before I attempt any description of this place, I have to tell you something, and ask what you think about it. Don't laugh, Uncle Vin, but Mr Joyce and Jimmy Sullivan want me to try and act a girl called Clemency in Mr Joyce's last play (the one act you saw in London, which is not yet done in New York). I have agreed to try and learn to do it, and tomorrow we are to start working on it. They could not find anyone they wanted for the part in New York, and Mr Joyce says the girl in London is not right and has turned it into another kind of play from the one he meant. The idea is that we should spend a month or six weeks here as Mrs Joyce needed a holiday, and then go back to New York. The thing is, Uncle Vin, that I have not broached this matter with Papa, because I feel that he may not like it, and also it is likely that they may find I am no good, in which case I might as well not worry him at all. I telephoned him from New York to explain to him about coming here, and he was delighted about it. If only I could see and talk to him I would tell him at once, but I am not used to using letters for this purpose, and am afraid that I shall not know from his reply what he really feels. But I am not used, either, to deceiving him – it's becoming like a smudge on everything else I tell him. Of course if it is found that I can act I should love to do it, and Jimmy has explained that if the play is a success, I would be earning enough money to fly home and see him. What do you seriously think of my chances, as it is your profession after all, and you know me so well? And do you think I should tell Papa, or do you think it would be possible for you to go and see him and tell him about it, or find out what he feels? If Papa really hates the idea, I won't do it, although I shall mind enough to want to know the reason for his disapproval. Please write to me as soon as possible about this because it is worrying me.

Uncle Vin, I must begin by describing the bathing here, which exceeds anything I have ever read about. The water is sea green or sea blue, absolutely clear and warm; there are rocks right down to the water, so that one has to go straight in – I can't dive, but I don't mind plunging as it is so warm. We have masks to put over our faces and a tube for our mouths which sticks up in the air so that one can breathe while one is swimming face downwards. You can see the most marvellous things – fishes, and sponges growing to rocks, and anemones, and little octopus and seaweed of many kinds. The colours are far better than on land, or perhaps they are just new to me. The fish do not seem to mind one watching them at all; I found a great cloud of tiny silver ones hanging at all depths in the water like a sequin veil. The rock sometimes goes sheer into the sea, and it is extraordinary to see the sharp division of what grows on it above the water and what below. You do not have to be a good swimmer to do this, thank goodness we have two sets of masks, and take turns – the rest of the time one lies on burning rock. Mrs Joyce has an umbrella, and gave me a lot of sunburn lotion, but I don't think it has done much good, as I feel as though my shoulders are on fire. She can only bathe for a short time which is a pity as she is clearly the best swimmer of the lot of us. We spent the whole morning on this piece of shore – one can't call it a beach, thank goodness – and had a picnic lunch there. We are all beginning to like the wine, which is very odd indeed, but suits the climate. They also have the most delicious orangeade – slightly fizzy – in bottles, and Jimmy says very good beer. Then there is stuff called *ouzo*; it is transparent, but when you put it in a glass and pour water over it, it goes milky – like the stuff you drank in Paris, but I can't remember its name. I tell you all this, because I know you are interested in drinks. People drink in a quite different way, here – I mean they sit for ages at little tables with an enamel mug full of wine: they pour it into small glasses, and they talk a great deal. The foreigners all drink together, but with the Greeks it is only men. The women sit on chairs outside their houses or serve in the shops which never seem to shut, and the children run about, silently, like a crowd of birds. I mean they call and shout and chatter to one another, but the actual running is silent as they luckily do not have to wear shoes. I'm so sorry, Uncle Vin, but I shall have to stop, I am *so* sleepy, but I will write again soon and try to tell you better what it is like when I am less drunk with the newness and *so much* sun.

Your loving Sarah

This morning we started Clemency. It is a mysterious business. Mr Joyce and Jimmy were there. They made me sit on a chair and read one little bit two or three times very quietly, and then Jimmy told me what sort of place I was in while I was doing this bit and then he made me walk about while I was reading it which was much more difficult. Then he suddenly said: 'Make as much noise as you can.' I tried, but it felt all wrong, as the things Clemency says are all quiet ones in this bit, and I felt exceedingly foolish. Jimmy just said do it again and I tried – it was even worse. I said the words felt wrong for shouting, and Jimmy said nonsense the boy stood on the burning deck three blind mice one could say anything – just make a noise. Mr Joyce was staring at the ground and not saying anything. I took a deep breath and tried to shout three blind mice and it came out breathless and squeaky but was apparently no laughing matter to any of us. Then Jimmy said pretend you are a man shouting that, telling 500 other men about the mice. This was the odd thing. I did: and I had an entirely different voice – heavy and rather hoarse. Then Jimmy smiled at Mr Joyce, and Mr Joyce smiled at me, and Jimmy said, now, don't shout, just tell them about the mice, but be sure they hear. Then Mr Joyce said he'd leave us to it, and the rest of the time was spent on Jimmy making me feel my body while the noise was coming out. We didn't do any more Clemency. Jimmy said that we'd leave her for the moment, but that I would read some of her with Mr Joyce every day, and he and I would practise counting and breathing together. He is quite different when we are working – very business-like and rather stern, but by the end of the morning I understood that he was right to make this distinction, and that in the end (even of one morning) it made it easier to work if we behaved to-

gether as though that was all we did. At the end he said:
'Now, we won't discuss this when we aren't working – there's
nothing to say about it. Try during the rest of the day to be
aware of how you breathe; that is all you need to do.' Mrs
Joyce wants me to go and see if there are any letters as the
boat has come in.

3. LILLIAN

I was sitting on a rock at the edge of the sea with the sun
like a burning fan on my shoulders, and I looked alternately
up into the sky and down into the water for the origin of the
beautiful reflection one cast upon the other. It was a small
bay – almost a semicircle scooped out from the steep rocks –
and the others had swum out of sight round the coast: I sat
by myself. I had meant to sit or lie there until their return,
and was half-heartedly trying not to feel envious, but inside
I was poor Lillian putting a cheap brave face on her dis-
ability. I looked down again at the water that was only a few
inches below me – lucid, sinuous bulk that heaved and broke
its colour against the rock with something between a slap
and a stroke: patched in jewelled greens and blues and shot
with diamond fish who casually pursued their geometric
sense of direction. Looking, I knew that I had only done so
to make myself unhappy (really, Lillian, at your age!) and I
thought, 'If I wept now the tears would scald on the rock in
this heat.' Then, without thinking, I swung my legs over the
sea and waited before putting my right foot in the water; it
slipped in without seeming to break the surface and gleamed
whiter than my leg in the sun. The water was smooth and
softly cool after the burning rock: I stretched my foot in it,
and as I did this a forgotten, overwhelming sensation began.
It started with my foot: I began to feel its length and weight,
and the separations of my toes, the water on my skin and my
blood under it, and then, through the joint of my ankle this
discovery travelled slowly up my body until I reached the
palms of my hands pressed down on the rock each side of
me and the roots of my hair hot with sun. The difference be-

tween *seeing* my hand or my foot, and *knowing* them – feeling absolutely contained within all of my body at once, was marvellously new and clear, and for some unknown quantity of time I remained alive in this way, until my foot – idle and cold in it – turned my attention to the sea. Now it seemed so beautiful that I was freshly struck by its shades of light and mysterious melting depths – its irresistible movements, its enormous, effortless continuity ... I was still joyfully self-contained when I flung myself in to meet and join it.

I did not bathe for very long; but it seemed to me then that time was a secondary consideration which I had used to measure partial enjoyment, and now, in the sea, I did not need it. I was out of the water and drying in the sun before the others returned. Jimmy said: 'Lillian, you've been swimming!' and Em came and sat by me to say: 'You weren't in for too long?' and I felt my face relaxed and easy for smiling when I said that I'd had a perfect bathe.

I lost this feeling of my body: I don't know exactly when it went, but I was suddenly aware that it had gone, although now I could remember it, and everything I saw and heard continued to be affected – to be more sharply true. This is a place for sight. Now that we have been here long enough to establish some kind of routine, and I need not be concerned with the order of events, there seems to be even more chance of simply being here. In the morning, early, some of us go and swim – usually then I stay behind on the terrace where the sun has come up over the little nearby hill, and the colours on the rock are soft, and fresh and delicate – cinnamon, tawny, agate, crystalline – with grey-green cactus, signal cypress, and the pure white houses, and the pale blue of the sky glows with morning sunlight. To the left is the sea – a denser blue mark and, at this distance, still; and to the right, the warm and savage shoulder of mountain, already stripped of mist and naked to its bones for the sun. I look down at the tops of the olive trees in the little field below our terrace; the leaves are like moonshine, oblique, almost apologetic in this young light. The others come back, and Jimmy lights the Primus to boil water for our coffee which we drink black. The island butter is rancid – we eat the bread with honey and melons. Jimmy works with Alberta, and often I persuade Em to walk into the port with me. We buy food for lunch, and beautiful sponges and silk made in the monastery at the top of the mountain. We collect letters and drink more coffee or orange juice at one of the cafés and watch the people and the caiques unloading vegetables and the butcher bringing back scrawny and dripping haunches of goat from the *abattoir* at one end of the harbour. Em makes me ride home and I acquire a favourite donkey. It is very peaceful; we do not talk much except about what we need to buy or to point out people to each other. Sometimes we meet Aristophánes and then we are chocked full of island gossip and incident. The very old lady who walks slowly up and down in a pale pink coat and skirt and pink high-heeled shoes – bought, Em feels, to match the marble – owns the richest house; it is floodlit at night and she is always trying to fill it with important people, only hampered by continuous and haunting uncertainty as to who they are. Once she turned a man out of her house because his clothes were poor and he was very dirty: he proved to be a painter with an international reputation, and ever since then she has courted the dirtiest and poorest men she could find, with – Aristophánes tells us, contorted with glee – the most murderous results. He would talk to us until the boat came in with fresh hordes of travellers and tourists whom he could waylay with instructions and gossip, but Em gets restive and wants to go back to the house. There are two ways back. One, climbing up through the village, steps and narrow paths and houses all the way; or, round the coast, a switchback path edging the island for the short distance between the port and our village. The first is all whites and stones and shadows on white – enclosed, angled, domestic, made and built and used: the second is wilder, emptier – rock and sea coloured, with few houses, with the air like the clearest honey, and the rocks declining steeply into the water – flowers and sea-birds, and that curious breathless calm that on a fine day lies over the brink of land and sea, but this is

218

the longer way, and we use it more in the evening. We get back to find Jimmy walking up and down the western terrace, smoking, with his worried, professional expression, and Alberta nowhere to be seen. I think he reduces her to tears, poor girl. Em asks how it has gone, and Jimmy shrugs and looks black. Em's tic round his eyes begins, and for a moment there are echoes of the organized tensions that I associated with empty half-lit theatres and hotel bedrooms late at night, but here, suddenly confident and detached, I can say something which disperses them; Jimmy smiles and Em smooths his face with his hand and we all set about preparing for our picnic in the charming bay which we have come to look on as ours. Alberta appears; in shorts and an Aertex shirt she looks about fifteen, and I feel that it is hard that Jimmy should have been making her cry. She looks solemn and subdued; I feel protective and take her to pack the figs and tomatoes and melon and eggs and cheese and bread and wine for lunch.

We go slowly down to the bay. The path is steep and rough, and by now it is very hot – the mainland quivers over the glistening sea – the engines of the daily boat – like a crescendo of heat – can be heard even before she can be seen: it is delicious to feel sweat pricking out all over my skin with the sea so near. The last bit has no path – we simply scramble down with stones rattling ahead of us; they sound shrill and pretentious beside the huge boulders, and some of them even fall into the gentle water waving at our feet. The rocks are so hot that one can hardly walk on them. Jimmy slings our wine bottle into the sea and we float melons in a pool we have made. Jimmy and Alberta swim off with the goggles: Em stays and smokes with me. He is browning more easily than any of us; has never bothered with oil or sunburn, but he still looks tired. I wonder about his new play – whether it is worrying him; but somehow, here, I have learned not to ask about it. We watch the other two until they have swum out of sight round the coast: then, on the third morning, I said: 'Wouldn't you like to join the young? Because I am quite happy in the sun until I have my bathe,' and he said: 'No, no; they're better as they are: I haven't their capacity for swimming – started far too late in life.' After a moment he said: 'Did you notice at what point in your life you began referring to the young?'

'No.'

He said: 'For quite a long time during middle age, the young simply seem to be getting younger – and then there suddenly comes a day when you look at them and see that really they're at least thirty-five and still much younger than you, and then you see what that makes you.'

'Darling, how *morose*. Jimmy's not so very young, he always seems to be one of us. It's the girl who is.'

He heaved a sigh and looked mournfully at me. I said: 'After all, *I'm* younger than you, and you count me as the same age.'

'When really I am an exceptionally old man?'

'Not *old*. Late middle-aged.'

'Late middle-aged,' he repeated: 'how perfectly beastly.'

'Very wise and experienced, of course. And attractive, and successful.'

'Distinguished is the word.' He said it with such distaste that it made me laugh. We lay in silence: I was soaking up sun, and not thinking about anything we'd said, but when I got up to bathe, I saw that he was staring into some distance beyond the rock a few feet away.

'What is it?'

'I was just wondering what the hell I'd *done* with all my time.'

I was sitting with my foot poised above the green bewitching water with the memory of when I had first done this fresh in me. I smiled consolingly – I still felt detached and protective. Poor Em – worrying away in this beautiful place. 'Never mind, darling – you've got lots more time.' And seeing his face, I added: 'Well, at least you've got time to do one splendid thing. What more could you want?'

'What more indeed?' He had turned so that I could not see his face because of the sun. Just then, the others returned, and I wanted to try the goggles. Em made Jimmy go with me as it made him nervous if I was alone and he swam like an old-fashioned frog, he said, which was quite true. Jimmy took me to see a charming fish who lived in a particular crack in the rock with his head sticking out to watch everything that was going on; then I saw a sponge and he tried to dive for it, but it was too far down: then we found a ledge in the cliff large enough to rest on and we sat and talked. Jimmy adores looking under water – I've never known him so enthusiastic about anything. He wants to try with an aqualung and talks earnestly about the possibilities of learning until he suddenly remembers, and turns impulsively to me.

'It's too bad you can't do that when you'd love it so.'

'I don't even want to, Jimmy. I did want to bathe, and that is being so lovely that I am quite content.'

'You look it. You look marvellous. Do you know, you've been looking lately like you were when I first knew you?'

'Have I? Was that a good way to look?'

'It was. You feel good as well, don't you?'

I nearly told him then about my foot in the water, but something warned me to keep that to myself. Instead, I said: 'I feel like a battery being recharged – more and more energy every day.'

'That's fine.'

'The only thing is I don't know what to do with it.'

'Do with it? Why enjoy yourself, I guess.'

'But I *am* – and it's simply making more energy.'

'Well, that's fine.'

'No, Jimmy, you don't understand. If I could write plays, I could write one now. If I was an actress, I could act. If I was a politician I could fight an election, if I was Alberta's age I could fall in love. At the moment I could do so much of anything that I was. The only difficulty is that I don't think I'm anything – in that sense. There's no need here to do more than exist – like a plant or a fish.'

He didn't say anything for a moment but I knew from his face he was thinking. Eventually, he said slowly: 'It's how I think of you, Lillian – not doing anything particular, but just being someone. It's like casting a play and that's the role I see you in. Of course you have to be right – you can't just be *anyone*, but if you were right you could just be Lillian.'

'Is that what you feel women are *for*?' I was teasing him and he didn't like it, as he said: 'I don't know. I don't express myself very well – that's clearer to me every morning. Come on, let's go back and eat.'

We wetted our masks before putting them on, and as we did it, I realized that usually I would have asked him what he meant, but that I seemed to have lost some of my aimless curiosity; wondered why, and almost laughed. We smiled at each other before setting off and I patted his shoulder. When we got back I found Em gay and peaceful – he and Alberta had unpacked the lunch and were drinking wine. We talked about English picnics, and Em said they were nothing but sand and gooseflesh, and Alberta suddenly said that all her best picnics had been far too hot – and Em said surely not too hot – in *Dorset*? And she said yes, because they'd had them in the boiler house that worked the central heating for the church.

'It was a very old boiler and used too much fuel to be run all the winter, but when it was on, everything steamed with heat and Papa said it was injurious to the church and to people, so whenever it was on we had picnics in the boiler house in order to make the most of it. The fumes were awful, they made Serena cough and none of us wanted to eat much, but Clem said it provided us with a touch of evil so we all did it.'

'Why, were you forbidden to go there?'

'Not exactly, but soon after Clem had asked about it, Papa put "Strictly out of Bounds – Private – Dangerous" on the door in red ink and that made it worth while.'

I knew by his questions that Em was amused, and I remembered how he used to question me, wanting endless details about my childhood, and how much more vivid and desirable a great deal of my youth had seemed when I talked to him about it. I had always thought of his asking about it because he was interested in me, now it occurred to me that he had simply been fascinated by an age of life that he had missed.

'Surely, Em, you're not going to have a lot of children in your next play?'

'It had not occurred to me. Why?' He looked both startled and reserved.

'I thought you were collecting data.' Nobody said anything so I went on: 'They're always ghastly – awful mincing little creatures – not children at all although everybody pretends they are.'

'Well, I promise not to put one in any play,' he said, and lay back with his eyes shut.

Alberta and Jimmy began packing up lunch, and I wondered why I spend so much time talking and thinking about things I disliked, and whether I did this more than other people and whether they had always noticed it.

We climb very slowly back to our house – Jimmy and Em ahead with our baskets, and Alberta with me. Half-way up the rock I come upon a few cyclamen growing out of a crevice. They are pale pink, about four inches high, and the flowers are prefectly to scale with their height. I show them to Alberta, who kneels beside them with a cry of delight.

'They are wild,' I say; 'wild cyclamen.'

We both look at them: they are calm and delicate and sweet, and they make me smile with pleasure at finding them, but when I look at Alberta, her eyes have filled with tears. She touches one flower as though it is precious or imaginary, and says: 'I had always thought of them as tremendously looked after, in pots and greenhouses . . .' and I remember feeling just as she is now when I first found some gentians; the same joy at my miraculous discovery of something that has always been there to be found – that's half the miracle – but I do not tell her this because these are her cyclamen. Instead, I ask her whether she wants to pick them? She says no, she doesn't want to, and I remember that I picked my gentians and they wilted before I got them home.

On the coast path we pass a young man – he wears faded cotton trousers and a torn cotton shirt and he is carrying a stick with a string of tiny birds slung to it and a long, thin, archaic-looking gun. We greet him as we have learned to do; he replies, and there are the two shades of our being women, but foreigners, in his voice. I say: 'I don't think I should like being a woman here,' and Alberta thinks that although it would be different, it would be quite all right. I tell her what Aristophánes has told us – about the women having to provide the house and all its contents for the marriage, which meant that if a man had too many daughters, the younger ones would have little chance of marrying until they were about forty if at all. The man had only to bring his virility to the match, and he was hardly dependent upon his father for that. Alberta says, well, in a way he was, and we agree that Greek fathers had to be strong in every sense. And after all, she points out, the moment the man had married, he had to start providing for his daughters – so it came to much the same thing in the end. I wonder what the little birds were, and she says they are quail. We plan to search for them in a port restaurant that evening. 'How did you know they were quail? Do you know about birds?'

'No. A little boy told me. He speaks English and Greek and I met him in the Post Office.'

'What is he like?'

'A prodigy,' she answered seriously. 'He said he would take me for a short adventure if I liked, if I would discuss some interesting subject with him while we were on it.'

'What does he consider interesting?'

'He said he would give me a list of topics when we went and I would choose from it. He is compiling it today.'

We have passed the place where I have rested before – our house is in sight. . . .

Afternoon . . . I lie alone on the hard bed with all the shutters closed excepting those on the small shady window behind my head: from it there come occasional movements of air smelling of hot fig leaves. The room is very bare and simple; there are curious pieces of stone and rock lying on the window ledges and the chest of drawers to hold down the linen mats which are the only concession to essential detail. Somebody must have collected them, having once found them curious? beautiful? and then perhaps bought the mats to provide a use for their collection. I lie on a sheet – it is too hot for covering of any kind – I am like a larger stone on more linen; my limbs are heavy with sun and exercise – sinking into a rock-like immobility of sleep I am not even a plant or a fish. Fragments of what Jimmy said circle lazily in my mind looking for the roost of my conclusions about them. Looking as I used to look – my energy – my just being Lillian – what did that mean? I try to remember being her, and suddenly, the one time is quite easy because I had been so intensely aware of it then. . . .

I was twenty-four; it was December, and I was staying with my uncle and aunt in Norfolk – supposedly for Christmas, but really no term had been set for my visit because nobody knew what to do with me. My parents had left me enough money to provide me with an education as protracted as it was useless; my aunt had eventually presented me, and I had spent a long hectic summer eating cold salmon and strawberries to the seasonal accompaniment of horses, boats, tennis-balls, dance-bands, and fresh-faced young men who had just changed their size in collars and whose conversation would have read very like an engagement book with a narrow column for remarks. Although nothing was actually said about it there was a tacit admission between my aunt and myself that my season had not been a success. It was known, for instance, that I had been dubbed delicate and brainy, and my only conquest had been an extremely dissolute old peer called Sandlewood who had pinched my thigh most painfully and asked me to go to Majorca with him.

In Norfolk, my cousins shot duck and geese and hunted, whilst I, debarred from these pursuits by ill health and indifference, went for sodden, solitary walks, wondering sometimes, with a kind of numb hysteria, what was to become of me. I had one secret from everyone: I had met the playwright Emmanuel Joyce – twice: once at a party, and once when he had taken me out to lunch and then to Kew Gardens for the afternoon. On both occasions I had been dazzled – aware that I had never met anyone like him, and that there was a different taste to both these times from any that I had had with anyone else. At the end of the afternoon at Kew he had taken me back to the house in Lowndes Square where I had been staying, and said that he hoped to see me again, soon, and gone. Months later, I plodded across frozen ploughed fields remembering Kew at the height of the summer – recalling what he had said and how he had looked when he had said it – wondering whether I had said too much or too little (curiously, I could remember none of my replies to his questions and confidences), for I had heard no more of him and no longer expected to do so. But unwittingly he had opened the world a little to me by showing me something beyond the familiar element that I knew – like being shown the sea for the first time: one is conscious of the end of land and the beginning, but not the end of something new. He had represented change, creation, experience, and freedom to me, and I knew that if I never saw him again, this would still be true: so I hoarded these two meetings as my secret treasure, to be recaptured and examined again and again in private. I lived on this and on Matthew Arnold whose poetry touched some melancholy yearning spring in me. The rest of the time I drifted in the domestic, communal vacuum; large regular meals, violent exercise, amusements made up of repetition, and some play on any particular character's idiosyncrasy of the 'Keep still, Sally, there's a spider on you' variety; round games, dancing to the gramophone, everybody changing their clothes, getting bathed and fed, having fun, doing things all together every day, every evening ... until this particular evening when the telephone rang as usual at half past six, and as usual Sally leapt to her feet, tripped over the setter Moll, and dashed away. Sally was in love and spent twenty minutes on the telephone talking to her young man every evening except at week-ends when he came down. But she returned round eyed with curiosity and amazement. 'It's a personal call from *Stockholm* for *Lillian*' – as though she didn't know which surprised her most, and an extraordinary feeling – like an electric shock – ran through me. It must be he, but of course it could not be – nobody else I knew could possibly be in Stockholm; but he did not even know my address in the country. I reached the telephone room and shut the door carefully behind me. If it was he I was right, I had known it was the moment Sally came back; if it was someone else of course I was right, he could never have traced my telephone number – would not want to, had forgotten me.

'Lillian?' he said: his voice was faint, but perfectly clear.

'This is Lillian.'

'This is Emmanuel Joyce. Let me hear you – say good evening to me.'

'Good evening.'

'Thank God. I've been thinking so much about you – I haven't been able to get you out of my mind. How are you? You are not ill, are you?'

'No. Are you really in Stockholm?'

'Only just. I'm catching a plane back tonight. Before I catch it I must know one thing about you.' He paused, and afraid that the line would go dead, I said: 'What thing? What do you want to know?'

There was another pause, and then his voice, still faint, and very deliberate, said: 'Do you think you could possibly marry me?'

Then I heard my own voice simply asking: 'When?' and heard him give a delighted laugh.

'Oh – I *was* right to ask you like this. As soon as anyone will allow us. I'll be back tomorrow. Are you wearing something blue?'

'Yes.'

'I thought you were. Lillian!'

'Yes?'

'I'm forty-one. Is that all right?'

'It's quite all right.'

'Not much background, I warn you – it's all foreground with me.'

'I've got no foreground at all.'

'We can share in that case. Would you like a sapphire?'

'What for?'

'To bind you to me, of course.'

'Yes – yes I would like one.'

'Dark or light?'

'Not dark or light.'

'Not dark or light,' he repeated as though that pleased him.

'Where are we going to live?'

'We are going to live with each other.' (I remembered how simple and charming that sounded then.)

We made a plan about meeting; then he said: 'Lillian! Do I have to get anyone's permission to marry you?'

'I'm twenty-four: I'll just tell them. I'm sure they'll be pleased.'

'I shouldn't count on that.'

I said: 'It doesn't matter.'

'Say good night to me now – I've got to go.'

'Good night, Emmanuel.'

There was a pause, and then his voice – faint and gentle.

'Good night, darling Lillian.'

Then he had gone; I put the receiver down, and walked slowly back to the family and told them. We were both right. They were far from pleased: dumbfounded, incredulous, horrified, suspicious, angry, and embarrassed. But they couldn't stop me, and nothing they said mattered in the least. This was when I felt who I was: felt distinct, direct, without choice, calm, and able to do exactly what was needed. Everything they said – and they all said a great deal – simply uncovered more of my own purpose to me, without changing it. I found no need to argue with them; that they did not frighten or divide me, nor make me unhappy or angry. For once I felt something steady, like a firm seed, growing in me – reaching the extremities of my eyes and fingers, so that I saw what a suspended creature patched up of imagination and invention I had always been – the whole of my life until this moment (I was packing my clothes with an economy of neat movement that made even this part of it enjoyable). For once, then, I neither planned nor imagined what marrying Em would be like: I packed all my clothes and dined and slept, breakfasted, said good-bye to the family, and caught the train to London, and all the time I was contained in the movement of each minute. I remember feeling almost physically as though my life had suddenly turned towards the sun, and perhaps there is some connexion between then and how I am now – so many years later, on this hard bed with the sun striking me on this island of Greece.

But if it is just that there may be some connexion, what is it, and what is different between now and then? Surely it is not simply the years? Only the energy is recognizable all this time apart; then there seemed to be so much to do with it, and now? What place is there for my generosity, or target for sacrifice, or time for my patience, or – with Sarah gone – person for loving? If I continue as I am, I must find this out or I shall be wrecked and energy will explode in rockets of distress ... All this makes me unbearably sleepy and sleep now is like a kind of holding my breath in my heart – I can wake, so to speak, where I left off: and so I sleep.

4. JIMMY

THE first time I noticed that something was wrong was in the middle of the night two days after we arrived on the island. There are two small bedrooms at the top of this house we've taken; Emmanuel has one – ostensibly for writing, but he's taken to sleeping there – and I have the other. We all go to bed late, as the evenings are cooler for walking about, and most of us rest in the afternoons. We'd had a good evening; gone down to the port and eaten at one of the restaurants. The food is lousy, but what travel bureaux call atmosphere – and I don't know what else to call it – is gay; and the brandy although it tastes cheap actually is. There was a young girl playing an accordion; it's a queer instrument for a girl, but she played it very well, and what looked like all her family stood around and shouted and sang and she never said anything back – just smiled and smiled. Well – we walked home along a path overlooking the sea; the fishing-boats were out with flare lights to attract the fish and the moon was coming up, shining, someone said, like pewter on the sea; I remembered this because it bothered me, I couldn't think what pewter was. Then Lillian said: 'When we have our house, darling, we'll have pewter in the dining-room – it is so much more beautiful than silver.' Alberta asked what kind of house, and where were they going to have it, and Lillian said, England; in the country, but they didn't know where, and Alberta must help to find it, but, oh no, she would be in New York, wouldn't she – for years and years if the play ran? And Emmanuel said just nothing at all.

When we got back I went straight up and feeling I shouldn't sleep until I heard Emmanuel quiet in his room next to mine, I lay on my bed and smoked. I heard him come up after saying good night to Lillian, and waited for him to settle down, but he didn't. It wasn't that he made much noise, or even that I could hear everything (the wall was thin but not that thin); it was just that a strong feeling of restlessness seeped through it to me and made me anxious. I wanted to go into his room, but didn't feel that he'd like that. I lay there arguing that he'd come in to me if he wanted to talk, but he didn't come, and I knew he wasn't asleep and I couldn't sleep either. It was his play, I thought, gnawing at his vitals, and it was then that I realized that I got a kind of vicarious excitement out of Emmanuel starting a play, and didn't like that somehow.

It must have been much later – I realized I'd been dozing – when I came to because I heard his door open and his steps on the creaking stairs. Then another door opened, and then silence. Surely he hadn't woken Lillian? She was sleeping so well these nights that I didn't think he would, and knew I didn't want him to; after all, what was I for? But when, minutes later, I got out of bed and went to my window overlooking the sea terrace, I saw him sitting on the parapet with his knees drawn up and his head on them – he wasn't looking at the moon on the sea. I went down.

When he heard me, he raised his head and made a motion of silence with his hand towards the window a few yards away: Lillian slept there.

'Is the play on your mind?'

'Which play?'

'The new one.'

He shook his head. We were whispering, which seemed to make us say less.

He made another motion, and we moved farther along the terrace away from Lillian's window. I offered him a cigarette, and he took it: I waited for him to say something, but he didn't. After a while (I was watching him, and he was looking at the sea) I said: 'This house in England. Is that Lillian's idea, or have you decided to settle down?'

He said: 'She wants the house to be in England.'

There was another pause, and then he broke out: 'Which part of one decides to settle down? That's what I should like to know, and what happens to the rest of one?'

'Lillian wants to do it?'

'*I* think it would be better for Lillian – for both of us.'

'Is that what is worrying you?'

He smiled, and it gave me a shock, because it made me notice his eyes – which didn't change – had still a kind of desperate hunger which was accentuated by the smile.

'You know, Jimmy, when I am anxious, anything that comes into my head attaches itself to my anxiety. I'm just Anxiety Inc. People always think that one has a good reason for feeling as one does if philosophy could find it out, and often one has no reason, or a damn bad one. Perhaps that is what philosophy is meant to find out, among other things. More and more I sympathize with Marlowe and his allegorical figures. I could wake up in the morning and say "I'm sloth today" and everything I touched would be affected by what I was.'

He stopped abruptly, but I felt his thoughts going on and

on. I was right about this because a minute later he said: 'If I had to describe the whole of life on this earth by marks on a piece of paper, I would make circles.'

'*Circles?*'

He looked at me almost impatiently: 'Yes. The serpent's tail in his mouth, the links of a chain, the sun – the paradox, the fitting connexion of one thing with another – the difficulty of understanding what is a beginning and what is an end – dimensions always seem to be scaled down in an attempt to conceal this difficulty, so it's almost impossible to see anything whole – even one's life.'

'Do you want to see that whole?'

He smiled again, and said gently: 'It might help, Jimmy, it might help.'

'Yeah, I see what you mean,' I said, after thinking about it. 'It would make a hell of a difference to what one did.'

'Or a difference to who one was?'

'I suppose so.' I wasn't with him there, and I had thought of something else. 'Look here – what about the girl?'

He drew deeply on his cigarette without replying, and then he gave a curious little start as though he'd only just heard what I'd said.

'She's going to be good, don't you think, Jimmy?'

'I don't know yet. What I do know is that it's no good her being the perfect Clemency inside, if I can't get it to come across, which it isn't doing now.'

'You don't expect that in two sessions. Give her time.'

'Of course I don't expect her to learn everything at once.' I heard the trace of anger in my voice – for some reason I was unaccountably nervous. 'What worries me is that she's unexpectedly self-conscious – and while she's like that she sets up a block and I can't get past it. I can't get her to understand why I want her to do what I want.'

He didn't say anything, so I went on: 'You've seen it: she blushes, and looks miserable, and tries again, and it's farther off the point than ever.'

'You've established the fact that she's got a big voice.'

'Yeah, I know, but she doesn't know how to use it. She'd

lose it in a week the way she is going at present. That's what
I've got to teach her. How to relax and keep herself balanced
so that she knows what she's doing and where it is coming
from.'

'Well? I don't disagree with you, but what am I supposed
to say?'

'Well, so I think it would be better if I had her to myself
for a bit. I think it's easier to outgrow this self-conscious
thing with one other person. Even two people make an
audience, and with you there she's worrying the whole time
about the sense of the part – the matter rather than the
manner.'

'I see.'

'Just for a bit – until I get her loosened up and with more
confidence.' Something was wrong about this conversation,
but so help me I didn't know what.

He threw his cigarette away, and smiled at me, but there
was something wrong with that, too. 'Well, Jimmy, if you
feel that it would make it easier for you to have her to yourself you must have her to yourself. We must all bear the
main point of the exercise in mind, after all. What else are
any of us for?'

'Speaking for myself, I have no idea.'

After a bit, he asked: 'Did she say that she didn't want
me there?'

'She hasn't said anything at all; it's my idea. Let me have
her for a week, and then come and see. She'll need you later
on. This isn't an easy way to do things after all – it's forcing
someone, like a hothouse plant. She'll need you when she
knows a little more how to say the lines; then she'll have to
understand why she says any of them.'

'I doubt it. I expect I shoot my bolt when I write a play;
the rest is up to the rest of you – producers and the like.'

'Look here,' I said desperately: 'I'm *not* the rest of them –
I'm on your side, to do things exactly as you want. If you
don't think it's a good idea for me to work on her alone, I
won't . . .' I was raising my voice, and he made a move for
silence.

After we'd both listened for a moment, he said: 'No –
you go ahead. You'd better get some sleep if you're going to
work in the morning.'

I felt dismissed, and like most people who have got their
own way in something, I was anxious to make an irrelevant
gesture. 'Sure you wouldn't like a hot drink or something, to
help you sleep?'

He smiled again. 'Hot milk, on a Greek island? Don't be
absurd Jimmy. You go up: I shan't be long.'

And that was that.

Well – I started the next morning working with Alberta
alone, and he went to the port with Lillian, who was delighted.

Alone with her on the same terrace where we had talked
about her in the night, I looked at her carefully – trying to
think of the best method. . . . She stood in front of me in a
cotton skirt and shirt with the sleeves rolled up: she had
bare feet. She looked tense and apprehensive, and when she
realized I was looking at her she shifted her weight from
one foot to another and looked at the ground – like a kid
about to recite a lesson she doesn't know. She had nice feet; I
hadn't noticed them before.

'Let's sit a while and talk.'

She smiled obediently and sat down: I wasn't getting anywhere.

'Look – what's the matter? When we work on this, you
get kind of frightened so I don't know what to do with you.'

She didn't answer at once; then said hesitantly: 'I don't
seem able to do anything you tell me to do. I just seem to
repeat the same failure again and again. I feel all the time
that I am being most trying, but I don't know how to
change.'

'Do you think perhaps you are taking it all too personally?'

She looked startled. 'How do you mean?'

'Well, what you do or don't do isn't done to please me.'

'But you are the person who's teaching me.'

'That's incidental. *What* am I trying to teach you?'

'To act this part in this play, I suppose.'

'That's it.'

'Yes, *but* – I don't understand all this part of the learning. I don't see what it is for. So I don't know how else to take it but personally – as you say.'

'What don't you understand?'

She looked at me thoughtfully, although she had gone rather pink, and there was a mixture of embarrassment and determination in her voice when she answered: 'You asked me just now what I thought you were trying to teach me. I said to act this part in this play. You agreed. Nothing has been said about turning me into an actress – supposing that to be possible.'

'I agree.'

'But what you are teaching me doesn't seem to have anything to do with Clemency. She doesn't go shouting about breathing deeply with a book on her head.'

She said all this deadpan enough to make me laugh.

'She wouldn't be very convincing if she crept about staring at the floor and muttering under her breath, would she?'

'I don't regard any of this as a laughing matter.'

'Right: well, we'll both try to take a serious, but not dedicated, point of view.'

We looked at each other in wary silence: she didn't know how to take me any more than I knew how to deal with her. Finally I said: 'Look: I know you aren't an actress, and perhaps you don't even want to be one, but you've agreed to try and act this part which, to prevent any further quibbling, is going to involve your doing a little acting. Right?'

She nodded.

'Right. From my point of view, as an actress, or as material, you've got a certain amount of equipment. My job is to teach you how to use it, so that it works as much as possible. You might say that you already know this, one way or another, and that it's your own business. It is, as far as you are concerned, while you are being Alberta, but when we come to Clemency – to you being anyone else, in fact – it's not the same. To be Clemency, you've got to act: acting is not life, it gives the impression of life – if you act well, it gives a very strong one. In this part – like all good parts – there are a certain amount of externals pre-arranged: you have to follow them. You have to say certain words, move at certain times, and part of you knows beforehand that this is going to happen. You also have to do this in such a way that apparently intimate words and movements are none the less carried out so that they can be heard and seen at a distance, while preserving their apparent intimacy and spontaneity. You can't start giving these impressions until the knowledge of exactly what you are doing has really sunk into you. I was starting with your body. Until you are aware of that – of your voice and how you move, nobody will be able to take in anything else about you on a stage – however right it is inside you.' I cleared my voice – it was quite a speech for me, and I hadn't known that I had so much to say. 'There are different schools of acting. But you're not a student with several years to learn all about it, and you're not at any of the schools – you've got a couple of months and me. It's urgent, and between us we've got to find the best way of your learning. You must trust me not to be personal or we shall get nowhere.' I stopped, and then said: 'How does that seem to you?'

'Much better: I do begin to understand what you mean. You mean that I probably do understand more at the moment with my mind, and the rest of me is a bit behindhand. Something like that?'

'For this particular work – yes.'

'And it's also a question of scale, I suppose. I mean it all has to be a bit larger than I realized?'

'Yes – but not at the expense of sharpness or depth.'

She was silent for a bit: she still looked nervous, but she was natural with me again. Then she said: 'Jimmy – I don't see why you think I'll be able to learn all I need to learn: it may be a disastrous gamble, and you will be angry and he will be disappointed . . .'

'Who's he? Emmanuel, do you mean?'

'Mr Joyce – yes.'

Something about the way in which she had said 'he' made

me watch her now, but she looked back steadily – her face calm. If she developed a crush on Emmanuel, I found myself thinking savagely – *my* relations with her can be as impersonal as hell – it won't make the slightest difference. I decided to narrow the chances any way I could.

'Don't worry about Emmanuel,' I said, 'he understands the situation. He's an old hand at gambling, which means he's prepared to lose out on a hunch, but also that his hunches are often good. He's got a new play on his mind, and the only thing to do then is to leave him alone as much as possible. The best thing we can do for him is to get Clemency into your blood. You've got what it takes all right – believe me – we've just got to get everything working. Let's start – yes?'

She smiled warmly at me. 'Yes: thank you, Jimmy.'

Then I made a fool of myself. 'Anyway – any time he has left over for social intercourse ought to be kept for Lillian. This holiday is largely for her benefit, and heaven knows it's long enough since she had him to herself.'

She started to speak – checked herself, and put her hands in her lap: the colour which had flooded into her face slowly went away again. Already angry with myself, I could not help asking: 'What were you going to say?'

She shook her head.

'Maybe I shouldn't have said that. It sounded disloyal – I was thinking of Lillian: what *were* you going to say?'

'Nothing that has anything to do with Clemency.'

'Forget it,' I said miserably; 'I'd do anything for Emmanuel – you know that.'

She looked at me then with such a kind of sweetness – she didn't say anything, but the cheap, nasty feeling I had just went – she got to her feet and simply said: 'How do we start?'

And that was *that*.

CHAPTER SIX

*

I. EMMANUEL

HE had taken to sleeping on the eastern terrace: it was far
enough from Lillian, and out of Jimmy's irritating, anxious
clutches. Jimmy had twice followed him down in the night
when he had tried to sleep in the room upstairs, and he
could not stand any more of it. He had to be alone; he had
himself become so crowded that he could not manage these
deputations of himself that he seemed forced to meet, if
there were other people there : excepting her.

They had been nearly three weeks on the island, and his
insomnia had settled to three or four hours' sleep from about
2 a.m. until the sun slid up from behind the hill gradually
gilding the early grey air : the gentle warmth was like a
waking caress on his skin – he could not sleep after it. Then
he got up and went down to the sea, pausing outside her
window, because once she had come too. He went to the
beach where they all went each morning for lunch : sometimes he forgot to bathe. A great deal of the time he thought
he was mad, and wondered with a kind of reckless irresponsibility what would happen to him next. He lived alternately
with her image and her presence: with the first he became a
starving rabble, all crying their separate hungers – with the
last he seemed to collect into some adoring, accepting unity.
Her presence was like air to him; essential at the time, but
of no avail as a mere memory; it was only on the rare occasions when he managed to be alone with her that he could
store something with which to bear her absence.

Any shreds of control that he still possessed – and perhaps
they were substantial shreds – were spent on concealing his
state from the others. This meant particularly being a
charming, accommodating companion to Lillian during the
first half of the morning, and leaving no outward expression
of his feelings in Jimmy's way. With her, surprisingly, he

found it easy to be 'natural' and passive. Alone, he beat off attacks of terror about the future – the frightful evening when some casual remark had introduced the idea of her being thousands of miles away in New York while he struggled with English country life – attacks of desire that occurred with such sudden force that they ruled out any consideration for anything or anyone else – and attacks of humiliating fear when he felt that if anyone knew of all this, they would simply find it unbearably funny and em-barrassing – when even she would laugh. His ability to reason, to analyse the situation with any degree of detach-ment, had vanished: the state of dogged calm which he had reached through his conclusions on the boat might have been reached by someone else, since they seemed to have made not the slightest difference. Alone, he counterattacked his fears with imagination, invention, and a kind of transla-tion of his memory; these three active ingredients easily idealized the future, transformed the present, and distorted the past. Thus he would declare himself to her, and she, he would reflect with amusement both cunning and tender, she would almost certainly blush and resort to language that she had gleaned from her papa's library ... she would be deeply sensible of the honour he did her – and she would turn those marvellously clear calm eyes upon him with her consent. ... Later he would confess that he was sixty-two, and ask her whether she minded. She did not mind at all – it was quite all right. (Anxiety in these scenes was like salt – only adding to their taste.) The week in New York with her became encrusted with dreams of moments ... her head on his shoulder in the taxi, his touching her hair, her smiling peacefully in her sleep. Her confusion when she realized all he had bought her in the store – his taking her hands and explaining to her that there was nothing unseemly in accept-ing anything if one was loved as he loved her. ... But there were moments, also, which needed no embellishment: her walking into the crowded room at the party and answering his public question – steadily denying his wisdom – he had loved her then, or he had loved something true in her which she had made suddenly recognizable. In the flat, when they had been talking about the play and he had pressed her for her opinion: she had given it and touched some spring in him – illumined some part of himself that he thought had died in his early days. ... The part of him that needed reasons for loving her was satisfied by the purer memories – by this steady core of truth in her – some inner unchanging beauty that he had not recognized in anyone before, and this was the only discovery he made through comparison; the rest of him seemed to forget or ignore any other experience. In the same way, in the scenes with which he decorated his solitude, only he and she were there – and occasionally an anonymous conglomerate crowd – but no single other person; even Lillian seemed not to exist. All this was when he was alone – chiefly the nights, the early mornings, and some of the hot afternoons.

But there were hours without her, spent with Lillian, and sometimes Jimmy, and these he found interminable. Then, all the words that he had read and heard applied to his state, were not, he discovered, merely elegant eighteenth-century turns of phrase, but painfully, bitterly apt. Love *was* a fever – it burned and consumed him as he tossed and ached through burning delirious nights: it was a snare, a trap, a gin – injuring and imprisoning those it caught; then, sick with an impatience like pain, he would endure the leisurely mornings with Lillian – the cup of coffee that he did not want and which was too hot to drink, the amble back beside Lillian's donkey. Once, she had a headache, and did not come out to dinner with them: he thought the evening would never end, and when, at last, they were back at the house, Lillian had looked in at her room and said that she was fast asleep, and the disappointment at not seeing her brought unexpected, confounding tears to his eyes.

Time seemed now to have a life of its own – double-edged, airy, and malignant. On the few occasions when he was alone with her, it was gathered together into a whole – like a jewel in his hand – each moment with her was a facet reflected in his shining content. When they were four, it flowed over him in a flowery inconsequent manner – neither here nor there so to speak; but when he was alone or without her, it assumed thunderous, sullen, immovable proportions: it hung like a stone round his neck; it was like an eternal black sea with no shore – his restlessness had no relation to it. He would sit in the afternoons at the wooden table in his room at the top of the house while the others slept. This was when he was supposed to be writing. Once, then, he wrote her a letter beginning 'My darling love', and when he had written even that part he wondered how many million letters had been started like that, and how many dozen truths were embedded in the tradition. In spite of his desire to write the letter, he wrote it slowly and painfully – each word of it seemed to be wrenched and wrung from his heart, but also, it seemed a strangely impersonal business. It was extraordinary, but the effort and effect of putting down exactly what he had intended, neither adding nor leaving out anything, somehow removed him from the enterprise: it was necessary that the letter could be to no one but her, but it did not matter who had written the letter – this was the measure of his praise. When it was finished, he read it very carefully to see that it was right, and then burned it. Afterwards he had a feeling that he knew from good writing-days – when he was empty and light with a kind of exhausted peace, until energy from the work done slowly refilled him. But all the other afternoons he did not write anything.

In the late afternoon, when the sun was still simply shining, but the shadows on the Peloponnese – like a giant kneeling on the mountains – had turned violet, he would go down to the western terrace, and often she would come out from her room at one end of it and join him. Sometimes she came only a few minutes before one of the others, sometimes not before them at all, and every day now he was trembling, praying that she would come first. But when she did come, and walked softly on her bare feet across the marble towards him, warm, honey-coloured, entirely unconscious of changing his world, all his tension, his parched breathless waiting and longing for her transformed to a joy like sunlight in his blood.

She would drop down beside him with a brief friendly smile, but unless he asked her a question, they were usually silent.

Sometimes he asked about the child – the prodigy – with whom she went for walks.

'How was Jules Verne today?'

'In a very calculating mood. He was estimating how long the world would last – but it is all done in millions and partly in Greek, so I find him difficult to follow on the subject.'

'Has he references for his calculations?'

'Oh yes, but he says he is a critical statistician, and therefore will take nothing for granted. He said it was a thousand pities that I was not better informed, as our duologue on the subject was unbalanced by my ignorance, and then we talked about other things.'

'What did you talk about next?'

'Fish, and marriage.'

'Has he proposed to you?'

'He had mentioned the matter, but he feels that I am far too old, and he does not approve of too great a discrepancy in age. He is only ten, you see; that makes nine years between us. He feels that looking after his animals – he is very zoophilic – and his children and cooking for him might prove too much for me by the time he is of an age to marry.'

'I see. And what about fish?'

'I was asking him if he had ever seen a shark here. He said yes, he had once, and that there were stories of people being eaten by them from time to time – about four people since the war, he said, which made it a distinguished, though horrible end.'

'And then what?'

'I told him about learning your play.'

'I should like to meet him.'

'I'm afraid it would be no good. He does not want to meet

you as he says that the Greeks wrote far the best plays and it might hurt your feelings if this fact were to emerge.'

That was one kind of conversation that they had. Occasionally, he asked her how she was getting on with Jimmy. Then she was always serious, even when she answered, as once she did: 'He says that I am improving. He has managed to get my head in the air and my feet on the ground, and he says that is something.'

'What does he mean by that?'

'Oh – I hung my head and muttered and shuffled about with my feet all the time whenever he wanted me to stand still.' She stretched out her foot on the parapet as she said this – flexed it, and let it lie. She had the most beautiful feet that he had ever seen – small, with neat round heels and articulate toes, and a pretty arch between them.

'You have Trilby feet,' he said aloud without thinking.

She looked up and smiled, and blushing a little, said: 'Do you think that Jimmy is Svengali then?'

'I don't know. How do you feel about it all? About Clemency, I mean?'

She didn't answer for a moment – she never answered idly, he noticed. 'You see, we've been concentrating on such beginnings that I've rather lost Clemency. Jimmy says this doesn't matter.'

'But it worries you?'

'Yes – it does, rather, I feel that I ought to be learning about her as well, but there doesn't seem to be time for it.'

'Would you like to read her with me again?'

'Very much.' She looked up with sudden gratitude, and her forehead cleared. He wanted to take her face in his hands and shower endearments upon it: he put his hands in his pockets, and said: 'Right: well, we'll do that tomorrow. Afternoon?' When the others were there, they drank *arezinata*, ate the luscious black olives, and watched the evening triumph. Watching the sun set was a long, beautiful sight. It sank with heroic brilliance – the sky a great map of its tumult: they had none of them ever seen sunsets like these. It turned the rocks the colour of a leopard's eyes – the

243

white houses tender, delicate pinks – the sea an inky blue but broken and furred with gold as the evening winds silently echoed over it.

They would sit until the nearby island bloomed mysteriously like a whale in the sea, and a pale crocus cluster of lights trembled from the Peloponnese; the vine against the house was black, and he could watch her face less secretly. Then, sometimes, he would cry a private supplication to some god; that it should stay like this – not perfect – she was not his, and she knew nothing of it, but simply that she should be always there. In the flushed calm of the hour, with the long evening before him – even his night alone seemed distant, anything beyond it a dream, and this seemed a possible prayer.

He did not suggest reading Clemency with her until she had had a clear two weeks with Jimmy. This was chiefly because, in some odd way, he was far more frightened of Jimmy discovering about him than he was of Lillian – who seemed safely wrapped up in her own enjoyment. But Jimmy had this streak – which until now he had been grateful for – of acute perception where he was concerned; of anticipating his wishes, of understanding his smallest requirements, of attending him through every kind of crisis. He did not want the precipitation of Jimmy knowing – his intimate blind eye, his almost aggressive loyalty. …. There was, in any case, a slight strain between them – very slight – hardly definable – but something to do with the night when Jimmy had followed him down on to the terrace, clearly expecting him to talk himself into the new play, and he hadn't, because he had had nothing to say about it. Then, quite suddenly, Jimmy had switched – to her, and in a few moments of professional reason, had taken his mornings away from him. He had felt then like a child who has had something most precious to it firmly and with maddening kindness put out of its reach. Only Jimmy hadn't even realized what he'd done – poor Jimmy – he was simply trying to do his best with a raw girl in a big acting part. It was absurd, after all these years, to blame Jimmy for doing his job properly. The prospect of reading the play with her sharpened the whole evening and softened the night, when he was actually able to invoke these kinder, more reasoned considerations. . . .

The next morning, Lillian remarked as they walked on to the port, was exactly like a Dufy. There was a stiff breeze; the sea was petrol blue and neatly choppy, the coloured caiques – painted pinks and scarlets and greens – were frolicking at their moorings, the sky overhead was crowded with small, hurrying, white clouds; canvas awnings over shops and cafés were flapping with unrhythmic gusto, and the dozen or so harbour cats were all behaving like theatrical gangsters or secret agents. Only the mules and donkeys stood with lowered heads and expressions of cynical calm, looking – as Lillian said – as though they were trying to hold their breath to recover from hiccoughs. They had now a routine for the morning's shopping. They bought all the food together – Lillian choosing, and he carrying the baskets: fruit, vegetables, Nescafé, rice, tinned meat, eggs, and cheese; then she went to buy cigarettes from the ex-sponge diver who had had the bends and was hopelessly crippled, and he went to the Post Office. He was not interested in the possibility of letters, but Lillian – in theory, at least – adored them, and he knew that *her* letters from Dorset were important to her. So he went every day with the bundle of their passports, and helped the internationally crabbed official with 'Young' and 'Joyce' (he clearly felt that one ought to stand for the other, and the other should not exist at all). This morning, there was a good haul: two letters for her – one from Dorset and one from London, a bulky letter for Lillian, two for him, and a packet from New York for Jimmy.

'Darling, what a lot! Anything for me?'

He handed her her letter, and she fell upon it.

'It's from Peg Ashley – I wrote and told her about this heavenly place. I haven't seen her for ten years, but I thought that if we were going to settle down it would be nice to take up with her again. I've asked her to look for a house for us.'

He did not reply – afraid that it might involve actually discussing the future. With one of his own letters in his hand he was looking at the packet for Jimmy which now lay face downwards on the table. On the back of it, in bold sprawling writing, was the name and address of the photographer to whom Jimmy had taken her for pictures in New York. He had an overwhelming desire to see the pictures: he looked at Lillian; she was engrossed in her letter which was a very long one – but the packet was addressed to Jimmy. He opend his own letter and looked at it: it was from Willi Friedmann, and quite short, but difficult to read. With his mind on the packet he skimmed through his letter. Matthias had had an accident of the hand – Friedmann was not thence going to buy the fiddle as it would not be useful – something about destiny (very Germanic, he thought impatiently) and machinery at school – the boy was in hospital – then an almost illegible paragraph about the boy's feelings which he did not read. Bad luck for the boy, he thought absently – and reached for the packet. Lillian was still reading – it would be hours before they were back at the house, and the thought of having to see the pictures with Jimmy suddenly nauseated him. He opened the packet. The pictures were in a folder, and pinned to it was a note from Stanley to Jimmy. 'Roughs – only. She's a natural, your girl: congratulations. Stan.' Trembling, on fire with wordless thoughts, he ripped open the folder, and there she was. There were eight pictures and they gave him another shock. He had not known that anyone else could see her with such clarity and understanding of what she was; he had thought his image a private one made by his love – it was the only sense of possession he had had about her. At the bottom of the set was a small replica of one plate with another note. 'For your pocket book'. Anger roared in him like a drum-roll: he felt when it stopped he would be forced to see something terrible, and clung to the anger, which at least blinded him. He put the small picture in his pocket, and gathered up his own two letters saying savagely to himself: 'Time I did some letters with my secretary.' He must get back to the house;

this desire repeated until it became almost a shout: he turned to Lillian. She was wearing a wide-brimmed red hat which particularly suited her complexion, and now she was bent over the photographs. . . .

'. . . well – *really* – he is the most astonishing photographer. I mean, she has a nice little face, but who would have thought that this could be made of it!'

He did not reply, but smiled absently at her and looked about for Spiro to pay for the coffee – must get back.

'Whenever you smile at me like that, I know that you aren't listening. Seriously – I should think that she'll get film offers if she's any good at all at acting and photographs like that; wouldn't Jimmy be furious if she accepted them!'

'Why should it make any difference to him?'

'My dear, his protégée! He's been one all his life, he's never *had* one. Haven't you noticed how it's changed him?'

'In what way?'

'He's growing up.' Lillian said it with a kind of satisfaction.

Walking up the hill through the village, he kept behind Lillian's donkey. The stone steps – seemingly so shallow, and cut with wide enough treads for the whole donkey to stand on one of them – this morning were endless: as soon as he got his breath on one level, there was another to be climbed. He had never needed to wear a hat, but now the sun was boring down into the back of his neck in painful, uneven pulses – like the electric current of toothache. Beyond these physical discomforts his mind hunted his worst fears; refusing to consider exactly what he would find, it nevertheless pursued some dangerous track started by those confidential scraps of writing which had not been addressed to him. With this there was the most frightful sense of unreality – the feeling that he did not, could not exist in circumstances which had seemed to descend on him from nowhere, without warning or consideration for what he had thought that he was, making him feel old, and irrelevant, and disassociated. The sky burned, the houses dazzled, the stones had no flesh on their bones under his feet: he was sixty-two, and his wife sat on a donkey ahead of him. She was nineteen on the cool terrace, and her future stretched illimitable, like the sea round her. The gap between wanting and giving widened with each step that he took, and each step was bringing him nearer the sun, inviting its violence. He walked – his heart like a sledge hammer – collecting panic, as ideas, facts, likelihoods, and comparisons reared up and sheered off in his mind, each one irrefutable, each not to be borne: he clung only to the shreds of his anger and the illusion that whatever he found could be changed.

When the house was in sight, Lillian called back to him and talked the rest of the way – some long reminiscences about something they had done together; he tried to listen, but it made him feel still more unreal. At the door of the house he gave her the wallet to pay for the donkey and told her to get the man to bring the food in: he wanted to find them alone.

Jimmy was alone on the terrace, stretched at full length on the parapet – she was nowhere to be seen. Jimmy heard the door opening and sat up and said 'hi!', he seemed half-asleep.

'Where is your pupil?' Trying to say it lightly made his voice tremble.

'Alberta? She's somewhere around. It got too hot and we called it a day. She said something about writing a letter and she couldn't do it in the sun,' he added.

The donkey man padded quietly across the terrace with their baskets: unreality began to ebb; he noticed that a plant on the terrace had suddenly flowered with one great scarlet trumpet. Then Lillian appeared and paid the man, who received the money in his customary manner made up of indifference almost bordering on compassion, and went, closing the terrace door behind him. It was all the same, and I am a little mad, he thought wearily; he had to sit down. Then Lillian said: 'Have you shown the photographs to Jimmy?'

Jimmy said lazily: 'What photographs?'

'The ones of Alberta that Stanley took.'

Jimmy swung his legs down off the parapet and said: 'Did Stan send them to *you*?'

He said: 'As a matter of fact he didn't, but I couldn't resist looking at them. I hope you don't mind?'

Jimmy did not answer; Lillian had gone into the house. As Emmanuel held out the packet, Jimmy burst out: 'I should think you've enough letters of your own without opening other people's!' He did not take the packet. Then he added: 'It's extraordinary that I shouldn't be expected to have any privacy at all.'

'Sorry, Jimmy. I didn't know you felt so strongly about it, or of course I wouldn't have opened them.'

But they had known each other too well for this kind of lie: Jimmy said: 'You know damn well that you never stopped to think what I might feel.' For the first time they looked at each other. Jimmy had never in his life been like this to him, and as their eyes met he saw Jimmy realizing this; a flicker of astonishment marked the resentment in Jimmy's eyes and disappeared as he turned to his anger again for support, saying: 'I suppose you think that because you pay for the pictures . . .'

'Oh, for God's sake, Jimmy, I think nothing of the kind. Idle curiosity – that's all.' Lying made him angrier. He slammed the packet down on to the parapet between them, and stood up: he could never relinquish the small picture now. He turned towards the house, and as he did so, she came out of it.

'Mrs Joyce said there were some letters for me. And she said that my photographs had arrived from America.'

'They have.' Jimmy did not turn his head, but she looked at him and said: 'Are you satisfied with them?'

'Ask Mr Joyce: I haven't looked.'

She looked inquiringly at both of them – sensed something – he felt her retreat, and quickly held out her letters. 'The pictures are very good. Jimmy is angry with me because I opened the packet and it was addressed to him.'

'Oh,' she flushed slightly: Jimmy still didn't turn round.

Then, in spite of himself, he said: 'Jimmy seems to think that pictures of you are his personal property, when really, if they belong to anybody, they belong to you.'

'They're nothing to do with *me*,' she said cheerfully: 'Surely they were taken for Clemency?'

Jimmy said suddenly: 'Has he opened *your* letters?'

'Of course not.'

'Of course not.'

She and he said this at once, and Jimmy echoed satirically: 'Of course not.'

There was the uncomfortable pause which occurs when lack of proportion becomes manifest; then she put her letters into the pocket of her cotton skirt, and said: 'Mrs Joyce has prepared the lunch. Shall we leave the pictures now, and go to bathe?'

It struck him, walking down to the beach with her, that Jimmy had not even realized clearly the cause of his own anger – that *she* had certainly no idea of it: it was almost possible after these two conclusions to imagine that he had been wrong – that Jimmy was sulking on general, harmless grounds. He took the opportunity to apologize again to Jimmy with more truth in his apology. It was accepted.

2. ALBERTA

Darling Uncle Vin,

You are quite right, and what Papa says about life consisting of ranges of molehills is true also: I had forgotten it, as usual, because sometimes one draws far too near a molehill. I will write to Papa forthwith : I am merely charging up energy in agreeing with and thanking you. As you say, the whole question turns on whether I am good enough. I realized suddenly, yesterday, that I am learning a good deal, which was cheering, as I had been in despair. But yesterday Mr Joyce read some of the play with me (I have been working with Jimmy, learning to walk and speak and stand still and listen) and I had thought that the part was getting farther and farther away, but after one false start I read it much more easily, and didn't get a sore throat or a thumping heart or feel breathless and unreal – *so* – perhaps I shall be suitable in the end. What you say about the salary is staggering, Uncle Vin. Do you think, if I bought him one, Papa would use a little car instead of his awful old bicycle? Or do you think that that would constitute an even greater danger? If you do, at least I could buy him an ageless mackintosh like you have and have some of the draughts in his study stopped up which he has always said would need a team of experts from London. Which do you think would be best for him? It seems extraordinary to think that I could ever earn enough to do anything so *old* with my money – but perhaps this is all some kind of dream – if you saw this island you would see what I mean. It's something to do with everything in my life having changed, except, in some way, me inside it. It should be 'I', I think. I must say that Charlotte Brontë did not write nearly such good English as Jane Austen. Oh, by the way, I quite understand what you say about telling Papa myself, and not hiding behind you – that this is the wrong way of telling things: I should have told you this earlier, or perhaps I don't need to at all, but you know what a hotbed of misunderstanding letters can be – literature has taught me that, at least.

I'm so sorry that you didn't get the part of the card-sharper in the film, what bad luck, it would have made a change – still, I expect it will be very peaceful being the Rev. Clamber in *The Unashamed*, and it will help you with the instalments on your *Mixmaster*, and your portable canoe.

I have got quite sunburned, although nothing like Mr Joyce or Jimmy, but at least I've passed the shrimp colours and don't burn any more and my swimming has improved immeasurably. Some photographs of me for the play that were taken in New York have arrived; they are very like me, but I don't think they can be much good, as they seemed to make everybody rather cross. I was hoping that they would be rather glamorous, but I daresay that that was not possible in my case (Jimmy said that the man was a first-class photographer). I will remember what you say about a hare's foot, but at the moment that seems a distant piece of equipment. Jimmy is extremely interesting about acting – both sensible and arresting, and it certainly won't be his fault if I am no good. I wish you could be in the play too. What a good idea, it does not smack of corruption as you are a much better actor than I shall ever be an actress.

Love from Sarah

I have written to Papa, and it was not difficult at all. Only – now that the envelope is lying beside me with his name and address on it – I wish that I was the letter and going there. It was never an address before – even when I went to Paris with Uncle Vin – it was here and home, and now I feel very far away. June is one of the best months at home: grass up to your knees, hedges high and strung with wild roses; buttercups like money in the fields; thick dew in the mornings, a smell of honey and heather on the heath and the bees seem to dance in the air. All the Junes I have ever known there seem to have become one time, so that I don't seem to have any particular age in my memories, and everything I remember seems always to have been happening. Picnics, adventures with the brothers, waiting up for a ghost, putting a hen in Aunt T.'s cupboard, trying to tame a toad; hot stilted afternoons with Lady Gorge's nieces, walking round her garden, asking names, saying what we had been given for Christmas and what we would do when we were grown up; the atmosphere of cautious competition, the marvellous tea, and our riotous escape to play what Lady Gorge described to Papa as a very rough and dirty game; reading to Serena in the apple tree – she always liked sad stories and cried nearly all the time; evening walks with Papa when somehow whatever we talked about touched me and touched something else, so that I remember most clearly the tone of his voice, the feeling that he was giving me something that it was worth my trying to understand, and the smoothing of the ripe grasses against my legs ... loving him, I love to remember the reasons for it. I've never thought of spending years of my life away from him, which perhaps I shall do – but it doesn't matter how far I am or for how long because I can always remember that he is there – steady and gentle and true. I've thought very carefully about those three words, and they are the best I can find to describe him. The other side of it not mattering – which may be a piece of grandiloquence due to this being my diary – is that I just wish that I was with him *now*. I just wish that.

Friday

One thing I am learning is the difference between family life and living with other people: the latter is a much more groundless affair, so that sometimes one has to seek reasons for it, and then they seem to be outside reasons like money and work and things to be done. Things are not always easy here, but I don't understand what makes the difficulties. I thought that perhaps either Jimmy or Mr Joyce had decided that I was unsuitable for Clemency and that the other one didn't agree. Reading the play with Mr J. made me think of this. Half-way through, Jimmy joined us – he didn't interrupt by saying anything but the kind of way that Mr J. had been listening stopped – like the lights going out – and I couldn't read properly any more. I tried, because I felt it was wrong for me to become hopeless the moment Jimmy arrived, but it was no use, and when I stopped I saw that Mr J. was staring at the ground looking very sad and Jimmy was staring at him, but he didn't look sad, he just had a kind of violence in his face.

Stopping, seeing their faces, I had an extraordinary feeling – almost a smell, like gunpowder after an explosion, only there hadn't been one: I thought that perhaps we were before it, and without knowing why, I said: 'What is to become of all this?'

They both looked at me then, and seeing that they were not startled and had no ignorance in their faces, I thought: 'They *know* that something is wrong, and they're aware of disaster, but they are not avoiding it or telling me', and I wanted to say that I would not do what they wanted, but I couldn't speak, so I left them. I left the house and went out, starting for the port: I had such a longing for home that without thinking I ran nearly all the way, but when I got to the Post Office, it was too late and shut. Then I saw Julius walking slowly along reading a huge book, and without looking up, he stopped and waited until I caught up with him. We both went and had an orange drink although we hadn't any money, but the man never minds when we pay, and Julius took an envelope out of his *Outline of History* and said: 'I was going to bring this up to you when you had finished your acting work' and it was a letter from Papa. We finished our drinks and went up the hill of the village where I knew that they wouldn't find me. Julius said: 'I wish to read today but I do not mind your silent company' and I felt exactly the same, so we went past the houses up a gully where there was a fig tree with enough shade for two people and I read the letter. I read it twice and the second time I could hardly see his beautiful clear writing. Julius looked up and said: 'I hope no member of your family has died?' and when I said no, he apologized most courteously, and said that it had not occurred to him that letters could otherwise distress people, and went on reading. It was not simply that I was so glad to hear from him: it was that I could understand so much from what he wrote. I knew then that he had known that I was concealing things, that he trusted me about the concealments, that he had even foreseen the difficulties and differences which would occur for me; he did not say any of this in outside words – simply made it plain that he had used his thought for me rightly – putting any of his concern into the future.

You will feel that you have many decisions in this different life that you are leading, but they are always fewer than they seem: it is a kind of obedience to God not to think or imagine yourself into action but to wait until what is true in yourself picks out the reality in your life from any false contrivance or scene of your invention. Very little external action is required – the energy and courage is meant for other uses. You know this, and I know that you know it, I am only wanting at this distance, to prune you of unnecessary anxieties such as any you or I might have for each other.

At the end of the letter, he had written out his full blessing to me.

There were no birds, no clouds, no movement of the shadow from the tree, but a yellow and black-and-white butterfly – the largest I have ever seen, was silently examining the figs on the lower branches of our shade: Julius was watching it too, and said: 'Do you think it remembers when it was a caterpillar? Would you like me to catch it for you?' I said no, because it had such a short life anyway, and he said that I shouldn't be too sure of that – supposing an hour for us was a year for a butterfly – and then he was off on one of his immense calculations in Greek. I felt so calm and happy about the letter that I was hungry, and asked him whether he liked figs, but he only said: 'I prefer condensed milk' and went on reading. So I picked some figs and a leaf to put them on and ate them very slowly and carefully, and then went to sleep.

When I went back it was about five o'clock. Mr Joyce was by himself on the terrace, sitting at a small table with paper in front of him, but he didn't seem to be writing anything. He looked up and said 'Alberta!' as though I'd been away for days, and I began to feel rather ashamed of having simply run away without saying anything in the morning. He asked me if I wanted anything to eat, and said that the others had gone for a long walk with donkeys; he didn't say anything about the morning. I got some bread and cheese and olives and we both had a glass of wine and he smoked and we didn't talk much, until he asked me whether I would do his letters with him which had been piling up slowly ever since we got here. It took him a long time to find the letters, as he had been opening them himself since we came to the island and they were all stuffed in various pockets of his clothes. In the end he said, well, we had quite enough to be going on with, and dictated in his rapid quiet dictating voice – I have got quite used to it, although I still find the people we have to write to extraordinary. Then, when I folded my notebook and stood up, he said: 'You aren't going to type indoors on such a beautiful evening surely?' so I brought my typewriter out on to the terrace, and after I had done some of the letters I looked up and he was smiling at me and said: 'Were you going to say this morning that you didn't want to play Clemency?' and I said yes: I didn't say any more, and after waiting a moment, he said: 'But I think you've changed your mind since then – haven't you?' I told him that I had decided not to come to any decision about it, but what did he think? Or Jimmy? He thought for a bit, and then said that he'd come to much the same decision as me – not to make one. He explained that there were many other factors besides getting Clemency right, and that he'd been considering our leaving Greece a little sooner than we had planned and all going to London before New York. Then he said that he felt I should have the opportunity of talking to my father and that Mrs Joyce wanted to make inquiries about buying a house in the country. I told him that I had written to Papa, although he would not have got the letter yet, but the prospect of going home before we went to America added to the feeling Papa's letter had given me. I looked out over the sea which was absolutely calm and the colours of a delphinium, and thought that I would bathe when I had finished the letters. Then Mr J. laughed and said did I think that there would be a pretty house in Dorset for him to buy? I said that I would write to Aunt Topsy and inquire, but he said no don't it was really no more than an idle thought. Then I finished the letters. Samples – to a lady who wished to call her champion Boxer puppy Emmanuel Joyce: another who wanted to spend three months with him telling him the story of her life in order that he should make a play of it. A club who wanted him to talk to them about Renaissance drama and poetry for two and a half hours with lantern slides 'and other expenses' provided. Two girls who wanted to be his secretary. A furious man who was collecting copies of a certain play of Mr J.'s and burning them as he went. He had got to 122 copies and wished to know how many more there were. Another lady who said he looked awfully like somebody she had met on a boat in the Red Sea once and was he? Then there were the ordinary business ones – asking for material, or asking for permission to act or reproduce scenes or bits of plays. Mr J. is tremendously patient and brief with the mad ones, but as he said nearly all his letters were variations on a negative theme. At the end he said he knew that these weren't all the letters, but he couldn't find any more, but would I make a note of Friedmann in my book, and if the letter didn't turn up, we would have to write to him.

I felt nervous of seeing Jimmy again, but he came back from his expedition in tremendous spirits, and so was Mrs Joyce. It was a very hot night, and we ate in the café belonging to our village and didn't go into the port. You go into the back of the café and look at huge black pots on charcoal stoves and choose what you will have. There isn't much choice and nearly everything is fried, but there is always marvellous fruit and I have got very attached to Turkish coffee. After we had sat for a long time, Jimmy suddenly asked me whether I would like to go bathing by moonlight, and not having bathed all day this seemed a delicious proposal. Mr J. said should he and Mrs J. come and watch us, and Mrs J. said, no, she was tired, and wanted to talk to him, so we all went back to the house, and then Jimmy and I went off with our bathing things. It was the kind of night when the moonlight was golden and the stars were like great shining drops: we walked down to the bay and settled on the piece of rock where we usually sit before bathing and Jimmy said: 'Let's talk for a bit before we bathe.'

We sat for what seemed a very long time and he didn't say anything. I nearly asked him if he had any particular subject in mind, but I had a feeling that he had something he wanted to say so I just waited. Eventually, he said: 'You're nineteen, aren't you?' and I said, yes. Then he said: 'I'm thirty-three: I've been thinking about it all afternoon.'

After a bit, he went on: 'I want to talk to you, but if you interrupt I'll get so thrown I won't be able to explain anything to you. O.K. you won't interrupt?'

I agreed, and folded my hands so that I could pinch myself if I forgot.

'About your career. I think that you could make it – could be a good Clemency and a success in New York. If you make a hit there it will lead to other things – you won't be a secretary any more. But you'll need help – you wouldn't find New York on your own with a big and tiring part that easy: not if you were all by yourself.'

'But I *shouldn't* be all by myself, surely?'

'Wait.' I wanted to apologize, but that would have meant further interruption, so I didn't.

'Lillian doesn't want to go to New York. And she doesn't want Emmanuel to go either. She wants to buy a house in England and settle down for a bit. She doesn't want him to go either,' he repeated: he was staring at me. I didn't speak until he said: 'Well? Have you thought of that?'

'No I haven't.' I began to feel alarmed at the prospect. 'I had not thought of trying to do new kind of work without all of you at all.'

'Well, it's probably time you did.'

Something in his voice irritated me, and I said: 'I haven't thought about it, because I didn't think that it was even decided that I should do the part. If I did, I suppose I thought that everything else would be the same.'

'You mean you thought that you'd still be his secretary? We'd still be a nice cosy little foursome?'

I asked him what was the *matter* – he sounded so odd.

He lit a cigarette with exaggerated care before he said: 'I find it difficult to talk to you because I never know what you understand. You floor me every time. Leave the foursome for the moment. It would have to come to an end anyway. Let's concentrate on you in New York. I rehearse the show – perhaps they come over for the opening, and then there you are in a run, with the rest of us maybe on a slow boat to China or some place. You may be there for *years*! You haven't any friends in New York – you don't know your way around – the work is killing – hotel life will get you down – you'll miss your family – awful old men will keep trying to take you up country for a week-end –'

'Jimmy, *don't*!' I was laughing, and then I saw that although he meant me to laugh, he was meaning some of it, and even part of that picture of me alone in New York for years was dismaying. I was just about to broach the question of Uncle Vin possibly having some part in the play, thus providing me with a friend and some family in one stroke, when he said: 'Now I'm coming to the important part – I mean the part I really want you to understand. The best solution seems to me for me to stay in New York with you right through the run. You see, I know how to take care of things for you all round. I know the city, I know theatre people, and I could see to it you have the right sort of time.' He paused, and looked at me expectantly.

'It is exceedingly kind of you. But what about Mr Joyce?'

'What about him?'

'I thought you were supposed always to be working for him – with him, I mean.'

'Yeah – but if you married me the situation would be different, and I might make a change.'

I stared at him. I wanted to say: 'If I *what*?' but felt it would be rude and I couldn't think of anything else to say. Then he said almost angrily: 'I *told* you I had some complicated things to say, and you have interrupted so much that I *have* got them in the wrong order. You don't understand. I'm making you a perfectly businesslike proposition. You need looking after, I know how to do it, and it would all be much simpler if we were married. I like you very much,' he added.

I wondered whether this sort of thing happened to a great many people, and what they did about it: it wasn't at all how I'd ever thought of people proposing to each other. He seemed serious – even nervous about it: it occurred to me that possibly he was just trying to be very kind, although it did seem to be carrying kindness a very long way.

'I don't want to marry somebody simply to make things more comfortable: I don't think that is what marriage is for, but it is extremely kind of you to suggest it.' I thought for a bit, but I couldn't think of anything to add.

He was silent for a while; then he said: 'I wish you'd think about it some more before you turn me down. I don't feel I've put it at all well: it's not just what I think about it all, but I've never met anyone like you before and I don't know how to put it – that sounds corny: it's honestly true.'

I said I would – indeed it would be very difficult not to think about it. He said: 'Well, we'd better forget it now, and bathe.'

We bathed; but I found myself unable to put what seemed such an extraordinary matter out of my mind, so that at one moment I found myself floating on my back facing the stars, in the warm dark water which at night seems to be scented more strongly of the sea, and thinking, 'Really Sarah, here you are bathing at night off an island in Greece, and your thoughts are much of the kind that they have been when you are pleating Papa's surplice on a rainy Saturday morning in Dorset.'

We came out and sat on our towels, and Jimmy had another cigarette. Before I had had much time to consider how to say it, I asked him how he would feel if some time after we had married one of us fell in love with somebody who we would rather have married. If we *were* married, of course. He said: 'I've thought of all that, naturally. I figured you'd have more opportunity to fall in love with me than with anyone else – if you were married to me, of course.' Then he added: 'A lot of phoney marriages happen because the people have the idea that they're wildly in love. Don't you think it might make sense to start with respect and affection – compatibility of interests and a few other things like that?'

When I said, but what about his falling in love with somebody else, the mere thought seemed to embarrass him as he went rather red and said I needn't worry about that – that wouldn't happen to him. We left it at that: it all seemed a bit cold-blooded to me, but to accuse somebody of cold-bloodedness is something which I feel should not be lightly done. He said he wished he'd brought some drink down with him, and we decided to go back.

When we were climbing the cliffs, which seemed much steeper in the moonlight, I said something about worrying about Mrs Joyce climbing them in the heat of the day, and he answered: 'Lillian is pretty good at knowing what she can do really. It would be more like life if Emmanuel cracked up over them. He's not so young as he was, you know. He's in his late sixties.'

'Is he really?' The thought surprised me so much that for a moment I didn't remember that of course he was sixty-one – it was on the potted autobiography sheet that sometimes got sent to people. So I said: 'I don't call sixty-one "late sixties",' and he didn't reply.

Just as we were reaching the house he put his hand on my arm and said: 'That was a terrible lie about Emmanuel's age. I don't know what made me tell it.'

I said it didn't matter and I expected he'd forgotten, but he went on holding my arm, and said no, he hadn't forgotten – he knew perfectly well, and I was the last person he wanted to lie to. He looked quite desperate so there didn't seem any point in telling him what Papa says about the least important part of lying being who you tell the lie to, so I didn't – I simply begged him not to worry. Now I've been back in my room, read Papa's letter again, and written all this – an enormous amount. Then I looked at other bits I've written, and I see that I haven't made a portrait of him.

Portrait of Mr Joyce. (This might be very interesting after we are all dead – a bit like planting trees.)

He is quite a small man with a sallow complexion and wiry thick hair which is dark except where it is a shining grey. He has a rather low forehead, but it is quite wide and he has surprisingly delicate eyebrows – they seem to indicate a line rather than be one. He has very dark brown eyes with heavy eyelids: the expressions in them always seem to be more than one at a time and often at variance. He has a jutting, but simple nose, and two lines run from the side of it down to his mouth, which is wide, with clearly cut complicated lips. He has magnificent ears – that sounds rather like an elephant, but they are – large and delicate. He has quite an ordinary chin – I mean it just seems to go with the rest of his face without being a feature on its own. He has veins and freckles on the backs of his hands, and thickish wrists and his shoulders are rather hunched. He has a gentle voice which very occasionally squeaks when he gets indignant:

he is also exceedingly good at imitating people – he just does it suddenly for a few seconds, but it is always startlingly accurate. He walks in a rather jerky manner – taking short springy steps – not at all like Papa's silent tread, but he does give one the same feeling of terrific energy. Perhaps it is because I am sleepy, but I really can't think of any more to say about him, except that I quite understand why Jimmy has been so devoted to him; he is such a kind man to people. An *excellent* employer as Aunt T. would say. Enough, but I begin to wonder whether this diary is suitable for Mary.

3. JIMMY

IN all the confusion which I seem to have gotten into one question goes on like a drumbeat setting the rhythm to something I don't begin to understand. What does she think of him? What *does* she think of him? I don't feel that asking her would tell me: maybe I don't have the courage to ask her, in case she did tell me and it was the wrong answer. I've never seen Emmanuel show any interest in a girl without its being returned – he's never had to make much effort for his pounds of flesh – all these years I've sat back and watched it, I haven't cared a damn one way or the other: I've protected him, soothed Lillian, and comforted the girl: there was nothing in it for me. I've watched everyone's behaviour rotate, as regular as clockwork – there's a kind of off-beat reliability about people's emotional extremes – so that sometimes I've even known beforehand what was going to happen and have been able to soften the blow for somebody. . . . Well, I don't know now. . . . His affairs have always been some kind of escape: once or twice he was infatuated – with that whacky girl who was so good in *The Top Drawer*, and with the one with wonderful hair who sang in a night-club that awful summer we spent in Cannes – but generally, as he once said gossip columns should say: 'I'm not good friends with her – we're just going to bed' – it was like that. Although he never talked about the situation with Lillian

I knew it went round in circles: she wanted children, they weren't possible, so she didn't want Emmanuel; he strayed, she got frightened and did anything she could to get him back, and after a short interval it all started again. I've seen all that; it's been the background to nine years' hard work; I've loved working with him, and as he once said to me: 'By God, Jimmy, we don't choose our backgrounds: if we did, mine would be so dull and respectable that nobody would have a word to say about it.' But supposing he isn't seriously interested in her, what does she feel about him? Enough, maybe, to start something she isn't old enough or experienced enough to stop. But he is interested. He waits on that damn terrace every afternoon for her: I've watched his face when she comes out and sits on the parapet. They don't talk much, or she talks a bit and he watches her although she doesn't seem to realize it. They never look up to my window, or even across to Lillian's – you'd think they were the only two people in the house those times. I didn't think much about this – just happened to see them once or twice – until those pictures arrived. That was what triggered the whole thing off. I'd never have believed he'd open Stan's packet to me, and if I had thought of that, I'd never have believed how angry it would make me. In all these years for the first time I felt, 'That's *my* packet – *my* life you're interfering with – and nobody, not even you, has the right to do it.' It was worse to feel it with him: for the first time with him I felt back in the orphanage – that dead sea of equality; of owning nothing and not being owned. I didn't want to look at the pictures – I just wanted to throw them over the parapet, but when I saw them it was worse – it was as though I'd never seen Alberta in my life – she'd been there all the time and I'd been too blind to see her. I wouldn't have shown them to anybody – just kept them to myself and got Stan to take another lot for everybody else.

She just isn't the kind of girl for a routine seduction – that's all – it wouldn't happen to her unless she mistook it for something else: and that wouldn't happen unless she was deliberately misled. But I can't say I find these conclusions exactly restful, and when I knew she was to spend the morning reading the play with him, I couldn't keep away. I'd got involved with going down to the port with Lillian, but I made an excuse without worrying too much if it was a good one, and came back. That walk, if you're worrying, is murder in the sun – it seems to go on and on, and I had time to remember all the hot marching I'd done in the Army – only then you never seemed to be going to anything, you were just going – forward they liked to say.

I was a fool to go back: she was reading quite quietly, and he was listening in the way he has that makes you think nobody has ever done it before, but when she saw me she tried to raise her voice, his attention snapped, and I thought, 'Now – if he's innocent, he'll be angry – now I'll know,' and waited for him to lash out as I've seen him do to people who've succeeded in interrupting him when he's working. But he didn't: he glanced at me – tried to look at her and stared at the ground, and she stopped, and said something that for a moment made me think she knew everything about us – we hardly had time to stare at her before she had gone. I would have gone after her, but he got to his feet and then stood, listening, as I was, to her footsteps running on the stones outside. He said: 'She's gone': he said it stupidly – as though it was what he was thinking and he was not sure what it meant. Then he said: 'What on *earth* do you think you are doing barging in like that? I keep out of your frequent sessions with her – I should have thought you'd know better than to interrupt my rehearsal?' But it was all a tremendous effort – it didn't wash. I said: 'I think it's time we talked.'

'My dear Jimmy, we've been talking for years. Can't you think of any new means of communication?'

'Not with you I can't. I want to ask you one or two questions.'

'Are they pertinent?'

'I don't know or care. I just have to ask them – that's all.'

He sat down and it made him look very small: I had to remember her face a few minutes ago to get on with it.

'Are you interested in that girl?'

He said at once: 'Naturally. I would hardly be risking her in a leading part if I wasn't.' I was going to interrupt, but he went on: 'Although, at this rate, I don't think I shall be called upon to take the risk.'

'What do you mean?'

'I mean that you are making it so clear to her that you and I have different methods for preparing her that she will be confused and embarrassed into giving up the whole project. I shouldn't blame her at all if she did that now.'

'Look – you know as well as I do that we've worked together for nine years and our methods have never seemed different until now. It would be queer if they were, seeing that you've taught me. The confusion is not coming out of that, and that wasn't the kind of interest I was asking you about.'

'Are you implying that I have other, more personal interests in her?'

'Yes I am! And I'm not implying it, I'm asking a straight question: I'm not even asking any more – I know!'

He was so still that he looked as though he didn't breathe. Then, he said: 'What do you know?'

'You're in love with her. I know that because I've seen it so many times before; I know the signs. You aren't writing, you don't sleep, you hardly exist unless she's around. It's all very well at the moment, because you can see her every day, and it isn't easy for you to be alone with her. Remember Virginia? It was just like this then. All right – so you're in love with her. But what about *her*? She's nineteen – she probably hasn't been in love with anyone – may not even have been kissed, she's led such a secluded life with that family of hers in the back of beyond. You come along and change her whole life – everything is new and glamorous – she travels, she has clothes, she gets the opportunity most girls would give their eyes for – and all because of you. So far she's taken the whole thing very well – she enjoys it; but she doesn't seem to have let it go to her head. I call that a remarkable dignity – do you remember what that Miriam creature was like after you picked her up? But if you make a pass at her, she doesn't stand a chance. She's not old enough, or spoiled enough to do things by halves – she'll be madly in love with you – there'll be nothing she wouldn't do. So then, what? We go to New York – we go into rehearsal; the normal publicity starts up. She'll have the double strain of doing the part and being in love with you. Sometimes this will make her act twice as well – sometimes it won't. Then there'll be more publicity – you'll never get away from that. They'll never come out into the open – just the usual sly little cracks – she'll be hurt and angry, then she'll be hurt and frightened, and finally – and by this time it will have got back to her family, she'll be hurt and ashamed. And then there's Lillian. Have you thought about her, at all? You should have – you ought to know the pattern by now. To begin with, when she kicks up, you'll be clever enough to blind the girl into thinking it's certainly not her fault, and probably not yours. We'll have the whole neurotic story of Lillian's neurotic life trotted out, and everybody will be terribly sorry for everybody else – excepting Lillian. All this time that girl will be playing eight times a week not counting any other public appearances, and the gossip columns will really be minding your business for you. You'll find it harder and harder to see her alone, and all the time they'll be saying things – about her, and about you – comparing your interest in her with your interest in various back numbers – mentioning your age and hers whenever possible – they might even get Mary what's-her-name to give the kind of interview they can blow up into an article, 'My Six Weeks with Emmanuel Joyce', if she's hard up and still feels the way she did last time I saw her. Lillian will be ill – the girl will be living on tranquillizers and pep pills, and out of all this, at some point, you'll start to write another play. When you get really stuck into it, you'll ease out of the whole situation: you'll take Lillian away somewhere to recover and you'll write, and *she* will be nicely left with a dazzling career and a broken heart.'

I'd run out of breath and felt my heart pounding about,

but there had been no choice about what I'd said to him. He had sat like a stone, with his eyes fixed on me and no expression in them that I could recognize or label. I stared back at him until I couldn't bear his silence any more and said: 'It's only because I've seen it so many times before that I know all this.'

After what seemed a long time, he said: 'And this is what "having a private life" has meant to you all these years.'

'I haven't blamed you; I'm not blaming you now. How can I know what is right for you?'

'But you've known that that kind of "private life" was not for you.'

'I don't remember thinking about that. I just feel now that it wouldn't be right for her.'

There was another long silence, and then he said: 'You are quite right, of course. And everything you've said has been quite true: there is no argument.' He fell silent again; then suddenly he yawned, and after it he looked utterly exhausted. Then he blinked, shook himself, and tried to smile at me. 'You make me feel my years – or rather my wasted age.'

'I didn't mean to do that.' I wanted to be gentle now, and felt awkward – but he said heavily. 'Oh yes, you did. The whole exercise would have been wasted if you hadn't made me feel that.'

'Then you do agree about it?'

'Agree that I have no business to seduce Alberta, encourage her to love me, and then abandon her? I do agree. For what it is worth, I entirely agree with you – it is out of the question. Now you know that I know that: will that do?'

I said 'Of course.' I didn't feel at all good about him. I was just about to go, when he roused himself to ask: 'Is this the first time that you've felt like this about me – and anyone else?'

I nodded. 'That's what I mean about not blaming you. Hell that sounds awful, I just mean it's been your business and theirs and certainly not mine. They weren't the same sort of girl as Alberta to start with – that's all.' I didn't want to pursue this, but he went on: 'You feel that she is not someone who should have casual and irresponsible passes made at her by *anyone* – is that it?'

I didn't reply at once, and he repeated more sharply: 'Is that it? Or do you make exceptions below a certain age?'

'It's not a question of making exceptions, and I don't feel that she can't look after herself at all: I don't feel that most people would meet with any response: you would; that's what I mean.'

He regarded me steadily – he still looked sick. 'And if she doesn't do the part, you still feel that?'

'I do – yes.'

He got to his feet. 'Right – Jimmy – that's about all, I think.' He looked about him as though he was trying to think of some place to go and made for the house. At least I knew better than to follow him.

When Lillian came back with plans for an afternoon expedition I told her he'd gone to his room. She went up and came down a few minutes later: 'He's asleep! He's lying on his face with his head under his arm – that usually means he has a headache. Did he say he had one?'

'He said he was tired. How about you and I take the donkeys and leave him to sleep?' So we did just that.

We went to look at a little church Lillian had found, built fairly high up in the village. When we got there, she sent the donkeys away, because she said she couldn't talk to me with the donkey man there. There were old women with white cloths round their heads sweeping in and outside the church which was very small indeed. The inside was entirely covered with paintings of people with rather sad, simple faces, but the whole effect wasn't simple at all. Lillian loved it – she said it was like being inside a casket of jewels. There was a wooden gallery at one end and I climbed up it. That gave me a shock. All around the walls were sacks – open at the top and stuffed with human bones; I knew they were human because of the skulls. I told Lillian who was unexpectedly calm about it, and said yes, she had been told that some favoured people were allowed to keep their family's bones in the church when they had been buried for long enough. She said she thought it was a friendly idea, and I discovered that I hadn't really thought about it at all, and she was right. 'You're just a mass of preconceived notions, darling Jimmy,' she said, and we both liked her saying it.

After the church, we wandered slowly down through the paths and streets to the port again, but got lost, and found a small square with a café running along one side of it. There were two old trees growing out of the stones and we sat at a table under one and had a drink, and then, eventually, lunch.

'Well,' I said; 'how's your energy?'

She said: 'I'm storing it up. I've thought what to do with it, you see.'

'*Have* you?' She didn't answer, so I said: 'What are you going to do, Lillian?'

She had her elbows on the table; now she held her face with her hands as though to keep it steady and spoke rather fast.

'I'm going to *find* this house in England, and furnish it, and stock the garden and learn to drive a car again and to be nicer to Em's theatrical friends so that they will all want to come and stay and he won't feel cut off. I'm going to concentrate on this – on somewhere steady for our future – and not think about the past so much. I'm going to take up the piano again, and unpack all my books after all these years: I thought I might even buy a pair of labradors – they need not worry Em if he doesn't have them in his study – I thought I might breed them – try to get really good at it. Really stop the kind of thinking I do as I am, and try to have some kind of life, if I can find the right place to have it in.'

'What made you come to all this?'

'It started with Em offering me the house. He doesn't really want one – it was a gesture, you know. No – it started with his making me remember something good before Sarah: that's what I've found so difficult, you see – to remember anything good properly before her. Or perhaps it was something that Alberta said – honestly, Jimmy, I just don't know – all those things, I think, and probably more; this is a beautiful place to accumulate in.'

'What did she say to you?'

'Are you curious about that? She said. "I'm so sorry that you lost your daughter" ...' Her eyes had filled with tears, but they stayed in her eyes. 'That's all. But she said it in the kind of way that didn't detach Sarah's death from everything else – for me, I mean. Isn't it odd? She touched it in exactly the right way and I found it didn't feel the same as I had always thought it would. That's a step, isn't it?'

'Sure. You like her, don't you?'

She smiled, and a tear fell on to the table. 'Not as much as you do, Jimmy, but I do like her. That brings me to something else.'

'Don't rush yourself: the last time we had lunch was in London.'

'So it was. It wasn't nearly as nice as today. Jimmy. You asked me in New York to help in any way that I could about Alberta being tried for Clemency. I haven't helped much, because there haven't been many ways that I could, but what you really **meant** was "don't sabotage" and I haven't, have I?'

'You certainly haven't.'

'Well – you *could* help me about having the house in England, and you could certainly sabotage it. Don't you think it would be a good thing if Em had a home somewhere to live and work in between trips?'

Remembering what he had said about it that night on the terrace, I said: 'I think it would be a very good thing if *you* had one.'

'I wouldn't want it without him.'

'I didn't mean that. I meant it would be especially good for you. I don't think he minds where he is – it depends what he is doing there.'

'He might *get* to mind,' she said wistfully. 'And it wouldn't stop us going on trips from time to time – once we were settled in.'

'Lillian, I think it's a fine idea, but what about this play? Won't he want to go straight to New York for that?'

'That's what I wanted to ask you,' she leaned forward while I lit her cigarette and I smelled that scent I've known ever since I've known her: something to do with lemons – I've always liked it.

'Couldn't you manage the play, and Alberta, if you're going to use her, with*out* Em? Surely he doesn't have to be there all through rehearsals? We could just fly over for the opening, and fly back, if he wants to go very badly.'

'He may want to be there,' I said – I was beginning to feel trapped.

'But you could manage without him, if he didn't?'

'Yes – yes I think I *could* do that; but I wouldn't want to if he didn't want me to.'

She was watching me carefully for the evasions I was trying to avoid.

'Alberta is going to be good, isn't she? You've really decided to use her?'

'*I* should like to. I don't know what he thinks. I was going to see this morning, but she walked out on us. I think I upset her.'

'That's a good sign anyway.'

'Why? Surely it's better for a producer if an actress holds her ground and keeps on acting.'

'Temperament,' she said vaguely: 'or perhaps Em put her off.' She was thinking of something else. Then she asked suddenly: 'What do you think of those pictures?'

'Very good. Very like her too.' I'd planned what to say about them by now.

'Oh Jimmy, is that all you can find to say?'

'What else would you say?'

'I'd say that Miss Young is going to have quite a time in New York. I think everyone will be after her if she isn't protected. I think you'll have your work cut out to keep her mind on her work.'

'She's always seemed to me reasonably conscientious.'

'My dear, you forget how young she is. She's never lived

in a city before, and certainly nowhere where every other young man in town will want to date her. If you don't take pretty drastic steps, you'll find yourself without a lead because she'll have married someone, or be having a breakdown through lack of sleep or something.'

'What steps do you suggest I take?'

She put out her cigarette and started hunting in her bag. 'Well, you could always marry her yourself, couldn't you Jimmy?'

I felt the back of my neck start to burn, which, damn it, I'd give anything to stop. 'She'd never marry me.'

'Oh, I don't know. If you made it clear to her that it was for the sake of her career, and pointed out the vicious and dreary alternatives, she might. After all, whatever you are, you aren't a fate worse than death.' Then she stopped, and said: 'Jimmy – I'm teasing you – perhaps in very bad taste. It's *your* life – you do what you want. Only, if you want something, do something about it.'

I said I'd see about paying the bill and walked flaming into the cool café. As I walked I thought – really I could go anywhere just like this and not have left much behind. I didn't seem to have anything excepting nine years' experience at directing Emmanuel's life and his plays. A future as insecure as my past was uncertain, and nothing tangible about the present unless you counted some nice luggage which just about held my clothes. However you looked at it, it wasn't much to offer.

When I got back to Lillian, she gave me her hand to pull her up, and said: 'You should count up your assets one day, Jimmy dear. You'd be surprised.'

I didn't tell her that I had, and I wasn't.

On the way back Lillian said: 'Let's go by the sea'; so we did, and half-way home she said: 'Let's bathe'; so we did that too. We were peaceful and didn't talk much; once she said to me, 'I wasn't teasing you in a bitchy way, darling Jimmy. I was trying to infuse you with the kind of courage I'm afraid you haven't got. Like you have kinds I haven't got.' Then she went on dreamily: 'I wonder how many of us

272

it would take to make one whole person? Even the four of us wouldn't do. Hundreds, I expect.' Then she yawned, and it made me remember Emmanuel in the morning and wonder where Alberta was, but I didn't want her to know that I felt anxious about either of them so I waited for her to suggest our return.

We found Alberta kneeling on the terrace with the typewriter in front of her and Emmanuel signing the letters she had finished for him; everything very calm and businesslike, but I noticed that Emmanuel wouldn't look at me, and I felt somehow nervous of meeting Alberta after the morning, although Lillian had so obviously enjoyed herself that she filled any gaps there might have been.

After dinner I took Alberta for a bathe. I'd had what seemed to me at dinner a very good idea, but when we got down on the beach and I was alone with her – although it still seemed good, it seemed much more difficult. I'd decided that the only way to do it was to be perfectly practical and level-headed and not make too much of the whole thing. Then, although that couldn't frighten her, she might see the sense of it, and I might get some sort of line on how she felt. After all, if she said she couldn't bear me, or she was in love with someone else or she didn't want to marry anybody, I'd know where I was. I'd also thought pretty carefully about what Lillian had said, and decided that my only asset was that I did know how to look after people – so I plugged that part of it fairly hard. The only trouble was that she didn't say any of the things back that I'd expected. She didn't say she couldn't bear me, she didn't say that she was in love with anybody else (although she didn't say she wasn't); she kept saying that was extremely kind of me – as though I was offering her a job. I nearly got angry with her, she was so damn polite: she also said something queer about not wanting to marry in order to be more comfortable ... what the hell does she think I'm for if it isn't to do every single goddam thing I could to look after her in every way I can think of? I suppose I *didn't* put it to her right; once I'd felt that, I felt sure of it and said so – in order to give myself some kind of loophole to raise the matter again. We bathed, and her hair got wet so that it was stuck in little wet triangles on her forehead and the rest of it was like a neat gleaming cap: I spread out my towel for us both to sit on and put hers round her and for one awful moment I wished she was very unhappy so that she wouldn't even notice who was comforting her. Then she asked me if I'd thought what it would be like if she fell in love with some-one else after we were married: this was good; at least it meant she was thinking about it, but naturally I answered her very calmly and finished by making a few general (rather good) remarks about marriage, but I've noticed that women aren't much good at generalizations, they always come back to a personal view: she said what about *my* falling in love with somebody. The utter impossibility of this clearly hadn't struck her – I didn't feel that I could go into that so I just brushed it aside. Then I felt we'd said just about as much as I could manage without losing control of the situa-tion, so I said I wanted a drink. I made her climb in front of me in case she slipped: alone, I could say this to her – even with Lillian it would be possible, but somehow, after this morning, not with Emmanuel. This made me angry and I told her an idiot lie about him, and she knew it was one although I think even if she hadn't I couldn't have stuck to it. I wanted to take her by the shoulders and stare into her eyes and ask: 'What *do* you feel about him? Just tell me so I'll know and I won't ask any more questions'; because I know she wouldn't lie to me – she's about the most truthful person I've ever met – but I couldn't do it: I just apologized, and went to bed feeling lousy with anxiety that I'd never be worth her the way I was acting. She's the last person in the world I want to lie to, and he's the last person in the world I want to lie about – and so what? I still did it. That kept me awake some time, and I came to the conclusion that what with one thing and another I'd been taking my own character for granted.

4. LILLIAN

APART from giving Jimmy a chance to be alone with Alberta, I really did want to talk to Em. He'd been almost silent at dinner, excepting when he'd done a set piece – one of his filmscript conference stories with everyone calling him Mannie – I know them all but they still make me laugh; the rest of the time he seemed hardly to be with us. At one point, when we'd been talking about Greek myths, I said why didn't he make a play of one – in contemporary terms, and he said the idea had a kind of whimsical vulgarity that nauseated him. And that, as Jimmy said, was that. Alberta asked whether there were any new ideas that hadn't been written about, and he said no, but occasionally somebody discovered something for himself, and then, if he could write, it became a fresh translation, and, to people who hadn't made the discovery, something new. But in three hours that could hardly be described as a fair share of the conversation. It irritated me because I felt he was casting a gloom on all three of us and the whole day.

After the others had gone for their bathe, I got glasses and our house-bottle of brandy which we hardly ever drink because it is so full of fire and vanilla, and lay on the one comfortable chair that we keep on the terrace. 'Really, Em, that was a most tactless suggestion.'

'What was tactless?'

'Couldn't you see that Jimmy wanted to be alone with her? The last thing they want is a pair of old chaperones: I'd have thought you would be the first person to notice that. Give me some brandy, darling.'

He poured the brandy in silence, and lit a cigarette.

'Is something worrying you? Is the new play on your mind?'

'Not in the least.'

'Are you worrying about Alberta?'

'Alberta?'

'Clemency, if you prefer. Jimmy seems quite happy about her.'

'Has Jimmy been pouring out his heart to you?'

'He's much too shy. He doesn't have to tell me – I know.'

He sat on the parapet and turned to the sea – I could hardly hear what he said. 'What do you think she feels about him?'

It was odd, I hadn't thought of that. 'I'm not sure. She's got the kind of reserve that makes it very difficult to tell. It's obvious she *likes* him, and after all, she agreed to go bathing with him. Do you remember that time in France when we found that wonderful little beach one night and took off all our clothes and just plunged in?' He didn't answer, and I knew it was no good getting angry with him when he was like this, so I went on: 'and the next day when we tried to find it again in the light, we couldn't: it didn't seem to be anywhere. Do you remember?'

He said: 'I didn't – but you've reminded me.'

'Darling, do turn round, or I shan't hear a word you say, and could I have one of your cigarettes?'

He bent down to give me one, and when he lit the match I saw his face. He looked dreadful – collapsed and exhausted like he used to look after bad asthma. 'Darling! What is the matter? Are you ill?'

But he only blew out the match and said crossly: 'Not in the least. I'm deadly tired – that's all; I didn't sleep last night.'

'You slept this morning.'

'As you've so often told me, that is hardly the same thing.'

'Do you want to go to bed now?'

He smiled then, and said: 'Oh no – the last thing I want to do is to go to bed.' He drank some brandy and sat on the parapet again. 'What was it you wanted to talk about?'

'I'm not at all sure that you're in the right mood for it.'

He said nothing: I've noticed before that he gets these attacks of silence: they annoy me because I don't understand them – whatever he is feeling doesn't take me like

276

that when I feel it, and the most I can do is to provoke him into a contradiction or a retort. That would be useless now; I was just about to try again, when he said: 'You want to talk about returning to England and buying a house – is that it?'

'Yes. Would they be wildly unsuitable topics?'

'Not if you will do most of the talking.'

I said: 'I've adored being here: it has been a perfect holiday, but I feel it is coming to an end.'

'The perfection?'

'No – the whole thing. I feel that it is time we went back – almost I feel I know we *are* going back. I'm not bored, and it has been wonderful to bathe again and live in this air and the marvellous, continuing sun – but I was wrong about one thing.'

'What thing?'

'I thought that an island would be a good place for you to write, and it hasn't been. I feel this must be depressing for you, and that you would be far happier in one of the old places that you associated with writing. If we went back to London – Jimmy could get you that nice room in Shepherd Market and I could start house hunting, and only take you to see one if it really seemed a desirable residence. If it is humanly possible, I should like to find a house and get a bit settled before we go to the Bahamas in January.'

'Why on earth are we going there?'

'Because Leonard and Jo asked us. Oh, don't start being difficult about that – you said you wanted to go when they asked us. If we've just got a new house it will probably be torture to go, although one can't do anything much to a garden in January, whereas the autumn is the perfect time to start. But it may take months to find the right house.'

'In which case?'

'In which case, the sooner we start the better. Then you'll be able to get on with your play, Jimmy can go on training Alberta until they have to go to America – perhaps she could have a short holiday at home as well, I know that she wants to see her father, and I can look for the house.'

I waited for him to say that he wanted to go to New York, but he didn't: he didn't say anything.

'What I do need to consider much more with you is the kind of house we are looking for.'

'What kind do you want?'

'It isn't simply what I want. I mean do *you* want it to be near or far from London; what sort of size, and how much land – things like that. And also, how much can we afford it to cost?'

He finished his brandy and reached for the bottle. 'My dear, I haven't the slightest idea about any of this. I think you had better get what *you* want. I don't know how to approach such a plan because I cannot think about life in your terms.'

'But it was *your* idea that we should buy a house!'

'I know. But the idea started from something else. I can't explain to you, but the difference is something like you starting to paint a picture by designing its frame, and I wanting to start at whatever is to be the picture's centre and then discovering what surround it may need. Something like that.'

'Well?'

'Do you remember saying to me that the trouble with you was that you didn't know what you were *for*, and that that made it very difficult for you to know what you wanted because you never wanted the same thing for very long?'

'Did I say that?'

'In New York in the morning.' He smiled. 'Isn't it extraordinary – what we remember and what we forget? Well, you assumed then, that it was different for me – that I did know.'

'Yes?'

'I don't, most of the time. That's all. But when I don't, there is nothing I feel I can safely do. I can't fabricate results with no cause.'

He drank some brandy and stood up. 'But *you* go on with it; you find a house that you like: I am not trying to stop you.'

'But I can't possibly do it all by myself!'

'You may have to.' He paused. 'I may have to go – to New York for this play.'

Somehow I had known he was going to say this ever since I had talked to Jimmy, but that just made it worse. It was no good simply being angry, because I wanted him to change his mind – seeing this, I saw how much I really wanted the house with him: so I waited until the worst things I was going to say had cleared off.

'You don't feel that Jimmy could manage on his own just this once?'

'No.'

'But you haven't even decided whether she is going to do the part, have you?'

'No.'

After a moment, he added: 'When I've decided these things I'll tell you, of course.'

It was the 'of course' that did it. 'Do you have to say things like that to me?'

He looked deliberately surprised – I knew that he wasn't and felt suddenly furious.

'Do you have to treat me all the time as though I was a sick child? Can't you ever discuss what we are going to do – or even what you are going to do – reasonably with me? Or does it satisfy your dramatic instinct to have little secrets all the time? I suppose you know that that dreadful Gloria Williams wrote me a mad letter just before she took all those pills? You thought that that was quite all right as long as I didn't know. Well, it wasn't. It was just as awful, and worse in the end when I did. While we're about it, perhaps you'd explain what on earth this means.' I knew the letter was somewhere in my bag, but I couldn't find it: really it would have been better if I hadn't even tried for a second to be reasonable. . . . I found the letter and held it out for him to see.

He said: 'Where *did* you find that? I've been looking for it everywhere.'

'It was on the floor in your room. I saw it when you were

asleep. I read it while I was changing for dinner. Who are
the Friedmanns? You obviously know them well – have
known them for years. Don't you under*stand*, Em – I don't
mean it is like Gloria Williams – I realize that this is a man
writing to you about a boy and that you saw these people
when you were in London, but why don't I know anything
about them? When you say that you may go to New York
when we have something very important to do together in
England and that you'll let me know when you've decided
about it you make me so angry and *despairing* about us that
I lose my head and my temper at once. You don't take me
into your confidence at all.'

'Perhaps I have no confidence in your confidence.'

It was exactly like being slapped for hysteria. I found
myself staring at him – my hands with the letter dropped
back into my lap. He sat down on the bench beside my
chair, took the letter from me, and said: 'Sometimes you are
very stupid and then there is no reason why I should trust
you. If I gave you certain confidences, you would do something stupid, and when things turned out badly you would
fall back on your good intentions, when, in fact, you had
had no intentions of any kind. The Friedmanns are the
people who took the two children you would not adopt.
They are Jews: they understood what these children had
endured, and like you Mrs Friedmann was childless: but
they have given them what was needed. I have continued to
see them because when they undertook the children they
had very little money, and although I could not keep the
most serious part of the promises I had undertaken I could
at least help somebody else to do so. That's all. But remember how we last talked on this subject – years ago now – and
see why you are the last person I would consult. Last time I
saw her, Mrs Friedmann said children should be above luck
– they were beyond your notice – you simply did not consider them at all. What was there for me to tell you about
them, if they were only to provide fuel for your resentment
and self-pity?'

There was complete silence. It was as though all my blood

had turned and was trying to move in a different direction: I heard myself asking something. . . .

He smiled then, and gave my hand a little, absent pat. '. . . do about them? Why nothing, now. They are much better off with the Friedmanns than they would be with us.'

Soon after that, we went to bed – he upstairs, I to my room, the best room in the house, on the ground floor. For the first time in my life at any such moment, I did not cry – just lay – with what he had said printing itself again and again. It was as though a thought, like a piece of paper, was pressed on to me and torn off – painfully – as though I was publishing this truth about me alone in a room, dark, excepting for the shallow, childish strips made by the moon, which seemed only an echo of light. One piece of the letter recurred: about the boy: 'a child who survives what he has survived, and with his gift, only to have it taken away suddenly by a foolish accident – what is his destiny? All day he looks at his hand. He does not speak not even yet has he wept.' I did not need to understand the situation to recognize this.

I woke in the morning feeling wonderfully light-headed and calm, and with a great desire to begin the day; but before getting up, I lay and remembered how I had lain in the night: Em's voice, the shock, the pain which was still not an ordinary kind, as some locked-up part of me had almost welcomed it – the only part which plainly hurt was when he had said: 'Why nothing, now.' I could nearly have again that curious, physical jolt inside me with the feeling that everything, at that moment, was changing direction. . . .

It was the most brilliant and beautiful morning: cloudless sky, heraldic sun, and the sea the smoke-blue of distant flowers. I found Alberta in the kitchen hut at the end of the western terrace, making coffee: she had already boiled a pan of water for us to wash. She was the only one of us who could get a full bucket of water out of the well. She was wearing a blue cotton skirt and a pink cotton shirt I had given her, it had faded, but it suited her more like that than it had ever suited me.

'It is remarkable the way you always make very old clothes look their best. Oh dear. That sounds like the remark of a prize bitch – I really meant it: it is a great art – usually only men have it.'

She said: 'I can't tell you what fun it is having such a choice of clothes. I lie in bed and choose them every morning.'

'Did you have a good bathe last night?'

'Yes. The water seems even warmer in the dark – more salt, too. The ants have got the old figs – we'll have to eat the new ones, but there's a new melon as well. The honey is in the washing-up bowl.'

'Why?'

'Ants! There've been more every day since we've been here.' She blew out the stove and said: 'We must get more paraffin today – there's just about enough for one more morning.'

'Are the others awake?'

'I don't know. They usually seem to hear when I take the coffee on to the terrace – it's a bit like the ants when we move the honey.'

We took the breakfast out of the kitchen hut. Already the sun was stronger, and one of the scarlet trumpet flowers was dying. She said: 'Julius said that it would get hotter nearly every day. He is making a list of the advantages of winter. He's going to read them to me this afternoon.'

Jimmy came out: he did not look as though he had slept very well. He and Alberta seemed calm with each other so I am afraid Jimmy cannot have mustered the courage to tell her what he feels.

Em did not join us until the middle of breakfast: he looked as though he had not slept at all, but when I saw him I had such a rush of warmth, of affectionate gratitude towards him, that I could not stay where I was. He saw me rise, came over, and pushed me gently down again. Alberta poured his coffee and he asked about the bathe. Jimmy answered him – they looked at each other, and I had the feeling I often have with them, that they are talking to each other without words. The end of breakfast was friendly and serene – as though we had all known each other all our lives, and I thought, 'How well Alberta has fitted in with us,' and then, rather rashly, said so aloud. It was very silly; she blushed, and Jimmy began slowly going scarlet, the way he does, and Em said 'She has indeed' in a mechanical sort of voice to fill the gap.

As I didn't have to go to the port to get food for lunch, we agreed to bathe as soon as possible. Jimmy said that Alberta must do her minimum routine stint – he is a great stickler for discipline; Em said that in that case he would go on to the other terrace to read, and I went to the kitchen hut to clear up breakfast and collect our lunch. It was very hot there. I opened its one window and the door: for a moment I considered opening the heavy gate beyond the hut which is our entrance, but when I looked out the sun was already on the gate.

It was so hot by now that I did everything slowly, with half my attention on the exercises that Jimmy was directing. On the steep rocks outside the kitchen-hut window a goat was trying to eat bits of cactus – moving with light, uneasy footsteps on the rocks, its bell muttering round its neck. I threw it a piece of bread, but it didn't seem able to find it. I leaned out of the window with another piece; it looked at me with its stuffed animals' eyes and nodded irritably, so I threw that piece too. I was watching it eat, and listening to all the sound of the small valley made lazy by heat when there was suddenly a brief pounding outside – although I had not heard anybody approach – but there was a sense of violence in the sound which made me run to the gate: as I reached it, it burst open, and there was the little boy I knew must be Julius. He wore simply a pair of faded jeans – his face and his shoulders were streaked with sweat. He stared at me with frightful urgency for a second – I just had time to wonder why he was not scarlet after running so hard because he was panting, gasping for breath – when he pushed past me and ran to the terrace. He went straight to Alberta and said: 'Here is a tragic telegram!' gave it to her, and burst into tears.

She seemed to open it very slowly, and read it for a long time; and then she looked at the boy crying, and he looked at her with tears streaming down his face – then he raised his fist clenched, and shook it in the air, crying: '*That* – to the driver of the car!'

She put the telegram carefully away in the pocket of her skirt: she was still looking at the boy – had gone very pale: she put out her hand and touched his fist – he flung his arms round her with such a cry, that for a moment I thought that the telegram had been his – his grief was so intense, and she was so still. But then – I think it was Jimmy – said: 'What *is* it, Alberta?' and she looked out over the boy's head that she was holding, and said: 'He was knocked down by a car. He is dead: my father.'

Now she was dead white: we all seemed to be frozen: then I saw that she had been speaking to Em, who was standing in the doorway of the house. He was staring at her, and I saw on his face what I had only seen before in the barest shadow at odd seconds of our lives – that he loved her – and I was struck by it.

CHAPTER SEVEN

*

I. JIMMY

WHAT struck me was the kind of courage she had. She didn't cry, or faint or make a scene or even say anything very much. Emmanuel made her sit down and I got her some brandy, but she didn't want it. She was even soothing the boy who sat shivering beside her. He'd had quite a time, poor kid; apparently they'd called to him from the Post Office because they couldn't make out the message – he'd written it out for them and then run all the way here in this heat. She hadn't talked to me much about her father, but somehow I knew it was far the worst shock she'd ever had in her life, by the way all her reactions seemed to have slowed down, so that it took her time to understand what you said: she stared at the brandy and held the glass for a minute before she said she didn't want it. It was Lillian who drank the brandy. She'd gone a bad colour – for her to have an attack now was just *all* we needed – but she pulled herself together. The only thing Alberta said was that she had to telephone, and the boy said he would help her. Emmanuel said: 'You'd like to go back wouldn't you?' and she looked up at him as though she hardly knew him and nodded. He wanted me so we went on to the other terrace.

'Jimmy. You'd better go down to the port with them and ring the airport. Get four seats – I don't think there is much point in any of us staying here now.' He thought for a moment and said: 'We might all go to the port.'

So we all went. There followed an hour of sheer nightmare in the Post Office, when all we did was to put through the call to England and establish the fact that it might take all day to get through again to the airport – I did manage it once, but couldn't find anyone to speak English and then got cut off. There was nowhere to sit; Lillian had to go outside; the boy argued with the operator until they weren't speaking to each other, and Alberta leaned against the counter absolutely white and speechless. The place reeked of dust and sweat, and all the windows were closed. Something had to be done about it. I led Emmanuel outside and said that I would catch the boat when it called and call the airport from Piraeus. He said again that we might all go. 'You can ask her, but the only thing she seems to want is that telephone call and it may take all day to come through.' He agreed, and went to tell Lillian, who was waving anxiously from her café table.

I went back to her. She was standing exactly as I had left her, and I remembered how we had waited in New York for the call to come through to her father – and her saying after she had spoken to him 'It's simply that I've known him all my life' as the tears ran down her face. I put my arm round her shoulder and told her that I was going to Athens to get plane seats and she listened with that same strained expression, and said 'That is extremely kind of you, Jimmy' – and then I remembered wishing last night that she would be very unhappy so that she would not notice who was comforting her. I said: 'I'll come and say good-bye before I go' and let go of her shoulder which seemed somehow light as well as stiff.

When I got outside again, I was going straight up to the house to fetch our passports and tickets, but Emmanuel waved and I went over to them. He looked kind of surprised and very nervous.

'Lillian says she wants to go with you.'

I looked at her. '*She* says so?'

Lillian looked me full in the face and spoke very fast – so I knew something was wrong. 'Yes, Jimmy. If we are leaving so suddenly, there are one or two things that I want to do in Athens, so I'd rather come over with you today if you don't mind. Em doesn't mind at all, do you, darling?'

I didn't catch his reply.

'I shan't hold you up at all. I'll go straight to the hotel, and do my things on my own. Are you going back to the house? Because we haven't got much time, and I don't think

I could make it, but I want my light coat and my little square travelling case – it's got most of my toilet things in it.'

'When is the boat due?'

'In about half an hour, I think, because people are already beginning to collect. You'd better go, Jimmy, if you're going.'

She was quite right: there wasn't time to argue with her. I did that walk in the fastest time I've ever made it, and by the time I'd finished packing what was needed, I saw the boat in the distance, and ran part of the way back. How that kid ran the whole way I can't think. I didn't even have time to think why Lillian was so mad to go, but the craziest part of it was that it wasn't till I was back in the port that I realized that her going meant that Emmanuel would be staying with Alberta. For one moment I thought of thrusting all the papers and his wife's bag at him and saying: 'You make the arrangements – just this once!' but I knew I wouldn't when I saw him. I'd always made the arrangements – it was what I was for: it may have been then that I swore I'd be for something else: at least for making my own arrangements or, maybe, hers.

She was standing just as I had left her, with the boy squatting at her feet.

'Any luck at all?'

She shook her head, and the operator clicked his teeth and smiled and closed his eyes, and Julius said: 'Regrettably there is not time about telephone calls.'

The boat was hooting now and very near. I walked down to the quay with Emmanuel and Lillian where the row boats were waiting to take us out.

'I'll get seats any time from tomorrow evening, and I'll either try to call you this evening, or send a telegram.'

'Won't tomorrow be too soon?'

I looked at Lillian grimly and thought that nothing would be too soon for me. Emmanuel said: 'I'll wait in the Post Office from six till seven this evening for you to call. All right?'

'o.k.'

Lillian said: 'Well good-bye darling. I hope her call comes through. See you tomorrow.' She climbed into the small rocking boat and I put her case on her knees. She was smiling brightly – the last thing I wanted was a boat trip with her.

'Good-bye, Jimmy. Do your best.'

'And you,' I said; for a moment our eyes met and he had that creature-of-circumstance look I knew so well and had come to dread. But I had to go. I jumped in; I was the last, and we were off. The boat was swooping into the harbour like a great white gull emitting shrill hoots. Emmanuel waved once and walked slowly away, back towards the Post Office, where, I thought, she would still be standing. . . .

'Get her a chair!' I yelled suddenly, and he turned round, but I don't think he heard me.

A lot of that day I had to remind myself that the feelings I was having simply didn't count beside Alberta's – and that in a way I was doing something for her that she needed. To begin with, we were no sooner on the boat and steaming away full bat when I discovered that we weren't going straight back to Piraeus at all – far from it, in fact we returned from a protracted tour to our island at about four and then went back to Piraeus. So all our mad rush had been completely unnecessary. The hope that the others would join us on the boat at four was dim – I felt viciously that if the telephone operator didn't succeed in messing up her call until long after that time, Emmanuel would somehow avoid catching the boat. I couldn't tell Lillian why I felt so anxious and frustrated by the whole thing – I knew from repeated experience what it was like being with her when she thought or knew that Emmanuel was with a girl he was interested in. As she didn't know, she took the news about our boat quite calmly. Once, she said: 'Don't worry too much about Alberta, Jimmy. Em's the best person in the world to be with when you've had a bad shock – he'll look after her.' As if that made it any better. Everybody on the boat was so damn gay – we careered along like some kids'

Sunday outing. I put Lillian in a chair and told her I needed some exercise, and mooched around for what seemed like hours. I ended up just leaning over a rail, feeling bluer than the sea, until I felt someone touch my arm, and it was Lillian saying why didn't we both have a drink. 'You can disown me afterwards if you like, Jimmy dear, but I'm parched and I do so hate bars by myself.' I noticed then that she had dark marks round her eyes, and thought that perhaps she hadn't wanted to come at all – she'd honestly thought it would be easier for Alberta to be alone with Emmanuel: somehow that touched me and I found the whole thing better after that.

Going back to our island was a bad time, though. We got there about a quarter to four – we didn't come so far in to the harbour as we had in the morning, and the row boats seemed to take an age to reach us. Lillian and I leaned over a rail on the boat deck watching the small laden boats, but long before they got near enough for us to see people's faces we knew that Alberta and Emmanuel weren't there. The port otherwise seemed deserted, and the Post Office looked shut.

'Perhaps the poor girl didn't get her call through before they shut at midday.' Then she added: 'Probably she didn't.'

I glanced at her face, but she gave no sign that she noticed me. Suddenly she pointed to the top of the mountain. 'We never went up to the monastery. The day we arrived here, I planned to do that, and we never did. That is something we *could* have done.'

'What couldn't we have done?'

The boat was leaving, and she turned away from the rail. 'Oh – anything from preventing her father's death onwards.'

We decided to settle somewhere for the rest of the trip, and found two chairs in the bows which seemed to have the right amount of shade and shelter. As we sat down she said: 'If only one knew at the time what one *could* do!'

'What would happen then?'

'Well, at least one would try to do it; one would be better occupied.'

She gave me a queer little smile – something appealing about it – not at all how I usually saw her.

The journey to Piraeus seemed very long – partly because it started at a time when the light begins to change, from hot afternoon sun – a bright, impartial light on everything – to the beginning of evening when all those colours start up in the sky. We both slept the first part of the journey, and when I woke it was cooler and softer and Lillian was awake and gazing into the distance. I woke with such a strong feeling for Alberta that it was almost as though I was actually with her and it was a real moment in my life – much more than any other – I couldn't remember anything better. I thought: 'So *this is* my life,' and saw Lillian looking at me and said:

'I love her now. I know it. I don't just want to look after her – I want life with her on any terms at any price. Anything else would just be existing and playing – a waiting game.'

Lillian leaned towards me and took my hands: 'I'm glad you know – I *do hope* you get it.'

She looked like crying and I felt so wonderful – I couldn't bear her to cry. 'There's nothing sad about it – I'll find a way. Everything is different – if one knows something.'

Lillian was very quiet after that, and we sat, hardly speaking, while the light sank slowly into the sea. It was beautiful, and I thought that any one of these things would from now on remind me of her – the sea, the evening sky, a boat, the warm breeze coming off the land – but she would make me remember all these things at once – the whole world could come to life for me because of her.

2. LILLIAN

THE lights of Piraeus were strung out in a shallow half-circle in grey dusk like a jeweller's necklace on velvet. They looked pretty, neat, and inaccessible, but somewhere in the future we were going to tie up in a gap between two beads

and they would seem far apart. This was a kind of future –
the only kind that I could envisage – something already
drawing to its past. But my own life stretched out round
me like a sea – it seemed illimitable. Jimmy was silent –
wrapped in his dreams, and I, knowing so clearly what
would shatter them, was at least silent to him.

The morning already seemed another life away: since I
had seen Em's face, so radiant with concerning love, I had
lived my old life almost out: it had now so many threadbare
patches where I could find no substance, that I could see
through myself in it. ('You have a kind of indefatigable stu-
pidity – all your life you have been rehearsing for this
event when you thought you were playing the lead in an
ancient tragedy.') Now, understanding perhaps for the first
time in all my years of living with him, something that
mattered to Em, I had left him to decide what he would do,
and tell me afterwards what he had decided, of course. Even
then, I had hardly done it. Jealousy – no, a searing envy for
that girl who had shown me his face – had blasted me so
that I had stood on the terrace with the rocks going round
me like lumps of brown sugar, and I had had to drink the
brandy she hadn't wanted. Then we had all gone down to
the port – in single file, with the boy leading; the boy,
Alberta, Jimmy, I, and Em last. All the morning, I knew
that what dignity, what resolution I had was stiffened by
hers – I could not bear this acknowledgement, but I could
not escape it.

Sitting by myself at the café table while the others were
in the Post Office (*I* was the one who could not stand the heat
and smell of sweat and nowhere to sit) all my resentment
and grievances for the string of his infidelities – known and
guessed – were stripped off, revealing such a shocking inadequacy that it even seemed astonishing that I should have
been given the chance to recall so many. The times that I
had stormed at him – the false righteous indignation that I
had managed to employ – about his vulgarity, his coarse and
partial views of love, his lack of discrimination, all that I
had contrived to twist into peculiar insults to me and my

marriage with him unravelled, until I saw that the real confusion had always been mine. He, at least, had known what he was doing: it had had nothing to do with his view of love, he must even have used discrimination to make sure of this. But I, standing upon rights which were not mine and a deprivation which had not been his, had refused to recognize any loyalty in his behaviour to me; for, looking back on these affairs, I was forced to understand that he had not sought love from them. He had not sought it with *her*: the fact that he had looked steadily more and more desperate since we had been here, and had made no attempts to be alone with her, all pointed to his having struggled. ... I might never have known; might have gone on thrusting Jimmy down his throat, speculating idly and aloud about his fatigue, if it had not been for the telegram. It had taken the shock of the telegram for me to know anything. ...

I did not plan to go to the boat; I was too raw and confused to have plans, but when he came out to tell me that Jimmy was going to Athens to get tickets for the aeroplane, I suddenly felt that I should go with Jimmy – that it was one thing that I could do for him – to leave him in peace to make his own decision, and I looked at him thinking how much patience he had had with my difficulties. His face had closed to an expression of conventional waiting and concern, and I thought, if I leave him with her and he tells her – what will become of me? Then, because I felt almost intolerably diminished to myself, I wondered what he had ever admired in me, and there was one answer to that. He had admired my courage – the only time that I ever had any – which was when I had gone on carrying Sarah after they had said that it would almost certainly kill me, and had not told him that I knew this. That had been the end of my courage, it seemed. There must have been many occasions for it, but it was too late to regret them: I could, at least, go to Athens, now. I told him I wanted to go: his reply confounded me.

'Jimmy may not want you to go.'

I said what had it got to do with Jimmy, in my most wilful voice – the only difference was that I heard myself this time. But when Jimmy joined us, I could see that Em was quite right, and Jimmy did not seem in the least anxious for my company. That was a final slap: I had not thought of myself as so generally tiresome: the sensation of doing something which I found difficult and having somebody else irritated with me for doing it made it all at once more real, and more unpleasant. I talked Jimmy into agreeing – haven't I had years of practice at getting my own way? – and in no time, it seemed we had left them.

I watched Em walking away from us on the quay, and then Jimmy shouted to him to get Alberta a chair, and I thought, Jimmy loves her too, and he's left her with Em, but then, of course, he doesn't know what he is doing. On the boat, we found that we need not have left the island until the afternoon, and this made poor Jimmy desperate, but I was grateful that we hadn't known, and I hadn't had all those hours in which to change my mind. Jimmy left me in a chair and went off by himself, and I had the whole day again with the stark ungratifying pictures of myself that it presented. There was plenty of time for review; the trouble was that the more ordered I became in it, the more clearly I saw what I was, the less I liked it, and the more inexorably everything I noted or could remember added up to my standing little or no chance now. It seemed to me that, presented with the choice of living with Alberta or me, nobody in their senses would hesitate. In the end this made me think of Jimmy. The relief of finding that I could actually do this was extraordinary, and I went to find him. Knowing more than he, I felt a need to relieve him somehow, if only from the feeling that I would be a deadweight to him in Athens. We had a drink together, and he talked in a guarded, deliberately practical way about her. Did I think that she would now want to give up doing the play? Did I think that she would just want to go back home and stay there? I said all I could think of – that her father's profession meant that the family would no longer be able to live in the vicarage after his death, and that it would also mean that there was far less money so that she might have more incentive than ever for doing the play. He said it surely was tough on her, but he looked reassured.

When we found ourselves returning to the island, we both went to the side of the ship where we could watch the rowing-boats. I knew that they wouldn't be there, but I felt him hoping, and when we had both searched the boats and the port for them and found nothing but the Post Office looking absolutely deserted, I had to comfort him. I felt him turn to me, and it seemed another confirmation of what I was, that when I honestly tried to think of someone else it only made them suspicious. But what could I *do now* about it all? I longed then to go back – to have another chance at my opportunities – but then, if I went back, I should not know what I know now; I should be the same clutching, hysterical creature – laying waste to chance – hoarding sensations until they went bad, making my world smaller and smaller in order to keep myself the centre of it. . . . I think I was more frightened then than I had ever been; everything else of that kind that I had felt had been only little gestures towards fear – it was the difference between losing one's way and there being no way to lose. . . .

Jimmy was saying something about finding somewhere sheltered. I followed him. I said something to him about wanting to know what one could do, and as he always does to any general or thoughtless exclamation, he asked a question of such ruthless simplicity that he made one feel as though one had asked for something which one would not be able to use. But he was there: he was trying to be patient and kind in spite of his own anxieties. It occurred to me that perhaps even my leaving Em on the island with her had been an entirely selfish idea – designed to tell me where I was, without the slightest reference to Jimmy, and that what I had thought was self-control in not spilling out my fears to him was just a kind of self-enlightened cowardice. I shut my eyes and tried to swallow this, but it was too much: I sank into an apathy where thoughts droned and flitted through my mind without my seeming to have anything to do with them, until I suppose even they got tired of the lack of response, and I must have slept.

When I woke it was twilight, and Jimmy was asleep. I thought of us reaching Piraeus – found I couldn't think of anything beyond that – looked at Jimmy's peaceful, trusting face, and decided not to think about anything excepting the sea – its always moving, always remaining – its continuity and comforting size. . . .

When Jimmy woke up he suddenly told me that he loved her: he was unmistakable and resolute: he said that everything was different if one knew something – *he* said that. I could not warn or protect him; I could only cling to the papery intention of keeping silent.

We arrived. Then we had to find a taxi to take us into Athens: the heat of the day was still in the streets. I lay back in the cab with the hot, dusty air blowing on my face in small, sluggish wafts, thinking 'Now we are going to a hotel.' But we arrived there, got rooms and were at the door of them, and then there seemed to be no future at all, until Jimmy said that I had better have a bath while he telephoned the airport and in half an hour we would have dinner. He did not ask me, he simply arranged it, and I fell gratefully upon half an hour with a future of dinner.

At dinner he told me that he had got two seats on a plane leaving the following evening, and two more for the day after that. 'I'll take her back to her family, and you and Em can go together.'

'Good,' I said: I was feeling sick by then. Then he said that he had tried to get through to the island, but had completely failed. I said that of course we were two hours later than we had told Em that we would be, and I thought the Post Office closed at about eight. He said yes, he'd thought of that too: we would call in the meantime, but meanwhile he'd sent a telegram.

Some time after dinner he said: 'You look absolutely done in! Don't you think you'd better get some sleep? We don't have to hurry in the morning – except I've got to check on those tickets and take them to the place to be filled in.'

But I didn't want to go to bed. He ordered some brandy for both of us and we had another cigarette. As he was lighting mine, he said: 'I suppose losing a father is just about as tough as anything that can happen to a girl, isn't it?'

'It depends what kind of relationship they had. I think it is hard on Alberta.'

'What was it like for you? Or do you mind my asking?'

I shook my head while I was thinking.

'You see I didn't just lose a father. I lost both parents at once: they were drowned sailing together. So I lost my home at the same time, and it is really impossible to separate the losses. It was just that everything I knew came to an end, suddenly, without warning.'

'That must have been awful.' He looked really concerned.

'It's probably less awful to have had all that and lost it than never to have had it at all. I had a very happy childhood, and I adored our house and its country.' It was odd how distant all that seemed now – I heard myself telling it in the voice I used for talking about other people.

He said: 'It must be a strange feeling: I shall have to think carefully what it is like. You said she will be losing her home, too, and her mother died years ago, so it's a little like you, isn't it?'

'Yes.' I realized that until now I would have said, no, it wasn't. I was only fourteen when *my* parents had died – I would have competed with Alberta about loss when it had nothing to do with Jimmy wanting to know how she felt. If there was to be any competition, it was Jimmy who had undoubtedly suffered most, and there he was, thinking about her.

'I've been thinking,' he said: 'do you think it is about time I struck out on my own? I mean, I've spent years now just sticking around having things handed me on a plate. Your asking me whether I could handle the play in New York on my own started me thinking that maybe it's time I stopped doing just what came easiest; I never thought about the future – when I think of the *dough* I might have saved!'

I could not help smiling at him. 'If that is the only thing

you regret about your past, you're not doing so badly. I
should think about it, and wait and see.'

'I wouldn't just walk out on Emmanuel, if that's what is
worrying you. Unless he wanted me to.'

'He'd never want that.' I tried to sound convincing, but I
couldn't look at him.

He said: 'Oh you never know – he might want a change;
people do sometimes.'

Then he said we must get some sleep.

I was half-way through having another bath, before I remembered that I'd had one before dinner. The rising panic
that I had felt when Jimmy said good night to me had re-
sulted in my not having the least idea what I had been
doing: I came to, as it were, lying in warm water, looking at
my body and thinking. 'You washed it all two hours ago!'
and feeling faintly irritated and ridiculous, but I also found
I was looking at my body as though it belonged to someone
else. All my life I had been dominated by this body – poor
Lillian's frail and unpredictable frame – however much care
I took of it, it never seemed to be enough, and I discovered
then that I had always lived with a picture of somebody
called Lillian for whom I would do anything – make endless
allowances, flatter, soothe, commiserate with, and comfort.
She was highly strung, sensitive, intelligent, delicate, deeply
emotional, and vulnerable – she was anybody's sickly romantic picture of a young girl – perpetually in need of protec-
tion and encouragement, guarding her damn feelings so
carefully that they never had a chance to operate: she was
demanding, dishonest, and dull … I could just imagine
reading about her in a short, brilliantly written novel, but
any longer, or more direct association was really too tedious
and absurd … And yet this picture had never left me. Even
though my body had changed until it in no way fitted with
this picture, I had somehow arranged the split. I had not
actually fallen into the crude trap of continuing to dress as
though I was eighteen – had adapted myself externally with
ingenious taste and managed all the time to put up with,
even to nurture, this ageless bore, who, if she was anyone else

but Lillian, I would not have tolerated for a week-end. Now, whoever 'I' was, I was faced with living entirely alone with her for the rest of my life. I got out of the bath, wrapped myself in a towel, went into the bedroom with its twin beds, and sat on the one that had already been turned down for me. Supposing I go back to England alone, she will have to help me find a house and furnish it. It is no good her weeping and wanting everyone to be sorry for her all the time, because nothing will get done like that. I can't take her back to what remains of my family in Norfolk, although they would be delighted to hear that she'd parted with Em, because the moment they stopped being sorry for her, she'd become intolerable. If I found her work, she'd never keep it – she'd be ill, or she'd bore everyone so much that they couldn't work with her. In spite of her 'needing affection so desperately' she's incapable of giving it, or even of engendering it in anyone but me. I wouldn't want her to meet people, she'd let me down so terribly – she simply isn't interested in anything but herself, and although she thinks that I've led her a 'hard life', she hasn't got any experience at all. She has absolutely no sense of proportion, so nothing makes her laugh – she's neurotic to the point of madness, and if we hadn't turned out to have the same name, nothing would have induced me to have anything to do with her. I would really rather be alone. Just because she was so kind and understanding to me about Sarah, doesn't give her the right to drag at me now. And I suddenly realized that if Sarah had lived, I would have just had to get rid of her because she would have been so bad for Sarah. The possibility of ever having been able to get rid of her was extraordinarily bracing: on the strength of it, I got into the other bed without a sleeping pill.

It was good to lie down: I felt my weight making its shape in the bed, and shut my eyes. Immediately, as though in some other sense I had opened them, there was a picture of Alberta – still in her faded pink shirt – thrown into his arms and weeping so bitterly for her father that I longed to comfort her too.

3. ALBERTA

If I write this out – just what has happened – it may get a little clearer, and if it did, I might know how to bear it. Now that I've spoken to Uncle Vin, I at least *know* what has happened – it's just that I cannot think about it – I cannot think at all: everything looks the same, life goes on from minute to minute and I go with it, only it all feels quite unreal, and just as it begins to feel ominous and odd that everything should all look the same and yet feel so unreal, the fact about him suddenly explodes all over again as though I hadn't known before. He is dead: he was knocked over by a car in the little lane by the church on the corner they were always going to widen. *The car didn't stop.* He was on his bicycle – Aunt T. said he'd been to see old Mr Derwent who was ill, and he'd gone after supper: this happened on his way back – about a quarter to ten, they think, but they don't know, because they didn't find him until some time after eleven. He was dead when they found him. I asked Uncle Vin whether he had been killed at once by the car and Uncle Vin said no, he didn't think that he had been. So perhaps he had a little time which I know he would have wanted – without too much pain – oh! that part of it *is difficult* – not knowing that, and I may never know. I cannot write about the driver of the car because I know too well what Papa would say about that, and now he is dead and will never speak to me or write to me again, I shall have to remember more than ever what he has said. Otherwise there will be nothing left of him – I shall lose it all.

There seem to be two sides to this. I don't see why Papa of all people should be subject to such an accident; he wasn't old, he was very useful. He must have noticed that Papa was one of the more useful people, he was so much loved and depended upon. I could understand it a little better if he had had to die *for* something – to save somebody's life, or for some greater cause, but it wasn't like that. He simply gets knocked down on an evening because there wasn't a moon and I don't suppose the tail light of his bicycle was working – I was the only person who ever got it to work – and is left to lie in a ditch and die by himself: *why*? This makes me feel violent: the only person who understood about that and ever helped me to get past it was Papa, and this is the second side of it. It seems to me that losing him is something which stretches round me in every direction – there is no end to the loss – starting from quite small things like calling him in the house and hearing him answer, to feeling that wherever I was or whatever happened, he stood in the same relation to me: he said 'We cannot do without help', but it was *he* who helped me, and I loved him for that too. Supposing he had not died but I had this aching shock about someone, what would I do? I would go to him and tell him about it – everything that I have put down here: I would say: 'The one person in my life – the only person who is really necessary to me has been killed in a useless, silly accident. There is something wicked here – that somebody so loved and useful should be murdered out of carelessness.' What would he say to that? He would ask me what this person had stood for in my life. I would say that apart from his being a most important part of my family and my having always known him and loved him, he was the only person who gave me any sense of direction, because what he felt and thought and did was founded on what seemed to be an unshakeable integrity which gave them a sense of purpose and proportion. I found this utterly reliable, and loved it.

Now I have had to think most carefully what Papa would say to this – I have to imagine, out of all the other things that he has said to me, what he would say to this; but I don't think he would really say things, he would ask me a hard question: he would say was it reliable of this person to die and leave me so bereft? The answer to that, of course, is that he couldn't help it. He would agree with that, wouldn't he? Yes, he would; I remember now what he said about examples – he said that if one threw one's arms round a signpost one might become so devoted to it that one forgot what it was for – he said this was a discouraging thing that happened to signposts. What he's really meaning is that people aren't designed to be the kind of reliable that I'm talking about: or perhaps they were designed to be but none of them manage it. If somebody gives one a sense of direction that one wants, the direction cannot die – it would still be there even if one lost it. If he gave me that, I don't want to forget what he said or what he was, but somehow, I must try to go on by myself.

Did he feel like this when my mother died? Because all these years *he* hasn't had anybody who meant to him what he has meant to me. I don't think he has even *tried* to make another person reliable – he just went on by himself: I know that, so that in some way it hasn't stopped because he is dead. So: I am supposed to *make use of his death* – that is how he would see it: he once said: 'It takes *far more* love to be impersonal – not less; will you think about that possibility, my dear Sarah?' But I never did: he has actually had to die to make me consider it. I am the last person to try and pick out wickedness when I don't understand what is good. He always said that was a mug's game.

So the real question about Papa is not what did he die for at all. It is the opposite, and that is what I must try and understand. Otherwise, it is very like having to be on a cliff with no head for heights.

4. EMMANUEL

HE turned his back on the boat and walked slowly across the quay away from them. He had at once the sensation of being entirely trapped and entirely free. He had just become aware of this when he heard Jimmy shouting to him: 'Better beware!' He turned round, but Jimmy didn't shout anything more. He was free now to make his decision in peace: he was trapped into the necessity for making a decision. He had never expected an opportunity to look after her – from the moment the telegram had arrived he had foreseen nothing but her shock, his responses choked by convention, and endless, wearisome arrangements made by Jimmy. He had fallen in with this – what else could he do? He had got Lillian out of the Post Office before she fainted from the heat, and after that he had simply fallen in with Jimmy's determination and Lillian's whim. Now they were gone, and he was left with her. He had almost reached the Post Office when the certain knowledge, that he wanted to marry her and live with her always more than he had ever wanted anything else and more than he cared about deserting Lillian, struck him. It had not been tangible before – he had felt suspended, first by the shock of finding that he loved her, then by his circumstances and the need for concealment. But now, in some way, action had been taken for him by her father's death, now if she was ever to be his it was necessary that he make some move, now whatever she might feel about him had become relevant. He did not have Jimmy's cynical confidence in his powers – about them, he simply felt that it was easy to achieve something that one did not very much want – one was detached enough for the right kind of intellectual consideration – but he did feel that something which was so profoundly and startlingly true for him could not leave her disaffected. . . .

In the Post Office he discovered that she was standing exactly where he had left her over an hour ago. The boy, who was sitting on the floor, said: 'We have had one false alarm' and she tried to smile at him, but he saw from her eyes that she was not seeing him clearly.

'If we go and sit outside for a bit, would you call us if the call comes through?'

Julius nodded, and she made no protest when he took her arm and led her outside, until they were almost at the café table, when she said: 'It will be all right, won't it? I must speak to them.'

'I promise you.' He arranged his chair so that he could see the Post Office door and saw Julius looking through the window to see where they were. 'It's all right: he's seen us. All he need do is wave. Have a cold drink.'

She nodded, and then asked: 'Where are the others?'

'They've gone on the boat,' he said gently: 'to see about the plane tickets.'

'Oh yes.' She said it as though that had nothing to do with her.

When her drink arrived she said: 'I do realize that this has disorganized everybody: I'm so sorry.'

'We were all ready to go back anyway,' he replied with what he hoped was just the right note of callous cheerfulness.

She had not touched her drink; she stared at it quite calmly, and then said: 'I'm afraid I can't drink it: I feel too dizzy.'

He got up, turned her round in her chair by her shoulders, and pushed her head down between her knees, catching her just as her body started to go limp.

After a very short time he felt her head pressing up against his hand and released her.

'All right?' She had some colour in her face now, and he realized how white she had been.

'Yes, thank you. I haven't done that for years – I used to know exactly when to put my own head down.'

He handed her her drink. 'You sound as though you have had a great deal of practice. I should drink some of that.'

'Years of it. Nearly every week at Early Service. You need practice to kneel with no food inside you. Could you get some more orange?'

'You haven't finished that one.'

'I should like to take some to Julius; he is a kind boy, and exceedingly fond of orange juice.'

'I'll take him some: you stay where you are.'

Julius received the drink gravely – he had picked up a number of Greek manners. There were more people in the Post Office, as the mail from the boat had been sorted, and a letter was handed to him. He asked Julius if there were any more, and Julius asked and there weren't. As he walked back to her he saw her put her hands on each side of the small table and grip it, and he knew that she was using the table to make something real for herself and his throat ached with pity, but when he reached her she looked up and said: 'Was he pleased?'

'I think he was. There was only one letter – for me.' He put it on the table. 'Do you think it would make it any easier for you while you are waiting for this call if you talked about it?'

But she answered stiffly: 'I haven't anything to say.'

A moment later she said: 'I didn't mean to sound ungrateful. It is just that I am trying to get used to the idea: it seems to be all I can do.'

'Telegrams are winding. It will be better when you have talked to your family.'

She said in a low voice: 'It will seem more real, anyway.'

He had never felt so powerless: everything he longed to do was either useless or impossible. He wanted to take her in his arms and hold her head until she wept and released some tension of her feeling; he wanted to tell her that there was nothing that he would not to do help her – now and always; he wanted to tell that he knew how she was feeling, that he loved her and would never allow anything again to hurt her as this was hurting, he would prevent, or at least share it. But he knew that he wasn't even sharing it: he leaned towards her, impelled to say something, and as suddenly she smiled and looked down to her feet.

'I wondered what this was.' She had bent down and came up with an extremely small, very dirty kitten in her hands. The moment that she put it on her lap, it rose on to its hind legs, climbed up her and thrust its bullet head under her chin, emitting an improbably noisy irregular clockwork purr.

'Oh really! It seems quite frantic for affection. Isn't it a curious colour? Like a black cat dipped in flour. It's rather ugly, in fact.'

But she was still smiling at it: it was a filthy little creature, with long legs, a rat-like tail, and its ears still looked as though they had been stuck on to its head, but he felt so grateful to it for making her smile, that he said: 'I'll get it some food.'

They gave it some bread and cheese on the table, which it

ate in frenzied tearing gulps. Two other full-grown cats arrived like magic; one of them jumped on to the third empty chair, but the kitten put one paw over the bread, fluffed out its meagre coat, and swore with such appalling violence that the older cat washed a hind leg and retreated. When it had eaten everything, it walked twice round the table for crumbs, neatly avoiding the letter, looked them both in the face, jumped on to Alberta's lap and went to sleep with hiccoughs. She said: 'It has the most honest expression, quite unlike Napoleon, who always makes one feel rather uncomfortable on purpose. She's our cat at home.'

'This is a little guttersnipe: it's learned all it knows the hard way. It doesn't look as though it has learned much about washing.'

She stroked its back and said serenely: 'No: it is probably covered with fleas. I wonder whether ...' but even before him she had seen Julius waving. She said. 'Please keep the kitten,' put it on his knee, and went.

He kept the kitten and waited: it seemed a long time. Eventually, because he had to find something to take his mind off waiting for her, he picked up the letter and opened it.

It was from Mrs Friedmann and it was about the boy, Matthias; the writing was enormous, but difficult to read.

I am needing to explain something which is hard but you are so much the good man you will have little difficulty of understanding.

There followed a long and pathetic account of Matthias's state of mind. He had lost one finger at the second joint, and damaged two more so badly that playing the violin was out of the question for him. He was shocked, and inconsolable about this – wished to die – he had tried to attack the surgeon and after that seemed to have no interest in anything or anybody. The sight of Mrs Friedmann or Becky reduced him to floods of tears, and the sound or even the idea of music made him hysterical. He was still in a hospital although they had moved him: they had tried to have him at home, but it was clear that he needed continuous attention, and as he seemed not to endure Mrs Friedmann it had not proved practicable to keep him there. Then came her astonishing suggestion.

You will not know how it is to feel that there is nothing for him I may do his needing so much to be helped and I helpless. Hans too has tried and tried and the doctors talk with him at first they say a little time but now the talking about time have they stopped. We have agreed Hans and I that he must another chance now have and this is why dear Mr Joyce I now write to you – to say that I must ask you now to take Matthias out of his hospital and away with you into life as you have so much more to give in changing scene and full life of peoples and interest than for us is possible. Last night I am speaking with Hans and say I am so sad and unhappy because I so much love Matthias and he say 'You love Matthias? Or you love having a son?' *This is true*, Mr Joyce – too *much* – and now I am knowing it so must write and ask you. We are agreed that there is no other person so full of trust because your goodness to us we will never never forget and know we can have no ways of paying to you our deep thanks. I have also to say that for this one time I write the letter instead of Hans as I think you will not believe that I mean to bear giving up Matthias unless you read my writing with your eyes. Hans will be writing as there is much finances to be under discussion as he will be wishing to pay all for Matthias supposing in your great kindness you agree to what I am asking. Forgiving my shocking English and all I am asking which I would not do except for the boy.

She was his faithfully, B. Friedmann. For a while he sat, shocked by the enormous simplicity of her suggestion. That she should calmly – well, not calmly – but that she should simply suggest handing the boy over to him! She had, of course, exaggerated ideas of his goodness since it was he who had provided her with the children and the means to keep them in the first place, and she had wanted them more than anything else. But still – to suggest handing over a hysterical desperate child who had just lost what he clearly felt was the reason for his life just because she felt it would be better for *him* and that he, Emmanuel, was the best person to take on this delicate and trying responsibility because he was such a wonderful character leading such a full, interesting, and good life! 'She doesn't know', he thought grimly, 'that I am in process of trying to get rid of my extremely difficult, sick wife, and marry a girl more than forty years younger than myself – if she'll have me. The uproar that these two moves will create is hardly conducive to the recovery of a highly strung boy.' He would have to go and see the Friedmanns, however, as soon as he got to London, and explain to them. He crammed the letter into his pocket – trying to feel angry, trying to feel amused by Mrs Friedmann's guileless presumptions. Then Alberta returned, with Julius following her. She was very pale again: she didn't say anything – just sat down as though she was very tired.

They walked across the port to a restaurant for lunch – it was only because Julius said he must go home for this, that they realized that it was lunch time. The kitten followed them, and in the end she picked it up and settled down at a table with it. They ate tiny little tepid fried fish and stuffed tomatoes which were served a little cooler than they were themselves. Neither of them ate much, but the kitten gorged and swore until it was a triangular shape and its whiskers were sticky with rice. Then, belching heavily, it settled again on Alberta's lap and tried to clean itself up. She said: 'I like the way its life goes on.' She was holding its wretched little tail for it to wash. They had reached the coffee rather gratefully: their silence, except for talking about the kitten occasionally, had lasted all through the meal. Now he said abruptly: 'Will you tell me what your family said?'

'He was knocked down by a car in the lane by the church – in the evening. He was dead by the time they found him.'

'They? What about whoever was driving the car?'

'They didn't stop,' she said: her voice had no expression

at all when she said this, and something about her face checked his angry exclamation.

'My uncle is there – I spoke mostly to him. I told him that I was coming home as soon as possible. Is that all right?'

'Of course. Will you want to stay there for a time?'

But she looked as though the question was utterly beyond her, so he did not pursue it. Then she said: 'I'm glad that I talked to them, anyway. Do you think we could go back to the house now?'

He paid for lunch, and said: 'What about your kitten?'

'I thought I'd take it up to the house with me. It doesn't seem to belong to anybody, so no one will mind where it spends the afternoon. Do *you* mind?'

'I think it is a good idea.' He meant it: it could at least be something real for her for the day, although he had a pang of jealousy that this creature could collect her attention. But on the way home, she said: 'You are being so exceedingly kind and thoughtful to me. I do really notice it, I simply find it difficult to discuss.' Her voice shook a little with the effort of saying this.

He looked at her walking up the hill beside him. 'It is nothing, my dear Sarah – don't try to talk about any of it.' His heart was pounding: she looked at him with a gentle expression when he used her name, and suddenly he could not stop. 'Sometimes', he said painfully, 'I love you: sometimes you seem a part of something that I love.' He stopped abruptly; it was enough – more than enough. She gave him an odd abstracted little smile and their silence closed over these words, so that a minute later they might never have been spoken. He did not know what she felt; minutes later, he wondered whether she had even heard them.

When they got back to the house, they found Julius sitting outside their door. He was reading a very large book which proved to be Wells's *Outline of History*: he wore his usual jeans supplemented by a huge sheath knife, and his back was the smooth and tender brown of an egg.

'I thought you might have further telephoning and would need my services in Greek.'

'Jimmy Sullivan is going to call me between six and seven this evening: will that be difficult, do you think?'

'Is he the man who went this morning on the boat?'

When they said he was, Julius said ho, well he wouldn't arrive in Piraeus until well after eight in the evening, and explained to them about the boat's circuit. When they realized that the boat was due back to their island in about half an hour he asked her whether she wanted to catch it.

'I don't know. We haven't packed – I mean there is everybody's packing to be done . . .'

'If you like, I will try to arrange that a caique takes you over tonight,' Julius offered.

He looked at her. 'Would you prefer that?'

'I would. But if Julius can't manage it, won't we be rather stuck?'

'There are many caiques going over in summer – it will be all right, it will be fine and wonderful and much better than going in the big boat. Is that your cat?'

She had put the kitten down on the terrace and it lay on its side, gazing at them with fierce innocent eyes. 'Not really. I just found it. Does it belong to anyone, do you know?'

'I will find out. I will go now and leave my book here.'

When Julius had gone, he said. 'You're quite right. We couldn't get packed up in time and we'll need at least one donkey to get it down to the port.'

She picked up the kitten, and said: 'If you don't mind, I would rather leave the packing for a bit. Could we do it later?'

Although she said nothing about it, her need to be alone was now so apparent that without a word he opened the door of her room for her and shut her into it.

He went back on to the terrace, and stood a while staring through the hot restful scene before him. It was one of the hours when the age of this country rose up to the eye: sun burning on rock and sea: animals still – people absent – houses shuttered – the few trees still in the windless heat, and the sky so wide – so spread past a vault or a canopy, of such penetrating height, such boundless distance that it was immortally beyond space and eternally above time: he looked up at it, and as his eyes left the sea and rocks of the island a picture of the whole world placed itself naturally between him and the sky; only now the seas were like single drops of water, the lands small crumbs of earth – the sky was loaded with other stars, with invisible suns and unknown moons, and this world was a grain of dust and water, a particle, an incident so small that it would demand absolute attention for its notice. And yet this same earth contained a multitude of life about most of which he knew nothing; it was of an antiquity that he could not honestly envisage; its variety and size seemed too great for him to explore, and his existence upon it was not significant. Inside that insignificance he thrashed and machinated and obeyed an authority made up tomorrow, the next generation, and once upon a time. Inside that authority he used words from one of many languages for a small specific purpose of communicating – what? only what he could feel or perceive – the fruit from his little personal shrub of knowledge; he did this and expected to be paid for it in happiness collected off other people, a lavish change in his material scenery, and any other trappings that helped to make him swell. 'And there I am, in my nutshell,' he thought: 'and I can't write a play about the stars, because I don't understand them; nor can I become a star. I don't even know what it feels like to be a tree, let alone a star. I don't really know what it feels like to be anybody else.'

He was upstairs, in his room: he had not noticed going there, and it seemed to him extraordinary that, in the middle of discovering the minute size of his life, he should fail to be aware of even one moment of it. Some part of him must have decided to go, and his legs then carried him and here he was – almost as though he had missed out a minute of his life by not existing in it. But if one noticed this kind of thing, then one must be living in a more slipshod manner than was intended – he was, perhaps, rattling about in his nutshell. This was too much: insignificance was one thing –

inadequacy was quite another – he did not feel that he could afford it: it made any regrets or desires about understanding the stars utterly absurd. Quite suddenly her criticism of Clemency that she had made in New York came into his mind. She had said that all the things that Clemency had to give up didn't seem to matter much, because she hadn't herself valued them. He had been going to rewrite that bit, and he'd done nothing about it. Why? It was partly laziness, of course, but it was also because although he'd agreed with her, and thought she was right, he hadn't felt what to do about it. It wasn't a piece of writing where one could rely on what a lot one knew about how to write a scene. So rightly, in a sense, he had left it. The trouble was that with his experience of doing without, he'd tended to avoid giving up anything – in case that left him utterly deprived.

He felt now extremely restless, and decided to pack. For weeks now he had been longing for a whole day alone with her, and now that he had got it, every single thing was wrong. She was deeply unhappy, unreachable in her present state: and yet for weeks he had thought of nothing but her, and on top of that his recent thoughts had further diminished and disturbed him, until he felt that, without her, his life would cease to have any meaning at all. He packed all his own things with a kind of angry speed. At some unknown point in time he would be packing to go away with her – the tears, the recriminations, the public yelps of disapproval, the years trying to compensate somebody for something which wasn't his fault – all of it behind him; he would start a new life – he would use everything he had learned to make it different and good for her. . . .

He went downstairs quietly, in case she was asleep: her western shutters were closed, but he had such a desire to see that she was there that he went round to the other terrace, where her room had another window. She was sitting on the floor, leaning against her bed, and she slept with her head against her arm. On the bed was a letter, a large open book, and her pen. He was afraid that if he looked at her too long he would wake her.

He went back upstairs and packed Jimmy's things. Jimmy felt curiously distant; like someone he had once known, but had not met for years. It did not take him long to pack up Jimmy's things.

Now – Lillian. She had left a certain amount of luggage in New York, but she still seemed to have brought an incredible amount. He started methodically with her shoes – mostly sandals of every shape and colour: they all had to be packed in separate linen bags embroidered with her initials. The chest of drawers was full to overflowing with underclothes, shirts, sweaters, shorts, scarves – what on earth could she want with forty-eight scarves, he counted wondering, the wardrobe was crammed with skirts, dresses, jackets, duster coats, hats, belts, trousers, and dressing-gowns. The top of the chest of drawers was littered with bottles and pots, little fitted cases, brushes and combs, jewellery, sun glasses, scent, toilet water, and all kinds of lipsticks and rouge. There was also the small red leather folder that had the photographs of Sarah which she was usually never without. He opened it: there she was – two pictures of her, one laughing, one serious: they were rather blurred as they had been too much enlarged: Sarah sitting on a table in a pale dress, with a mere coxcomb of hair: her head looking too large for her body, her bare arms just creased at the wrist, her fingers joyfully articulate. In the serious picture her eyes looked dark and enormous, in the laughing one her forehead was charmingly wrinkled: dear little Sarah – but she was dead: she had been dead for fourteen years and Lillian could not let go of her; pined and brooded over these pictures for hours of her life, and never forgot about them. Whatever she thought, she felt about nothing but Sarah. Really, compared with Lillian, Mrs Friedmann's view that naturally he would do anything for Matthias was hardly obsessive . . . Why had he thought of her, of Mrs Friedmann? It wasn't because of Lillian and Sarah, he realized, it was something else – it was nearly everything that had happened since he had read her letter: he hadn't really stopped thinking about her at all – only he hadn't thought in words. A picture of Mrs Friedmann rose before him: fat, a vulgar shape, overdressed, plastered with wildly unsuitable make-up, her rather hoarse but musical voice saying things that made her own eyes fill with easy tears – he realized that some of them had dropped on to the letter that she had written him – he had to read it again. He cleared a place on the bed, and sat down.

He read it very slowly, and sat for a long time afterwards, unable to move: it might have been another letter that he had read in the morning and he another man reading it. Now, he had no words of any kind – he felt simply, entirely exposed, and seized by some unnameable emotion as though his heart was blushing a deep red. He did not know how long it lasted, but at the beginning of its end he heard himself finding that past a certain degree emotions did not need separate names – they were all one – or at least a part of all one. This discovery seemed to be tremendously important; it brought with it a sense of truth and triumph: for a moment he was filled with elation like a soundless fire which silently consumed all his dead, heavy rubbish until he no longer felt like a stone inside his body, and his mind was a poised feather rising and falling over the warm breaths below it . . . Afterwards, or perhaps even before it had died, he started to see his life as though he was on some height, and it lay on a distant plain below him; occurring without chronology, but with amazing swiftness and certainty: events – pursuing – caught up with and overcame his imagination of himself. So – the man in New York who had remembered the boy who swore to rescue his mother in a carriage with horses was now faced with the young man who had let her pine until he had to lift her into it, and now the black plumes on the black horses nodded and told him so. The man who could move Jimmy to a most tender concern for his romantic story of one fine day in the country with a beautiful girl whom he had then lost, was faced now with the man who had lied to the girl, had forgotten her, and only discovered her plight by accident and too late. His implications to Jimmy of his grief, his fate, and misfortune were now ruthlessly transplanted – to the girl – to Jimmy himself. The figure he had designed who enjoyed his reputation for patience and loyalty to a woman who had disappointed him, was faced with the man who had chosen – in a fit of curiosity and solitude – to marry her: the little reasons for doing so crept out now from the vault of his true memory where he had kept them incarcerated: she attracted him because ten years before she would have been unattainable – she represented a kind of life that he thought he would never understand and it was flattering at more than forty to have this young beauty turn her first attentions to him. Everything that happened to Lillian with him had been touched by these considerations he employed about himself in their beginning, and he resented their deserts on behalf of a man who did not exist. 'My wife is as good as she is beautiful,' Friedmann had said, and his saying it recurred – the first words spoken in this silent panorama. He had never in his life felt that about anyone until now; and as he understood this, he saw all his desires and intentions and his behaviour about them, like two sharply serrated edges, clash as though they had never been formed to meet, annihilating all possibility of love. But now, as he approached *her* – she who seemed in a sense to have given birth to his heart, who he thought had entirely transformed him – he was halted by pictures of past approaches in his imagination – of holding her bare shoulders in his hands – of her whole body like a young unexplored country – of her youth that could not compare him with another man – she was to give him transfusions of life; she was to nourish him with her impressions; he was to live on the virtue of her discoveries, since he had forgotten or discarded his own. It was then that he saw her separate from himself. He saw her whole – her promise, her dangers, her degree of life, what moved and what slept in her, what shape what colour what sound of a woman she was now; he saw everything that she was, and not she but the truth of this sight made him see both of her and of himself what was eternal and what could be changed. This knowledge of her, which gradually became more and more brilliantly illuminated – endured past his astonishment (was she, who he had thought entire perfection, only this?) – and past his pain, the disorder, the abuse, the entire *lack of necessity* for her, the quantity of suffering which in ignorance of her he would invoke in order to get what he wanted, was suddenly perfectly plain to him – it endured until its reality met with his acceptance: there was a moment of bliss in this recognition, and then imperceptibly he became aware that it had happened – that it had finished. He was sitting on the bed looking into empty sunlit air with Mrs Friedmann's letter crushed in his hand.

Julius stood in the doorway, and it struck him as an interesting piece of order that he should arrive just then – not a few minutes earlier, and not much later when, alone, he might have succumbed to bitterness at the difficulties ahead. Julius said: 'Your caique is arranged – it will cost you 500 drachmas. It leaves at somewhere after half past eleven tonight; I have come to an arrangement with my parents whereby I am enabled to see you off. Are you in favour of vengeance?'

'I don't know.' He felt truthful and startled.

'It is very much done here: of course it is dull compared with the old days.'

'What was it like then?'

'Oh – embroidered cloaks stiff with poison and poisoned wine and swords and things – poisons were generally fashionable, but I don't think people are very well up in them any more. I have been told you write plays: it must make that much more difficult. No wonder,' he added kindly.

He did not feel equal to being unfavourably compared with Euripides, so he said: 'It really is kind of you to have made all the arrangements for us: there is one more thing. Do you think when you go back to the port you could arrange a donkey or two for us for the luggage?'

His face fell, but he simply said: 'What time?'

'I thought about nine. Then we'll lock up here and come in and perhaps you would have dinner with us at about half past at whatever restaurant you think the best. Could you do that?' His eyes shone and he gave a little hop, but he said solemnly: 'I should be charmed and delighted and – charmed. I'll meet you at Jannis at twenty past nine.' Then he moved closer and said in a piercing whisper: 'I have paid for that kitten myself as a parting present for her. It will be a surprise to cheer her up: we might have a discussion on English literature at dinner, mightn't we?'

'We easily might.'

He gave a shout of joy and chanted: 'Alternative subjects – astronomy, history of civilizations, or whether it is necessary to get to the moon. The donkeys will come.' And he went.

He folded up Mrs Friedmann's letter and put it carefully away – he felt that one way and another he was going to need it.

By the time she appeared he had finished Lillian's packing and was sitting on the terrace. She walked slowly across the terrace towards him rolling up the sleeves of a faded shirt that he remembered had once belonged to Lillian: he looked at her face – she was a little flushed from her sleep but her eyes had not changed – they had still the distant look of strain about them which made them too large and dark. 'Would you like to have one last bathe?' he said: 'all the plans have been excellently made by Julius, and we are dining with him at nine thirty.'

'What about the packing?'

'It is all done excepting yours and whatever I have forgotten. We have plenty of time. Where is your kitten?'

'It has gone to sleep in my hat.' She stood aimlessly by the parapet. 'It is still very hot. Perhaps it would be a good idea to bathe.'

They walked in silence down to the bay where they had always bathed: he found that he was intensely aware of his surroundings; of the late afternoon sun turning amber on the rocks – the sea below them streaked with dark purple patches – the hot, somehow antique smell from the land – but he felt that she was simply following him – she hardly knew where she was. They had all taken to getting up in their bathing things, so she unbuttoned her shirt, pulled carelessly at the zip on her skirt, stepped out of it, and moved towards the water. He said: 'Please wait for me,' he was afraid that she would swim miles away, and he was too poor a swimmer to be any help if she needed it. She sat down on the rock with her feet in the water and waited, without answering. When she saw he was ready she slipped in and he followed her. The water was marvellous after all the sweat of the day, and for a few minutes he simply floated and let it wash him, and looked up at the sky, and when he looked he saw that she was swimming furiously to the point where Jimmy and she used to go with the goggles, and, worrying about her, he started laboriously to follow. When he was less than half-way there, he saw that she had climbed on to a ledge and was sitting with her back to him looking out to sea. He had not swum to this point before, and it took him a long time; he was out of breath and exhausted by the time he reached her. He clutched the sharp edge of the rock and painfully hoisted himself out of the water, but she did not turn round.

'Phew!' he said, feeling nervous and absurd; 'that's the longest swim I've done here.'

She didn't answer for a bit, and then said: 'I'm sorry – but I haven't got anything at all to say. I think I'll go in now,' jumped off the rock and swam away.

He watched her go; he was too tired to swim back at once – and she was swimming back to the beach anyway. The sleep had slackened the hold she had over herself and it was the first time she had had to wake with her father's death. He knew about this from seeing Lillian struggle with it, but it had caught her unawares. He watched her land and put her towel round her – he could almost see her tenseness from here: he had to get her over this bit of it. 'My poor darling,' he thought, and it was a simple thought, charged only with gentleness.

The swim back seemed interminable: he tried to take it slowly and easily – but in the end it just became a matter of getting there somehow. He climbed out at last and sat gasping on the rock feeling too weak to reach his towel. She had dressed and was drying her hair.

'Throw me my towel, like a kind girl,' he said: 'I'm not built for swimming and I'm far too old to learn now. Did your father like swimming?'

She stopped towelling her hair, and said: 'He never had much time for it. Besides the water is awfully cold at our nearest bit of sea.'

'Women are supposed to be much better at it than men: especially indoor men like me. Although I don't suppose he had rickets as a child as I did.'

She said: 'I don't think so' in a muffled voice and tried to go on with her hair.

He continued to talk and to dress as though he was completely unaware of her. 'Do you remember when you first told me about your father? It was on the aeroplane going to New York: you told me all kinds of things that he had said to you, and instead of that being irritating or dull, you made me feel what a delightful man he was.'

She had stopped even trying to dry her hair – her head was bent so that he couldn't see her face, but she was shaking from head to foot. He got up, drew his belt round him, and moved closer to her before sitting again.

'I was thinking how difficult it was for you to have this shock without having him to help you about it. I was wondering – if this doesn't sound too strange to you – what as the person who has always helped you most he would say if you told him that your father, whom you loved, had suddenly died. I was thinking that if you could manage to separate these two things *at all* – it might make a difference. What do you think about that?'

She looked up at last – her face white again – a tumult of misery and recognition: he said again very gently: 'What do you think?' and held out his arms. . . .

He held her in silence through the worst of it – until he felt her beginning to return from her abandon – to come out of her maze of grief; then when she was quieter and beginning to be aware of him, he pushed her hair out of her eyes and mopped her face with her towel – with an intentional clumsiness so that she smiled like watery sunlight and sat up. When he had found her a handkerchief, she said: 'If one loves somebody very much indeed – it is difficult to be impersonal about them, isn't it?'

'Very.'

She blew her nose again. 'You know what you said about trying to separate the two things?'

'Yes?'

'Well – I agree with it. It is just that I was finding it very difficult to do.'

'Easier now?'

She nodded. 'I just needed to cry for him once.'

'You may need to again: you are very young, dear Sarah; you have a great deal ahead.'

She looked at him uncertainly.

'I mean – cry because you love him – don't feel too bitterly deprived.' That's enough of that, he thought, and got to his feet.

On the way back to the house the thoughts that he had held her in his arms and that tomorrow she would be on her way back to England occurred with random wildness – he couldn't stop them occurring, but he found it possible to jerk his attention to something else: it would be easier when there was some distance to them: when he had to say 'last week, last month, two years ago'.

When she had packed, she joined him on the terrace: she was carrying the kitten – squirming with appreciation – in her arms. Her tears seemed somehow to have cleansed and simplified her face: she was beautiful after them – her eyelids swollen and smooth as cream, her eyes clear as washed slate, her mouth and forehead gentle with the tensions gone. She had changed into a dark blue shirt with the sleeves rolled up – there was a white stripe on her wrist where her watch had been.

'It has slept all the afternoon. It seems so fond of me that I cannot help reciprocating. Do you think it will mind awfully being returned to its guttersnipe life?'

319

'We'll give it another enormous dinner anyway'; he did not want to spoil Julius's surprise. He had brought out the large wicker-covered jar which was still half-full of wine, and now he handed her a glass.

'We might as well drink until the donkey man arrives.'

'And watch our last sunset.'

'Yes.' He wondered painfully what that meant to her. 'You have not got your watch on.'

'I'm going to give it to Julius. It is the only thing I can think of that he would like. I've put it in a box – the one that had my evening bag you gave me in it.'

'Isn't that far too big a box for a watch?'

'Yes, but I've wrapped it in a good many fig leaves, so it doesn't rattle. It's not a very girlish watch. Do you think he will like it?'

'He is sure to. Sarah!'

She pushed the kitten down into her lap and looked up.

'Shall you be going to New York, do you think?'

'Have you both decided that you want me?'

'We have both decided that we want you.' He smiled to ease the words for himself. 'But I may not be able to come over with you as I have things to do in England. You may have to go with Jimmy; will that be all right for you?'

'Would you come and see the play in the end?'

'Oh yes, I expect so. But Jimmy would look after you: or will your family need you at home?'

'I think my family will need me to earn some money more than anything else.'

'Jimmy would look after you,' he repeated, pressing the point.

She blushed a little, and said: 'I know.' She was silent for a moment, and then added suddenly: 'He even said he'd *marry* me in order to look after me better in New York.'

'What did you say to that?'

She spread out her hands. 'Well – nothing – except thanking him. He asked me in the sort of way you advise people to go to your dentist, because he's so much better than the one they've got.'

'I don't suppose he felt like that at all. He hasn't got much confidence in people liking him, unless he feels he's useful to them. That is probably my fault.' Then, suddenly, he told her about the girl in the country – the whole story, with all its truthful uncertainties: including the search he had made, for years, but too casually, for Jimmy: how he had thought when finally he discovered him and sent for him in London that he would be sure when he saw him, and hadn't been – had never been sure, and had therefore (therefore? he wondered) never told Jimmy. He considered nothing but the truth while he was telling it, not even his own motives for telling it to her, but at the end he was conscious of some lightening of this particular weight on him, and looked nervously to see whether it had transferred to her. But she, who had listened quietly making no sound or sign, now looked back at him with an impersonal friendliness and said: 'I should think anybody would be glad to know that you might have been their father.'

'You mean you think I should have told him?'

She hesitated: 'I don't know whether you *should* have. I meant only that he might be glad to be told.'

They watched the clouds, like a veiled chorus, gather and turn iris in a sky flushed to cloth of gold by the brilliant sun which suffused as it sank and left streaks of greens and pinks – both tender and piercing, like a lament, in the air – the sea like burnished steel – the land mysteriously shadowed – and the air turning to velvet, sparked with stars and the yellow domestic lights.

'Would *you* tell him for me?' he asked after a long and companionable silence.

'Don't you want to do that yourself?'

'I – no, no I don't. Unless you think I must?'

'The truth, you see,' he said a minute later: 'I should find that peculiarly difficult with him after all these years.' He looked at her almost pleadingly: 'If I *knew* precisely one way or the other whether he was my son it would be different. As it is I am afraid of simply kicking up a lot of dust about his mother – and, also, it is my fault that I don't know, of course.'

She said: 'Yes – I will tell him when the right moment comes. If you trust me.'

'I would be very grateful to you.'

'So am I to you. Does it seem to you a very long time since this morning?'

'A very long time.'

'And tonight this house will be as though we were never in it.'

'Oh,' he said, 'shall we have left no mark?'

He felt her looking at him gravely in the dusk: 'I very much doubt it. It may have marked us, but I don't think we have marked it: its time is too long.'

They heard the delicate, hesitant tapping of a mule or donkey's feet on the stone outside. 'This is the end of being really alone with her,' he thought: 'even the boat won't be quite like this: this is an end.' He got to his feet: 'How are you going to manage the kitten?'

'In a sling round my neck. It is the most adaptable creature. It made a very neat mess in a flower pot in my room.'

When the mule was laden, he came out of the house to lock the door, and she was standing where she had stood that morning on the terrace when she had told him the contents of the telegram, and the rush of feeling that he had had for her then recurred. He turned away quickly to lock the door: in the morning he had been silent because he had felt restricted by other people – now, at least, he was restricting himself – and he tried now to stiffen himself with this difference.

They walked behind the mule to the port, facing a young moon that lay couched in little clouds like a young beauty on a bed of feathers. The man spoke to his mule, but they were silent until they met Julius who was waiting for them. He wore a spotless shirt and his bleached and tufted hair had been smoothed, his face was solemn but discreetly decorated by a little smile of excitement.

'I have commanded quail – small roasted birds. Ho! that's a good way to carry a cat. I should think you'd be desolate to part with it, wouldn't you?'

'She's very sad about it,' he said firmly before she could answer Julius.

Dinner was a great success. He found their combined company charming: Julius drank four bottles of orange and the kitten crunched up so many quail bones that it had not even energy to swear at other cats. After dinner she gave Julius the watch: he was very impressed and told her about the kitten. Then he rushed away into the restaurant and came back with a roll of white paper.

'I am also presenting you with this.'

It was an elaborate and spirited picture of marine life – drawn in indian ink with a remarkable assurance and care. In the corner it had 'With love from Julius Lawson' written in red ink. At the top it had 'Some Life in the Red Sea'.

'I drew it this afternoon. It is quite the best of my collection. You did say you were interested in marine life?'

'Yes: it's beautiful.'

'Five of the specimens are not accurate: I haven't seen them, so they are simply how I thought they would look from their names.'

She admired it again.

'You haven't noticed the chart of depths.' He showed her the side of the picture which was neatly ruled out with fathoms marks deepening down the picture. 'Nobody is swimming out of their depths, you see. I think many painters would forget to do that.'

She thanked him very solemnly and he relaxed. 'It is not a slipshod affair – you could easily have it put in a frame, and hang it on a wall if you have one.'

She rolled it carefully up again and promised to frame it when she got home.

When the time came for them to board the caique, he became very silent. He hopped to and fro off the boat like a small bird, helping them to stow their smaller belongings. Finally he shook hands with Emmanuel, and bowed his thanks for the splendid dinner, and when Emmanuel said rather awkwardly: 'I didn't know what you would like, so would you choose something for yourself?' and gave him a hundred-drachma note, he looked at it with awe and muttered: 'Fifty weeks' worth of pocket money! I am speechless with gratitude at your munificence.'

When she said good-bye he clung to her with a sudden intensity, hugged her and whispered something, but the engine had been started and he had to go. He jumped back on to the quay, his eyes blazing with sad excitement, and shouted 'Come back! Come back!' and not knowing they said 'Yes!' Then they were cast off and chugging away and leaving him looking much smaller – a small boy – and forlorn.

They were settled on a hatch amidships: there seemed to be several passengers – all Greek – crouched about the boat among boxes of fish and jars of wine, who talked quietly to one another and called to a second boat that was leaving with them. He and she had been looking at Julius; now he turned to see her face which was still turned towards the shore: she looked grave, almost stern, but he felt her give a little inward sigh: he asked. 'What were you thinking?'

Still looking she answered: 'I was just trying to accept our departure. I mean – we're leaving the island *now*; it is a moment. And yet, years from now, we may have difficulty in remembering it.'

He was about to deny this, since leaving the island meant so much to him, but the essential truth of what she said was undeniable. Years hence, he would remember something of what he had felt while they left the island, but he would not remember exactly what this moment was like – it would all be lost in the ashes of other experience. So he said nothing.

They chugged gently out of the small harbour, and then increased speed. Behind them the island loomed in mountainous bulk above the lights of the port which gradually became diminished until they were like stamens at the heart of an enormous flower. Ahead was dark sea and, above, a

midnight sky crowded with stars. Voices had lowered in the
boat – the other caique remained a constant distance from
them. The kitten lay inert in the sling she had made from
a cotton headsquare. She said: 'You know, Julius has
changed this cat's life. Will they let me take it into England?'

'There is a quarantine, I think. We'll have to think what
to do.'

They were sitting on the hatch: suddenly she said: 'Now
we have left the island.'

'Then we must be in the boat.'

She smiled; then yawned and answered: 'I think I will be
asleep in it.'

He made her a pillow of his coat and covered her with
her own. The kitten, let out of its sling, stretched, yawned,
and lay down round her neck. 'Young creatures,' he thought;
'they have both simply had enough of the day.' She put up
a hand to him and said: 'You have been so kind: you've
changed it for me so that I see one isn't entirely alone – one
does meet people from time to time.'

He took her hand, and knowing what she did not know,
he kissed it. She said drowsily: 'Nobody has ever kissed my
hand before,' and seemed really, he thought, as they say, to
fall asleep. He had time to put her hand back under the
coat, and that was all. The kitten lifted its head, and moved
itself closer to the shelter of her neck, and they were both
gone.

He thought that he wasn't tired: he had imagined himself talking to her for hours: but now this did not seem a
deprivation, she was there, herself, and he could see it. He
lit a cigarette, and watched the island recede to a blurred
murmur of lights and no outline against the sky. They had
left it: soon, he would be leaving her – it was all a matter
of departure. Where was he going? This was a question all
of one's life. They would arrive, leave the boat, and go – to
what? For some long time he tried to understand what any
arrival had meant in his life – the cigarette was finished:
he made a pillow of her bag – slippery and hard for his

head. He was tired, tired, tired: the boat throbbed with his tiredness – on and on – getting nowhere, although the sea was all round him and he knew that they were travelling upon it. He looked at her – rapt and attentive to her sleep – and the kitten – its head curled, curved in her neck, its eyes slits of concentration upon the matter in hand, and wanting to join them in this if nothing else, he lay down. He looked up at the stars, and thought: 'They can bear to be there all the time: I can hardly bear to be here at all.' He put his hand on the kitten's back which lay against her shoulder, and shut his eyes. . . .

CHAPTER EIGHT

*

I. ALBERTA

In the boat I seemed to wake up suddenly – and completely. It was very cold and grey, with mist and still water round us; all rather ghostly and unreal, and that may have been why I started to think about home, and to imagine myself there. I thought of unhitching the white gate and walking round the weedy curved drive to the front door which is always open in summer and looking up at the house – the stone which is the most beautiful warmed worn grey, and the wistaria and blowzy roses and cracked white paint on the window sills with Serena's tennis shoes drying a toothpaste white on one of them: waiting to look, and walking up the steps into the hall which is the size of an ordinary room and somehow cold even in summer with all its doors and the staircase. The dining-room and the drawing-room doors are open and the baize door leading to the kitchen is hitched back, but the door of his study is shut, and the thought of opening it and finding his study exactly as it has always been, but without him, is one which I cannot bear. If I go past the baize door and along the stone passage and out of the garden door by the kitchen it will only be to walk round the back lawn to his study window, because perhaps if you look in at a room through a window you half-expect to find it empty. And there is everything – his glass-fronted bookcase, his desk covered with papers and presents like ink wipers that we made him as children, the photograph of our mother in a silver frame with blue velvet inside, the leather armchair and the long battered sofa with the springs broken at one end, the coconut matting and the black woolly rug in front of the fireplace which we used to use for bears, and the really horrible jar with metal snakes writhing round its outside that he will keep pampas grass in – he said it was the kind of jar that was made for pampas grass and any-

thing nicer would have been a waste – and the coat rack
next to the door which Aunt T. had put there to remind
him to wrap up when he went out, and the dark green wall-
paper that he wouldn't afford to change, and the unfortunate lampshade that a parishioner made him for a Christmas present which he said it would hurt her feelings not to
use, and his First-Aid box with two divisions, a large one
for children and a small one for animals, and the funny
smell like stamp albums with a touch of moth balls thrown
in ... every single thing is there as it seems always to have
been ever since I can remember – only when I go back to it
now, although I can see him sitting in his chair and looking
up when he sees me and just smiling without saying a word
– he won't be there – and now I have to go back and the
feeling of dread that I woke up with on the boat has grown
and grown until I don't know how to bear going back.

This is hopeless. It isn't as though I'll ever have to do it
again, because we shall have to move to make room for a
new vicar. The others have had this ever since he died: it is
what Aunt T. would call morbid and it is where Papa would
say 'Courage, Sarah' in his firmest voice. . . . Oh dear, at least
I *know* what he would say perfectly well, and from now
onwards I must just say those sort of things to myself. It *is*
better having written it out; partly, I suppose, because I can
see how silly it looks. It is no good going back in the wrong
way; I must be firm and calm and helpful to poor Aunt T.,
because Humphrey isn't practical, and Clem isn't calm, and
poor Uncle Vin is in the middle of a film so I don't suppose
he can be very helpful. And Mary and Serena are too young.
I simply must be my age, as Jimmy would say.

This morning I tried to thank Mr Joyce for everything:
it was after we'd left the boat and staggered ashore with all
the suitcases and the kitten. We went to a small café and
had bread and coffee as we both felt pretty cold and empty:
the kitten kept escaping and of course it doesn't understand
in the least about traffic. The sailors gave it a garfish out of
one of the fish boxes – they are a very long, thin fish with an
intellectual expression – and it ate like somebody typing

very fast down a long line. The food seemed to make it frisky which was most unfortunate. I was beginning to despair of its control when Mr J. said: 'We'll have to get it a basket: we'll try and buy one on our way to Athens', and it was then that I tried to thank him. The trouble was that trying to say something I really meant and felt, simply made me want to cry. He was very patient and sympathetic about it; which nearly made me laugh; for a moment, with his face blue from not shaving and circles under his eyes and a bar of smudge across his forehead, he looked like a clown – funny, and somehow terribly sad at the same time – but of course I didn't tell him that. In a way I've got to love him – not like Papa, of course, but a feeling of considerable affection, and I have a feeling that, unlike Papa, he *minds* his age, so that although with Papa or someone of my own age I could have said: 'You look like a clown, my dear X', with Mr J. this would be wrong. Papa used to say that I was not nearly sensitive enough to people's feelings, so that is another thing to start remembering. In the taxi driving into Athens to the same hotel where he said we would be sure to find the others, he suddenly asked me to say good-bye to him then. He said he hated airports and collective farewells and anyway it would probably be raining in London which made everything worse. So we solemnly said good-bye: we shook hands and then kissed each other's faces: 'Like French Prime Ministers,' I said, and at first I thought he hadn't heard, but then he said not in the least – they never stopped shaving. Then he offered me help of a practical nature: he said if I found that there was a money crisis at home, I must tell him, because financial help was his long suit, and he looked both bitter and kind when he said it. I thanked him and he said: 'Now there is nothing more that we need underline; let's look for your basket.' We found it, and came here, and now I've bathed and changed out of island clothes and am waiting to hear the plans which Jimmy is out making apparently, and the dread of the journey home keeps bouncing towards me and away again – it has just come back like a tiresome ball that seems both unerring and silly; there is a considerable difference between knowing what to do and actually doing it, I suppose one spends most of one's life in this gap?

2. LILLIAN

I woke late with the telephone ringing, and as I propped myself up to answer it I saw the turned-down bed that had not been slept in beside me. It was Jimmy, sounding harassed.

'I'm at the Air Terminal, we've a problem on. This plane leaves tonight at six-thirty. If they catch the boat – and it seems to be the only one – that we caught yesterday, they can't possibly arrive in time. I tried to call the island before I came here this morning, but I can't make any sense out of what they say. They should have gotten the cable by now, but what difference will that make? Should I cancel today's plane, and try to get two more seats for tomorrow?'

This wasn't the kind of thing Jimmy usually asked anybody, and really wondering, I said: 'What do you feel about it?'

There was a pause, then he said: 'That's the funny thing. My instinct is not to, but I haven't explained the practical situation here because it would sound crazy and they wouldn't *let* me book it.'

I said: 'I should stick to your instinct.'

'O.K.' He sounded relieved. Then he said: 'I've heard of a place out of town where I thought we might have lunch. Would you like that?'

'Very much. When will you be coming back?'

'After I've been to American Express. Don't go out, Lillian, in case they call from the island, will you?'

'No.' We hung up. I felt sure then that Jimmy was right – although not in the way he thought: they were going to call from the island and say they were going back together, and it was Jimmy and I who would use today's tickets. I got out of bed and went into the bathroom – I suppose that was instinct too because my stuff was in there – but I was caught before I could reach it off the shelf – skewered on a circle of pain that constricts until there's no room for anything but the skewer . . . . I was on the tiled floor – still upright, leaning against the bath clutching my left side where the skewer was embedded and waiting for the extraordinary choking gasps to give me air. I'd never reach those capsules now – in any case nothing in the room was keeping still – even the floor was heaving at me so that I couldn't see properly and there seemed to be something cold, heavy, and unpleasant pressing on the back of my neck. I shut my eyes and concentrated upon the gasps and on pushing the skewer right home and that seemed to work, as the pain died down and the gasps brought air. Then it was just a question of time – of waiting until I dared lever myself up to the shelf with the capsules on it. If the telephone were to ring now it would be a pity, but it would not make any real difference. The facts would be the same; it would only be that I shouldn't know them. After one false attempt I thought that by the time I was able to get up to the capsules, I shouldn't need them, and that somehow seemed to fit with everything else just now. I was very thirsty, but that would have to wait too. If they did not get here until after we had left, I would have to leave without my pictures of Sarah. Perhaps that would not make a real difference, either. After that I concentrated upon my breathing and relieving the extraordinary tension in my chest until I was able to get up.

I drank a little water and then took the glass and the capsules back to the bedroom: even that effort made me sweat: there was nothing for it but to lie down. It had been the thought of facing poor Jimmy with these changed plans that had struck me after he had been talking. I felt that he might well have accused me of being both a fool and a coward to have left Em on the island with her, knowing what I knew and not telling Jimmy. This was confusing; I no longer felt able to attach anyone's judgement of me to the last thing I had done, and therefore Jimmy would probably be right. I hadn't meant it like that (had I? I wondered), and with these weak and uncertain reflections I fell asleep.

I woke again as the door opened with a rattling of keys – Jimmy, I thought, let in by the chambermaid – but it was Em. I was so astonished that I lay quite still, looking at him without speaking.

'Lillian? Were you asleep?'

'How did you get here?'

'We came over on a boat last night.'

He stopped, and I waited for him to say something more, but he didn't. I sat up and looked at my travelling clock: it was nearly twelve.

'It is rather stuffy in here,' he remarked, and went to open a window. Near the light I saw his face more clearly: he looked calm but absolutely exhausted. He saw the capsules by my bed and said: 'Are you just keeping them by you, or have you been ill?' His voice was sharp, edgy with anxiety, and remembering how I had used these attacks, I said: 'I'm just keeping them by me. Have you seen Jimmy?'

'No. I've just had a shower in his room and changed, but they said he was out.'

'He's coming back to take me out to lunch,' I said, wishing desperately that he would tell me something.

'You'd better get up then.' He put my dressing-gown on my bed, and lit a cigarette. As I got out of bed, he said: 'Why don't you tell me the plans?'

I got into the bathroom before replying – held on to the basin and seeing the glass over it looked myself firmly in the eye: once in the day was enough, for heaven's sake. I looked terrible – with purple circles under my eyes and all my skin too thin. I said: 'What did you say?'

'What are the plans?' I heard him moving restlessly about the room.

'Jimmy has succeeded in getting two tickets for a plane leaving this evening and two for tomorrow. He couldn't get four for today.'

'How on earth did he know we'd be here in time?'

'He didn't. He just got them to be on the safe side.'

'Well – she wants to get back quickly. We'd better go tomorrow.'

I couldn't see the face in the glass any more: everything blurred as though I had been looking into a stream that had been still and was starting to move. He was not going with her – not going. . . .

'You're very quiet in there – hadn't you better get dressed?'

He had come to the open door of the bathroom. I seized a sponge and turned on the cold tap: I seemed to wash my face for hours, until it was numb. The water stopped him talking and he retreated. When I came out, I found that he had sent for my luggage.

'You hate wearing the same clothes for two days running. You may want to change into your other scarf.' He tried to smile, and that, too, made me want to weep: in that attempt he exposed himself: I knew all over again that I had been right about his face on the terrace.

'Do you think we might have a drink up here while I dress? I missed breakfast and I'll be giddy by the time we get to lunch if I don't have something.'

He ordered drinks. In the top of the first suitcase I opened was the folder which had Sarah's pictures. He was sitting on the unmade bed, and I felt him watching me – knowing that I would pick up the folder and put it, open, on the dressing-table; he must have watched me so many times. I picked up the folder and opened it – knowing what I would see by heart – like the print of seaweed against certain kinds of stone, these pictures were indelibly printed into my memory – I did not need them in the folder. I looked round the room: for the first time in my life I realized that certain gestures, if they are to be honest, must be made without any appearance of drama – that they must be quiet and light or they lose any value: but it was an extraordinary feeling, to know quite well what I meant to do, and be at a loss about how to do it. Eventually, I tossed the folder over to him and said: 'Darling – I really don't *need* these any

more, but I can't quite bring myself to throw them away:
could you dispose of them?'

He said: 'Are you sure you mean me to throw these
away?'

'Yes. After all, there is the whole album that I left in
New York if I ever want to look at it, but I'm not sure that
I do any more. I think I've changed a little in this way.'
It was very odd: I could not look at him and felt myself
actually blushing: luckily, then, our drinks arrived, and he
put the folder into his pocket. I found my shantung suit,
and while I was burrowing for a shirt, he brought me my
Americano and said: 'When we have a house, I shan't
allow you to travel with so much luggage. I'm afraid I
didn't pack it very well.'

'Did *you* pack it?'

He got to his feet abruptly. 'Yes. Now, I'm going to see if
Jimmy is back so that we can arrange things. Shall I fetch
you, or will you meet us in the bar?'

'I'll meet you in the bar; won't be long.'

He went leaving his drink behind: he had not wanted
it in the least – it had been simply another concession. Now
that I was alone I could afford some of the relief out of
this extreme and light-headed change that he had unwittingly made for me – it would not matter if I laughed or
cried or became intoxicated by this – it seemed to me –
miraculous reversal. But because my fears for myself had
melted – had so instantly dissolved – I could turn in their
absence, naturally to him . . .

He was very unhappy: he had not said her name and only
referred to her when I had told him about the two tickets:
had she, I wondered, failed him with no response? Or had
he, deeply touched by her, recognized her requirements
as separate from his own, and made his decision as the best
he could do for her? Whichever it was I felt he had been
struck in some different way – that he was suffering a new
and difficult pain – and there was nothing inconclusive
about it – he had made up his mind. I tried to imagine him
making it up: could feel the instant's warmth, almost in-

spiration that would come when he resolved it – like a new laid fire with its paper burning, before the paper becomes black ash and the fire has to live on its own. How rare it was to live any promise out; how hard to keep every minute of any decision; how painful to reach even to the height of one's own nature . . . Were he and I going to live with the image of her always before us, as we had lived for so many years now with Sarah? If we were to be so haunted, it was I who had taught him the trick of it. But perhaps he was trying to do more than I had ever tried, and this thought gave me a great gentleness for him as I discovered that one does not only want to protect what is weak. This was new, unmistakable, and I could recognize it: a movement and warmth of concern and joy for him that still, I thought, after all these years of my life might be a very beginning of love.

3. JIMMY

On the way back from American Express, I bought her something. I don't know why I was so sure she would be back in time for the plane, but I was sure, and I bought the bracelet as a kind of proof to myself. Oh, I bought it for other reasons, but the idea of buying it *then* – even if I wasn't going to give it to her for months – came out of the feeling of being so *sure* – how I've never felt about anything before except getting to England when I was a boy. Even not getting a call through to them on the island hadn't thrown me. I'd felt crazy booking the seats and I'd called Lillian because I'd felt mean at going out without seeing her and I suppose I'd wanted backing over my hunch. She's been sweet, Lillian has: more and more I've wondered, since we've been in Athens, whether she doesn't know just as much about Emmanuel's feelings as I do – she's just dumb about them to me because she doesn't want to upset me; but it isn't just her courage – she's been sweet with it, listening to me last night when she was dead tired, being patient and kind of *good* about it all. I'd offered, on the spur of the moment, to take her out to lunch at this *taverna* out of the city because I know she adores trips and new places to eat, but walking back from American Express I began to regret the offer. I didn't want to go that far away on account of my hunch that the others were going to turn up. That's the trouble in life: you make a plan, or offer something, and you're sincerely thinking of the other person at the time, but then you start thinking of yourself, and if the plan doesn't suit you you're in trouble. But maybe if I was right about her knowing, Lillian wouldn't want to go out to lunch either.

I'd decided to walk back to the hotel to use up some of the morning. It was a wonderful day and in spite of anxieties, uncertainties, and wondering how she was I couldn't stop the feeling of being light-hearted and the world all before me and containing her. Just the sheer certainty that I would see her before the day was out was enough to make it a good day: after that, it was up to me, and I found this a new and exciting way to look at anything. I've never had much sense of direction, and wasn't thinking about it anyway: Athens is a small place, and you have the feeling that you can walk to anywhere in it – but after quite some walk I knew I was lost. This made me twist about into narrower streets where an automobile has to hoot and nudge its way through the people, who don't walk like they do in New York, like they're going some place – nor like they do in London where you feel they're taking exercise-never-mind-the-weather, but just as though they are on the street because they like it that way. I started looking in the shop windows and that's how I saw the bracelet. It was just a circle of pale pink beads with pearls fixed in between some of the beads: it was hanging on a nail at the side of the window which was so stuffed with all kinds of jewellery that afterwards I wondered how I'd ever noticed the bracelet. I went in and got the man to show it me. The pearls were pierced by some kind of golden wire which made them hang stiffly – the pink beads were coral. He wanted 1,500 drachma for it – when I asked him where it had been made he shrugged and said something which I think just meant that it hadn't been made in Greece. It looked somehow as though it had been especially made for somebody, and, whoever she had been, I felt that it had also been made for Alberta, so I bought it. I did try to argue about the price but it didn't work, and he knew I didn't really care. He wrapped it up in very thin foreign kind of paper, and within a few minutes of seeing it I was outside the shop again with the bracelet in my pocket. Then I just had to get back to the hotel and took a taxi. In the cab I unwrapped the bracelet to be sure it gave me the same feeling of being the right one for her, and it did. I'd never bought a serious present for a girl in my life: flowers and scent and scarves and candy – anyone could buy those for anybody and that was just how I'd bought them. This was different – this was an antique, something that she could always wear; I wanted to laugh out loud, I was so lit up about it.

When I got to the hotel they told me that Mr Joyce had arrived and was using my room. I said I'd go up, and got them to give me her room number – she was a floor above my room; I took the elevator to my floor, waited until it had gone, and walked the last flight. Now that my hunch was proved right, and she was actually here, I found myself breathless – not only with impatience to see her – but fear of the kind that I had had when we left her on the island with Emmanuel. How did she feel about him – all that again, plus her being unhappy – perhaps sobbing her heart out on his shoulder. . . . I knocked, and at once she let me in.

She was wearing her prettiest dress – the one Lillian got with her in New York and she looked marvellously fresh and neat and clean.

'How *are* you,' I said, and that was just all I could think of to say. She said she was very well and thanked me – just how I might have known she would.

'Do you mind me coming up? I wanted to know how you were.'

'Not at all.' She seemed nervous. 'Come and see something.'

She led me into the bathroom. There, crouched in the bath, was a small kitten, looking very neat and lost.

'Julius gave it to me as a parting present. Mr Joyce said he thinks there may be trouble about quarantine, but I'm afraid we're committed to this cat now. It is much nicer than it looks, but I'm keeping it in the bath because it can't get out and it won't matter if it makes a mess there. Of course it has been fed.'

'How did you get here?'

She told me, and somehow I felt that everything had been all right. We went back into her room: there was the big book she writes in lying open on the bed.

'Are you writing a novel or something?'

'A kind of diary, but I don't think I shall go on with it. I won't, in fact.' She shut the book and put it inside her suitcase.

'Aren't you going to ask me about the plans?'

'Yes: what are they?'

I told her: she didn't look as pleased as I'd hoped, although she thanked me in her prim way for all the trouble I'd taken.

'What's the matter, Alberta? You wanted to get home as quickly as possible didn't you?'

'I do, of course.'

In spite of her fresh clothes, her tanned skin and clear eyes, she looked pale and as though something was worrying her, and as though she couldn't decide whether to tell me or not. I waited; if I asked her, I guessed she wouldn't. Then she sat on the bed suddenly, and said: 'It sounds awfully silly, but I simply *dread* going back. I can't explain it. I would have thought that my father being dead would stop anything else mattering – like places, or things one had to do, but it doesn't stop this at all. I just don't want to go back, and see them and hear all the story of him – how they found him and what people think of the driver of the car, and sort papers in his study and write letters to people I don't even know about him and clear up his house and all the traces of him so that somebody else can live in it, and

338

we all pack up and leave and that's that. I just don't want
to go back,' she repeated, and then in a rather shaky voice
added, 'and you needn't tell me that all this is both childish
and selfish because I know – and that makes it worse.'

'I wouldn't dream of it . . .' but she interrupted: 'Well, it
is, both childish and selfish,' and stared angrily at the floor.

'I meant I wouldn't dream of telling you anything about
it. Except that I'll come with you, if you'd find that any use
at all. There's sure to be a pub near where I could stay and
not be a worry to your family, but just be around if you
needed me?' I was standing in front of her at the end of
the bed – there was nowhere to sit so I knelt because I had
to see her face. She looked up and simply said: 'Oh Jimmy
– it would make all the difference!' Then more and more
colour came into her face and she said: 'If you are quite
sure that it wouldn't inconvenience you?'

'It wouldn't.' I handed her my handkerchief and she blew
her nose.

'It is most odd. It wouldn't have occurred to me that your
coming would make all the difference at all. I don't mean
to sound rude, of course: I mean I truly wasn't trying to get
you to come or anything.' She looked at me anxiously: 'I
really do thank you for taking all this trouble. So it won't
just be the aeroplane, it will be the train down and everything else?'

I managed to make an airy gesture: 'Aeroplanes, trains,
boats – they're all the same to me.'

Her eyes shone: 'And people? Do you find them indis-
tinguishable?'

I put my hand to her head: 'Some of them have wet hair
which is one way of telling. If I really want to make it easy
for myself –'

She sneezed: I got my packet out and unwrapped it. 'I
put a little distinguishing mark on them.' The bracelet
exactly fitted, and she wasn't wearing her watch. 'Then it is
perfectly easy for me to tell even at a distance . . .' She
looked up from her wrist. 'That they are different from
everybody else.'

She looked solemn and sparkling and her head was very close to mine; but it was odd, I was loving her so much that I knew this had to be done in a different way to any way I'd tried or imagined. So I picked up both her hands and kissed them, and then fetched her big book out of her suitcase. I put it on her lap and unscrewed my pen.

'There's just one more thing for you to write.'

'What should I write?'

'All good young diaries end up with a proposal: I'll dictate it. "Today, Jimmy asked me to marry him. He says I may take as long as I like to decide about this as long as I come to the right decision in the end." That's all.'

She wrote it: then she looked at the bracelet and finally said: 'Is that true?'

'Quite true – only it's a secret: it's a secret diary, you see: so nobody else knows.'

She looked awed: 'You see – I'm not quite sure about it: it is rather a momentous step where one should consult all one's feelings.'

'It's a case for considering every single one of them.'

'And that takes time?'

'Well, naturally, I don't know how many feelings you have, but you take your time.'

She sneezed again. 'I love my bracelet: it is truly the most beautiful object. Do you think we could change the subject – I haven't got much presence of mind left about this one?'

'I haven't got another subject to change into right now. But I ought to go and find Emmanuel and tell him the plans.'

'Not our plans? I mean any plans we might make?'

'Not them – no. I'll meet you in the bar.'

When I was at the door, she said: 'Jimmy. About Mr Joyce. He told me that if we go to New York, he may have to stay in England for a while: he sounded very sad about it. I think he has a great devotion to you.' I waited, because I thought she was going to say something else – but she didn't – she just said: 'That's all. I just wanted to tell you.'

Walking down the stairs feeling so rich with life I seemed to float, I suddenly thought of what she'd said about Emmanuel: in all the years I'd lived and worked with him I'd never thought of the devotion as being that way round. I'd thought of him as powerful, casually generous, brilliant, and generally, somehow, a romantic character, and I as painstaking and faithful, his devoted dog-eyed boy. I'd really lived it that way regardless of results because I'd had no particular sense of direction – but now that I felt this changing I didn't have the need either to make a religion of working for him, or a political cause out of working for myself. . . .

4. EMMANUEL

THE whole day had been stamped with finality for him – all the events had the poignant unreality of a dream – of ends and departure. He had burned the pictures of both the Sarahs together down in Jimmy's room which he had found empty, and he had watched the paper curl and discolour ahead of a flame hardly detectable in the bright sunlight. Very soon they were gone, and he was left with the empty red folder and nothing to conceal. Jimmy had arrived, remarked incuriously on the smell, and told him that he was taking her to her home: he was grateful on the whole, not to have to make a gesture to Jimmy about that. They had gone down together to the bar with so much unsaid that the illusion of their being in complete accord returned, or – possibly because he felt that was an end to a certain kind of relationship with Jimmy – it had merely ceased to be an illusion. They had ordered a drink, and Jimmy had told him more about the arrangements: he had listened as though these motions were already past, and had never had anything to do with him, but he had observed Jimmy's elated confidence and it had touched him somewhere with a sharp sense of separation. Lillian had joined them and her approach across the room was tentative, had a softness about it which marked her behaviour throughout the day – he noticed that in all the time she had spent upstairs, she had not really made up her face.

And lastly, she came down, wearing the dress in which he had first desired her, and carrying the kitten's basket. As she put the basket down on the floor, he saw a new and pretty bracelet clustered on her wrist, about which, throughout the day, nobody said anything. Lillian was introduced to the kitten who responded with ferocious affection – it wasn't until much later in the afternoon that he had realized that Lillian was the first person to notice a new bracelet and remark upon it. . . .

They had lunched at a *taverna* in the country – out of doors in a grove with the mountain of Hymettus behind them. Sprigs of verbena were laid on the table; the hot air was impregnated with their dry lemon sweetness. They were served with a meticulous leisure – the meal ending hours later with a dish of walnuts steeped in honey. He could not remember what they talked about: any gaiety had the quality of an Indian summer, as though, separately, they were all acknowledging the end of something together. He saw each one of them with the clarity of detachment, and with the affection of a farewell, as though their lives together hung upon a thread; they were all going to leave one another and themselves in this hot silent place and were already aware of the changes to come. He thought of the years he had known them and the hours that he had loved them and the moments that he had understood them – and he included himself in this plural. He saw her, a little shy with Jimmy, friendly to Lillian, and grateful to himself. He saw Lillian gentle to the girl, almost tender to Jimmy, but here there was a blank – he felt only that she was acutely aware of him – he could put no name to her manner. And he saw himself – the oldest, who in some way had provided the pivot on which they had all turned to one another, whose function where they were concerned might very well now be fulfilled and who had now to discover some private direction for the rest of his life. In these last hours he felt calm, disengaged, and concealed from them.

It did not occur to him – until they were standing round their table preparing to leave it – that perhaps there were dimensions to this concealment, and that they might each, separately, have some different thing to conceal from each other one. This, sharpened by the urgency of departure – there was just time now to drive to the hotel, pick up the luggage, and drive to the airport – heightened his perceptions. One does not give up anything, he thought, she was never mine: it was a notion I had of myself with her. He remembered years ago telling Jimmy something of the kind – when the boy had his orphanage chip on his shoulder – he'd told him that afterwards he would find that it had never been there, and this would make him feel light, and a bit of a fool. My God, he thought, the difference between what one thinks about how things are and the actual living through of one's discoveries!

He waited in the car with Lillian while the others collected their luggage. He looked at her and she smiled so hesitantly that he said: 'What is it?'

'It is horrid seeing people off. I was wondering whether I'd stay here, perhaps?'

He said: 'I think we should both go.' He did not know why he said it, and sounded perfectly determined. He glanced at her to see whether she was going to demur, but she simply nodded.

He said: 'I burned those pictures,' and she answered: 'Thank you, darling.'

When they came out of the hotel, Jimmy went in front and Alberta sat between them with the kitten's basket on the floor in front of her. After a while and as though she had been thinking carefully, she said:

'I don't really know how to thank you both for the wonderful time that I have had, and your kindness about everything. As it seems likely that I shall be going to New York eventually, I wondered whether you would care to adopt this kitten? I thought perhaps it could live more happily in your house than being carted about the world by me. It isn't that I don't like it – I think it is the most personable and strong-minded cat I've ever met. But there is its future to be considered.'

Lillian looked at him, so he said: 'You must decide, but personally I think all houses should be furnished by at least one cat.'

So Lillian seriously accepted: she seemed to understand Alberta in this matter, who said: 'It will be much more compatible than that eccentric little monkey,' and they reminded each other of its speedy and terrible behaviour, while he watched the road slip past, marking the time in seconds now.

At the airport they all got out and waited while the tickets were checked and the luggage weighed. They were late, they were given to understand: the bus passengers had already been waiting half an hour, and the aeroplane was actually in – they could see it being refuelled. In the hall where all the stalls sold their trivia, they seemed to split up: Jimmy took Lillian's arm and walked her off to buy cigarettes. He was left alone with Alberta. She said diffidently: 'Shall I see you again before we go to New York?'

'I don't know, Sarah. Do you dread going home?' he added abruptly: the idea of her dreading it had suddenly occurred to him.

'I do, rather. But it will be so much of a bridge to have Jimmy.'

'Is he going home with you?'

'If you can spare him?'

'Oh yes. I shan't be needing him – except for the New York production – for some time.'

'Until you write another play in fact.'

'Yes,' he replied discovering this. They were silent until minutes later she said: 'We've said good-bye, haven't we? So we can't say any more.'

'Remember what I asked you.'

'I do: it may well prove possible in the aeroplane.'

Their flight was being called. The others returned. Lillian kissed Alberta and Jimmy. Jimmy looked anxiously at him:

he put a hand on Jimmy's arm, and felt himself smiling, heard himself say: 'Take care of her.' And Jimmy said: 'Yes. I'll call you at Claridges the day after tomorrow.' Then they had to go. He stood by Lillian to watch them walk through the doorways and become diminished by the crowd outside, who already stood with the afternoon sun in their eyes and white dust circling round their feet, waiting to be led to the aircraft. Lillian said:

'I'll join you in the taxi in a few minutes,' and disappeared.

Now they were being led to the aircraft. He walked to the window in order to see them better. As they reached the steps, Jimmy turned round, saw him, and waved, and then she did the same. She was wearing a yellow coat and her head was bare. He raised his hand and dropped it again. Now they were up the gangway and out of sight. He watched the plane taxi out to the head of a runway and crouch there, and he remembered explaining to her that they ran the engines up one by one: he remembered her gravity, her smooth hair with the black band, her friendly excitement, and was wrenched by a moment's anguish as though he was dragging something out of his heart. They were off: he watched the collection of speed until the moment when they actually left the ground when the speed seemed, as it were, to be dropped on to it – they were just airborne, suspended a few feet from the earth, and then – as suddenly – moving again, climbing up into the blue air towards the sun. He watched until they turned away to make the wide circle and head west, the aircraft glinting and small, like a lucky charm in the sky.

They were gone: no longer part of his present: to steady himself, he tried to see this loss at it might be seen. A boy who might be his son, and a girl whom he might have loved – would have married if circumstances had been different. Now, although they would be unstrapping themselves from their seats, they could not leave the aircraft: they could make what they wanted of the journey, but they could not escape it. This balance of what was inevitable, and what could be changed occurred again to him now as he tried to see his own framework; immediately, the taxi outside, containing Lillian whom all day he had scarcely recognized, although all day she had still been his wife, the mother of the Sarah who died. ... What had been her concealment during this day which had begun with her relinquishing her daughter? That had been bravely done and, as he understood this, something more of her revealed with courage in it which amounted almost to the beginning of something else.

When he reached the taxi she was already sitting in the back of it. He climbed in, the driver mentioned Athens and they thundered off. At the appropriate moment the driver said 'Akropolis' and they both turned to see this eminent beauty. She said then:

'Do you find it astonishing that it has been there all our lives and we have not seen it until now?'

'Tomorrow morning I will take you to see it before we catch our aeroplane.'

'Oh yes,' she said: 'it will be our last chance.'

He put his hand in his pocket for a cigarette, and felt the letter that for the last twenty-four hours he had needed to keep with him: when he turned to her she looked at him steadily, calm with her knowledge of the day, and his spirit rose to her serenity as he recognized that these were his circumstances: opportunities, neither easy nor impossible, lay under his hand – were simply facts of their small matter waiting to be transformed.

MORE ABOUT PENGUINS, PELICANS
AND PUFFINS

For further information about books available from Penguins please write to Dept EP, Penguin Books Ltd, Harmondsworth, Middlesex UB7 0DA.

In the U.S.A.: For a complete list of books available from Penguins in the United States write to Dept DG, Penguin Books, 299 Murray Hill Parkway, East Rutherford, New Jersey 07073.

In Canada: For a complete list of books available from Penguins in Canada write to Penguin Books Canada Ltd, 2801 John Street, Markham, Ontario L3R 1B4.

In Australia: For a complete list of books available from Penguins in Australia write to the Marketing Department, Penguin Books Australia Ltd, P.O. Box 257, Ringwood, Victoria 3134.

In New Zealand: For a complete list of books available from Penguins in New Zealand write to the Marketing Department, Penguin Books (N.Z.) Ltd, P.O. Box 4019, Auckland 10.

In India: For a complete list of books available from Penguins in India write to Penguin Overseas Ltd, 706 Eros Apartments, 56 Nehru Place, New Delhi 110019.

AFTER PURPLE
Wendy Perriam

Thea Morton is an ecstatic St Teresa, the Wife of Bath and Erica Jong's Isadora Wing rolled into one, forever hoping to bump into God in a final, pleading climax which will turn slattern into Soul. Disillusioned with mortal men and obsessed with the Catholic Church, she sets out in pursuit of celestial/carnal unity – on a punch-drunk, purple odyssey that brings shocking and hilarious consequences.

'Spectacularly exuberant . . . uninhibited and exceptionally entertaining' – *Sunday Times*

RABBIT IS RICH
John Updike

Rabbit has made it, he's got it all wrapped up – sex, marriage, fatherhood and a secure niche in the wonderland of Middle America – except for the slow, creeping onset of decay . . .

'Updike has fulfilled the fabulous promise he offered with *Rabbit, Run*' – *The New York Times Book Review*

'Brilliant . . . Updike revels in his great gifts of style and social – I mean domestic – observations' – *The New York Review of Books*

ADULT EDUCATION
Annette Williams Jaffee

Despite their difference Becca and Ulli are friends, united by a bond that defies failing marriages, small children and the ravages of time. It is a friendship that nourishes and comforts and Becca, hovering rebelliously on the edge of true maturity, draws increasingly on Ulli's self-contained strength, until Ulli slips away . . . and Becca is irrevocably pushed into adulthood . . .

'Tenderness and a swift, light hand . . . A fine commentary on the generation that just missed out on liberation' – *Punch*

A Choice of Penguin Fiction

THE LONDON EMBASSY
Paul Theroux

Hero of *The Consul's File*, Theroux's American diplomat has now been promoted and posted to London. In these episodes from his career – dinner with Mrs Thatcher, meeting a Russian defector, gossip, love affairs – he infiltrates the public lives and private events of the capital's rich and famous and, in doing so, draws us a new map of London.

'Fiendishly entertaining' – *Guardian*

OCCASION OF SIN
Rachel Billington

Rachel Billington's tender and subtle novel encapsulates the dilemma of contemporary woman. Successfully married, a loving mother, clever career woman and staunch Catholic, Laura imagined that her life was safely under control. Then, to her dismay, she falls passionately in love with Martin and her secure existence fragments into chaos, leaving her buffeted by elation, guilt and desire . . .

'Brilliantly charted, set down with freshness, conviction and psychological truth' – *Daily Telegraph*

LESSONS
Lee Zacharias

'I went home from my first solo contest bedecked, deflowered, betrothed, and depressed . . .' Jane Hurdle's musical gift lifts her above the ordinary. But in her struggle to become a musician, through her husband, lovers and family, she finds that life and art are often at odds . . .

'Symphonic . . . wonderfully readable' – *The New York Times*

STATUES IN A GARDEN
Isabel Colegate

This subtle and graceful novel, by the author of *The Shooting Party*, opens during the summer of 1914 . . .

As the aristocratic Weston family prepared for the wedding, they seemed blissfully unaware that something was going wrong. Then Philip, the insouciant, callous nephew, loses his uncle a small fortune on the Stock Exchange, but Aylmer Weston, distinguished member of Asquith's cabinet, is too involved in the Irish question to really acknowledge this threat to his ordered, privileged life. Then Philip sets his dark sights a little further – on Cynthia, his beautiful aunt and a most desirable lover . . .

'Beautifully precise . . . with just the right mixture of doomed fun, melancholy and faintly lascivious despair' – *Observer*

Also by Elizabeth Jane Howard

GETTING IT RIGHT

A hairdresser in the West End, Gavin is sensitive, shy, into the arts, prone to spots and, at 31, a virgin. He's a classic late developer – and maybe it's getting too late to develop at all?

Then one night Gavin finds himself at a posh penthouse party and, caught between Joan and Minerva, suddenly he's developing very rapidly indeed . . . Comedy sparkles, touches and seduces us through the next whirlwind fortnight as Gavin begins, at last, to get it right.

'Her very best novel to date' – *Options*

SOMETHING IN DISGUISE

May's second marriage to Colonel Herbert Brown-Lacey is turning out to be a terrible mistake . . . Oppressed by his presence, her children leave home; Oliver to drift from one affair to another, and Elizabeth to follow him to London in search of love and security. Even Herbert's own daughter, the shy and lonely Alice, is driven into marriage to escape her father's sinister behaviour.

'Has all Elizabeth Jane Howard's particularly feminine perception . . . yet what lingers in the mind is its delicious funniness' – William Trevor in the *Guardian*

Also adapted by the author into an acclaimed Thames TV serial

and

AFTER JULIUS
THE BEAUTIFUL VISIT
THE LONG VIEW
ODD GIRL OUT
MR WRONG